APPROACH

First Printing, Zeva Enterprises Publishing, 2022

Book Design: Kelly Noel Zeva
Cover Design: Kelly Noel Zeva
Cover Images: Aleksandr Korchagin via Canva Pro (girl in panties);
Luminas_Art via Pixabay (galaxy); Jeff Pearcy Photography (headshot of Kelly Noel)

empowerederotic.com

Approach

CRYSTALLINE KINK SERIES, BOOK #1

Kelly Noel Zeva

Zeva Enterprises Publishing

To James —
Thank you for co-creating art with me.

Contents

Preface

In April 2021, I received a crystal-clear insight to begin a new novel. That very evening I wrote a two-page scene, which eventually became part of *Approach.* It was the scene where the protagonist, Nicky (Nicole) Rivera, first meets their romantic interest, Kieran Jackson.

Instantly, I knew I was being called to do something *big.* The titles of the first four books of the *Crystalline Kink* series were downloaded to me with very little effort, within a day or so. And unlike other writing projects, where I hit a roadblock about 3,000 to 10,000 words in, I wrote the first 60,000 words for *Approach* in only four months.

See, *Approach* is based on my real-life experiences. It's fiction, yes, but the vast majority of it mirrors my own life from the end of 2019 through the first year of the COVID-19 pandemic.

Back in 2016, one of my mentors shared that I'd be doing channeled writing in the future. I never imagined it would be BDSM erotica based on my own life; I'd have laughed and felt so much resistance. To be so visible, so vulnerable about my own challenges, to share traumas I'd experienced in such a detailed, visceral way… it's not what I thought I signed up for.

But the more that I wrote, and as my relationship with my partner progressed, the more I saw how much the world needed this novel. How, in many ways, I wasn't even channeling the novel. I was channeling *my life* for the purposes of writing this series of novels. Much like *The Celestine Prophecy,* this novel is designed to help awaken the rest of the world.

I'm humbled and honored by this task. It has challenged and stretched me, and caused me to revisit uncomfortable, even painful moments, to really capture the fullness of Nicky's thoughts, emotions, and experiences. It required me asking challenging questions of my partner to more fully understand his love for me and how that evolved.

Unlike the films that we see, the regurgitated rom-coms we could all recite from heart, it hasn't been a linear path. It's never a linear path in real life. And the conflict isn't always petty arguments designed to create sexual tension. Often, the deepest conflict in life arises from our fears and our traumas. That's what I've strived to depict within *Approach*, to create multi-dimensional characters who have experienced trauma and yet choose to overcome it, to acknowledge it, to grow, and do better. Even when it's uncomfortable. Even when it requires support and accountability and someone calling bullshit every now and then.

Creating a superconscious relationship requires ongoing effort and commitment. As Nicky learns in *Approach*, it begins by "doing the work." It begins by healing your past trauma, compassionately communicating your needs and desires, gently stretching your edges and doing what's uncomfortable. It continues the same way: healing, communicating, stretching.

As I finish drafting the final quarter of this novel, I'm grateful for this journey. I'm grateful to be a messenger, to share my relationship experiences with others to help facilitate their growth, empowerment, and healing. Like Nicky, being a healer has been my calling. Being a writer has been my calling. Being an educator, activist, and advocate has been my calling. And to combine all of those callings into a single endeavor has brought me more joy than I can express.

What I wish, dear reader, is that this novel empowers you, provokes you, inspires you in a deep-reaching way as only stories can. That you feel capable of holding your life in your hands, creating your relationships more consciously. That you identify and break free from the toxic trauma loops that hold you in place.

As both Nicky and I can attest, it's not an overnight process. Healing deep trauma of any kind takes time, and practicing compassion toward yourself is paramount. If you learn to do that, you will heal more quickly, accelerate your process exponentially, fly higher, and shine more brightly than you can imagine.

Should you want support along that journey, I'd be honored to assist you. A great place to start are the 'Notes' and 'Glossary' at the end of *Approach*. In the 'Notes,' you'll see information about and links to different resources and programs that Nicky and other characters reference throughout the novel. Likewise, the 'Glossary' defines words related to trauma, conscious relationships, energy healing, and kink/BDSM that may be unfamiliar to you.

I've also included a QR code below, which links you to free and paid resources to help you take your healing journey further. While reading *Approach* is a great place to start, the only way to create healthy, fulfilling relationships is through practice. And more practice. And even more practice.

May this novel inspire you to begin or continue that practice. May it remind you of your own inherent power. May it remind you of what you deserve, and what you are capable of attracting.

That is my prayer for you.

"Our flesh shrinks from what it dreads and responds to the stimulus of what it desires by a purely reflex action of the nervous system. Our eyelid closes before we are aware that the fly is about to enter our eye."

— James Joyce, *A Portrait of the Artist as a Young Man*

Prologue

Ever since she turned twenty, Nicole Rivera was utterly convinced she would meet the man she would marry at the age of twenty-five.

Nicole wasn't sure how she knew, just that she *did*. She was sitting in her college's cafeteria eating breakfast, mulling over her most recent English essay, when it happened. It was as though God had dropped a clear bubble of insight directly into her mind, just as she was shoving a forkful of overcooked scrambled eggs into her mouth.

The vision was so obvious, with a clarity that rivaled the most expensive diamonds, that it could be nothing but heaven-sent truth. Nicole would meet this man when she was twenty-five. They would be friends first, before they dated. And she would meet him in October, shortly after a break up. Nicole had no doubt about *any* of it.

That very afternoon, Nicole told her father about the vision.

As they were chatting on the phone, she was lying on her stomach in her dorm room, looking at her recently acquired poster of Ryan Reynolds as the Green Lantern.

"I'm going to meet the man I marry when I'm twenty-five, *papa*. I know it, I just know it," she said. "And I think he might have brown hair and green eyes. He'll like craft beer. He'll be Catholic. And he'll like sports, but not too much."

"It sounds like you're certain, *m'ija*," Nicole's father said.

"Yes," she said emphatically. "I *am* certain. I don't know *how* I know. I just know."

Yet, despite knowing with absolute certainty that she would meet this person in five years' time, Nicole longed to be in a relationship sooner. *Much* sooner. She'd wanted a boyfriend since the age of ten, and she was still very, very incredibly single. And had been her entire life.

She'd never kissed a man. And she'd certainly never had sex.

Hell, prior to college, Nicole had never even masturbated (the Church had said it was a mortal sin) or known what an orgasm was. And it was only last summer that she'd finally stopped wearing her sterling silver purity ring.

By all accounts, twenty-year-old Nicole was as innocent and inexperienced with men as it was possible to be. And while she no longer believed she had to wait until marriage to have sex (what if they were incompatible that way?), she very much wanted to be in love when it happened.

Completely, utterly in love.

The kind of love her maternal oh-so-Catholic grandparents possessed. They'd been married nearly sixty years, and they were constantly laughing, joking, and teasing each other. Playing cards. Socializing at church. Spending time with family. Reminiscing about the day they had met in Chicago in the early 1950s, and it had been love at first sight. Four days together in-person, then love letters between Baresi and Milton for nine months. Then a wedding that marked the beginning of the rest of their lives.

Six children. Ten grandchildren. And still, they loved each other.

Nicole *knew* they still loved each other, *really* loved each other, because her grandpa's dark eyes sparkled mischievously when he looked at her grandma. Then, he would wink at his grandchildren, as if he had a secret he couldn't quite share. And in quiet moments, when he thought no one was looking, he gazed at his petite, frail, silver-haired wife with complete and utter reverence. Almost as though he were kneeling before a monstrance, adoring the Body of Christ itself.

Nicole wanted *that*. The kind of love that was the stuff of epic romance novels, a love that took her breath away. She wanted to look into the eyes of her beloved and know, beyond a doubt, that this was the person she'd long-since been destined to marry, to be with, to honor and cherish and celebrate for all of eternity.

And to be with a soul who felt the same about her.

For a while, Nicole held firm to this insight that she'd had. She would meet Her Future Husband (as she began calling him) at twenty-five. In October. Shortly after a break up. After her practice relationship, which would last one to two years. And nothing anyone would say could possibly shift, shake, or erode that belief.

She believed it even when she studied abroad in Spain and had her first real feelings for a woman—a beautiful, wise, and cultured spirit.

She believed it even when, after returning home, she came out as bisexual.

She even believed it when her dear grandpa fell ill and passed away during her senior year of college. And seven months later when his petite, frail, silver-haired widow followed him.

Eventually, though, her belief in the message faded. Two boyfriends later, Nicole barely remembered that fateful day in her college cafeteria. She just recalled the message, and even that seemed fuzzy. Ghostly, airy. Ephemeral.

Nevertheless, it was October. And Nicole was twenty-five.

Her second boyfriend, Camden, had ended things just three months earlier.

Nicole was sitting across from her travel companion, Bailey, in a small room at a bed and breakfast in Urubamba, Peru. Bailey and Nicole had taken Reiki Master training with each other six months earlier. During that class, they'd connected easily, and Bailey shared she'd wanted to do this trip to Peru's Sacred Valley for years. But she didn't want to do it alone, and her husband wasn't interested in going with her. Nicole had jumped at the chance to be Bailey's travel companion, to go hiking, see Machu Picchu, and add to her crystal collection.

And to experience the powerful, healing energy of Peru, of course.

It was Nicky and Bailey's first full day in Urubamba, after spending a single night in Lima, and already, the trip was stirring and awakening intense emotions.

Bailey perched on the end of her bed in their small *casita* and pulled her long blonde hair into a bun. "He's not the one you're supposed to be with. You know that, right? Your ex, the one you're holding onto?"

"But I love Paco," Nicole said desperately, raking a finger through her long, loose, dark brown curls.

Nicole had met Paco three years earlier, just a couple months after graduation. A good-natured programmer and web app developer, Paco had grown up on the East Coast and moved to the Midwest just a couple years after getting his Masters. On their first date, at a riverfront park in Madison, they spoke for *hours* about their families, their most atrocious experiences with online dating, and what they wanted in a relationship.

More than that, Nicole had even shared with him something she'd *never* shared on a first date: that she was a virgin and had never had a sexual partner.

And he'd responded kindly.

So, at the tender age of twenty-two, Nicole had fallen completely, and utterly, in love.

Just like her grandparents.

The problem was, even as the relationship started falling apart months later, and even as she'd been dating Camden, Nicole had *stayed* in love with Paco.

After all, Paco had been so many firsts for her. Her first boyfriend. Her first real kiss. Her first sexual partner. Her first love.

Three months after meeting, she'd given him her virginity. It was beautiful, and Nicole could barely have planned it better. Years later, she still looked on that moment with fondness. They made love in the gentle glow of candlelight as snow fell gently outside. It was slow and connected and precious. Intimate. Nicole cried and Paco had held her; she felt as though time ceased to exist.

Then three months after that, on Valentine's Day, he'd gotten special baking supplies so the two of them could make red velvet cupcakes (Nicole's favorite) and have an intimate night in. More than that, he'd made a scrapbook for her with notes and photos from their first six months together.

"Thank you! I love it. It's the most thoughtful gift I've ever received. I love you so much," she cried, flinging her arms around him, tears rolling down her cheeks.

He patted her on the back, gingerly. "I love you, too," he had said.

For the first time, Nicole thought that maybe she'd gotten it wrong. That she *hadn't* correctly interpreted the vision she'd had when she was just twenty years old. Had somehow not *quite* understood the message she'd been given. Started fudging and justifying where the details didn't quite line up.

Perhaps she wouldn't meet Her Future Husband precisely at age twenty-five. Or in October. Or after a breakup.

Because she wanted to marry *Paco*. But he had arrived three years too early. And while his *birthday* was in October, she definitely hadn't met him then. And they hadn't started as friends, and she'd never had a breakup.

She was attached to him, attracted to him. She *loved* him. He'd become her dearest friend.

They laughed and joked, just like her grandparents had. She enjoyed their dates together, had fun with him. And he wrote the sweetest notes in his cards to her.

She wanted him to be The One.

So, so badly.

But just as quickly as they'd built the relationship, it began to unravel.

First, Nicole noticed she was initiating physical intimacy far more than Paco was. He never kissed her in public (he hated PDA, he explained), and they often sat on separate couches when they watched movies or TV shows together. Their relationship felt routine, settled; sex felt mechanical. They began disagreeing about nothing and everything. Paco complained they talked about their relationship all the time, and once he'd snapped at Nicole to stop being so sensitive.

He apologized afterward, though, and Nicole knew that she'd been clingy, so it was probably *her* fault that the relationship wasn't working. She began evaluating every single text she sent to Paco with laserlike precision, rereading the language over and over before she sent it. Then, Nicole felt her chest squeeze tight until he responded; even then, she still felt on edge. Or, she would compulsively send him three messages in a row, before he'd responded, and she wondered if she was overdoing it. Once, she gave him new towels to replace his older, bleach-stained ones, and he responded angrily that he hadn't asked for them and she wasn't his mother.

More than everything else combined, though, Nicole realized they had very different spiritual philosophies.

While Paco was also raised Catholic, he identified more as an atheist or agnostic. Science and data trumped all. Nicole, meanwhile, had begun dabbling in tarot as a senior in college, and she was curious about energy healing and reincarnation.

Ultimately, Nicole had squelched those desires to explore further. She knew that most arguments a couple had were about sex, money, and religion.

She didn't share finances with Paco, so it was generally a non-issue.

If she *didn't* explore New Age spirituality, religion wouldn't be an issue, either. After all, she *did* believe in science. They could agree to disagree. But if she *did* explore beyond the veil, she was certain that would be the end of her relationship with Paco.

As far as sex, Nicole began reading. A lot. Along the way, she went down a rabbit hole and researched kink and BDSM voraciously. She went to a sex shop and picked out toys she might use with Paco. She asked Paco what he wanted to explore. She suggested that she and Paco fill out limit lists together and asked him to do reading and research. When he didn't, Nicole became frustrated and tearful and pronounced that he didn't care about improving their sex life.

Paco became resistant. He declared their sex life was fine, and he stopped initiating sex all together.

After a few months, Nicole started asking if they should break up. She had the conversation with Paco three, four, five times. Each time, it ended with, "I love you, and I don't want to break up."

But the problems were still there. Nicole became unhappier, more anxious. And the thing she'd once dreamed of became a fear...

What if she ended up marrying Paco?

What if this was the only relationship she ever knew?

What if this was the only *sex life* she ever knew?

The thought made her heart race, her fingers go numb, and she began to hyperventilate. Once, the edges of her vision blackened and she had to lie down on the sofa for several minutes.

Finally, though, Nicole decided that she couldn't *not* explore spirituality any longer. She wanted, no, *needed* to feel connected to something bigger than herself. Something other than Catholicism. Purely on impulse, she registered for a group meditation series that started the very next day.

That first night, in an empty yoga studio at a local juice bar, Nicole sat in a sacred circle with eight other participants. Their facilitator, Octavia, a beautiful, dark-skinned Black woman with full lips and kind eyes, was an angel intuitive. She explained that she could connect with angels and archangels, that she could visually see and hear them. Once everyone arrived, Octavia explained that she would narrate what was happening during the group meditation and share what the angels and archangels were doing in the space to support their healing.

"I may touch you during the meditation," she said. "If I don't have your permission to touch you, please roll up the end of your mat, so I don't disturb you."

Hesitating, Nicole left her mat unrolled. Then settling in, and allowing the facilitator's voice to lull her to near-sleep, Nicole breathed in. And exhaled out. The pressure she'd been feeling on and off in her forehead began consolidating, mounting, building. Intensifying.

It was painful, and a rigid ball of wax. Solid. Immovable.

"Archangels Michael and Uriel are moving around the circle to support you," Octavia said, in a soothing voice. "Michael will wrap you in..."

But Nicole didn't hear the rest. At that very instant, she felt a solid, physical, energetic presence standing right in front of her. It hovered there for a moment, then delicately touched her in the center of her forehead. The pressure immediately dissipated, spread through her head, and settled.

Nicole breathed a sigh of relief she hadn't known she was holding.

As the meditation came to an end, and Nicole came back to the room, she immediately raised her hand.

"Yes?" the facilitator asked.

"You mentioned you might touch people during the meditation," she blurted out. "Did you touch anyone?"

Tipping her head to the side, Octavia nodded. "Just one person," she said, pointing across the room, to a red-haired Asian woman in her mid-40s.

Nicole was flabbergasted.

She'd quite literally been touched by an angel.

Archangel Michael, to be exact.

The next morning, a message came through loud and clear. It was just like the message she'd received nearly four years earlier that one day in the cafeteria.

Except Nicole swore later to anyone who would listen that she heard it, just like someone had spoken to her, whispered in her ear. Back when she was twenty, she just *knew* it.

The voice said firmly, "You're to stop drinking alcohol and stop having sex."

And that was it.

The voice didn't say anything else.

But it was enough.

Later that morning, Nicole knew that this was the final rupture. That if she honored the voice's words, that she and Paco would end their relationship.

Immediately.

Sure enough, after she relayed the painfully clear message she'd received, that she wouldn't be having sex with him any longer, she and Paco finally had a new ending to the conversation they'd been having for several months: "I think we should break up."

Despite that, though, Nicole still loved him. She'd stayed in communication with him for the past eighteen months, minus the six weeks immediately after their breakup. She'd even met Paco for dinner once a month the entire time she was dating Camden.

And when she and Camden had ended their relationship three months ago, Nicole had reached out to Paco almost immediately. Because Paco was always there for her.

True, he rarely initiated, but he always responded to her texts or answered her phone calls when she needed him.

After Nicole had gotten through the worst of the healing from her breakup with Camden, she and Paco had begun seeing each other more frequently. After all, he was single, too. They began cuddling. Then kissing. Then… Nicole didn't know what it was, but Paco insisted they weren't dating.

Nevertheless, Paco was the last person that Nicole had texted before getting on the plane in Chicago to fly to Mexico City and then Lima to begin this two-week trip in Peru. She let Paco know she'd be out of contact for the duration of the trip and had wished him a happy birthday. He'd wished her a safe flight.

Now, Nicole looked at Bailey and saw that her eyes had glazed over. Sitting cross-legged, Bailey's hands were resting on her knees in an open posture. She was clearly receiving a psychic message of some sort.

"Your guides and my guides are having a conversation about this all. Talking about the person you are meant to be with. Would you like me to share the message I'm receiving?" she asked.

Nicole hesitated. Bailey was more intuitive than Nicole was, or she had more experience at least. Nicole was still pretty new to this whole world. Either way, the rawness in Nicole's heart center was pressing inward painfully, and she wanted it to stop. She wanted to feel better.

Maybe I'll meet him when I return home from Peru, Nicole thought desperately. *My future primary partner. Maybe this message will help me find him.*

Nicole no longer called this person Her Future Husband because, quite frankly, Nicole no longer *wanted* to get married. She saw how many relationships ended in divorce and how messy and expensive it was. It was impractical. Besides, Nicole was far more interested in kink and BDSM than she'd been at the age of twenty, and she'd accepted that she would probably be happiest if she had multiple partners.

It was still a new concept to her, but she'd been in two monogamous relationships now, and each time, she'd raised the idea of polyamory. Neither of her partners had been kinky. Not really. In fact, that was a big part of the reason Camden had broken up with her. He wanted to date as a single person… not as someone with another partner.

Plus, Nicole was bisexual. Or pansexual. Queer. She wasn't really sure.

In any case, she was polyamorous.

At the same time, Nicole still wanted that deep, scorching, soul-merging relationship that she'd imagined five years ago. She wanted her own version of what her Catholic grandparents had had. A lifelong love. Her best friend. Someone with whom she could explore spirituality and kink and past lives and grow deeper. Someone who knew her, understood her, accepted her, and loved her at the deepest levels. A relationship that grew and deepened over time into something that was powerful beyond words.

The stuff of epic romance novels.

That wasn't what she had with Paco.

And she knew it.

Nicole nodded toward Bailey, wrapping her arms around herself. "Yes, I'd like to hear the message that's coming through right now. Thank you for asking."

Bailey smiled serenely. "Your person is someone you wouldn't pick for yourself. In fact, you'll resist being involved with him. He won't be your type at all."

Nicole raised an eyebrow. "What do you mean, he won't be my type?"

"Physically. You always go for skinny, dark-haired boys with glasses. He won't be that."

Suddenly, Nicole received her own visual. A tall, muscular man with light blond hair looking down at her with a smile. Football player physique. Yeah, *definitely* not her type. Not bad-looking. Handsome in his own right, in fact.

Just not her type.

At all.

"I'm getting a visual right now, too," Nicole said. "Muscular, like a linebacker. Blond."

"Yes, he'll be strong. Very strong. And he'll have a goatee that you'll hate at first, but it will grow on you."

"And he'll be thirty-four when I meet him."

"I'm getting thirty-five," Bailey said, pulling down her sandy tresses, combing through them, and piling them back atop her head.

That was a substantial age gap if they would meet before she turned twenty-six in two months' time, Nicole realized. Ten years' difference.

She made a face.

Bailey chuckled, then repositioned herself so that she could continue channeling. "My guides also want you to know that he'll be a client. I don't know what that means, but he'll be a client. And you'll resist it. But then it will hit you like a ton of bricks. It'll have something to do with crystals. That's what I'm getting. That's how you'll know it's him."

Nicole's head was swimming. She couldn't process anything beyond the very first comment Bailey had made. He would be a *client?*

That was unprofessional. No wonder she would resist it.

"Well," Nicole said slowly, doubtfully, "I *do* work at a marketing firm as an account executive. We have clients there."

Bailey just smiled.

"Is there anything else?" Nicole asked.

Grinning, Bailey nodded. "Oh, loads. Your guides are *super* chatty about this. I'm also seeing you out at a bar. For drinks or something. In a group setting. Also, there's something about a necklace that he wears," Bailey responded.

Even more to take in. It was *overwhelming*.

But, yep. It was probably a marketing client. They often went out for dinner and drinks with their clients after work. Generally at that ritzy place with the gorgeous view of the capitol.

Besides, Nicole didn't see how else she'd come into contact with prospective clients.

"Great. Thanks, Bailey." Nicole stood up then folded at the waist to stretch.

When she stood up, she saw Bailey was looking at her very seriously. "There's one more thing," she said. "Be open."

"Be open?"

Nodding, Bailey repeated, "Be open."

Then she shuddered and the glazed look in her eyes disappeared. Bailey hopped off the bed like a cat, leaving Nicole very dazed and curious indeed.

Chapter One

Two years later...

"That's a hell of a story, Nicole," Bailey said, laughing, wiping tears from her eyes. "What an intense ride you've had."

"I know, right?" Nicky said, taking a sip of their drink. "Also, just a reminder... I go by Nicky these days."

"Oh, right. My bad. Sorry about that."

Nicky quirked an eyebrow and took another sip of their cocktail. Then, delicately, they pulled out the cherry and gently placed it on their tongue before biting into it.

Juicy.

"So, let me reflect back what I'm hearing," Bailey continued. "Over the course of the past two years, you left the marketing firm you were working at, started your own business, became a Reiki healer full-time, and *now* you're working full-time as an intuitive relationship coach?"

Nodding, Nicky took another sip. "Yup."

"And you're dating *two* people? And one of them is a woman."

Nicky smiled. "Wild, isn't it?"

Bailey frowned thoughtfully. Nicky had told her snippets of their journey, especially having drifted away from doing marketing and doing more energy healing. But clearly a lot more than that had happened since they had traveled to Peru together.

For a moment, Bailey just looked at Nicky, observing how her friend had changed. Nicky had traded in their shoulder-length hair for a short pixie, which had reduced their dark brown curls to just a few waves. In all truth, it was more becoming. Nicky had such intense amber eyes. So intense they could leave a lasting impression in just a few moments, and this shorter haircut drew more attention to Nicky's face.

"The new haircut suits you," Bailey said after a moment, eating a couple of her frites, dipping them into the aioli.

Nicky's face broke into a beaming grin. "Thanks."

"So," Bailey said, by way of a subject change, "Tell me more about your new partners. What are their names?"

"Arthur and Sofia," Nicky said. "Sofia's Latinx like me. Her mom moved them out here from Mexico back in the late 90s."

The two of them sat in silence for a moment, Nicky stirring the liquid in their drink, and Bailey munching on a couple more frites. Laughter, conversations, and the clatter of glassware filtered gently around them.

"Now that we've been fed and watered, I might as well get to it," Bailey said finally. "The reason I asked you here wasn't purely social."

Nicky looked up. "Oh?"

"I mean, I did want to reconnect with you, especially now that we're in the same city and all, but I'm also looking for someone to share an office space with me. Someone I trust who's also doing holistic work."

"And you thought I might be a good fit since I've been working out of my apartment," Nicky said slowly, setting down their drink.

"Exactly," Bailey said.

Folding their hands under their chin, Nicky looked at her. "Do you have a spot in mind? How much would it be?"

Bailey grinned. "Yep. I thought you might ask," she said, pulling several papers out with a flourish. "If I buy your next drink, would you be willing to go over this with me now?"

Nicky quickly downed the rest of their cocktail. "Hell yes!"

Over the next twenty minutes, Bailey showed Nicky photos of the office suite, which contained a classroom, and the two friends discussed the relevant details. How much the space was, and how they might split utilities. When they might move in. What it would be like to work near each other. While it was all hypothetical, Nicky saw the advantages to such a plan: it would allow them to expand their practice and leave their work at the office.

Best, it would be a dedicated space for in-person sessions, which was sometimes necessary. Yes, Nicky had a few coaching clients from other places in the country, but most of their Reiki clients were local. Connecting face-to-face, when possible, was always Nicky's preference.

It was more personal that way.

And from a healing perspective, Nicky could read body language much more easily. If one of their clients was having a trauma response, they could be more sensitive to it and to their client's energy system.

At long last, Nicky's second cocktail was full of nothing but ice cubes and bourbon-flavored water, and Bailey's few remaining frites were stone cold.

"So, what do you think?" Bailey asked at long last.

"I think you need some new frites," Nicky said, snagging one and sniffing it suspiciously.

"Not that, silly. The office," Bailey said.

"Oh, that? I'm in," Nicky said. "Just let me know what you need me to do. Thanks for taking care of the logistical stuff."

Bailey beamed. "Wonderful. And you're welcome."

The two friends chatted a bit more as they paid their bills, pulled on their coats, and headed toward the parking garage where they said their goodbyes.

* * *

Once Nicky reached their apartment, they poured themself a large glass of water. They might have overdone it just a little bit. But if they gulped down a few glasses of water now, they could probably still avoid a hangover tomorrow.

As they sipped their water, Nicky realized they'd omitted one key detail when they'd told Bailey about the last two years of their life. Just three months after returning from the Peru trip, Nicky had finally joined the local kink community. Nicky had been thinking about doing it for months. Had *almost* done it just before leaving for Peru, actually, but had talked themself out of it. But as the new year rolled around, Nicky pulled on their black combat boots and their best black jeans; put on some eyeliner, mascara, and lipstick; and had decided to jump in.

Their first kink event had been a New Year's Eve slosh. Because Nicky was still single, they didn't have other plans, anyway. Besides, the slosh was basically just a bunch of people drinking beer, wine, and cocktails at a bar and talking about kink and BDSM. To Nicky, it seemed safer than going to a play party right off the bat. Or, at least, more comfortable.

While at the slosh, though, Nicky *had* been invited to a play party happening the following weekend. It was one of the more experienced kinksters who invited them, a tall Black man with medium-brown skin and closely cropped curls named David. He was wearing black dress pants, a black dress shirt, a silver vest, and a matching tie. Because he was quite friendly and helpful, Nicky had decided to accept.

David had then described how, at this particular event, Nerds and Kinksters, there was a gaming space, a social space, a place to eat food and re-hydrate, and a dungeon. The dungeon, he explained, was the only place where any kinky play or BDSM actually took place, though nudity was welcome throughout the entire building.

"They have black screens that they put up just past the registration area. Once you get past the curtains, anything goes. At least as far as clothing."

"Good to know," Nicky had said. "But what about the dungeon? That sounds intimidating."

"It can be for people new to kink," David acknowledged. "But you don't have to go into the dungeon if you don't want to. No one will think less of you for it. Some people socialize the entire time they're there. It's a very accepting, non-judgmental space."

He then went on to explain that all sorts of scenes took place in the dungeon: massages, floggings, bondage, sensation play, food play, electric play, even public sex.

Then David's face shifted into a smirk. "I like to do needle play and piercings, personally. Or more intense impact. But there's lots of variety. There's also a bunch of mattresses so that people can fuck before they go home."

"They're also great for aftercare," piped up a petite brunette with ivory skin, who wrapped her arms around David's waist.

At Nicky's quizzical look, David supplied, "Any care that happens after a scene to help calm a person's nervous system. Aftercare is an essential part of kink, though what it looks like varies. Impact, power play, and other kinds of BDSM often cause an endorphin and adrenaline rush, and things like food, water, and cuddling help rebalance the brain."

Nicky nodded. That was good to know.

Overall, the conversation with David had been incredibly informative, and it was nice to meet someone personally who had experience—*real* experience—with kink and BDSM. David had then explained that only people who had been vetted were allowed to attend a Nerds and Kinksters play party, and that someone would need to vouch for Nicky before they could buy their ticket.

"It's a way to make sure that the event stays safer," he explained. "The admin team runs background checks to make sure that none of the participants at the event are registered sex offenders. There's also a mandatory orientation where the admins go over the ground rules, including safety protocols."

On the whole, it seemed like the perfect kind of event for Nicky's first play party, and having these safety checks in place calmed Nicky's nerves at least a little bit.

David agreed to vouch for them.

"This is the email you'll send the info to," he said, handing Nicky a slip of paper. "And that's my full name underneath. Tell them I'm vouching for you. You'll need to supply your legal name, your birth date. Then, if you pass the background check, you'll be sent a secret link where you can purchase your ticket."

Nicky had taken the slip of paper and gripped it both tightly and tenderly. Their entire body was charged with a crackling, electric current. It felt like a momentous occasion.

The vetting process went smoothly, and the following weekend, Nicky was in the orientation learning about safe words, consent, and other event protocols.

"The word 'red' is a universal safe word here," the director of the event explained. She had kind eyes, dark brown skin, long braided hair, and a cheerful but no-nonsense attitude. "That means that, even if you have a different safe word that you're using for the scene, calling 'red' will still immediately stop play."

The admin team had also explained that just because someone might give another person a hug, didn't give everyone the right.

"You don't know what their relationship is," the director explained. "They may have an agreement that they can hug in all spaces. Ask for consent before you touch someone. A hug, a handshake, even a shoulder touch.

"Consent is a fully-informed enthusiastic yes," she continued. "If you don't know what you're agreeing to, you can't give consent. If you're drunk or on drugs, you can't give consent. That's why we don't permit drugs or alcohol on the premises, and you're not allowed into the event if you're visibly intoxicated. If you ask someone to do a scene and they say 'no,' wait for them to bring it back up. Otherwise, you're putting pressure on them, and that affects their ability to give consent."

It felt like a lot to remember, but much of it was common sense. They'd all gotten a quick tour of the space after that, but as volunteers were still setting up for the event, it wasn't all-encompassing. Then, Nicky and the rest of the new attendees had been dismissed until the event was set to start.

Once Nicky returned to the event space, the very first person they had met was Arthur. Tall, long, lanky body, brown skin, dreadlocks. Kind eyes, playful smile.

Even though the night Nicky first met Arthur was two years before the two of them ultimately started dating, Nicky would be lying if they said they didn't have a crush on Arthur from the first time they met. That first night, Arthur had also introduced Nicky to one of his partners, Asa.

"We're going to be doing an electric scene later. Would you like to watch?" Arthur had asked.

Nicky thought back to the orientation. *Consent is a fully-informed enthusiastic yes.* "I don't know what an electric scene is," Nicky admitted. "So I'm not sure."

"Electric play is where you use a tool, like a violet wand, to run electricity through the other person's body. It's much easier to experience than it is to explain."

Nicky declined, but thanked Arthur for the offer. He asked to give Nicky a hug, and they'd said yes. *That* was definitely a hell yes. Then Arthur darted away with Asa, and Nicky had continued to explore.

That first play party was, in many ways, anticlimactic. Nicky poked their head into the dungeon, and decided it was a bit much. They met a lot of people, though, all of whom were friendly and very willing to share their experiences and give advice, when asked.

After that first event, it became easier. The second time, Nicky spent more time in the dungeon watching different scenes, and gradually, Nicky was even willing to negotiate and do scenes with people.

By the time a year had passed, Nicky had done several impact scenes; a couple electric scenes; a simple bondage scene; and even a suspension scene with Indigo, a very experienced rope top. Nicky had also connected with a few other people interested in ageplay who, as adults, liked watching animated movies, coloring, and cuddling with stuffed animals.

It was wonderful, Nicky realized, to simply be themself without fear of judgment.

As a direct result of joining the kink community, Nicky became far more comfortable in their body, and far more accepting as a person. The first time they'd been at a play party and had seen people of all shapes and sizes and skin colors wearing little-to-no clothing, Nicky had felt rigid and judgmental. How *dare* they not know what kind of clothing to wear based on their body size? How dare they subject people to seeing *that?* Their large stomachs, their fat, their flab?

Nicky still had those thoughts sometimes, but it wasn't the same. The thoughts were softer, easier to ignore. They'd also stopped critiquing their own body so harshly.

Moreover, Nicky started to trust themself more and more. Trust that they would speak up and use a safe word if things became too much. Trust that they would only do a scene with someone if they felt safe playing with them. And Nicky trusted they wouldn't actually share the critical thoughts they had about other people's bodies.

Gratefully, the Nerds and Kinksters admin team had spoken to this that first night at orientation, too.

"You may see people doing things you don't agree with or wearing things that make you feel uncomfortable. That's okay. Their kinks don't need to be your kinks. But keep your thoughts to yourself. Don't yuck someone else's yum," the event director had said.

Overall, getting involved with their local kink community (versus just reading about BDSM) was an empowering experience. As a way to give back to the Nerds and Kinksters events that had supported them so much, Nicky even started volunteering. Usually manning the front desk, sometimes helping with coat check, even assisting with setup once or twice. Sure, they received a free ticket as a thank you, but they really enjoyed meeting more people and interacting with them at a deeper level.

That was how Nicky had first met Saffron, Kitty, and Indigo.

As well as Hyacinth, Mason, and Stacy.

It was also how Nicky had first met Kieran.

About a year after Nicky had first started attending the monthly Nerds and Kinksters play parties, Nicky was working the front desk for one of the events. They had sat there in a sparkly purple dress, wearing a tiara and dangly silver earrings, greeting people, checking their IDs, looking at their waivers, signing them in, and folding neon green wristbands around their arms. Kieran grabbed their coats, hung them up, gave them a black plastic number in exchange.

Nicky and Kieran worked in constant drumbeat rhythm, barely speaking as the rush of people flowed through the space.

Eventually, the tide of new arrivals slowed.

Then practically stopped.

After a lone straggler headed into the event, now sporting a neon green wristband, Kieran cleared his throat. Nicky turned. Their eyes widened. He waved.

"Hi," he said. "I didn't have a chance to introduce myself earlier. I'm Kieran."

Nicky smiled. "I'm Violet." Their preferred scene name.

"Nice to meet you, Violet."

"Same," Nicky had said, taking off their tiara.

They still had about an hour remaining in their shift, so they chatted about several different things, including kink and polyamory, but the rest seemed like a blur. Overall, he was nice, and it was pleasant.

Kieran was older than Nicky, and married. He also had a girlfriend and a couple play partners, besides. He had broad shoulders; strong, thick legs and arms; shaggy, reddish hair; and a goatee.

Nicky *hated* the goatee.

"How long have you been part of the kink scene?" Nicky finally asked.

"Sixteen years," he replied. "I used to live on the East Coast, and I joined the scene out there in my early twenties."

Nicky's eyes widened. "So, you have a lot of experience."

"You could say that," Kieran said with a grin, chuckling.

The two of them talked shop about kink and BDSM after that. Kieran was a Dominant, a Daddy, a sadist. Nicky introduced Kieran to Ollie the Otter, their loyal stuffed animal companion, and shared that they were a Switch (a sub-leaning Switch, to be exact) and that they'd dabbled in ageplay and identified as a little.

Very neutral, common conversation to have at a play party. But then, the conversation turned to neotantra. Working with energy. Nicky's eyes lit up. It was exciting and unusual to have this kind of conversation with a fellow kinkster.

"I became a Reiki Master Teacher shortly before I went to Peru in 2017," they said. "So I've been doing energy work for the past two years."

Likewise, Kieran had been exploring different modalities that used energy work, and he'd also done some work as a massage therapist. Apparently, he was well-known for his massages, especially those that incorporated energy work.

"If you'd like, we could do a massage scene sometime," he offered.

Immediately, Nicky's body became rigid. That was *definitely* a no. "Um, I don't think I'd be open to that. Thanks for offering, though."

The two of them chatted for the rest of their shift, but moved onto other topics: their favorite spots in the city, the artistic photoshoots Nicky had done, polyamory.

"I identify as solo poly," Nicky announced proudly.

Kieran smiled. "Sounds like you're quite proud of that fact."

"I've rushed into monogamy twice now, and it hasn't worked. I just don't know enough about someone after only two or three months of dating them."

"I can understand that," he said.

Nicky fidgeted in their seat. Kieran was looking at them so openly. It was uncomfortable.

Pretty quickly after that, volunteers showed up to replace them. Nicky and Kieran said their goodbyes, and went about their way. They didn't see each other for the rest of the evening, but Nicky didn't think much of it.

He was nice, sure, but *so* not their type.

Overall, Nicky's relationship with kink had shaped their personal and professional journey in many ways. It was because of kink and BDSM that Nicky had decided to pivot and become a sex and relationship coach, rather than a health coach. There were so few people coaching on how to have authentic, joyful sex and relationships, and even fewer that were knowledgeable about kink and BDSM, ethical non-monogamy, or polyamory.

Yet they shared very little about the play parties, scenes, nudity, and erotic exploration with most people. While Nicky was close with their parents, they didn't know about Nicky's interest in kink until their business model started shifting in September, just two short months ago. Since Nicky's Italian mother was raised in the Catholic Church, just like Nicky's grandparents, her views had been fairly conservative.

Their mom's eyes bugged out of her skull when she heard what her eldest child was now pursuing as a career. "You're doing what?" she exclaimed.

Admittedly, Nicky was able to soften the blow by reassuring her that yes, Nicky was still providing sex and relationship coaching more broadly, and yes, they *were* still facilitating Reiki sessions. And yes, they still took the occasional copywriting job to help them pay for their apartment and other expenses.

But it didn't make the conversation *that* much easier.

September was also when Nicky started dating both Arthur and Sofia. That was a transition for their mom and dad... to be hearing about *two* romantic interests and partners, instead of just one. While both of those relationships were relatively new, Nicky genuinely cared for both of them.

With Arthur, Nicky would go to museums, discuss politics and social justice, and have lots of flirty fun. With Sofia (whom they had met at a local networking group), Nicky would exclaim about their shared interests (Star Trek, Harry Potter, and Disney) and empathize about being an entrepreneur. Sofia was a real estate agent and independent content creator.

Because Arthur and Sofia were very different, they each brought something unique into Nicky's life that made things richer and more joyful. Plus, it was nice to be dating people who were *actually* kinky, instead of falling for a person who wasn't really interested in BDSM.

But, truth be told, something was missing. Arthur had a live-in partner with whom he co-parented his daughter Eva, and Sofia was new to poly and had a primary partner of nearly six years. While Nicky's partners showed up for them and were often in contact, Nicky missed the nucleus that they associated with monogamy.

Having their person. Someone with whom they shared everything. Well, most everything. Someone who understood them completely. Someone with whom they could grow old, have fun, and heal and grow incessantly. Their best friend. Someone Nicky would be with for a very, very long time. Ideally, the rest of their life.

But maybe that was wishful thinking. Maybe that didn't even exist.

For now, being with Arthur and Sofia was enough.

Chapter Two

The Wednesday following their happy hour with Bailey, Nicky went to the library for their weekly co-working session with their girlfriend, Sofia. Per usual, the two of them locked themselves into the white study room that they'd reserved and quietly powered through some work.

For their part, Nicky was writing social media content for Instagram and their very new Facebook group. Meanwhile, Sofia was looking at new listings that she was planning to show later that week.

"Lots of new two-bedroom apartments available on the east side, Nicky, if you want to upgrade," Sofia murmured.

Nicky smiled wanly, and went back to their work.

Pretty quickly, though, Nicky and Sofia began getting distracted. It started when Sofia was swiping through her new matches on her dating app and continued when the two of them got to talking about the play party happening in two weeks' time. It would be Sofia's second time going to a public event, and she planned to do a scene with her partner, Ricky.

"I'm also leaving it open," she said. "Maybe you and I can do a scene or something."

"Yeah, maybe," Nicky echoed as they scrolled through FetLife, looking at the Dance Card for the event. Though some people used the kinky social media site as a dating app, Nicky used it primarily to connect with friends they knew in the kink community and to get details on events they were planning to attend.

"It does look like Arthur's going to be there, too," Nicky said. "So I want to make sure I spend some time with him."

Nicky was met with a silent, stony nod. Then Sofia plastered on a smile.

"Sure, that works," she said.

But Nicky didn't believe her.

* * *

The play party came quickly, and while Nicky was excited, they were also nervous. Nicky felt this way for a few reasons. Mostly, their stomach kept flipping because Nicky had agreed to do an electric scene with Arthur and Asa. It was the first time Nicky would be topping for this kind of scene, and they didn't want to screw it up. Typically, they were on the receiving end of electric play; they weren't helping facilitate the experience for someone else.

Yes, Asa would be there, and they were experienced at topping for electric play, which was helpful, but it was still new for Nicky.

Nicky's hair was bearing the brunt of their nerves, as Nicky kept fluffing it, swiping it over, brushing it down, and re-fluffing it.

Their hair looked *exactly* the same as it did five minutes ago.

"For the *last* time, Nicky, you look great," Sofia said with exasperation, swinging her legs as she sat on the kitchen counter. "Now can we *please* go?"

Nicky looked up from the mirror to see Sofia staring at them, irritation plain on her face. Because Nicky and Bailey had just signed their office lease, Sofia had suggested that they glam up a bit more than usual for the play party as a way to celebrate.

"I never get to see you be super femme," Sofia had said. "It would be fun. For both of us."

Eventually, Nicky relented. But boy, were they beginning to regret their decision to get ready at the same time as their girlfriend.

Sofia looked flawlessly beautiful, and it had been effortless. She was wearing a ruffled black skirt, a sheer gold blouse with a black tank underneath, and black wedges. Against her golden-brown skin, the black looked bold, powerful. Her long black hair was curled elegantly, precisely, and she even had some glitter spray gently running through it.

She looked like a goddess.

Night sighed. They knew it wasn't fair to compare, but they truly felt unglamorous next to her. Groaning, Nicky brushed a hand through their short, wavy hair then grabbed their wallet and shoved it into the back pocket of their black skinny jeans.

"I'm still learning how to style it," they said, flattening their hair a final time.

Sighing, then smiling, Sofia came up and gave Nicky a hug. "I know. It looks great, though. Very you. Even Ricky thinks so."

"You know, I still can't get over the fact that two of your partners have names that rhyme. It's something out of an 80s buddy comedy."

Sofia laughed, a gentle tinkle, her long black hair swaying as she walked. "I know. It's so delightful."

Nicky just rolled their eyes and locked the door of their apartment behind both of them.

"Ricky's meeting us there, right?" they asked once the two of them were in transit. Nicky flicked the turn signal downward. Blink. Blink. Blink. The light turned green, and they turned to the right.

"Yep. That's the plan," Sofia said. "So is the new guy I met on the dating app."

A pang went through Nicky's chest. They looked at their girlfriend. "I thought you said you were capping it at three partners."

Sofia shrugged. "Yeah, I mean, I don't think I would *probably* see a fourth person super regularly. But things with Ivan are *pretty* casual. Plus this guy seemed interested in meeting me. I figure there's no harm in seeing where it goes."

Nicky smiled. "Well, I hope it goes well," they said, facing forward, their fingers gripping the steering wheel.

The two of them rode the rest of the way in silence.

When they reached the club, the atmosphere shifted, and both Nicky and Sofia started chatting excitedly. What scenes they had planned, what scenes they hoped to do by the end of the night, who they hoped to see. Once they had checked in, signed the waivers, checked their coats, and gotten their wristbands, Sofia kissed Nicky on the cheek and gave them a hug. Then she darted off to find her primary partner, Ricky, and Nicky headed toward the food room.

Kink on an empty stomach, Nicky had learned, was not a wise decision. They grabbed a plate and started piling it with carrots, hummus, slices of bell peppers, cheese and crackers, and a pre-packaged bag of chips. They had just sat down when a pair of hands gently covered their eyes.

"Guess who?" a playful voice cooed.

"Arthur!" Nicky exclaimed, laughing. They set down their plate of food and turned to greet their other partner, a tall, lanky Black man with an easy grin on his face. His dreadlocks fell to his shoulders, and some of them were pulled back. "It's so good to see you! I thought you weren't getting here for another hour."

His grin widened. "Turns out I didn't have to get a sitter. My nesting partner Christie said they would watch Eva tonight."

Nicky kissed him on the mouth, and wound their fingers through his hair. "Mmm," he sighed, giving Nicky a big hug. "Missed you."

"Missed you, too," they said, hugging him back and giving him a kiss. After a minute, he broke the embrace.

"I better go find Asa and check in on them," he said. "They're already here, too."

Nicky nodded. Asa had been Arthur's partner for three years, and because they lived out-of-state, they didn't always make it up for monthly events. When they did, it was understood that Asa was Arthur's priority.

"Thanks for letting me know," Nicky said, dipping another carrot into the hummus. "I'll come find you later." And in a joyful flurry of energy, Arthur bounced out of the room. Nicky, meanwhile, continued to eat their snacks, hydrate, and prep for the night ahead.

* * *

Play parties were always interesting, Nicky reflected, as they strolled the dungeon later that evening. The air was crackling with erotic energy. Most of the equipment was in use, including the three spanking benches, two crosses, three massage tables, and four of the six mattresses.

Nicky sighed. They really should have scheduled a scene for tonight. While they had spent some time with Arthur and Sofia, so far this evening had been rather, well… flat.

Yes, a voice said, *but next month is your birthday, and you'll have a lot planned for then.*

True, Nicky mused. But even so, as they saw Sofia laughing with Ricky and Ivan on the other side of the dungeon, they couldn't help but feel just a bit envious.

Nicky tore their eyes away from the scene that Sofia was wrapping up and stopped to watch another flogging scene happening on one of the St. Andrew's crosses. Two planks of painted red wood slatted together to form an X shape. The bottom, Wei, a curvy woman with long, wavy black hair and light brown skin, was tied to it. The leather cuffs wrapped around her wrists were attached to the top of the cross. Her feet, spread apart, were also in restraints that were attached to the cross.

It was rhythmic, watching her be beaten. Wei moaned, leaning into the restraints, red marks appearing on her back and butt and thighs. Nicky glanced at the top for the scene, the one who was beating Wei. It was David. No surprise there. An admin and experienced player, David was well-known in the community as a top, Dominant, and sadist. Sweat glistened off his brown skin as he spun two floggers at once in a florentine pattern. *Fwip, fwip. Fwip, fwip.* Nicky allowed themself to sink into the rhythm of the flogging, watching Wei and David. Into the rhythm of the electronic music that pulsed in the background. In the dim light, the dungeon seemed mystical, magical. Anything was possible.

Nicky didn't know how long they stood there, watching the falls of the flogger land on Wei's skin, entranced. Until a vaguely familiar voice pulled them from their meditation and reverie.

"Violet?"

Nicky turned their head. A burly red-haired, goateed man was standing next to Sofia. Her arm was looped through his.

"Kieran?" Nicky asked incredulously. "It's been awhile."

"Yeah, it has been," he said. "April, I think. How have you been?"

Tilting their head, Nicky shrugged. "Started my own business. I left my nine-to-five and now I'm a holistic sex coach. Basically, I do sex and relationship coaching mixed with energy healing."

Kieran smiled. "Good for you. Congrats."

Sofia frowned slightly. "How do you two know each other?" she asked.

"We volunteered together at a play party back in the winter," Kieran explained, turning his attention to Sofia. "Violet was wearing a sparkly purple dress that evening."

Sofia's eyes widened. "I don't think I've ever seen you wear a dress, Nicky," she said.

Nicky shrugged, their gaze flitting from Kieran to Sofia. "It was before I came out as non-binary and trans. Over the summer, I gutted my wardrobe and trashed most of my skirts, dresses, heels, and makeup."

Relaxing visibly, Sofia delicately untangled her arm from Kieran's.

"I think I'm going to find Ricky in all this and let you two catch up. Ricky said something about wanting to do another scene with me later tonight." With a small smile, she began walking off.

Once Sofia had left the dungeon, Nicky sighed. "I'm sorry. I didn't mean to intrude."

"You didn't," Kieran insisted. "I was the one who called out to you."

Another moment of silence. "How long have you been dating Sofia?" Nicky asked. "I didn't realize she was seeing anyone new aside from me, Ricky, and Ivan."

Kieran smiled. "This is our first date. We've been talking for a couple of weeks but hadn't met in person. Sofia wanted to connect at a vetted event before talking about sceneing together. Very smart, of course."

"Yeah, smart," Nicky echoed, twisting their watch around their wrist. So this was the person Sofia had met on her dating app.

For some reason, Nicky felt the need to escape. Go find Arthur, wherever he was. Or just start watching another scene.

Breathe. Keep breathing, a voice said.

Instead, Nicky pinched the inside of their wrist, then wrapped their arms around themself.

"Violet—," Kieran started.

"Nicky," they corrected reflexively. "I go by Nicky these days."

"Even at play parties?"

Nicky nodded. "Yes, here too."

A small smile. "You got it. Nicky it is. Correct me if I slip," Kieran said.

"I also use they/them pronouns," Nicky blurted out. They winced. God, that was awkward. "Sorry… still learning how to weave that into conversation."

Whatever he had planned to say after that must not have been as important as Nicky thought it might have been, because he just kept looking at Nicky, smiling. Nicky felt a warm flush in their gut, their solar plexus. Embarrassment.

"No worries," Kieran said. "Thanks for letting me know. Let me know if I slip."

The two of them stood there for a few minutes, still in front of the St. Andrew's cross, and David set the two floggers down. He picked up a bat and began thumping it on Wei's butt, thighs, and back in time with the music. He held one hand over her tailbone and sacrum, protecting it. Wei's moans and sighs grew even louder, reaching a fever pitch. Nicky tore their eyes away.

"Do you want to do a scene?" they asked Kieran suddenly.

Kieran raised his eyebrows.

"Depends on the scene," he said slowly. "What did you have in mind?"

Nicky shrugged, then looked at the pair in front of them. David was setting down the bat to pick up a thin cane. Nicky winced. They had never been on the receiving end of a cane and never cared to. "Impact? Flogging, maybe?"

Kieran was just about to answer when Arthur appeared before the two of them, shirtless. "Nicky!" he chirped. "Asa just snagged a massage table for the electro scene. Violet wand all over my body. Are you ready?"

Nicky turned their full attention toward him. "Is that happening right now?"

Arthur grinned. "Yup, in about five minutes. Right over there. Once the cleaner dries." He pointed toward the other side of the room where a couple people, including Asa, were gathered.

Nicky leaned up to give him a kiss.

"Sure," they said. "Sounds great. I'll be over there in a few."

If possible, Arthur's grin got even broader. His dazzling white teeth contrasted so beautifully against his dark skin. "Perfect! It's going to be so fun." After giving Nicky a quick squeeze, he skipped away.

"Well," Nicky said, "I guess I better head over for his scene." So much for the flogging.

"Yes," Kieran said, chuckling, his hazel eyes sparkling. "A raincheck on the impact scene."

Nicky waved goodbye and headed off. As they walked toward the massage table, toward Arthur and Asa, they couldn't help but notice that Kieran was still looking at them, a half-smile playing on his lips.

* * *

That night, Arthur came home with Nicky. It was an impulsive, last-minute decision since Asa had decided to spend the night with a friend, but Nicky didn't mind. Surprisingly, Nicky could sleep peacefully in the same bed as Arthur. They were a very light sleeper and sensitive to the energy of others, so they often felt most well-rested when they slept alone.

Once Nicky locked the door behind the two of them, they both kicked off their shoes and collapsed on the sofa. Their limbs were entwined as they held each other.

"That electro scene was so fun!" Arthur enthused.

"Yes, it was," Nicky agreed.

They lounged for a few minutes, playing with each other's hair, kissing each other every so often, hugging each other tight.

"I saw you chatting with Kieran," Arthur said. "I didn't realize you two knew each other."

"Yeah," they said. "It was several months ago. The February play party, I think? We volunteered together. I was at the front desk, and he was on coat check. That's all."

Nicky kissed Arthur on the temple then moved to stand. They helped him up and guided him to the bedroom. Nicky flicked on their Himalayan salt lamp, and Arthur gently peeled off Nicky's top layers. He rubbed the sides of Nicky's chest, kissing their neck, before pulling off his own shirt, just wearing his boxers and black jeans.

Moaning, Nicky leaned back into Arthur. He reached his hands under Nicky's lacy tank top and began rubbing their breasts, gently brushing the nipples with the palm of his hand. Their nipples began to perk up under his touch, and Nicky's breathing started to become heavier. Their back arched, and Arthur held them, placing one hand at the curve of their hip.

Arthur pressed his groin into Nicky's ass, and they gasped. Even though Arthur was still wearing jeans and boxers, Nicky could tell that he was getting hard. Nicky's own pelvis seemed to be opening up, as they became wetter. The two of them fell into bed, climbed under the covers, and kissed and caressed and teased each other's bodies until they finally fell asleep.

* * *

The next couple of weeks passed in a blur. Nicky was swamped with work, especially sales calls. As a result, they didn't pause for a break until Friday, once their work week was officially over. It was almost two full weeks after the play party, and they were having their weekly date night with Sofia.

"That last play party was fun, don't you think?" Sofia said.

The two of them were walking outside, through the nearby park, holding hands. Nicky always got a bit uncomfortable when the two of them did this in public, non-kinky spaces because they never knew what someone might say and when. Just a few weeks ago, when Nicky was walking downtown with Sofia, someone bumped into them intentionally and whispered, "Dyke."

"Mhm," Nicky said, picking at a piece of lint on their coat with one mitten. They breathed out and saw the condensation, the whitish water collecting in front of them. "I really enjoyed Arthur's scene."

"Kieran and I had a blast," Sofia continued, as though Nicky hadn't said anything. "We've had three dates since the play party, and we've got our fourth one tomorrow. It's going really well, and I'm having a lot of fun. He's really great at teasing me."

"Well, he is a Dom," Nicky commented. "And he's had close to two decades of experience with kink and BDSM. So it doesn't surprise me he's learned a few things in that time."

"How do you know that?" Sofia said, frowning.

"We spent some time talking when we volunteered together back in February," Nicky replied simply. "We chatted for close to two hours, so we covered a fair number of subjects. Including our kinks. So, he knows I'm a sub-leaning Switch and a little, just like I know he's a Dom and a Daddy and a sadist."

A pause. "Well, anyway," Sofia repeated, "it's going really well."

The two of them returned to Nicky's apartment after that, and Sofia rested on the sofa while Nicky made hot cocoa. Once Nicky had flicked off the lights, Sofia curled onto Nicky's lap, and they watched their new show together. Absently, Nicky brushed Sofia's long, dark locks with their hand.

"I think I'm going to go to Late-Night Kink tomorrow," Nicky said. "At the larger kink space in town. Do you want to go with me?"

Sofia shook her head, stretching. "Nope. I've got my date with Kieran, and then Ricky and I have plans afterward. I'm completely booked tomorrow."

"Right," Nicky murmured. "You said that. I'm sorry."

Shifting their energy back toward the television, Nicky rested their hand in a single spot on Sofia's head as they watched the show together.

One episode, two, three. Finally, Nicky was ready to go to bed, and Sofia was ready to go home.

***

Nicky awoke to a dull, dark gray sky. They rolled over. Then, with resolution, they flung back the comforter and sheets, pulled themself out of bed and began to dress in their workout clothes. Binder, t-shirt, leggings, socks, boots. They wrapped a coat and scarf around themself and continued onward.

When they reached the gym, they went to the women's locker room and placed their bag, coat, and snow boots in the locker. Put on their sneakers. Looked in the mirror. Flexed their muscles. They almost passed today. How nice for once. In the reflection, Nicky saw a couple people staring at them, two young 20-somethings with long bouncy ponytails.

Then Nicky overheard it. "What a dyke. *It* might as well be in the men's locker room looking like *that.*"

Turning around, Nicky stared at them icily.

"This *it* has ears," Nicky spat. "Didn't you learn it's not nice to talk behind people's backs?"

The girls looked away, uncomfortable, muttering among themselves.

Angry, Nicky snatched their water bottle and face towel and pushed through the door into the main room. Walked through the rows of equipment and hopped onto the treadmill. Started at a quick clip for their warm up, and then pushed the pace to release the pent-up frustration, the cortisol and adrenaline pumping through their system.

Still not intense enough, so Nicky pressed the button on the treadmill up again. Then they ran until their muscles screamed, until the tears started flowing. Nicky placed their feet on either side of the still-moving treadmill so they could breathe through the wracking sobs.

It was a few minutes before their breathing settled, and they began their short cool-down.

Nicky went straight to the locker room, grabbed their stuff, shrugged on their coat, and exited the building. They would do the rest of their workout at home. Fuck those girls. Fuck bathrooms and locker rooms. Fuck the gender binary.

Thank God for tonight, Nicky thought later, as they soaked in the bathtub after they had done the rest of their workout: yoga and some strength training. Maybe they could top for an impact scene and work through some of this emotion. Or better yet, bottom for something. Surrender, let someone else drive for a while. Being different was exhausting. Conforming had been exhausting, but not conforming had its own challenges.

"Fuck them," Nicky muttered, and they sank further into the bath water, breathing deeply. Inhaling, exhaling. Inhaling, exhaling. Inhaling, exhaling. Letting the hurt, anger, and pain seep into the bathwater. And then, minutes later, swirl neutrally and disappear down the drain.

Once they'd stepped out of the bath and wrapped themself in a fluffy towel, Nicky started pulling together clothing for Late-Night Kink. Ultimately, they landed on a gold blouse, black skinny jeans, and a white blazer. Hoop earrings. Boots with heels. A push-up bra. Black lacy undies. Just because Nicky was non-binary didn't mean they couldn't look femme if they wanted to.

Nicky even dug through their old cosmetics and swiped some red matte gloss on their lips and smoky black eyeliner around their eyes. They glanced in the mirror. They looked fucking hot.

Mission accomplished, they thought, a cat-like smile gracing their lips.

Nicky placed their phone in their purse, grabbed their keys, and made their way to Late-Night Kink. Once there, they put their purse and phone in one of the cubbies up front and began walking through the space. They'd been here before on a weekday, with Arthur, but the two of them had been the only ones at the venue. This was the first time that Nicky had been here without a partner.

As they walked around, they noticed it was quite empty. Just a single group in the medical room, two couples in the dungeon. One person using the suspension rig, and a very small group sat on the bean bags, chatting. Overall, it was incredibly low-key for a Saturday night kink event.

Nicky sighed. Shame. Maybe they wouldn't be doing a scene with anyone, after all. Nicky started heading back toward the entrance to grab their purse. Maybe it was just better to head home and spend the night watching something on Netflix.

But then a flash of movement caught their eye.

"Hello, Nicky," said a soft voice, from behind them. "I thought that was you."

Spinning around, Nicky looked to see who had greeted them.

It was Kieran.

Chapter Three

"Kieran!" Nicky exclaimed. "Thank God there's someone I know here! I didn't expect you. Sofia said the two of you were going on a date."

"Yep," he said. "We met for lunch, and then I got ready to come here."

"It's pretty empty," Nicky said, looking around. "I thought this was supposed to be a big event. But there's three scenes happening, if that."

Kieran looked at Nicky curiously. "You've never been to Late-Night Kink?"

"Nope. Is it normally a big event?"

He laughed. "Normally, yes. But there's another event happening across town, and I suspect most people are there this weekend."

"Lucky us! We get the whole place to ourselves," Nicky said. "Well, almost."

Kieran grinned. Nicky was more relaxed and open tonight than they had been the last time he'd seen them. It was nice to see them smiling. They had a great smile.

"Can I cash in that rain check?" Nicky asked.

"Hmm?"

"For the impact scene? The flogging?" they clarified. "It's been at least three months since I've gotten my ass flogged, and that's *way* too long."

Kieran tilted his head to the side. "I'd be open to that," he said. "Do you have any agreements with Sofia about playing with each other's partners?"

Nicky shook their head. "No, we don't."

"Well, then, I'm happy to appease," Kieran said, chuckling. Nicky's enthusiasm was infectious. "Do you want to find a spot to set up? I can show you the toys I have, and then we can negotiate the scene."

Practically skipping into the dungeon, Nicky stopped abruptly in front of a St. Andrew's cross, their grin wide, hopping from foot to foot eagerly. Kieran couldn't help it; as he slung his toy bag onto the massage table, he chuckled.

Kieran soon began removing several impact toys from his bag that might work for this scene. Nothing too sharp or too intense. He didn't know Nicky well, and he didn't know what their pain threshold was. Besides, it was their first scene together, and while Kieran might be a sadist, he also valued consent. The last thing he wanted to do was put Nicky off from ever doing a scene with him again by unintentionally crossing their boundaries.

Once he'd pulled out all the toys, Kieran looked up at Nicky. Surprise and shock was etched on their face, mingling with excitement and just a touch of fear. A devious grin pulled at the edges of Kieran's lips. This was a greater collection of impact toys than Nicky had seen all in one place; that much was obvious.

He pointed to the right side of the massage table. "Any toys that you want me to use on you, put them over there. Anything that's not in that pile I won't even pick up."

Nicky tested the toys against their forearm, and set aside a paddle, finger floggers, a padded bat, and a couple other toys. No canes. Just as well. Canes could be intense for a first impact scene with any new play partner.

"What do you want from this scene?" Kieran asked.

Nicky bit their lip. "Aside from just getting my ass flogged? I don't know. I guess just an energy release more than anything. Today's been rough, and I just want to feel..."

"Safe? Held? Like you can surrender?"

"Yes, exactly that," Nicky said, jabbing their finger at Kieran excitedly. Or, more specifically, his words. "I've also been curious to experience subspace again. It's only happened a couple of times. The last time, I was super giggly, and it felt like I was punch-drunk."

This was going to be fun, Kieran thought. No, he wouldn't unleash his sadist side tonight. It would be a more sensual, gentle impact scene. Energetic. But to do an impact scene with someone that could appreciate energy play... *that* was exciting for him. It was rare that he had a partner that was as energetically aware as Nicky. After all, she was (*they were*, Kieran corrected himself mentally) a Reiki Master and energy healer.

Self-mastery and energetic awareness were sexy, Kieran realized.

"That all sounds good to me," Kieran said. "What do you want for aftercare?"

Nicky suddenly looked uncomfortable. "Well, I don't really know. When I scene with my partners, I typically cuddle with them afterward. Sometimes I go into littlespace. I'll probably want to be wrapped in a blanket and cuddle with Ollie. Have some water. Beyond that, I don't know. Conversation, maybe?"

Kieran nodded. "That all sounds good. And safe words?"

"I typically use the traffic light system," Nicky said. "Green, yellow, red."

"Great, me too. I want to give you another safe word, though, if that feels supportive."

Nicky shrugged. "Okay."

"It's blue. If you call blue on a toy, I'll stop using it immediately. It's different from calling yellow, which just pauses the play. I find it's helpful if there's a particular toy that becomes too intense."

His eyes focused on Nicky's face, and Nicky looked away quickly, feeling scorched. Nicky doubted it was just the toys that could be intense.

As Kieran set about preparing his toys, Nicky surveyed the cross and began stripping, taking off their heels, then their blazer. Shirt. Jeans. Then, at last, the bra. Standing in just their black lacy underwear, they crossed their arms against their chest and watched him prepare the scene. Yes, Nicky had been nude at plenty of play parties before, but this felt different.

After all, as Nicky scanned the dungeon yet again, there was only one other couple in their sight line. Even though this was a play party, the two of them were effectively playing alone.

There was something thrilling about that, Nicky had to admit. They were a little nervous, since the only time they had scened with someone in such an intimate way was with an established romantic and sexual partner, but Kieran was emphatic about consent. And safety. Nicky had learned that oh-so-clearly from their very first conversation with Kieran.

While it was standard protocol at play parties to ask someone for permission to hug them, Kieran had somehow (if that was even possible) taken it a step further and had not even requested to touch or hug Nicky upon the end of their volunteer shift back in February. He'd simply waved and stood in his own energy. Just as he did now.

"Just a couple other things," Kieran said. "Are there any places you don't want to be touched?"

Nicky bit their lip and thought. "I'm fine with toys being used from my knees to my shoulders, but probably not on my pussy."

"And spanking?"

"Off the table," Nicky said vehemently, shaking their head. "That's too intimate."

"Thank you for expressing your boundaries so clearly."

"You're welcome."

They lapsed into silence. Meticulously, Kieran wiped down the St. Andrew's cross, laid out the toys within reach of the equipment, and grabbed a few coils of rope, letting them thud on the floor. "Are you ready?" he asked softly.

Nicky nodded, swallowing. They stood in front of the red wooden cross, lifting their hands upward. Then, they watched as Kieran looped the purple cotton rope through the metal rings, then around their wrists and arms.

He checked it, ensuring he could fit a couple fingers in between Nicky's wrist and the loop of rope, eyed the setup, and made another adjustment. "How's that?" he asked after a moment.

"Good."

"If you get tired during the scene, you can always lean forward and rest on the cross."

A brief beat, barely a single measure of the music. Then, Kieran placed a hand on Nicky's shoulder, gently flowing some energy. Nicky sank into the energy and closed their eyes. The next thing they knew, they received a soft *fwip* on their butt. The flogger.

Nicky shivered and exhaled at the pleasurable sensation of stinginess. It had been so long since they'd done an impact scene.

The two of them sank into a rhythm. Nicky, slowly melting, leaning against the red wood, their arms above their head. Kieran, weaving his finger floggers in time to the pounding dance music, tracing infinity symbols along Nicky's back and ass.

Each stroke of the flogger both relaxed and awakened Nicky. And the energy flowing through was divine. Their focus began expanding, softening, spreading. "Mmmm," they murmured, sticking their butt in the air just a bit. It was unconscious, a completely instinctual response to the impact.

After several minutes, Kieran paused and set down his floggers, then picked up the padded bat and began thumping it on Nicky's back. They started at the change in sensation, and then sank in again. He grinned. This was his favorite part of an impact scene, watching for those body reactions. Subtle and obvious. Were they enjoying it? Kieran could very much tell from the gentle way that Nicky's ass swayed in time with the impact, that yes, Nicky was enjoying the scene very much. Slowly, *gently*, they were going into subspace.

He would be the maestro to guide them there. The conductor to orchestrate this masterwork. Build the scene to a swell, crescendo, peak, and then soften. Decrescendo.

Kieran paused after the first round of impact, about ten minutes, to assess Nicky's body responses. They were more sensitive but still just at the edge of subspace. Still very lucid. They could do one, maybe two more rounds of impact.

"How are you doing, Nicky?" he murmured.

Nicky raised their head, already a little groggy. "I'm doing great," they said, a slightly loopy grin on their face, lifting themself off the cross for just a moment. "This is *great.*"

"Excellent," he said. "Are you ready for more?"

Nicky nodded lazily, the dreamy grin still in place, and leaned back against the cross.

Kieran picked up the floggers again and began whirling them both, grazing the ends against Nicky's butt.

"Yellow," they said.

Kieran paused and waited.

"The floggers are a bit much for my butt, but my back is fine."

Continuing, Kieran began flogging Nicky's back and watched as their body softened, as they exhaled, as their energy relaxed and dispersed. Flowed. Even though he couldn't see Nicky's face from this position, just their back, he could tell that they were more relaxed than they had been in awhile. Gone was that pinched, perfectly controlled, rigid energy that he'd seen so often with them. Nicky's energy was more open, free-flowing, moving. It washed over Kieran, and he had to take a deep breath so that he wasn't swept away in it.

It was, Kieran knew, surrender. She was—dammit, *they were*—surrendering. Yes, it was within a very defined container, with very explicit limits. It was a single scene. Just a thirty-minute event from beginning to end. But a part of him began to roar, awakening deep from within his chest, his gut.

The energy and the scene continued flowing, with Nicky leaning into the impact more and more until finally, Kieran could tell that they were in a really good place. Loopy, high on endorphins, and unaware of their own pain tolerance.

And while there was a part of Kieran that wanted to stretch Nicky just a bit more, see where their edges really were, he reminded himself of Nicky's original intention for the scene. They'd had a rough day and wanted an energy release. That was it. They hadn't consented to stretching their edges with pain or pleasure. And while Kieran loved stretching people, he valued consent even more.

So, Kieran began the decrescendo. He slowed the thump of the bat, made it softer. Touched Nicky with a piece of fur, and with his hands (on their shoulders and back only), grounding them. Nicky was getting dangerously close to overstimulation. That much was clear. Kieran could tell by the way Nicky was shivering, and one of their legs was twitching. He continued the decrescendo.

Yes, Kieran was a quick study. But just like anything, it took time before he really understood a person's body. Before he could intuitively sense the edges before his partner could articulate them. And this was a casual scene. Pick-up play.

Except that it didn't really *feel* like pick-up play, if Kieran was being honest with himself.

Kieran had wanted to do a scene with Nicky ever since that night at Tapas when they were teaching about energy play. There weren't a whole lot of people in their local community who even knew about energy play, let alone practiced it like Nicky did. And to do an impact scene with someone like this was so fun. He could feel Nicky drinking in the energy, sense the subtle shifts in their energy field as they grounded, expanded, and reached new heights of pleasure and presence.

Kieran shook his head and turned his attention to the ropes still holding Nicky's wrists.

"I'm going to untie you now and then grab you some water," he said.

Nicky nodded slowly, their head heavy. Kieran loosened the rope so Nicky could move from the cross. Once they were untied, they stumbled toward their pile of clothes and began rummaging through a black backpack. After a moment, Nicky withdrew a gray robe and Ollie, wrapped the robe around themselves, clutched the stuffed otter to their chest, and plopped onto the floor.

"Stay here," Kieran said, gently but firmly. "I'll be back in a moment with that bottle of water."

True to his word, Kieran reappeared soon after. Nicky opened the bottle of water and began sipping it.

"I'm going to have you stay here for a few minutes while I clean the equipment we just used," Kieran said. "Then I'll walk with you over to the sitting area, and we can chat. And of course, Ollie is more than welcome to join, if that feels supportive."

Nicky nodded yet again, hearing the words, but they acknowledged that they only penetrated a specific part of their brain.

"I feel like I'm drunk," Nicky announced, the words rolling sloppily off their tongue. They pushed their backpack to the side and began giggling. Yes, Nicky was a lightweight (just a single beer could get them tipsy, and two or three did them in), but this was *fabulous*. It was like being drunk but better.

If they'd been in subspace before, this *really* did not even compare.

"Yes, subspace can feel like its own high," Kieran said, still wiping down the equipment. "I'm almost done here. Please make sure you have some of your water."

Giggling, Nicky opened their water bottle and took a few long, deep gulps.

"I've never had impact play feel like that before," Nicky said decidedly, twisting the cap back on. "That was fabulous. Very…"

"Grounding?" Kieran supplied, zipping his toy bag shut.

"Yes," Nicky said, jabbing a finger in Kieran's direction. "That."

"We can head over to the sitting area now," Kieran said, hoisting the toy bag over his shoulder. "If that feels supportive."

Nicky nodded, still drunkenly, and stood up, tottering just a little. With Kieran only a couple steps away, Nicky walked over to the nearest sofa and plopped down. Kieran handed them a fluffy blue blanket. Nicky blinked.

"Thank you," they said.

"You're welcome," Kieran responded, sitting next to them on the couch. "Did you want to snuggle?"

Nicky hesitated, looked at Kieran, then at the blanket.

"You don't have to if you don't want to."

"I know," they said. They hesitated another moment, then they tipped themself sideways, leaning their head against Kieran's shoulder.

Their entire body went rigid. Barely twenty seconds passed before they pulled themself off Kieran. "I'm sorry," they said, apologetically, "it just… it just feels *weird*."

Kieran smiled. "There's nothing to apologize for. Do you want me to move to the chair so that you can lie down on the sofa?"

Nicky nodded, and Kieran stood up. They talked some after that, about the scene, about Nicky's new business, and about kink. Specifically, what happened in the body and brain when a person entered subspace. That was one thing they liked about Kieran, Nicky decided. He was so knowledgeable about the biochemistry of kink.

It was actually kind of attractive, in a *super* nerdy way.

Nicky shook their head, clearing that thought, refocusing on what Kieran was saying.

"…want to make sure you eat some chocolate tomorrow. We just flooded your body with endorphins," he said. "Your body will need to rebalance and chocolate will increase your dopamine and serotonin levels."

"Thanks for letting me know," Nicky said. "I've got some cacao at my apartment, and I can make myself a chocolate banana smoothie."

Kieran smiled. "Great. I'm glad."

After a few minutes more, Kieran checked in. "Looks like you're more lucid. Do you feel okay to drive?"

Nicky nodded, standing up. "Yep, it's not that far from here."

"Can you text me when you get home so I know you arrived there safely?"

"Can do, *mon capitan*," they said, saluting Kieran with a wink.

"Perfect." Kieran started gathering his things, then paused. He turned and saw Nicky looking at him expectantly, biting their lip. "Yes?"

"I'm celebrating my birthday on Thursday, and I wanted to invite you. It's a group thing, and Sofia will be there. Arthur, too, if you've met him. At that new brewpub downtown, Mon Ami? It'd be great to have you there."

Kieran's chest felt warm and open, but then he remembered something crucial. Nicky had just had their ass flogged for the first time in three months. With energy play happening concurrently, no less. And it was their first time playing together. It was the subspace talking. It had to be. Any other explanation really didn't make sense.

"So, I just want to acknowledge that your brain is running on a cocktail of endorphins right now," he said. "I've had play partners offer to do things well outside their limits once they're in subspace. To have sex. To become a slave. You might change your mind tomorrow once you've come down from tonight's experience."

"I won't change my mind," Nicky said. "So you'll be there?"

Kieran didn't respond. He just nodded vaguely, swinging his bag over his shoulder. "Do you want me to walk you to your car?"

"Nope," Nicky said quickly. "I'll be okay. But I will send you a message when I get home."

"Excellent," he said.

Nicky gathered their things, exchanged numbers with Kieran, and began walking toward the parking lot. Once the two of them were there, they waved goodbye. Half an hour later, as he pulled into his driveway, Kieran saw he had an unread message from Nicky.

Made it home safely, it said. *Haven't changed my mind. Still want you there on Thursday. Good night.*

Chuckling softly, Kieran closed his phone, got out of the car, and headed toward the house, mentally replaying the scene from earlier—especially each of Nicky's reactions in those precious, sacred moments. Their smile. Their shivers. Their surrender.

Yes, Kieran looked forward to seeing them again. Birthday party or no, he hoped it would happen soon.

Chapter Four

When Kieran had first met Nicky back in February, he'd only known them as Violet. And to be totally honest, that meeting almost hadn't happened.

He wasn't supposed to be volunteering at the front desk that night. Kieran had offered to help with setup instead. But then, halfway through getting ready for the event, the person who was supposed to be on coat check messaged April, the event director, that they weren't coming in because of the snow.

"Well, looks like I've got an hour to find a replacement," April said grimly, pushing her braids over her shoulder. Then she called out to the room. "Hello, my setup people. Would anyone be willing to provide extra help and do the first shift of coat check? Otherwise, one of the admins will need to do it."

Kieran was closest, helping one of the other experienced players—his long-time friend, Indigo—set up the suspension rig. He set the piece of wood he was holding against the floor for a moment. "I can, April," he called out, raising his hand.

"Great. Thank you, Kieran."

Then turning on her heel, April left the room, presumably to see how the rest of the event space was coming.

By the time Kieran had finished setting up the suspension rig with Indigo, it was time to add the rope lights, hang the curtains, set up the mattresses, and bring out the chairs and tables in the food room. The DJ had arrived and began preparing what he needed to mix music for the event, dimming the overhead lights.

The yoga studio was completely transformed. It now looked and felt like a dungeon, with massage tables and crosses and spanking benches spaced apart, and mattresses along one wall on a raised platform. The wall of mirrors reflected back the equipment, so that the dungeon seemed to have even *more* equipment than it did, and only royal blue and black rope lights illuminated the space.

Kieran always marveled at the transformation. That's why he loved doing setup: he got to see the shifts and changes as they happened.

By this time, it was almost seven, though, the time the event was due to start. So Kieran picked up some lingering debris, wiped down the equipment, and headed to the bathroom to change out of his sweaty clothing.

For tonight, Kieran had opted for a simple outfit: an orange t-shirt and black athletic pants. He always had a black shirt and his kilt for later, just in case. He splashed some water on his flushed face, brushed a hand through his hair, scratched at his scalp, and changed his clothes. Then, hoisting his backpack up, he walked quickly to coat check to start his volunteer shift.

Kieran's first impression of this woman with whom he was volunteering was that she was very rigid. He saw the tension in her body, saw how she pinned her elbows to her side. Then gestured widely, her eyes lighting up. She was inexperienced. Nervous. Perfectly controlled. Still learning who she was.

The clothing she was wearing didn't seem authentic. She had on an almost floor-length sparkly purple halter gown, elbow-length satin black gloves, and a tiara. The only parts of her outfit that seemed genuine were the black fishnets and sneakers that she wore. The girl folded her feet beneath her, as though a princess shouldn't have edges.

But Kieran liked edges, perhaps too much.

He'd barely been able to wave hello when he first reached the desk because there was a line of people already waiting to check their coats and bags. After stashing his own bag in the back, Kieran simply began taking people's coats; giving them their plastic numbers; and holding out his arm for the next coat, bag, or purse.

The two of them worked in constant drumbeat rhythm, and Kieran found something strangely soothing in the way they flowed together as they served the people in front of them. Eventually, their strange duet changed tempo; the stream became a trickle, then just a drip-drip-drip as the tide of new arrivals slowed.

Then, eventually, stopped.

Taking a pause, Kieran sat down and looked at this woman, the 20-something in the sparkly purple princess dress. Youthful exuberance covered her face, so she *couldn't* be more than thirty. And in fact, she was probably several years younger than that.

From his spot at the edge of the coatroom, he could just see faint white lines on the inside of her forearm. He folded his lips together. He recognized scars like that all too well. She used to cut herself.

Kieran watched her as a single guest came in wearing no coat. After the lone straggler walked away from the desk, now sporting a neon green wristband, he cleared his throat. She turned. Her dark curls cascaded around her shoulders, and her eyes widened. He waved.

"Hi," he said. "I didn't have a chance to introduce myself earlier. I'm Kieran."

She smiled. "I'm Violet."

"Nice to meet you."

"Same," she said, taking off her tiara and shaking out her hair.

They chatted for the rest of their shift—about kink, the weather, their favorite spots in the city. The two of them even connected on meditation and energy healing. She was a Reiki Master. He was experienced in Tantric massage. And the relationships they had. She was single and solo poly.

"It's complicated," she added quickly, and he left that alone. He shared that he was married and had another committed relationship, too, plus a few play partners.

She stiffened at that. Just like the rigidity in her body, there was a guardedness in her eyes, judgment even, steel walls that she held around herself energetically. A sort of suspiciousness, *especially* when he offered to do a massage scene with her sometime. She declined politely, but her words held a frosty edge.

It contrasted so radically with her laughter, when her amber eyes became liquid gold.

Kieran loved her laugh.

The conversation and energy flowed easily, effortlessly. He chuckled when her eyes grew big and she exclaimed in surprise and excitement when he shared that he was a fellow Disney fan. She introduced him to her faithful companion, Ollie the Otter, and pressed the stuffed animal to her chest as she swirled around in the padded computer chair.

More than anything, he noticed, Kieran appreciated Violet's energy. Buoyant, light, fun. Joyful. A beam of white light that warmed and illuminated the room. Swirling, spiraling into itself. Glowing, expanding. He could see from the pinched way she held herself, grabbed her midsection every so often, and even the timbre of her voice, that she was still growing into herself, though. Shedding parts that didn't serve her.

Kieran didn't connect with just anyone. Yes, there were polite acquaintances, but this felt different. Yet it was abundantly clear that while the conversation and energy flowed easily between the two of them, Violet was *definitely* not ready to be in a relationship with him. Of any sort. As a lover, partner, or close friend.

Regardless, he wanted to see her again. Or, at least, stay in touch.

"Would it be all right if I add you on FetLife?" he asked as their shift came to a close.

She nodded, a slight smile on her face. "Sure."

Then, all too soon, the bell tolled nine, signaling the end of their time together.

Kieran waved goodbye to Princess Violet and Sir Ollie, and the girl in the sparkly purple dress darted away. Even though it wasn't a connection that was ripe right now, Kieran couldn't help thinking he'd like to get to know her more and better.

But because of the drama that soon began unfolding in his other relationships, Kieran only saw Violet once more before the two of them reconnected through Sofia. Before he came to know them as Nicky.

✳ ✳ ✳

Their second meeting was just two months after they first met, in April, during a festival night. On festival nights, the first two hours of the play party featured "tapas" stations where practitioners did short scenes demoing their specialty within kink and BDSM. Attendees walked from station to station and most tried a few new things.

This year, Violet was one of the teachers. *Neotantra and Energy Play,* her station was titled, according to the FetLife posts and the event description.

Kieran arrived at the dungeon that night with his wife, Jamie. He thought attending the festival night would bring them closer together.

"Are there any particular stations you'd like to explore?" he asked, as he stood next to her.

Jamie looked at him briefly, then shook her head.

"Would you be up for the Neotantra and Energy Play one? It might be a great way for us to connect. It says there's scenes for singles and for couples."

Jamie shrugged. "Fine," she said.

As the two of them waited in line, Kieran noticed—not for the first time that night, either—how lonely he felt even as he was standing next to his wife. He reached for Jamie's hand to feel some physical closeness, and she pulled it away.

Kieran tried not to mind.

Finally, it was their turn.

"Hello," Violet said brightly, waving the two of them forward.

Unlike a couple months ago, she was wearing a much more demure outfit: thigh-high striped panda socks, silky pajamas, and a black satin robe covering everything. There were no gloves or tiara in sight.

Overall, it seemed much more authentic.

Violet smiled, and there was a flash of recognition in her eyes when she saw Kieran. "Are the two of you ready?"

Kieran nodded. "Violet, this is my wife, Jamie."

Her smile became a touch wider, as she waved. "Nice to meet you, Jamie."

Glancing over at his wife, Kieran noticed that Jamie was smiling, too. He reached for her hand, and she didn't pull away. Maybe this would go well after all.

After ascertaining that the two of them wanted to delve more into neotantra, instead of receiving Reiki, Violet directed them to either edge of the mattress and then sat cross-legged next to them, making the third point of the triangle. Kieran could feel that familiar light, joyful, buoyant energy radiating from her.

It was soothing and peaceful.

"Okay, so I'm going to invite you each to get into a cross-legged position," Violet said, gesturing for the two of them to get closer. "From here, you're going to position your hands like so."

She knelt beside them and moved Kieran and Jamie's hands. By the time Violet was complete, their right hands were facing downward, and their left hands were facing up, respectively, so that each of their hands was hovering over or beneath their partner's. Satisfied, Violet took her seat again.

"Now, you're going to gaze into each other's eyes. The left, or non-dominant eye."

Kieran felt more open than he had in some time. Connected to Jamie, too.

But even as he was touching his wife, gazing into her eyes, he could still feel the pull of Violet's energy. He was practiced at tuning out certain stimuli, but Kieran noticed that he was curious what it might be like to explore this exercise with Violet instead of Jamie.

He shook his head and cleared that thought, refocusing on his wife.

From there, Violet guided them into another pose where Kieran placed one of his hands on Jamie's heart chakra, and his other hand was over Jamie's hand on his heart. Jamie occupied a similar stance. From there, the two of them began rocking back and forth, building energy between them. The goal of this pose, Violet said, was to feel more intimately and emotionally connected to each other.

As he began rocking in time with Jamie, Kieran felt a bit more of his energy come back to him. Over the past couple of years, he'd felt very disconnected from himself. Like he only had access to a fraction of his natural stores of energy. Maybe a third of it.

His third-eye chakra, which had once felt so open, connected, and expanded, felt like a black hole, a sucking void that snuffed out all forms of light and intuitive guidance.

But here, next to Violet, rocking back and forth as the energy was building between him and Jamie, it was like his energetic capacity was expanding from a small cup to a large mug. For the first time in a long while, Kieran had hope that things might change.

* * *

The peace and feelings of expansion didn't last long. Shortly after that night, Jamie went back to her existing habits. Barely engaging with Kieran, not keeping her promises to him. The tension in their household grew thicker as Kieran became more and more frustrated.

He suggested they go to therapy together. Requested it. Pushed for it, even. Any way to make this work better. Any way to feel happier with his wife in their home.

The blackness in his third-eye chakra continued creeping in.

In addition, things were becoming complicated with his other partner, Penny. They wanted to have a child with him, and while he was open to that possibility, Jamie was upset that he was even considering her request. One night, in a flash of anger, she'd said, "I'm your fucking wife. You're only supposed to want *me!*"

Kieran had felt a bit lost and hopeless after that. He'd entered this relationship as a polyamorous person; Jamie had known he wasn't wired for monogamy. And now, these new expectations were being thrust on him.

Just because they were married.

It was suffocating.

Meanwhile, Penny had just gone through their own breakup and very much wanted Kieran to be *their* primary partner. The writing was on the wall with his marriage, they said. One day, he'd see it too. And Penny loved him deeply. And wanted to have a child with him.

Overall, Kieran wasn't sure what to do, but it felt like each of his feet was on a tightrope, and he had to very gently bend and balance to make sure that Jamie's needs and Penny's needs were both met.

It felt as if any misstep would have him plummeting to his death.

As spring became summer, both relationships grew increasingly toxic, and Kieran noticed he was feeling more anxiety and depression. Arguments and fights started breaking out. Occasionally at first, then more consistently.

Weekly. Then daily.

With Jamie, the lack of intimacy was even more pronounced. More than that, the clutter in their home had become overwhelming. On several occasions, Kieran came home from work, entirely exhausted, only to see Jamie watching television listlessly, the house in disarray, half of a cold can of soup on the stovetop. When he greeted her with a kiss, she barely looked up. When he asked to sit next to her on the couch and watch TV with her, she asked that he sit on the loveseat instead.

It became an all-too-familiar pattern.

For a while, Kieran kept putting in the effort. He was going to therapy, and he requested that Jamie do the same.

She didn't make the appointments, as she promised to do, and nothing changed.

Finally, Kieran had had it. "I want a divorce," he said one day. "I've been trying for months. I've asked that we go to therapy together. You said you would schedule therapy appointments for yourself, and you haven't. This hasn't gotten better. You're not putting in the work. I'm done."

Jamie sighed, then shrugged. "Back in March, I gave it six months before our relationship ended, anyway."

Hearing Jamie say this so nonchalantly, Kieran felt a sharp pang in his chest. She'd given them six months. And here they were, six months later, filing for divorce.

It would have been nice to know this six months ago, Kieran thought testily. Maybe it would have saved both of them some grief.

Filing for divorce felt like a light breeze clearing through, moving the stagnant energy that had laid waste to the relationship. Even though it was time-consuming, Kieran continued forward with it, taking it step by step.

Meanwhile, Penny was frustrated that Kieran wouldn't commit more than he was. They screamed at him one night that he was too involved with his wife, and yes, the two of them were talking about having a child together, but it wasn't enough. It wouldn't be enough unless *they* were the most important partner in his life, that *their* needs came before everyone else's, and that *they* were his primary.

The anxiety that Kieran felt grew. He'd started shaking while he was sleeping in response to the trauma he was going through. But as things fell apart with Penny, he noticed that the tremors started happening even when he was awake if he became overstimulated.

In a final display of anger, Penny stopped communicating with Kieran and began dating one of their exes. They lambasted Kieran on social media, and even after he blocked Penny's number, they still managed to send him a few messages blaming *him* for their unhappiness.

Each message felt like a slice to the chest. Months later, even after the relationship was well-and-truly complete, a text from Penny would reactivate his entire nervous system, and it would take several hours to rebalance.

Perhaps the cruelest part of it all was that he *had* wanted to have a child with Penny. Kieran desperately wanted to be a father again. And to have that snatched and taken away, and to have that relationship end within the same stroke, was more than he could bear.

* * *

In the midst of his two committed relationships dissolving into chaos, connecting with Sofia—and reconnecting with Nicky—were two twin rays of sunlight. Kieran still remembered where he'd been when he'd matched with Sofia: he'd been in the basement, lying in bed, unable to sleep. So, pulling out his phone, he began scrolling through OkCupid.

He'd had a larger-than-usual batch of "swipe lefts" when he finally landed on Sofia.

Kieran loved her bright, joyful smile. The sparkle in her eyes. The photos of her laughing with her friends and her primary partner, Ricky. The way she spoke on her profile about her new and recent explorations into kink and BDSM, how her new girlfriend had introduced her to the scene and the local community.

Their first few messages back and forth to each other were light-hearted, just a touch flirty. She was sweet, kind. Equally passionate about Star Wars, and she was a cosplayer.

By day, I may look straight-laced as a real estate agent, she'd messaged him, *but don't let that fool you. I make a mean Princess Leia or Arwen.*

She'd proposed they meet at the upcoming play party, and he agreed. The two of them spoke on the phone beforehand, and the teasing lilt in her voice had drawn him in. She'd told him how she appreciated his kindness, his energy.

For the first time in several months, Kieran felt hope and maybe even joy.

He felt *seen*.

It was wonderful.

Then, when he'd seen Nicky, it had felt like a collision. That was the only way to describe it. Yes, he was dating Sofia, so he and Nicky were really just in overlapping social circles, but there was still some draw that he had to them individually. The ease and familiarity and comfort that had been present the first time they chatted was still there.

Kieran could tell that Nicky still wasn't open to a relationship with him, and that was okay. But something had shifted. After all, Nicky had been the one to ask him to do a scene together. Twice now, they'd asked.

So, as Kieran reflected on the night that he'd just had with Nicky, he was curious.

Curious to see what would unfold. Curious to see what came next. Happy and willing to be the observer. Because even though a part of him was definitely interested in Nicky, they weren't interested in him, so keeping this energy to himself was crucial.

After all, Kieran thought, consent was sexy. *Nicky's* consent was sexy. Nothing was worth compromising that.

Chapter Five

The morning after their scene with Kieran, Nicky felt blue, achy, and listless. Remembering Kieran's advice, they created their chocolate banana smoothie and went for a walk in the brisk December weather. By the time they returned to their apartment, cold and out of breath, their energy was lifted.

Nicky began alternating journaling with cleaning and organizing their apartment. Doing their dirty dishes. Meditating. Being.

It was, decidedly, a powerful, empowering morning.

That was, until Sofia called.

"I heard you did a scene with Kieran last night," she said, by way of greeting. Even without seeing their girlfriend's face, Nicky could tell she was upset. Her voice had a steely edge.

"I'm guessing you heard about that from Kieran," Nicky said, settling to sit on their bed. This was clearly not a conversation during which they wanted to be distracted with cleaning.

"Yes," Sofia said. "I'm upset that you got to scene with him before I did when *I'm* the one dating him."

Nicky felt a bit of impatience at that. "It was unexpected. He and I were both at Late-Night Kink, and it just seemed like a good idea."

Silence. Then, Sofia added, "He also said you invited him to your birthday party on Thursday."

"Yes, I did," Nicky replied, flopping back on the bed. "Do you have a problem with that?"

"No, but he was wondering if you were serious."

"Yes, Sofia, I was serious about that."

Nicky exhaled loudly; they could feel a sharp edge entering their own voice. Using one hand to massage their third-eye chakra and temples, Nicky silently counted to ten to calm themself down.

"Look, I'm sorry I didn't check in with you before sceneing with Kieran last night," they continued. "I didn't mean to upset you. I had asked Kieran to do an impact scene with me a couple weeks ago, and we decided on a rain check. We cashed that check last night."

There was a pause. But the energy softened, like a balloon slowly letting out its air. Instead of anger, judgment, and stony silence, it was contemplative, reflective. When Sofia spoke, her voice was softer.

"Thanks for sharing that," she said. "I'm still frustrated. Because I really wanted to do a scene with him and I haven't yet. And it sucks that you beat me to it. He's spoken a lot about his massage scenes. But you and I haven't discussed boundaries about doing scenes with each other's partners."

"Right," Nicky said slowly. They stood up. They needed to walk, move, do something. "Anything else?"

"Anything else what?"

"Well, are we good? Or is there something else you wanted to say?"

The pause was just a touch too long for Nicky's comfort. They exhaled again. "What is it, Sofia?"

"I don't want you to scene with Kieran as long as he and I are dating. I know that's my stuff, but that's how I feel."

Nicky was actively pacing their apartment now. God, they really wanted to clean. Even hand washing dishes right about now sounded wonderful.

"You do realize that I'm still coming down from last night's scene with him as you're telling me this, right?" Nicky said. "Like, just this morning I had *massive* sub drop."

"I know and I'm sorry."

From Nicky's perspective, though, Sofia only sounded *slightly* apologetic.

And that pissed Nicky off.

Immensely.

They *so* did not have capacity for this right now.

Regardless, Nicky took a few deep breaths, bit their lip. After all, Sofia *wasn't* the enemy. Sofia was their *girlfriend*. The woman they loved. Who was Nicky to say that Sofia wasn't being sincere? That could just be Nicky's interpretation. Besides, Sofia was going through the trouble to communicate what she wanted. The least that Nicky could do was listen.

"Does this include group scenes?" Nicky asked after a moment.

Another silence. The energy of hesitation.

"Sofia?"

"No," Sofia said firmly after a moment. "That doesn't seem fair."

"Okay. So, you don't want me doing any more scenes one-on-one with Kieran as long as the two of you are dating."

"Or having sex."

At Sofia's words, Nicky's gut began roiling. It had taken the two of them nearly three months to get to second base. And yet here Sofia was, moving so quickly with Kieran. "You're having sex with each other. After four dates."

"Well, no," Sofia admitted, "but soon, I think. Our makeout sessions have been pretty hot recently. Last time, he even—"

"I have to go, Sofia," Nicky said suddenly. "I'll see you at Mon Ami on Thursday."

The stony silence was back. "You're upset that I'm making out with him, aren't you?"

Nicky's head was swimming. "What? No, I just—"

"It's not that big a deal, Nicky," Sofia said coolly. "After all, he and I are dating. I don't know *why* you're being so sensitive."

"Right," Nicky said, anxiety overtaking their irritation. "I'm sorry. I have to go."

They hung up. As soon as they ended the call, Nicky kicked off their fuzzy socks, changed into their workout gear, and laced their running shoes. Slipping on a warm jacket, they tucked their keys into their binder, locked the door and began to run.

As their feet pounded on the pavement, Nicky felt their breathing settle out. They pushed their body harder, until their muscles protested, until the stitch in their side might burst. Only then did Nicky slow their pace from a quick jog, to a slow jog, finally to a walk.

They walked the rest of the way back to their apartment. There, Nicky grabbed a blanket, made themself a cup of hot chamomile tea, and watched Netflix until they fell asleep on the couch.

* * *

Thursday's party at Mon Ami came quickly, and the tension between Nicky and Sofia was still thick. To be fair, Nicky didn't particularly feel like discussing the issue further just yet. So, they kept the conversation light.

Nicky had a feeling that Sofia was also hesitant to bring up the conversation.

Which was just as well. Nicky was leading their first free online workshop this week, a three-day event about conscious communication and developing healthy intimate relationships. Nicky didn't need to be distracted going into leading this event since it would require their full presence and energy.

Truth be told, Nicky did feel a bit like a hypocrite speaking on this topic. But when those thoughts came up, and they felt anxious, Nicky just looked at themself in the mirror and said, "You can still help people knowing what you know now."

As a way to promote the event, Nicky posted a couple of livestreams to their Facebook page and shared openly about their story. How they'd been raised Catholic, hadn't masturbated until the age of eighteen, and had cut themself and had suicidal thoughts at the time. Then, at the age of twenty-one, they had begun unwinding their trauma around sexuality and had started passionately pursuing spiritual growth and personal development.

In the last week, Kieran had added Nicky on Facebook, and he'd quickly joined their private Facebook group after watching the video that detailed Nicky's story. Sofia messaged Nicky saying, *Kieran said anyone who's willing to be that vulnerable publicly is worth trusting.*

Kieran had actually been the *only* person in the very small Facebook group who had shown up live for the two trainings that Nicky had held so far. He'd even commented on some of the videos and was doing the optional homework that Nicky was assigning.

Truth be told, it was rather impressive.

Nicky was so enmeshed in the workshop series that by the time their birthday party rolled around on Thursday, they actually missed their girlfriend and were excited to see her.

Sofia arrived at Mon Ami and sat down at the table just a few minutes after Nicky did. She looked so beautiful, Nicky thought, her smile full and glowing. As she flipped her long black hair and planted a kiss on Nicky's lips, it seemed like everything would be okay. Sofia handed Nicky the card she had gotten them, and Ricky even showed up with flowers.

Everything would be fine. Everything *was* fine. Nicky had been making a big deal about things. Sofia and Kieran were dating, and the two of them could go at whatever speed worked for them. It was none of Nicky's business, and just because Sofia and Nicky hadn't moved as quickly didn't mean that their relationship was any less valid.

Smiling, Nicky glanced down the table to see who was present. Arthur was there, Nicky's parents were there, and Kieran was just walking in the door.

"Kieran!" Nicky exclaimed, getting out of their seat, almost stumbling. "Can I give you a hug?"

One beer in, and Nicky was already a bit tipsy.

Oops.

Kieran chuckled and held out an arm. "Sure."

After giving him a half-hug, Nicky returned to their seat and ordered their next beer.

Likewise, Kieran sat down and ordered his first beer. "I'll do Triple Karma. The Belgian," he said to the server, handing him the menu. "Thank you."

Perking up, Nicky turned away from the conversation they were having with Arthur and glanced at Kieran. "You're a fan of Belgian tripels?" they asked. "Aren't they good? I mean, really really *really* good?"

"Yes, they are good. What I like most about them, though, is the balance of the malt and the hops. Dubbels tend to be a bit too malty for my taste."

Nicky's eyes practically popped out of their sockets. This time Kieran's laughter had him bent practically double. Nicky was so entertaining when they'd had a bit to drink.

"You sure know a lot about beer," Nicky said. "Usually I'm the one in the room who knows the most about beer, but you might rival me. And that's saying something! I worked as a server at a Belgian bier haus a few years ago."

Kieran was still laughing, but he straightened up and let the chuckles subside. *Goddamn*, this was fun. He was glad Nicky had invited him.

This was *much* better than going straight home after work.

"Yes, I do know a fair amount about beer," he said. "There was about three months where I was learning to pair beer and wine with the food I made. I love cooking."

Nicky nodded, and then another person arrived, which pulled their attention away from the conversation. "Paco!" Waving, Nicky stood up and gave the newcomer—a Latino man with wavy black hair, glasses, and a winning smile—a fierce hug.

Kieran began chatting with Sofia, connecting with her, teasing her and holding her hand. She lit up as he paid her attention, and the intimacy was wonderful. The warmth and care. Sofia's eyes crinkled when she laughed.

Overall, Kieran thought, the evening was glowing a lot like the Edison bulbs that filled the pub. The beer and company were good. He felt cared for, desired. He was having fun, laughing.

He wished he could hold this moment just a bit longer.

Just as he was about to settle his tab and make the journey toward home, though, the conversation turned to kink and BDSM. Specifically, the event that was coming up that Saturday.

"So, who's going to be there?" Nicky asked the table. Nicky's parents had already left, as had Paco. Everyone still at the table was kinky and had been to this particular event before.

"We will, of course," Sofia said. "There's no way that we would miss your scene."

Arthur smiled and nodded. "I'll be there, too."

"Kieran?" Sofia prompted, squeezing his hand.

"What's happening Saturday?" Kieran asked.

"It's my birthday scene," Nicky said, between bites of cake. They'd snuck in their own red velvet cake and had everyone at the table sing to them. Nearly three beers in, Nicky was *quite* loosened up.

It reminded Kieran of the previous weekend, when he had done the scene with Nicky. They'd been relaxed, open, punch-drunk. And their energy had floated so beautifully, enveloping him with a beautiful white glow.

Damn, that had been fun.

"What are you doing for the scene, Nicky?" he asked, taking a sip of his beer.

"It'll be a group scene. I'll be tied to the massage table and blindfolded," Nicky explained. "People will be able to touch me, and I've asked Indigo to be the moderator for the scene. That way there's somebody who isn't participating that's overseeing what's happening. I've done a scene with Indigo before, and I trust him."

"Sounds fun," Kieran replied. "I'm planning to be there on Saturday, but I do have a couple other scenes planned that night. If I'm available, I'll definitely come by and join in, though."

After that, Kieran downed the rest of his beer, flagged the server, paid his bill, gave Nicky a quick hug, and walked to the door with Sofia, holding her hand the entire time.

"It was great seeing you," he said, pulling her into a tight embrace. They stayed like that for a few moments. Then, Kieran leaned forward and gave her a kiss on the lips.

"Great seeing you, too," she murmured. "And I'm looking forward to Saturday's massage scene with you."

"Me too," he replied.

"*And* I'm looking forward to having sex with you soon," she said, smirking, kissing him again.

Kieran noticed a bit of tightness in his stomach. With all the drama that had occurred in his relationships with Jamie and Penny over the past six months, he wasn't ready to have sex with someone new just yet. That step felt too intimate.

At least right now.

But for now, he just smiled. "I'll see you Saturday," he said simply, pressing a small kiss to Sofia's forehead and giving her one final hug.

As Kieran walked to his car and drove home, he wondered how he was going to tell Sofia that he didn't want to have sex with her just yet when she so was clearly wanted that kind of connection with him. He hoped she wouldn't get offended. It wasn't anything personal.

We'll discuss it after Saturday, he reminded himself.

Feeling calmer, Kieran pushed these thoughts aside, thinking instead about the chores he'd have to do when he got home.

* * *

Friday was the last day of Nicky's three-day workshop series. Even before Nicky's final livestream, Kieran knew he was going to sign up to work with them. Yesterday, they'd shared about their private coaching program, and Kieran instantly felt drawn to work with them. Nicky had provided such valuable content over the last few days. More than that, Kieran had this strange feeling that Nicky was uniquely qualified to help him through what he was healing.

When Nicky offered to connect over the phone with anyone who had questions about the program, Kieran reached out and requested they schedule a time to chat. When Nicky called him promptly at three-thirty as the two of them had arranged, he picked up on the first ring.

"Hi, Kieran," they said. "It's been great seeing you attend the workshop over the past few days."

"I've really enjoyed it," he said. "Thanks for leading it. It's really great content."

Even on the other end of the phone, he could feel their surprise. "Thank you. And you're welcome," Nicky said.

"Look, I'll just get to it," Kieran said. "I want to work with you, and I'd like to do the program. I just have a few questions, and I want to make sure we're on the same page."

"Okay, sure."

"First thing: my intention for working with you is to open my third-eye chakra," he said. "I've felt really disconnected from my intuition for a few years now, and it makes it more challenging to recognize patterns in relationships that don't serve me, to avoid potholes, if you will. I've tried doing it on my own, and I haven't made the progress that I want to."

"Sure, we can work on that together," Nicky said.

"Excellent," Kieran said. "The other thing is that I know you're dating Sofia—"

"Yes, and I have confidentiality clauses in all my contracts. Sofia wouldn't be privy to anything that you and I discuss."

"I figured as much," Kieran said quickly. "It was more that I don't want to make it awkward for *you*. You know, since she and I are also dating."

"Oh," Nicky said. "I don't think it will be much of an issue. I'm comfortable setting boundaries with her and playing Switzerland, if necessary. You know, being the neutral party."

"Excellent," Kieran said again. "Then I just want you to know that I'll make my first payment tomorrow. So you know to look for it."

"Okay, great!"

Kieran smiled. He could feel Nicky's joy and enthusiasm over the phone.

"Oh, and Nicky?" he said after a minute.

"Yes?" they said, a bit hesitant.

"Happy birthday."

Chapter Six

The next morning, Nicky sprang out of bed right away. Even though the kink event wasn't until the evening and they had hours upon hours to get ready, Nicky wanted the day to be perfect. To feel totally prepared in mind, body, and spirit for what would transpire. That meant going for a run beforehand, painting their nails turquoise (Nicky was in a femme mood today), taking a hot bath and shaving their legs, and plucking their eyebrows and facial hair.

Nicky even found some time to journal and do a short meditation.

They also packed and repacked their black backpack (their toy bag) a few times before they were satisfied. Ollie the Otter, check. Fuzzy, thigh-high panda socks, check. Backup pair of fuzzy socks, check. Pajamas, check. Comfy gray robe, check. Massage oil, check. Lube, check.

Condoms, just in case.

Check.

Finally, it was late afternoon, and Nicky started the process of getting dressed. They'd done their laundry, so they had the choice of all their clothing, including the laciest of their underwear. And their favorite black bralette.

Yes, it would all be coming off anyway, but Nicky still wanted to feel sexy.

At last it was nearly seven, and Arthur texted Nicky that he'd just arrived. Since he was planning to spend the night after the event, he'd offered to drive the two of them. That way, Nicky didn't have to think about anything except getting ready and having fun. Nicky appreciated the gesture.

"Are you looking forward to tonight?" Arthur chirped, his eyes wide with excitement, as Nicky climbed into the passenger seat and fastened their seatbelt.

"You have no idea," they said, leaning forward to press a peck on his lips.

Arthur grinned, started the car, and the two of them were off.

Even though Nicky and Arthur parked in the lot only a couple minutes after seven, there were several people already milling about the event space when they arrived. Hyacinth was there in rainbow neon strappy lingerie and white fishnets, and the DJ was spinning the music in time to the pulsing lights. Every other staccato drumbeat, he was illuminated in the dungeon.

No Sofia or Ricky. At least, not yet.

"I'm going to look for Indigo," Nicky said after a few minutes. "He said that he would moderate tonight's scene but wanted to talk about it first. He wants to know what to expect so that he can be most supportive."

Arthur nodded. "I'll see who else is here. Asa's not coming tonight, but it's always fun to chat with people in the food room. What time were you aiming to do the scene?"

"Before it gets too late. Probably eight-thirty or nine at the latest?"

"Okay," he said. "I'll come find you in an hour, then."

With that, Nicky was on their own to find Indigo.

It didn't take long; he was in the social area and very easy to spot. His neon green and blue hair was folded over on the one side, looking halfway between a mohawk and an elegant combover.

"Indigo!" Nicky called.

He looked up, waved, and headed toward them.

"I was just about to start looking for you," he said. "Ready to talk about your scene?"

The two of them sat down, and Nicky walked Indigo through what they wanted to experience that night: Nicky wanted to be bound to a massage table and blindfolded. From there, people would be allowed to touch them and use certain toys on them to enhance the sensations and experience.

"Okay, that sounds good, but it's a little vague. I'd like you to do me a favor," Indigo said. "Can you write out specifically what's a 'yes' for the scene, and what's a 'no' or off-limits? That way I can help enforce your boundaries a bit more."

"Sure, I can work on that and get it to you before the scene," Nicky replied. "I'll go do that now. See you soon."

From there, Nicky went into the gaming room, grabbed a piece of paper, a pen, and a few brightly colored crayons and began thinking about what they didn't want in their scene. No impact. No kissing on the face or neck.

But then they paused.

What did they *want* to experience?

Thinking, Nicky pursed their lips.

"Nicky!"

At the sound of their name, Nicky glanced up, then over, to see Sofia running toward them. Sofia pulled Nicky into a tight hug, and Nicky wrapped their arms gently around their girlfriend. They saw Ricky was just a few paces away, also smiling.

"Hey, it's good to see you, Soph," Nicky murmured.

"You too," Sofia chimed.

It was almost like last week's disagreement hadn't happened. Nicky was glad that this could be the energy tonight. They wanted their girlfriend to celebrate with them instead of the night being weird and uncomfortable.

"This is your list of what you want in your scene?" Sofia asked. She sat down next to Nicky and looked at the list. "Kind of empty, isn't it?"

"Yeah, I'm a bit stuck on what to include," Nicky admitted. "I know I don't want impact, but beyond that I'm at a bit of a loss. I've never done this kind of scene before."

At that moment, Kieran entered the gaming room and waved at everyone. Sofia stood up and gave him a side hug.

"I've got a few minutes until my next scene, so I thought I'd pop by and say hello," he said. He looked down at the paper. "I'm guessing Indigo asked you to write out what the boundaries are for your scene?"

"Mhm," Nicky said, nodding, tracing lines with the crayons. "I'm stuck, though."

Kieran sat down across from Nicky and studied the paper.

"Are you open to suggestions?" he asked.

"Sure," Nicky said. "That'd be great."

He smiled. "No problem. So, you have no impact, but what does that mean? Does that just mean with toys, or do you not want people slapping you, either?"

Nicky's eyes widened. "Ooh, good point. No slaps." They scribbled furiously.

"And where are people allowed to touch you?"

The two of them went back and forth like this for a bit, Kieran making suggestions, Nicky adding items or making additional notes on their list. Every so often, Sofia chimed in and suggested something, too.

Once the list was complete, Nicky realized it was quite thorough.

What was allowed: People using their hands, lips, tongues, and teeth on Nicky's body below their neck, including on their shoulders, breasts, arms, legs, ankles, and feet. People could massage those areas. Apply lotion and oils to those areas.

But something was missing.

"Are you going to let us give you orgasms?" Sofia asked at last.

Oh, yes. *That.* Nicky blushed.

"I think so," they said slowly. "Just partners and metas, though. I'm thinking it would be great to have you all touch my clit and play with my pussy with your fingers. Probably no toys, though. I don't know if they've been washed and sanitized before they're being used on me."

Nicky added this caveat to the list. Sofia, Arthur, and Ricky would be privy to touching their clit and pussy. They hesitated before adding one more name to the list of people who could touch them in those areas.

Kieran.

After all, he *was* a meta.

Nicky would be blindfolded.

He'd shown himself to be trustworthy.

And this *was* a group scene.

Besides, just because Nicky said he *could* touch them down there didn't mean he would.

With a flourish, Nicky added a fierce red crayon line under the "Not Allowed" heading and a green line under the "Hell Yes" heading on the piece of paper. They marched over to Indigo and handed him the list.

He looked at it, mouthing the words as he read it. Finally, he looked up. "I'll need to know who everyone on this list is before we get started… Sofia, Ricky, and Arthur. I know Kieran already. That way I can make sure no one else is touching your clit or pussy."

Nicky flashed a smile. "Sounds good."

* * *

It seemed only minutes later that Nicky was tied to the massage table, nude, a blindfold across their eyes, waiting for their scene to begin.

It was the first time they'd done this kind of bondage, the first time they'd be doing a group scene, the first time they'd let strangers touch them.

A lot of edges to stretch in a single evening.

Adrenaline pumped through Nicky's veins as Arthur made the final tie securing Nicky to the table.

"How do the ropes feel?" he asked.

Nicky shifted from side to side, moved their feet, tried to raise their hands. There was a bit of give, but they weren't going to be able to move a whole lot. "They're fine."

"Not too tight?"

"Nope," Nicky said. "We're good."

"Perfect," Arthur cooed into Nicky's ear. "Then just lean back and relax."

The next thing Nicky knew, they felt someone (presumably Arthur) running their tongue over Nicky's collarbone, shoulder, and breasts. Then another touch joined the mix, then another, until the single flute of touch became a full orchestra.

Nicky's mind started getting hazy at the edges of thought. An idea would come in like a wispy cirrus cloud and disappear before it was fully formed. Soon, all Nicky could feel, sense, and be present to was the various people touching them. More hands, tongues, and fingers than they could dare count.

A person sucking each of their tits. Someone touching their clit and pussy. People stroking their legs. Massaging their feet. Kissing their collarbone.

The multitude of sensations lulled Nicky even deeper, and it carried them away into subspace.

* * *

It was close to nine o'clock when Kieran finally wrapped up his impact scene with Hyacinth. It had been a caning scene, and Hyacinth had screamed oh-so-delightfully in response to the pain. She protested that she could keep going, could handle at least five more strikes, but Kieran could tell that she was unaware of her own pain tolerance.

That was a perfect time to stop. Otherwise, the endorphins might wear off, and later she might decide they'd gone too far.

So, instead, he helped her up from the spanking bench, got her water, fetched her a blanket, and held her. A few minutes later, Hyacinth's partner, Wei, came over from her own scene and took her to one of the mattresses. Kieran watched Hyacinth snuggle into Wei. Satisfied that she was being taken care of, he began to pack up his toys and wipe down the spanking bench they had just used.

As the cleaner was drying, Kieran scanned the dungeon. On the other side of the room, a small group was gathering around a massage table. He saw Indigo, interacting with the crowd, speaking to people as they joined.

That was Nicky's birthday scene, then.

Kieran set his toy bag off to the side of the room where it was out of the way and walked over, waving to Indigo. Indigo greeted him warmly, clapping him on the shoulder.

"You saw Nicky's limit list earlier, right?" Indigo asked.

Kieran nodded. "Yeah, I did. I was there as they were writing it."

He'd actually been surprised and flattered. When Nicky had decided to let partners and metas touch their pussy and clit, he hadn't been sure he'd be included in that group. But sure enough, at the bottom of the "Hell Yes" section, there'd been just a short sentence in cramped writing:

Genital touching (pelvis, clit, pussy, vulva) with fingers and hands, permitted only by partners and metas: Arthur, Sofia, Ricky, Kieran.

Kieran was surprised because he'd only been dating Sofia a couple weeks, and he and Nicky had only done one scene together. Plus, from the little he'd learned and observed about them, it seemed Nicky had pretty clear boundaries when it came to sexual touch.

Even though he'd already read over Nicky's limits earlier, he looked over the list for the scene again. Just to make sure he knew *exactly* what was a hell yes and what was off-limits. There was nothing worse than someone surrendering control and having that consent be violated.

Intentional or not, consent violations disrupted scenes and broke trust.

Handing the list back to Indigo, Kieran made his way into the group and surveyed what was taking place.

There were half-a-dozen people touching Nicky in various ways. Sofia was sucking at one of Nicky's breasts, and Arthur was massaging their pelvis, running his tongue lazily around one of Nicky's hip bones. Ricky was touching Nicky's other breast, and Nicky was squirming, moaning.

Sofia looked up then, gazing at Kieran as she was still sucking Nicky's nipple, squeezing it with one of her hands. She paused, lifted her head, motioned for Kieran to join her, then resumed sucking.

Kieran could feel the energy of the scene pulsing through him, a big swell of pleasure and passion, magnified because of everyone that was present. It was magnetic, powerful.

Almost overwhelming.

"I'm glad you're here," Sofia murmured as Kieran placed a hand on her back. "You've been missing all the fun."

She kissed him then, still squeezing Nicky's nipple, and he kissed her back. As he did, he placed one hand on Nicky's arm, running energy through his fingers.

Nicky shivered at his touch.

Kieran smiled.

As he continued kissing Sofia, Kieran stroked Nicky's body, first their shoulder, then their arm, then their right breast. He could feel their energy opening, expanding, coiling into and outside of itself as the orchestra, the fugue reached a crescendo. Reiki energy flowed through him into Nicky, and their breath hitched.

Accelerando.

The scene began to move more quickly after that.

Nicky was moaning, biting their lip, squirming against the ropes and restraints.

Kieran placed a gentle kiss along their collarbone, then their shoulder, then dipped down to their breast, moving his tongue in circles around their nipple. Nicky began to buck against the rope restraints and their moans became louder.

Really, it was a bit of a shame that he couldn't kiss them on the mouth.

Or on their clit.

Kieran wondered what Nicky would taste like.

Moving downward, Kieran began brushing his hands along Nicky's pelvis, their inner thighs. Nicky shivered again, then settled, as he flowed some grounding energy into them. Then, gently, Kieran began brushing his hands and fingers against Nicky's vulva, their yoni.

They were so incredibly wet.

Kieran brought some of that wetness upward, tracing small circles around Nicky's clit, centering the energy, focusing it in the center of their groin, and moving it upward. Root chakra. Sacral chakra. Solar plexus.

As he moved the energy upward, Nicky's pelvis and abdomen seemed to expand, as did their energy system. Their chakras practically floated above their physical body, suspended in midair.

Ritardando.

Time stood still for a single instant as Kieran glanced at Nicky's face. The pleasure and ecstasy that was etched across their cheeks and lips… that was something Kieran wanted to remember forever.

He'd only been touching Nicky for a few moments when Sofia was at his side and kissed him roughly, pushing her breasts into him. Her energy was different than before. Needy, almost insecure.

Finally, Kieran placed it.

"Are you jealous?" he asked, pressing a kiss to her cheek.

Sofia didn't answer, just kissed him even more deeply on the mouth, and Kieran sank into it. There was so much passion swirling around him, so much energy entering him and exiting him and flowing through him.

It was heady and intoxicating.

There was something in the energy of the scene, something here, as he kissed Sofia that he hadn't felt in a long time.

There was passion, yes. Power and control, of course.

But there was also love.

And lots of it.

Kieran couldn't remember the last time he'd felt this much love, the last time he'd felt this loved. Swirling white-light energy radiating through his entire heart chakra, opening him, expanding him.

He moved that energy, the energy building between him and Sofia, through his body into Nicky's body, softening and spreading it. Empowering Nicky to release even more.

Kieran opened his eyes. He pulled at Sofia's long dark hair, and her lids lifted slowly. There was such desire and hunger, but also tenderness, care, and warmth.

And with all the energy present, all the love, Kieran wanted to hold onto this moment indefinitely.

Fermata.

Chapter Seven

After Nicky's birthday scene ended, Kieran helped clean up the massage table and ready the station for the next users. As he waited for the cleaner to dry, he looked over to the mattresses. Arthur had guided Nicky there a few minutes earlier for snuggles and other intimate aftercare.

"Mattress?" Nicky had muttered sleepily after being untied. Kieran almost laughed because it was so adorable. Nicky was *so* deep into subspace that very little would shake them from it.

Now, as Kieran watched, Nicky laughed, leaning in and caressing Arthur's face and touching him as he kissed and touched them back. The two of them were pressed together, both lying on their sides, smashing their bodies toward each other. Even from here, Kieran could see the sweat glistening off Nicky's pale golden skin, could see where they dug their fingers into Arthur as he touched them.

Arthur must have been fingering Nicky, because they pressed their pelvis into Arthur, gripped him even tighter, and their mouth formed an expanding 'O' shape.

It would have been nice, Kieran thought, to have cuddled with Nicky after their scene, to bring them the pleasure that Arthur was. But that hadn't been negotiated. That wasn't something Nicky wanted.

Kieran continued watching the two of them, even as Arthur placed his head between Nicky's legs and started touching their tits. Nicky's head lolled back, and their back began to arch. While their muscles tensed, it was so energetically different from the rigidity Kieran typically saw in Nicky.

This rigidity was the slow, sweet build of climax.

Kieran wondered what it would take to push Nicky over the edge. He imagined that Nicky's moans and screams were piercing, but between the distance and the loud music, he couldn't hear anything that came out of their mouth.

A touch along his bare shoulders brought him back to the moment, and he tore his eyes away from Nicky and Arthur.

"Are you ready for our massage scene?" Sofia asked. "I'm excited to finally do a scene with you."

"Almost," Kieran said. He scanned the area, wiped down the side table they had just used, and rearranged things slightly. "There. Yes. Let's find a mattress."

Two mattresses down from where Nicky and Arthur were, Kieran set up his massage scene with Sofia. He pulled out his oils and creams and asked Sofia to strip down as much as she felt comfortable. She kept her lacy underwear on, but otherwise she was completely nude. Her golden-brown skin glowed under the rope lights, and she pulled her long black hair to the side so that her entire back was visible.

"A few questions," Kieran said. "Are there any spots on your body you don't want me to touch?"

"Nope. I'm even willing to take off my underwear and let you touch me there if you ask very nicely," Sofia said playfully.

"Mmm," he replied. "We'll see about that. Next question: what kind of massage do you want? Sensual, therapeutic, or sadistic?"

"What's the difference?"

"Sensual massage is the softest. If you want to relax, that's the kind of massage that you want. Therapeutic tends to be a bit more intense because the primary goal is to release tension and help the body relax deeply. Only a few people I know can handle sadistic massages."

"Let's go sensual," Sofia said with a wink, after considering it for a moment. "After all, I do enjoy being sensual with you."

"Excellent," Kieran said. "Do you have any allergies to oils or to scents?"

Sofia shook her head and rested her face into the mattress.

Just as a new song came over the speakers, Kieran began the massage, gently rubbing oil over Sofia's back and shoulders. There was such powerful energy still running through him, and Kieran allowed it to flow into Sofia's skin as he massaged her. She began moaning, sinking deeper into the touch. Kieran sensed that she was feeling the electric sensation of energy.

Even though it wasn't a neotantric massage that he was giving her, Kieran felt so full, so joyful.

Sofia's shoulders softened into the mattress, and Kieran was getting hard at the thought of touching her all over. Her breasts, hips, and stomach. Perhaps he would pass on her yoni and glutes for this scene. Save that for a time when the two of them could negotiate it more explicitly beforehand.

As he continued massaging her hips, legs, and feet, he continued running and feeling the energy. Feeling the energy. It was full of such deep love. Pure white light.

Kieran rubbed the oils and creams in deeper. When Sofia was finally purring, he asked her to flip over. He massaged the front of her, beginning with her shoulders, legs, and stomach.

Then, finally, her breasts.

He pressed a kiss to her lips, and Sofia deepened it, sliding her tongue into his mouth. Kieran continued massaging her breasts, pinching her tits. It was raw and wild and passionate, and Kieran gripped her, his fingernails digging into her shoulders, her hips. Moaning, Sofia held him just as desperately as their bodies twisted deeper into the sheets.

"We've been here for a bit," Sofia said at last. "Ricky will be wondering what's happened to me. He can get a bit jealous, so we better wind this down."

Kieran nodded, pressing one final kiss to her lips, and pressed his body into her from behind. He wrapped his arms around her and listened as she chatted about some new real estate listings. As he held Sofia tightly, Kieran thought back to the group scene. The way that Sofia had looked at him with such care. His cock pulsed even more.

"Kieran?"

Shaking himself from his thoughts, he looked at Sofia. "Yes?" he said.

"Are you ready to wrap up?"

"Almost," he said. He grabbed Sofia's hands, and pressed another quick peck to her lips. "I wanted to do that first."

She giggled. "Aw," she said.

Kieran squeezed her hands, and looked into her eyes. "Also, I love you, Sofia."

Sofia's eyes went wide.

"You love me?" she said slowly.

Kieran nodded. "I love you."

She blinked, looked down at where he held her hands, then gently pulled them back toward herself.

"Thank you," she said awkwardly, at long last.

"Of course," he said, smiling. "You've had quite the impact on me the last few weeks, you know. And tonight, seeing the love and care and tenderness in your eyes, I really felt it. Love, that is."

Sofia nodded, not quite meeting Kieran's gaze.

"I should check in with Ricky," she said quickly. "See how he's doing. Like I said, he can get a bit jealous and we've been over here for a while doing our scene."

"Sure. Do you want me to walk you back?"

She shook her head. "No, that's okay. You said something about needing to get home before it got too late anyway. Deer, right? Don't want to get into an accident."

"Right," he said.

They gave each other a hug, and Kieran leaned in for a kiss. Sofia's lips felt a bit more rigid than usual, but he didn't think much of it. She was probably just overwhelmed, which was completely understandable.

"I guess I'll see you for our date on Friday?" she asked.

Kieran smiled. "Yes. I'm looking forward to it."

Then, with a final hug, Sofia darted away, and Kieran went to grab his toy bag and got ready to leave.

* * *

"Nicky! I need to talk with you. Something major just happened."

Even after cuddles and other aftercare from Arthur, Nicky was still out of it. Wearing their pajamas, they were cuddling with a massive unicorn and watching an animated movie that was on in the gaming room for the littles. Bleary-eyed, Nicky turned toward their girlfriend. "Sorry, Sofia. What did you say?"

Sofia sighed. "I need to talk with you. Kieran just left, and I walked him to the door. But before that, as we wrapped up our massage scene, he told me he loved me."

Nicky blinked several times. "He what?" they said.

"He said he loved me."

"That's… pretty fast," Nicky said slowly, then yawned. "It's been… what? Four weeks?"

"I know," Sofia said, a bit grimly. "I said thank you. I wasn't sure how to respond."

"So you don't love him?"

Sofia shook her head. "I like him, for sure, and I *really* want to have sex with him. But I don't love him."

"Fair enough," Nicky said, yawning again and stretching. They were so glad that Arthur was spending the night. More cuddles were definitely in order after that group scene.

"And now things just seem so… serious," Sofia said, making a face. "And heavy."

"Because he loves you?"

Sofia nodded.

Nicky just stared at her girlfriend. "I could understand that," they said at last.

Crossing her arms, Sofia sighed. "I just wanted something light and *fun* with Kieran. After all, Ricky comes first, being my primary and all. I mean, we live together. Plus there's you and Ivan. I don't have capacity for more than something light. Especially with my career."

"Hmm," Nicky said, gathering up Ollie and their backpack. "I'm going to go find Arthur and see what he's up to. See if he's ready to head out."

"What do *you* think, Nicky?"

Closing their eyes for a moment, Nicky looked up at Sofia. "I think that Kieran's my client and I don't have capacity for this conversation," they said coolly.

Then, they flung their backpack over their shoulder and walked off, leaving their girlfriend a little stunned behind them.

* * *

The next few days were awkward, but eventually Sofia and Nicky reconnected and made up. Nicky apologized for their out-of-line comment, and kept their thoughts to themself, just listening to Sofia as she shared about things with Kieran. They still felt distant from their girlfriend, and noticed that when Sofia kissed them, they felt revulsion, like they wanted to pull away.

That made Nicky feel ashamed of themself, like they were doing something wrong.

After all, it wasn't Sofia's fault that Kieran was also Nicky's client and that Nicky needed to be neutral. And Sofia was still their girlfriend.

But Nicky had to admit it was just a *bit* messy.

Christmas came and went, and then soon, it was New Year's. Originally, Nicky had plans with Arthur, but they also wanted to spend time with Sofia. Arthur wanted to spend the entire night with a partner, so he'd decided to spend the weekend with Asa in Chicago.

Honestly, Nicky and Arthur had been distant since the night of Nicky's scene. On the way home from the play party, Nicky had snapped at Arthur when he'd asked why they were so quiet. They were frustrated that Sofia hadn't been more mindful of how and when she was sharing about Kieran's feelings, but they didn't want to talk about it. In hindsight, Nicky could have handled it better.

As things with both Arthur and Sofia were a bit rocky, Nicky had begun messaging their ex-boyfriend Paco again. True, he rarely initiated, but he always responded, and he still cared for Nicky. He had made that very clear. And when they cuddled with him or kissed him, it still felt *so* good.

More than that, it was *comfortable*. Like a soft, worn blanket, Nicky knew *exactly* where the holes were.

When Nicky asked Paco if they could come over to his apartment and hang out with him, it felt familiar. Like repeating a cycle, going along a dirt path they'd traversed a thousand times before. Something they could do on autopilot without thinking. Drive this way. Turn here. Park in the lot. Use the side door. Hit the buzzer. Greet him with a hug. Enter, catch up, and chat.

Rinse and repeat.

Nicky even brought over one of their remaining meal kits so the two of them could cook together. Then Nicky and Paco watched a movie while they sat next to each other on the couch, snuggling under a blanket.

It was almost like old times.

Almost like when they were still together, and things were still good.

"Is it alright if I lean into you?" Nicky asked.

Paco raised an eyebrow. "I know what you're doing," he said.

"What?"

"You want to cuddle with me."

"Yes, but only if it's something you're open to. I just want to know where your boundaries are tonight," Nicky said truthfully.

Paco looked at Nicky with an exasperated smile. "It's fine."

They stayed that way for most of the movie. At some point, Nicky found themself holding hands with Paco, then they were kissing each other.

Then they were in his bedroom, still kissing.

It happened quickly, unconsciously. Following that same familiar path, the same route. Completing the same cycle. The one Nicky had completed thousands of times over the past several years.

Paco grabbed Nicky's breast, and Nicky froze. They slowly removed Paco's hand.

"I need to stop," they said. "I don't want to go there right now."

"Okay. But you *are* wearing a dress tonight. I mean, you were practically asking for it," he said.

Sitting bolt upright, Nicky slid off the bed and stormed out of the bedroom.

"I can't believe you just said that," they said finally, as they started putting their shoes on.

"I don't understand why you're so upset," Paco said, chasing after them. "It was a joke, Nicole."

Nicky closed their eyes, took a deep inhale, and exhaled. "The fact that you don't understand *why* I'm angry is the bigger issue," they said tightly.

In a swift, sharp movement, Nicky grabbed their coat, flung it around themself, and cinched it tight. Paco was still standing there, his arms crossed, his own energy just as tight, rigid, and restrained as Nicky's.

"It was just a joke," he snapped again. "It's not a big deal."

Shaking their head, Nicky just grabbed their purse, closed the door behind themself, and began walking to their car.

Moments like these made Nicky remember *exactly* why they should never, ever, *ever* get back together with Paco. Perpetuating rape culture was never okay.

* * *

Because of this myriad of factors—the situation with Paco and the strained relationships that they had with Sofia and Arthur—Nicky decided to drink more than usual on New Year's Eve. It was just two days after the affair with Paco, and Nicky had deleted his number from their phone.

Not that it really made any difference. They had it memorized.

Once Nicky was at Sofia and Ricky's place, they hung up their coat, kicked off their shoes, and made their way to the kitchen to have some food and beer.

First, it was a single Spotted Cow with dinner.

Then one of their favorite dubbels from a local brewery.

Then a peach concoction that Sofia insisted Nicky try.

After that it was two or three more drinks. To be honest, Nicky lost count after five. They couldn't remember if they grabbed a sixth one or not. Their head was spinning only a little since Nicky had spaced out the drinks over the course of the evening, but their filter was pretty well gone.

Sofia was lapping up the attention that she was receiving from her multiple partners—Ivan was there, and she was flirting with Kieran, too—and somehow, Nicky had just had enough.

This week, Sofia had canceled her date with Kieran, telling him that she was beyond capacity with work. But she shared privately with Nicky that she canceled the date because she wasn't as attracted to him. He'd started messaging her more, telling her he loved her over text, giving her pet names she didn't want.

It was too serious. Too committed. Too much.

Even though Nicky hadn't even had their onboarding session with Kieran yet, they felt weirdly protective of him, and the mixed messages Sofia was giving him (alcohol or no) were just confusing and inappropriate.

"Hey, Sofia," Nicky said after a moment, "can I talk with you?"

Sofia nodded, ended the conversation that she was having and met Nicky in the kitchen. "What's up?"

"Can we go to the guest bedroom? It's sensitive."

The two of them walked to the bedroom, which was full of boxes, stacked high with papers, and completely covered in Sofia's work. Nicky cleared an empty spot on the bed and sat down.

"So, what did you want to talk to me about, *chiquita?*" Sofia asked, running her hand along Nicky's face tenderly.

Nicky jumped back as though they'd been burned.

"What's wrong?" Sofia asked.

"Everything," Nicky said. Their breathing was shallow, rapid, so they took a moment to inhale, exhale. Release. Then they continued.

"I don't like how you're treating Kieran and how you're putting me in the middle because he's my client. I don't like hearing you complain about your relationship with Ricky, and how you call me looking for support when the two of you fight, which seems to be every single week. And then in the next breath you say that Ricky is the most important because he's your primary and you're living with him. As if I don't already *know* that he's your primary and I need to be reminded of my place. Which is second. Or third."

Nicky's voice, which had started out evenly, was ragged and acidic by the end.

Sofia looked concerned.

"*Chiqui,* can we please talk about this more later?" she asked. "It's New Year's Eve. I have guests in the other room."

Maybe it was the way that Sofia was glancing at the door, or maybe it was that Nicky had had five drinks, or maybe it was just that Sofia hadn't checked in with Nicky for the past several weeks. But Nicky was beyond the point of politeness.

"No, we're going to have this conversation *now*. Because you haven't checked in with me about what I need from this relationship, and I'm *done* bending over backwards for you."

Sofia's eyes glinted at that. "Well, just tell me how you really feel," she said sarcastically, throwing her hands up. "Clearly, I can't do *anything* right in our relationship. But you're the one picking a fight while you're drunk, and in the middle of a party. You know, your age and inexperience are *really* showing here."

That comment sliced through Nicky, and they felt the sting in their heart chakra and pretty much everywhere in their body.

"I think it's best if you don't stay the night tonight," Sofia said coolly.

Nicky snapped to attention, and their body became rigid. "Yeah, that seems wise," they said icily. "See you later."

Storming into the kitchen, Nicky grabbed their coat and other clothing, slammed on their boots, and stomped out of Ricky and Sofia's house, letting the door close loudly behind them.

* * *

Getting a cab on New Year's Eve took a bit longer than Nicky had anticipated, so they just sat in their car with the heat on. It would be a thirty-minute wait, the dispatcher had said, so Nicky was grateful that their gas tank was full. *Never let your tank get below half in winter*, Nicky's mother always said.

Even so, Nicky's breath was crystallizing, and there was condensation with every single exhale. To occupy themself while they were waiting, Nicky turned on the radio, leaned their head back, and did their best to let the music wash over them.

Rap, rap, rap.

Nicky glanced in the direction of the sound. There was Kieran, tapping on their passenger-side window. He was wearing earmuffs and a coat, but he'd taken off one of his gloves. When he saw Nicky acknowledge him, he put the other glove back on.

The cab was still several minutes away. Nicky rolled down the passenger-side window.

"Is everything okay?" Kieran asked. "You left really quickly and didn't say goodbye."

It was such a simple question, but for some reason, it brought Nicky's anger back to the surface. No, clearly everything was *not* okay, because they were sitting idling their car in the freezing cold waiting for a ride home. Nicky almost bit that out, but caught themself.

Kieran was a client. While the two of them admittedly already had a non-traditional relationship, it wasn't appropriate for Nicky to lash out at him.

More than that, though, Nicky knew he wasn't at fault here and was just trying to be kind.

In fact, if Nicky were in any other mood, they probably would have thought it was sweet that Kieran was checking on them. Had taken the time to leave the party, get his coat and earmuffs and gloves on and rap on their passenger-side window until they acknowledged him.

But Nicky *was* in a foul mood.

"No," Nicky replied shortly.

"Do you want to talk about it?"

They hesitated, and glanced at the passenger seat. It had books and boxes on it—per usual—but cold air was leaking in and fast. Then they reminded themself: Kieran was a client. A *new* client. They needed to have professional boundaries.

As it was, he'd already seen them drunk and less than pristine.

And Kieran hadn't even had a single session with Nicky yet.

God, this was *such* a mess.

"No, it's okay," Nicky said quickly. "I'll be fine. I called a cab, and they'll be here in—"

They checked the app and sighed.

"Fifteen minutes."

"Can I at least give you a ride home, then?" Kieran offered. "That way you're not waiting out here longer, and you're only paying for a cab tomorrow when you come to get your car."

It was sorely tempting. The cab ride would be quite expensive given the premium surcharge for New Year's Eve, not to mention the cab would undoubtedly go slower because of the snow.

But Kieran was a client.

Nicky debated it for another minute.

Ultimately, their frugality won out.

"Are you sure?" Nicky asked.

Kieran smiled, a wide grin that lit up his face. "I wouldn't have offered if I wasn't. I was thinking about leaving soon anyway."

Nicky slowly rolled up the window, grabbed the overnight bag they'd brought to Sofia and Ricky's, and turned off the ignition. They took a deep breath, stepped out of their car, locked it, and waited expectantly.

"Let me just say some quick goodbyes," Kieran said. "I'll be right back."

A few minutes later, he returned, and the two of them walked over to his car, a big black truck. Nicky gave him their address, and Kieran began driving his truck toward Nicky's apartment, going slowly over the freshly fallen snow.

"You know, if you do want to talk about what happened at some point," Kieran said, "I'm happy to listen."

Nicky bristled at that. They breathed into their irritation.

"I appreciate the offer," they said, "but I don't think that would be appropriate. You know, since you're my client."

The two of them rode the rest of the way in silence. Upon arriving at Nicky's apartment, Kieran put the truck into park. "Thanks for letting me give you a lift."

Another rush of irritation. "Thank you for the ride."

"You're welcome."

Nicky unbuckled their seatbelt, but continued to stay seated. Kieran gazed at them curiously and noticed that Nicky's mouth was opening and closing slightly, as though they wanted to say something.

"Was there something else?"

"Yes," Nicky said after a moment. Their spine was straighter, and the rigidity was back. Nicky's body was perfectly controlled, even if their voice was prickly. "I think it's for the best that we don't do any kink or BDSM together moving forward since we're working together now. Just to keep the boundaries of our relationship a bit clearer."

Kieran paused. There was something a bit off about Nicky's request. He couldn't quite place his finger on it, but he knew they weren't really able to consent or make requests right now because they had been drinking.

"Can we revisit this in a couple days during my coaching session?" he asked. "Tonight, you're my friend. Besides, you've had a lot to drink tonight. If you really feel that way, you'll still feel it in a couple of days."

Nicky's shoulders slumped, and suddenly they looked exhausted. They smiled, the first time they'd done so since Kieran had come out to their car to check on them.

"Yes, we can discuss it during your coaching session instead. Thank you, Kieran."

"You're welcome, Nicky. Sleep well."

"Thanks. Drive safe."

With that, Nicky hopped out of the truck, gave one final half-smile to Kieran, and shut the door of the truck behind them.

Chapter Eight

Nicky awoke to the worst headache ever. Cursing, they told themself they would swear off alcohol for an entire year. Nothing good ever came of them having more than one or two drinks in a single night, anyway.

Kieran had texted Nicky that morning to see how they were doing, and it reminded Nicky of the day after their scene with Kieran. They told him they were doing well, then took some ibuprofen. Once their head had stopped pounding, Nicky called a cab to drive them back to their car, and then drove to the gym.

Workouts always made Nicky feel better.

The next day, Thursday, Nicky resumed their standard hectic pace. Sales calls, posting on social media, updating the website, engaging with their Facebook community, and coffee chats with new referral partners.

Then, it was Monday, Nicky's intake and first session with Kieran.

Other than the single message replying that they were doing fine, Nicky hadn't spoken with Kieran at all since New Year's Eve. Admittedly, they felt a bit embarrassed that he'd seen them drunk at Sofia and Ricky's party, and emotionally so out of sorts. But honestly, Nicky had been so distracted with the drama with Sofia to care very much.

At first, Sofia apologized. And when Nicky had called to talk with her, she'd been very warm and affectionate. But then she launched into sharing about a recent fight with Ricky—without Nicky's consent.

"Honestly, I can't believe Ricky didn't text me that he was going to be out later. He said he would be home at six o'clock after work, and he wasn't home until nearly nine. He'd had a bit to drink of course, but it was more that he was out with his new girlfriend without letting me know that he'd be home late. We got into a huge fight about it, and I'm still upset, and I—"

"Sofia," Nicky said tiredly, "I can't listen to this right now."

Immediately, there was silence. "You *always* go on about Paco and your mysterious Peruvian prediction, and I listen to you. But when *I* have something to share, you can't make time for it."

Nicky felt a twinge of guilt and anxiety. "I'm sorry. You're right."

And so, Nicky had gotten pulled into the familiar pattern with Sofia once more, though they ended the call as soon as they could while still being polite. Tension had been thick during the rest of the call.

Even so, Sofia insisted that the two of them meet in person that weekend. She'd been talking with her life coach and therapist about her relationship with Nicky. *I want to make this work*, Sofia had said, *but it isn't working right now.*

Overall, it was draining. Nicky wanted to be supportive, but emotionally, they were so done.

Nicky refocused. Kieran was due to arrive any minute. They grabbed a legal pad and pen and waited.

The door clicked in the waiting room. Nicky stood up from their desk to greet Kieran in the communal reception area.

"It's so good to see you, Kieran," Nicky said.

Kieran grinned. "It's good to see you, too."

Nicky ushered him into their private office, put a paper hanger over the door that said *Session in Progress, Do Not Disturb*, and closed the door. Nicky wheeled their office chair out from behind their desk and sat down.

"You can sit there, if you like," Nicky said, gesturing to a comfortable wooden chair, decorated with sky blue cushions.

Kieran glanced over at the chair, then Nicky. He'd been drawn to a bright, round, multicolored table in their office, which stood alongside the wall, partway between the chair and Nicky's desk.

The wood of the table was painted a deep indigo and a bright, almost noxious green with a pattern of interlocking circles stenciled along the top. Kieran didn't know what the design was, but it looked familiar.

But the most interesting part of the table was the arrangement of crystals on top. At the center, there was a spherical pink stone nestled in a shimmery gray tray. Around the center stone, there were crystals of various shapes and sizes and colors. While Kieran could hold most of them in a single hand, some looked quite heavy.

"You're missing two crystals, you know," he said, pointing to the grid. "One here, another here."

Nicky looked up from their notes.

"Yes. I loaned one to a friend, and another to a client." Their eyes narrowed. "How could you tell?"

Kieran shrugged. "The energy seemed off. Like there's a hole, and it's waiting to be filled."

Nodding, Nicky gestured once more to the chair. "Fair enough. Let's get started, though. We only have ninety minutes, and I want to respect your time and get through as much as possible."

They started by doing a short intake. Nicky asked Kieran about his past experiences with coaching, energy healing, and therapy before exploring his intentions for the next three months more deeply.

"After today, we'll have six sessions together to work through whatever feels most supportive. You mentioned that you wanted to work on opening your third-eye chakra. Can you tell me more about that?"

Kieran shrugged. "I used to be really intuitive. About three years ago, my third-eye chakra became blocked. Stuck. Now, it's really frustrating. I don't see toxic patterns ahead of time, and I feel like I'm flying blind in relationships."

Scribbling on their legal pad, and on the intake form, Nicky nodded absently. "And what would be a sign of success for you in our relationship?"

Kieran raised an eyebrow.

Nicky glanced up, saw his confused look, frowned, then blushed. "Oh, sorry. In our *coaching* relationship. Three months from now, how would you know that our time together has been worth the investment?"

"Feeling more connected to myself. Sleeping better. Having my third-eye chakra be more open."

"Okay," Nicky said. "Let's quantify that. On a scale of one to ten, how open is your third-eye chakra?"

"I'd say it's forty percent open," Kieran admitted. "Maybe thirty."

"Three months from now, where would you like it to be?"

"Fifty percent," he said decisively.

Nicky frowned. "You don't want it more open than that?"

He shrugged. "I've been working at this for a few years, and that's been with a lot of effort and meditation and healing. I'm sure we'll do some great work together, and I have faith in you. I just want to set realistic expectations. For you and for me."

"Okay," Nicky said. They set the legal pad off to the side. "Is there anything else?"

Kieran shook his head. "Nope."

The intake complete, Nicky began adjusting the Reiki table and the lighting in the office.

"Given your intention for the next three months," they said, "I'd like to suggest that today we do some Reiki, and maybe do a past life regression. How does that sound?"

"Great."

Kieran hopped up on the Reiki table, and Nicky placed the yoga bolster beneath his knees. They were about to toss the sheet and blanket over him when he brought his hand up.

"I naturally run very warm with my body temperature. I've been told I'm a space heater. So you don't have to worry about using sheets or blankets with me. I'm comfortable."

This time, it was Nicky's turn to shrug. They set the covers aside as requested and prepped the timer and ambient music on their phone before guiding Kieran into a relaxed state of being.

"I'm going to invite you to take three deep breaths," Nicky said. "Inhale in, exhale out. Release anything that no longer serves you."

Kieran exhaled deeply, and his body softened into the Reiki table a bit more.

"Again, breathe in, inhale, and exhale out. Great, you're doing great."

With the second breath, Kieran's shoulders dropped, and his eyes closed.

"And a third breath. Breathe in, inhale, sipping in that air—and exhale out. Good."

With the third breath, Kieran's breathing slowed even more, and his fists unclenched.

"Before we go any deeper," Nicky continued, "I'm going to share a framework with you that I use during my sessions—The Traffic Light Trauma Framework. It's designed to keep you safer within the session, to give you guardrails so you're willing to go deeper. Every so often, I'll check in with you and ask what color you're at, and I want you to tell me green, yellow, or red. If I ask for a color and don't get one right away, I'll assume you're at yellow. I'll also be watching your body language and check in if I notice a change.

"Green means you're good to keep going deeper, that you're curious and willing to explore more. Your autonomic nervous system is not activated. Yellow means you want to pause, and there's something coming up. We'll pause and breathe together until you get back to green. Red means you want to stop the process; it also means you're having a trauma response. If you say red, I'll pull you out of the process immediately and bring you back to a fully conscious state to process what you just experienced. If you're not sure what color you are, say the one that's more severe. So if you're not sure if you're green or yellow, you're yellow. If you're not sure if you're yellow or red, you're red. Do you have any questions?"

Kieran smiled, and shook his head. "It's a lot like the traffic-light safeword system in kink. And I'm very familiar with that."

A soft smile crossed Nicky's own face. "Great. Then let's dive in."

Nicky counted back from ten to one to help Kieran relax more, then asked him to imagine a beautiful woods in the middle of night where the full moon was shining, and the leaves on the trees were just beginning to bud. This was the mind map that Nicky used to help determine what kind of healing their clients needed.

Kieran must have needed a past life regression, Nicky thought, because he began heading down toward the river of time where Kieran could access any and all past and parallel timelines. By the river, there was a dock with a canoe tied to it. Once Kieran said he was standing on the dock, Nicky continued with the guided imagery.

"All right," Nicky said. "When you're ready, I'm going to invite you to step into the canoe, untie from the dock, and pick up the paddle."

Nicky grabbed a stool and sat at the head of the Reiki table. They held Kieran's head, cradling it in their hands. The heat that radiated from their palms scorched them, but Kieran didn't seem to mind.

From there, Nicky continued to guide him down the river, toward another dock that represented the timeline that they would explore today, the one that would most support Kieran's healing in that moment. He seemed calm, placid, and peaceful.

So Nicky guided him onto the second dock and through a veil of mist.

Into the past life.

Immediately, Kieran's whole body began to shake with violent tremors, from head to toe. Nicky felt their heart rate increase, and they took a breath. Panicking right now would not be supportive. For themself or Kieran.

Fortunately, they'd previously had a session with another client who had experienced tremors while on the table, so Nicky knew it was an automatic response of the nervous system, a way for the body to release and heal trauma.

It didn't necessarily mean anything was wrong.

"Kieran, what color are you? Green, yellow, or red?" Nicky asked timidly.

"Green," he said, with some effort.

"Are you sure?" they asked.

"Yes," he said. "We can keep going."

With his consent, Nicky began asking Kieran to see the past life in which he'd landed. He was a hunter, in the plains, moving through tall grasses, and it was hot. There was danger nearby.

All the while that Kieran was having that rich, vivid, multidimensional experience in his mind, Nicky sat at the end of the table, watching his trembling body, holding his head, flowing him Reiki, and scanning for signs that he might not be at green any longer.

But every time that Nicky checked in, Kieran insisted he was green.

Then, they guided him toward the spot where he was feeling dread.

His tremors intensified, and Nicky took a deep breath, holding the space, grounding themself, being the anchor for him in the moment.

"What do you see?" they asked quietly.

"I see—" and he just started sobbing. "I see—"

"Green, yellow, or red?"

Kieran took a deep, shuddering breath. His voice cleared. "I see my partner, my wife, and she's been killed. Massacred, tied up. I don't know, maybe hunted—"

Again, Kieran's voice broke.

"I'm going to invite you to leave this clearing," Nicky said. "We'll go into another scene."

They explored within the past life some more, but again, Kieran ended up in the same clearing, with the bloody image he couldn't quite fully explain, his tremors more intense.

"I want to come out of this process," he said. "I can't take any more right now."

Immediately, Nicky guided him out of the past life. They invited Kieran back to a waking state and asked him to wiggle his fingers and toes.

"When you're safely back inside your body, back inside the room," Nicky said, "you can open your eyes."

Kieran's tremors stopped, and after a moment, he opened his eyes. He looked utterly exhausted.

"Can I get you a glass of water?" Nicky asked mildly.

He nodded silently.

When Nicky returned with the glass, Kieran gulped at it. Eventually, as his breathing started to regulate, he began sipping it more.

That had been *intense*.

"How are you feeling?" Nicky asked. "You had some potent visuals."

"I need a few minutes to integrate from that," he said.

"Sure," Nicky said. "Is it alright if I flow you Reiki while you're coming down from that?"

"Yes."

Kieran continued drinking his water, and Nicky squatted down, a few feet away. They held their hands in front of them, cupped, as though they were a catcher. Even though Kieran knew Nicky was just flowing him Reiki, he smiled nonetheless.

"Can you work a little bit on my third eye?" he asked. "It's feeling clogged."

Standing up, Nicky began making circular motions with their fingers and hand in front of Kieran's forehead, still not touching him, about two feet away.

But then, they made motions like they were tapping something into his third eye.

Pain ripped into his forehead, like a hammer was splitting the center of his skull apart.

He winced.

"I can feel that all the way from here," he said. "My third eye is sensitive. Especially now. You don't need to be so forceful with it."

A red flush covered Nicky's cheeks and neck. "Sorry about that."

They softened their touch after that, and finally, Kieran was feeling grounded, back in his body.

"Are you good to drive home?" Nicky asked, their eyebrows furrowed. "I know it's been a while since you came out of the regression, but you went through a lot."

Kieran nodded. "Yeah, I'll be fine. Thanks for today. I can tell we started getting into something really deep."

"You're welcome. I'll see you in two weeks."

Once he closed the door behind him, Kieran took a deep breath.

This coaching relationship was going to stretch him; he could already tell.

* * *

Nicky wished they could have said that their session with Kieran was the most interesting thing that happened that week.

Unfortunately, it wasn't.

All too soon, it was Saturday, the day when Sofia wanted to meet in person to discuss their relationship. She'd requested that the two of them meet at Nicky's apartment. Ricky was home, and according to Sofia, he was upset at Nicky over what transpired on New Year's Eve.

Nicky lit a fire, grabbed their water bottle, and waited on the couch under a blanket until they heard the doorbell ring. They let Sofia in the building, then into their apartment, then took their seat again on the couch. Sofia joined them, perching on the edge of her seat.

She looked sober, stern, and a little defensive.

"I can't keep doing our relationship the way it is right now," she said.

"I agree," Nicky replied.

"I've spoken with my coach and I've talked it through with my therapist, and this is what I need in place if we're going to keep dating."

Everything that Sofia named that she needed was understandable; listening, empathy and compassion, Nicky keeping rude comments to themself, and not cutting Sofia off when she was speaking.

But the way it was communicated, it felt like Nicky had done everything wrong in their relationship. They did their best to keep listening, but at some point they began tuning out. Nicky slid to the floor. Their body was cold, even with the heat on and the fire raging. This was challenging, uncomfortable. Nicky took a deep breath.

"Thank you for the feedback. I'll sit with this all. I'm not sure if I can do this, but I'll take some time to think it over and let you know," they said.

Immediately, Nicky's teeth started chattering. They couldn't shake this chill.

Sofia paused for a minute, then nodded. A clear coat of surprise covered her face.

"Well, that went better than I expected," she said.

"Wh-what w-were y-you e-e-expecting?" Nicky asked.

"Honestly, when I walked in here, I wasn't sure if we were going to break up or not. It was all dependent on how this conversation went," Sofia said bluntly.

It felt like an icicle to Nicky's heart.

Did Sofia really have that little faith in them?

"I th-th-think I n-need s-some sp-space," Nicky said.

"Sure." Sofia stood up to leave, still holding her paper and notes that she'd been reading from.

"C-c-can I have y-y-your notes? As a r-reminder?" Nicky asked. "I wr-wrote it down, but it would be helpful t-t-to look at yours."

Sofia scanned her paper, then shook her head. "Your notes will be more useful, I think."

The two of them gave each other a quick hug, then Sofia left Nicky's apartment. Nicky pulled a big fuzzy blanket over them and huddled closer to the fire, trying to get warm.

* * *

Nicky took Kieran's feedback to heart. As a result, their second session with him went much better. When doing Reiki on him during his session, Nicky was very gentle with his third-eye chakra, gently touching the air above it. If they tapped in any symbols, they did so lightly.

"How did this happen?" Nicky asked at the end of their session, once they'd wrapped up the Reiki and sealed Kieran's chakras. "No offense, but it feels like your third-eye chakra is a black hole, this void or something. I've never seen anything like it."

Kieran smiled. "None taken. I don't know exactly. All I know is that I don't remember six months of my life. That was about three years ago. I don't remember *anything* that happened during that time. Afterward,

I had this blockage, sensitivity, and pain in my third eye. Every time I start to look into the depths, I feel terror. Pure terror."

Even hearing Kieran describe his experience made Nicky feel cold.

"Thank you for sharing," they said.

"You're welcome."

Nicky grabbed Kieran some water and guided him through some deep breaths. Once he was grounded and fully back in his body, Nicky checked in. "Do you feel safe to drive?"

He nodded. "Yeah. There's just one other thing I wanted to share."

"Okay, shoot."

"Sofia told me that she doesn't want to date me anymore," he said. "She said she's at capacity with her other relationships and she wants to tend to them. I just wanted to let you know."

Nicky folded their lips together. Sofia had messaged them this yesterday, of course. She'd even sent Nicky screenshots of her messages to and from Kieran.

From that, Nicky knew what Sofia had shared with Kieran wasn't the full story.

"Thank you for letting me know," they said simply. "Can I walk you to the door of the office suite?"

Kieran said yes, so Nicky joined him in the waiting area as he put on his coat, earmuffs, hat, and gloves.

"I'll see you in another two weeks?" Kieran asked.

Nicky nodded. "Yep, that works great. I can't believe it will be February already."

He grinned. "Me neither. This year is going to fly by."

Chapter Nine

No sooner had January melted into February than Nicky jetted off to Florida to attend a retreat for holistic entrepreneurs with Bailey. After the networking events each evening, the two of them watched cable TV in their hotel room, swam outside at the pool, or walked the grounds of the hotel. The night before they were to fly home, Nicky and Bailey spent nearly two hours in the hot tub, watching the sun set and the stars glitter.

"This is heaven," Nicky said, sinking deeper into the warm, warm water. "I never want to leave."

Bailey chuckled, a gentle tinkle of laughter. "Well, I'm grateful we head back tomorrow. Aidan, my husband, has been beside himself without me. Even though our daughter's been at school during the day, I'm usually helping look after her on nights and weekends. And I miss her. I miss them."

Nicky thought about what they were going back to. An empty apartment, a pile of dishes, and clothes strewn over the floor and couches.

"Well, I hope you've had fun at least," they said.

"Oh, yes!" Bailey laughed again, splashing into the water, her blonde ponytail getting even wetter. "It's been a blast. I'm glad we've been able to do this together."

"Me too," Nicky said. "Who'd have thought we would have ended up here?"

They settled into silence. As if by magic, lights in the pool and hot tub and on the pool deck turned on, illuminating the space.

"Bailey, can I ask you something?" Nicky asked. "As a friend? It's personal."

"Sure."

Nicky bit their lip, unsure how to describe this. "A few weeks ago, Sofia and I talked about our relationship. She shared what she needed if we're going to keep dating. During our conversation, I started shivering, and my teeth started chattering. It wasn't until after she left that I was finally able to get warm, and I was exhausted."

"It sounds like you were having a trauma response," Bailey said with a bit of a frown. "Like you felt attacked."

"Why would I feel that way?" Nicky blurted out, but even as they said it, they knew why.

From their perspective, Sofia was blaming them for what had happened on New Year's. Yes, Nicky probably shouldn't have broached that conversation with her after having so much alcohol and when Sofia had other guests over. But Sofia had made some hurtful comments that night, too, and she still hadn't acknowledged the frustrations Nicky had expressed.

Was Nicky really the villain here?

"It takes two people to create a relationship. Whether it's a delight or a disaster," Bailey said sagely.

"Meaning?"

"If your relationship with Sofia isn't working, it isn't anyone's fault, and it's both of your responsibility. The question is, do you want to keep working to make it better?"

No.

The answer inside Nicky was so strong, so fervent, so immediate. There had been some beautiful things early on in their relationship with Sofia, but recently, it hadn't been fun.

It felt hard. It was draining Nicky's energy, and honestly? They wanted to be single.

The idea of having space and freedom after several months was exciting. The amount of emotional support they were providing Sofia felt suffocating. Weirdly, Nicky had always resisted being single and had wanted to have at least one partner at a time, but now they craved being single. Focusing on themself sounded so nice. Comforting.

They were barely in contact with Arthur these days, so without Sofia, Nicky wouldn't be dating anybody.

"I want to be single," Nicky said, looking right at Bailey. "I want to be single. I'm excited to be single. And work on myself. Work on the business."

"That calls for a toast," Bailey said, lifting up her rumless strawberry daiquiri.

"More than that, I think," Nicky said. "I think it calls for alcohol. Just one, though. I *definitely* learned my lesson about overindulging on New Year's Eve."

As Nicky stepped out of the hot tub to go toward the bar, Bailey smiled, raising her glass again, taking another sip of her drink.

* * *

Upon returning to Madison, Nicky texted Sofia asking to talk. This time, at Sofia's place. That way, if there were intense emotions, Nicky could leave quickly without asking someone else to leave.

"Hey," Sofia said, leaning in for a peck on the lips, her customary way of greeting Nicky.

Nicky turned and offered their cheek instead.

Sofia stiffened, and her eyes widened, but she didn't say anything.

The two of them walked into the family room together, and sat on the green striped couch. It had seen better days, Nicky thought mildly. Sofia's dog had chewed a cushion at one end, and even with the fabric patch that had been expertly sewn on, there were still some threads hanging awkwardly.

"What's up?" Sofia asked.

"I've been sitting with what you and I discussed a few weeks ago," Nicky said. Might as well get straight to the point. Rip it off quickly and cleanly, like a bandage.

"And?" she prompted.

"I want to be single. I want to focus on myself and my business. Right now, I'm investing a lot of time and energy in our relationship, and it's not fun like it used to be. So, I want to break up."

Sofia nodded, an edge of steel in her movements. "I suspected as much when you didn't kiss me. And really, even when you asked to talk."

Nicky sat there awkwardly, not sure where to go from there. "I hope we can be friends," they said, "once some time passes, of course. Especially since we both go to the same kink space together. It would be nice to see you and not have it be awkward."

"We'll see," Sofia said.

The two of them sat in silence for a few minutes. Nicky's heart was beating rapidly, slamming itself against their ribcage.

"I mean, things have been on the rocks since New Year's Eve, if I'm being honest," Sofia said. "That's when we broke."

Biting their lip, Nicky said nothing. For them, there had been so many small moments earlier than New Year's Eve that were little fractures that had weakened the ice. The night of the party was just when Nicky and Sofia had slipped through into the dark, freezing water.

"Is there anything else you want to say?" Nicky asked at last.

Sofia shook her head curtly. "Nope."

"All right. Well, then I'll be heading out."

Standing up, Nicky put on their shoes, grabbed their coat, and put on their hat and mittens. They glanced at Sofia once more.

She had her arms folded across her chest, and it looked like she was torn between wanting to give Nicky a hug, wanting to cry, and glaring at Nicky in anger. Honestly, Nicky wasn't sure how they felt, either.

"I hope you have a great week," Nicky said awkwardly. They walked to the door and down the concrete steps toward their car.

Even though they didn't look back at the house, it didn't matter. Nicky knew the house, and Sofia's ambivalent expression, would be branded in their mind indefinitely.

* * *

In the days following their breakup with Sofia, Nicky poured themself into their work. It was a habit, of course, trailing over from their days as a high-achieving student. When Nicky was busy with work, they could bury their feelings more easily. But eventually, Nicky could see the familiar face of burnout looming near. They were snacking on meals quickly, only a couple times a day, unintentionally fasting until two o'clock in the afternoon, and they were cranky and extra-sensitive.

As a proactive measure, Nicky scheduled a session with their therapist and booked a mental health day on their calendar. Because Nicky's therapist worked an hour away in Baraboo, they would make a day of it. Drive up to Baraboo, have their appointment, and then go hiking at Devil's Lake State Park before driving back to Madison.

They laced their hiking shoes, readied their pack, and set off.

Once they reached the office of their therapist, Emma, Nicky parked and took a couple deep breaths. It had been six months since they'd last seen Emma. Money had been tight with starting the business last year, but Nicky knew that a session now was necessary.

Nicky had met Emma nearly two years ago, and she'd helped them immensely, especially as Nicky came out as queer, non-binary, and poly. Emma was polyamorous and non-binary herself and had supported Nicky as they'd come out to their parents, and as they'd started dating as an open poly person. Most of all, though, Emma was compassionate and direct; she'd learned to be fearless in the face of oppression. In addition to being non-binary, Emma was Arab-American, Muslim, and wheelchair-bound. As a result, Emma faced immense discrimination and vitriol simply for existing, let alone thriving.

Emma's bravery and continual commitment to helping others heal had inspired Nicky on countless occasions.

"People spew hate toward others because they haven't healed their own trauma," Emma had once told Nicky. "That's why I chose to become a therapist. I want to disrupt the cycles of abuse, ancestral trauma, and colonialism in any way that I can."

Today, after being whisked away to Emma's offices, Nicky was handed a bottle of water and a piece of dark chocolate, and they began to share what was going on in their life.

"I started dating a woman last September, and at first we really hit it off. We met at a networking event, and I liked that she was Latina, and she was driven, really ambitious. She's an independent real estate agent, and she's been making six figures the past few years."

"I can hear a but coming," Emma said, taking a sip of her own water.

"We started having disagreements. And… I don't know exactly… it just exploded. I exploded. She hadn't been polyamorous before dating me, and I think it was an adjustment. I got really tired hearing about her primary relationship, and the new people she was dating. At some point the magic we both felt at the beginning wore off. I couldn't keep doing it."

"So you ended it?" Emma asked.

"Yes," Nicky said. Their head was talking, but they felt completely disconnected from their body.

"How are you feeling, now that it's over?"

"Relieved," Nicky admitted, unwrapping the piece of dark chocolate. "It was more stressful than I realized. But I also miss her. I keep feeling like I did something wrong and I should try to fix it."

Emma made a note on the pad of paper in front of her.

"Nicky, you and I haven't talked about the placate trauma response, have we?"

Nicky shook their head. "Nope. I mean, I've heard of the fight or flight response. And there's freeze, too, right? Like how deer stop in the middle of the road and freeze to avoid being hit by the car?"

Smiling, Emma nodded. "Yep. Placate or fawn is a fourth possible response to trauma, and I've found it's common for people who have a history of anxiety, perfectionism, or overachieving."

Nicky grimaced. "That's me, all right."

"What I'm hearing is that your response to trauma in your relationship with Sofia was to placate her. To fawn. To fix things and make everything okay in response to her being upset. To over-apologize, or apologize for things that weren't your fault or responsibility. It's a coping strategy you likely learned in childhood. You placated your parents when they were upset, for fear that they would stop loving you."

Nicky's mom, Donna, had written detailed accounts of Nicky's childhood, and she had gifted it to them a couple years ago. Even at two years old, Nicky apologized profusely every time their mom said she didn't like Nicky's behavior. And then, little Nicky would ask if their mom still loved them.

Nicky had had those patterns with Sofia, too. Their first female partner.

The realization felt like a kick to the shin, and they didn't respond.

"Nicky," Emma asked after a minute, "are you okay?"

"I'm fine," Nicky mumbled. "Just a lot to take in."

"Okay," Emma said, and she didn't press any further.

From there, Emma and Nicky spoke more about Nicky's patterns of overworking and explored how Nicky might practice self-care consistently, eat healthily, and be kind to themself. By the end of the session, Nicky had identified how they could inject more fun into their life, set healthier boundaries with work, and begin to heal from their relationship with Sofia.

"Can you reflect back to me what you're putting into place this week, Nicky, before we wrap up for the day?" Emma asked.

Nicky nodded. "Yep. I'm going to run three times this week at the gym, and I'm still going to go to the local kink event this weekend even though Sofia might be there. I'm going to leave my laptop at the office so I don't bring my work home with me. And I'll set reminders to shut off my laptop by six o'clock in the evening so that I have time to clean my apartment, do a short workout, and relax."

"And as far as eating?"

"I'm not going to work on Saturdays or Sundays unless I'm leading a retreat," Nicky recited, "so I will go grocery shopping and meal prep on Saturdays. During retreat weeks, I'll ask my mom to make some freezer-ready meals for me. Or get sandwiches from Subway to fill in the gaps."

"Great. That all sounds wonderful." Emma gave Nicky a big smile. "Do you want to schedule your next appointment?"

Shaking their head, Nicky stood up to leave. "No, I need to let this integrate first. I'll see how I'm feeling in a couple weeks, and I'll probably contact you then."

"When would you like me to follow up with you if I haven't heard anything?" Emma asked.

Nicky thought for a minute. "Mid-April? In a couple months?"

"Sounds great. Talk to you soon, Nicky. I'm rooting for you."

* * *

Over the course of the next month, Nicky focused on giving themself exquisite self-care. They scheduled solo date nights, journaled, and consistently left their laptop at the office. Their sessions with Kieran were continuing to go well, and he was seeing some improvement in his ability to connect with his intuition and his authentic self. Nicky even took up weekly ballet classes, something that gave them so much joy.

But just as their new supportive habits started to take hold, there was even more to navigate. It was sudden and jarring, like the biting lash of a single-tail whip.

It started when Nicky was meeting with a prospective client at a local café. They both ordered coffee, but when Nicky looked for the creamer jug and the sugar packets at the self-serve station, they were missing. Confused, Nicky returned to the counter and asked the barista why the milk, cream, and sugar weren't in their normal places.

"It's according to the county's current health code," the barista said, handing Nicky a small creamer packet and a few packets of sugar. "I'm sorry. I know it's a pain. But we can't do the large self-serve items because of COVID-19. You know, the new virus?"

That was on March 5.

The flood started five days later.

First, there was an email from the local university canceling non-essential events. Then, the next day, an email canceling all classes. Nicky wasn't immediately affected by the closures, but the university was a big part of the city's social life, so they knew it was a big deal.

Emails from Nicky's gym and dance studio followed, announcing modified cleaning protocols and practices to keep everyone safer.

After that was an email from the kink event space letting people know that they *might* need to cancel the upcoming play party on March 21, and to stay tuned.

Then, social media exploded.

First, it was about a shortage of toilet paper. People posting pictures about stores being completely sold out. Steel racks were completely bare. Nicky raced to their bathroom. They didn't have any backup rolls, just the one they were using.

They panicked and called their mom.

"Mom, have you heard the news?" they asked, pacing their apartment, glancing at their newsfeed. "Stores are sold out of toilet paper. And I'm on my last roll."

That night, Nicky's mom went to three different stores before she found any toilet paper and purchased six big packages—two for Nicky, two for Nicky's sister, and two for her own home. Then, she met Nicky halfway between Illinois and Madison for the handoff. Nicky felt grateful they could do that; they knew not everyone had the same privilege.

From that day on, Nicky checked social media obsessively, hungry for updates and shreds of news. Over the next few days, they focused less on work, refreshing their newsfeed every twenty seconds. All so they could read the new articles about the virus, how it spread, who was at risk, and how to handle it.

Within a week, almost everything had shut down. Even grocery stores had instituted limited hours so that people could clean at night. Banks were drive-through only. Massage studios and other holistic wellness places closed, too.

The play party scheduled for March 21 was officially canceled, and tickets were refunded. Other kink spaces postponed their events, citing the pandemic. *We hope to be back next month*, the emails read. *Stay tuned.*

Finally, Nicky messaged Kieran, the one client with whom they had scheduled future in-person sessions. Given COVID-19 and the governor's executive orders, Nicky suggested they have future sessions remotely. Until further notice.

Kieran agreed. And Nicky breathed a sigh of relief.

They didn't leave their apartment for three days. Not even to go downstairs to visit their long-term pantry or wash their clothes. Nicky knew everything in their apartment was clean. Or maybe not clean, but at least only infected with *their* germs. They didn't know about the communal doorknobs in the building, or the ones in the basement. What if they contracted COVID-19?

With new anxiety and their most useful coping strategies—working out at the gym, ballet classes, kink—taken away, Nicky once again began to pour themself into the one thing that was most familiar: work.

* * *

After navigating three weeks of pandemic life alone in their apartment, Nicky desperately missed human contact. Hugs. Even being in the same physical space as someone else. Nicky decided to move in with their parents and immediately felt relief. When Nicky checked in with Bailey over video chat, though, Bailey shared that she was experiencing an *opposite* problem. Rather than feeling lonely and isolated, she was worried her family would argue more the longer the pandemic wore on.

"I haven't been going to the office like I had been, so I'm getting stir-crazy. Plus my husband is working remotely, and our daughter's school is virtual now. I think it's only a matter of time until our home feels like a pressure cooker."

"Like you can only outrun your problems for so long before they boil over," Nicky said, thinking back to their breakup with Sofia. "Yeah, I know that feeling."

"I just don't know what's going to happen," Bailey said. "The stay-at-home order has been extended through the end of May. That means June is the earliest we'll be able to open up the office and I'll be able to do in-person sessions again."

Nicky nodded grimly. "Yeah, I saw that update. I'm not thrilled. That's part of the reason I decided to move down here."

"How is it at your parents' place?"

Shrugging, Nicky glanced around. "Pretty nice. The basement here is my office, and I'm sleeping upstairs. Just not great that I'm paying rent for two spaces I'm not using—especially since we only moved into the office four months ago."

"I know," Bailey said, grimacing. "I'm sorry about that."

"On the plus side," Nicky continued, "My mom is respectful of my hours, and if she knows I have a meeting or a livestream, she'll take a break from sewing masks so it doesn't interrupt what I'm doing."

"She's making masks?"

"Yeah." Nicky scrunched their face up. "Cotton masks. Five hundred, I think, is her goal? She's donating them to local clinics, nursing homes, and hospitals since there's been a shortage of the N-95 respirators. But she's also making a few for family members. She's been working eight hours a day to get them done. "

"Snag me one if you can?" Bailey asked. "I've been looking at some on Etsy, but they're all on back-order."

Nicky laughed. "Sure, I can bring you one the next time I'm in Madison. Should be easy enough. Like I said, she's literally making hundreds."

They shifted topics then, and Nicky began sharing about their upcoming masterclass series, The Sexual Healing Challenge.

"It's going to be an energetic marathon," Nicky said, groaning. "I don't know how I thought I could do this by myself. My business coach does hers with three other team members. Even though mine won't be as big, I don't know how I'll get everything done for it."

"You know," Bailey said thoughtfully, "I've got a bunch of extra time on my hands since I'm not seeing in-person clients right now. If you tell me what you want me to do, I'm happy to support you. What you've been doing is amazing, and I'd love to be part of it."

Nicky was stunned. They certainly hadn't expected that.

"Really?" Nicky asked. "Are you sure? It's going to be intense. All hands on deck for nearly two weeks. Are you sure you can make space for that?"

Bailey chuckled. "If I can't make space for it now, I don't know when I could. There's nowhere to go and no one to see, unless it's virtually."

"Awesome, then let's set it up," Nicky said.

They began to hash out the logistical details, determining when they would meet next, and how and when Bailey would be compensated for her support. By the time that Nicky waved goodbye to Bailey's face on video chat, they were grinning. The Sexual Healing Challenge would be *great*. Thanks to Bailey, they would have the emotional and logistical support that they needed. More than that, Bailey was someone that Nicky really trusted. She was intuitive, and Nicky knew that Bailey would be attuned to Nicky's needs throughout the process.

All Nicky needed now was a few clients who would be willing to share about their coaching experience with Nicky and the benefits they had seen.

And Nicky knew *exactly* where to start.

Chapter Ten

"Hey, Kieran," Nicky said, waving at their webcam. "It's good to see you. Thanks for allowing me to interview you."

A smile crossed Kieran's face. "Of course. You're welcome."

It was just a few minutes before that day's masterclass was due to start. Nicky checked mic levels and practiced bringing them both on the stream. Everything looked good.

"You ready?" Nicky asked.

Kieran nodded. "Whenever you are."

Taking a deep breath, Nicky removed Kieran from the stream and hit the button to go live.

Show time.

"Hi, everyone! Welcome to our second bonus training of the Sexual Healing Challenge. Today we're talking about releasing trauma through energy healing. We'll be talking about different kinds of energy healing, and how those modalities heal the body, mind, and spirit.

"First, a few reminders. The video replays are coming down on Tuesday at 11:59pm, so you still have a few more days to watch any content you've missed. Second, if you need the workbook, please reach out and let me know, and our team will get it to you."

In the chat, Bailey was welcoming everyone, tagging people that had said they would show up for the livestream, even sharing a couple emojis. Thank God. It made Nicky feel less awkward since literally *no one* else was there yet.

Hope they're watching the replay, Nicky thought.

"Next, I've been getting a few emails and some questions about the coaching program, what it costs, and what's included."

This last part was a complete lie, and Nicky hated themself for it. Nicky hadn't gotten any queries, even though a few people had tuned in day after day on the livestreams. Nicky's coach insisted that this kind of response was normal, and it only took one person signing into the program for it to turn the tide and have more people sign up.

Most people will come in during the last day, or even once you take the content down. Keep building interest, their coach had advised.

God, Nicky hoped she was right.

"The information about the program is pinned to the top of the Facebook group, but I'll drop the link on this training, too."

Nicky cleared their throat, took a sip of water, and continued.

"Last, we have two more workshops after today. Tomorrow, I'm talking about healing shame from purity culture, and we'll do another healing process. Tuesday, I'm leading a masterclass on whichever topic is most valuable to all of you. There's a poll going right now, and the current winner is Identifying, Communicating, and Maintaining Authentic Sexual Boundaries.

"All right, that's it for the announcements. Without further adieu, I'm going to bring my guest, Kieran Jackson, on the livestream to join us for today's conversation."

Feeling flushed and shaken, and still doing their best to maintain composure, Nicky clicked the button that brought Kieran up onto the screen.

The two of them started with some small talk, and Nicky forced themself to feel their feet on the ground. Their shoulders were tight and rigid. Relax, they needed to relax.

All they were doing was talking with Kieran virtually, as they'd done several times during the pandemic. They knew Kieran valued the work they did. After all, he had decided to renew his coaching contract for another four months at the end of March.

But this time you have an audience, even if they're invisible, a voice piped up. *You're on display, so you need to be perfect. People can see if you're uncomfortable.*

Nicky *really* wished that voice would shut up.

"So, Kieran," they said smoothly, "before you became a coaching client, you already understood and practiced some forms of energy healing. Can you speak about your background with energy healing prior to us working together?"

Kieran smiled serenely. He was *so* much more at ease and grounded than they were right now, Nicky realized. Would that look bad? Could people tell?

"Sure. I came into energy healing through physical therapy and massage. I found that incorporating energy into massage helped people heal better when I was working on them. By doing that work, I became aware of my own energy system, my own chakras. Especially my heart chakra. Then, when I realized I had a blockage in my third eye, I understood how it affected me and what kind of support I might need to get rid of it."

Perfect answer. Brilliant, really. It set up the next question perfectly.

So why was Nicky so nervous?

"During our time together, we've explored a few different modalities... past life regressions, Reiki, and guided visualizations. What benefit have you seen from our sessions, especially with healing trauma? How has energy healing helped you heal trauma from your past and current relationships?"

Impassive. His face was impassive. Was that bad? No, Nicky assured themself. Calm. He was *calm*. Dammit, he was so hard to read.

"Doing past life regressions with you has been helpful in healing trauma from my marriage," Kieran added. "And doing the process where I spoke directly to my ex-wife's authentic self helped me find resolution. That wasn't a conversation that was going to happen otherwise. But I needed to have that conversation in order to let go of the anger and frustration I had toward her."

He smiled. A big smile. It made Nicky smile.

The tension in their shoulders began to release, and they scooted back in their chair.

Chatting with Kieran like this was almost *fun*.

Next, Nicky rounded back to the overall benefits that Kieran had seen during their time together. What had he gained? How had working with Nicky been beneficial?

"I definitely feel that doing holistic coaching with you, combined with therapy, has allowed me to heal faster," Kieran answered. "There were *a lot* of different issues going on, and with traditional therapy, it would take years to heal them. Being able to get right to the heart of the issue and understand the traumas and triggers that I had—sometimes within just a single session—that was huge."

"Why was that so important for you, Kieran?" Nicky asked.

"With my third eye being blocked, it's harder for me to identify the trauma patterns that I have," he replied. "Working with a coach or therapist makes that work easier."

He looked straight at the camera, and Nicky felt like he could see them, really see them. It was unnerving, and their back tensed again.

"Before I started working with you, I felt like I was only functioning at thirty or forty percent," Kieran added, still looking straight at Nicky. "I was looking at the world through a lens that was out of focus. I could still see things, make out shapes, but I didn't know where I was going. It was really disorienting. Because I wasn't connected to what I really wanted, I questioned all my major decisions, and I felt like I was making bad decisions because I wasn't in touch with myself and my true desires.

"After a Reiki session, it was night-and-day difference. I was able to think clearly. I was able to see patterns. I felt like myself again."

Kieran's gaze was penetrating. Nicky felt their breath catch ever so slightly at the back of their throat. They coughed and looked away from him.

"Thank you for sharing that, Kieran. So it was more challenging to make decisions from your authentic self, and to listen to that guidance."

"Most definitely."

"How has clearing your third-eye block affected other areas of your life?"

"Very positively. My work has improved, and I've recently created a new relationship. I'm seeing the patterns I've had, the decisions I made that created certain outcomes in my life. I still stumble. But as I've been healing, it's become obvious that whatever makes it through are things I want to hold onto, devote my time and energy to."

Nicky nodded. "That if something or someone can be there through the chaos with you and see it to the other side, they're meant to be part of your life."

Kieran's eyes locked on Nicky's through the screen. "Exactly."

* * *

Though the Sexual Healing Challenge was far from the raving financial success that Nicky had hoped it would be, they had one new client sign up to work with them. Nicky credited the enrollment to the interview they had done with Kieran. Later in the livestream, he'd talked about how—in conjunction with therapy—holistic coaching had helped him heal his trauma faster. He'd also encouraged anyone who was on the fence to strongly consider working with Nicky.

The next time that Nicky connected with Kieran, it was under vastly different circumstances. He'd been having issues with his wifi, so instead of connecting over Zoom, they did a phone check-in.

For a year that had started so quickly, it seemed to be ticking by slowly for both of them. Nicky felt like they were living in *Groundhog Day* alongside Bill Murray. Likewise, during their session, Kieran had shared openly about his frustrations with the pandemic.

"I hate that I can't go to the gym right now," he'd said. "That's typically how I work out, get my exercise in. Play racquetball, use the weight machines, go swimming. It was a big part of my self-care. I haven't found anything to replace it since the pandemic started, and it's definitely affected my mental health."

He was activated. He wasn't connected to his body.

Nicky barely noticed. They were frustrated themself because their sessions had turned into talk therapy of sorts—which Nicky wasn't qualified to do—and their conversations seemed to revolve around coping during COVID-19 rather than healing Kieran's deeper trauma.

It didn't feel as joyful as it had before.

"Tell me a bit more about what forms of self-care you've put into place over the last couple months that have worked for you," Nicky said. "What's supported you most?"

"It's been really hard, and I've been struggling a lot," Kieran complained. "Going outside and running errands make me feel anxious, and I don't have focus when I meditate. I haven't been able to see my therapist because she wasn't set up for telehealth."

Nicky was at a loss. "That sounds challenging."

"Yeah, it is."

An awkward silence fell, and Nicky felt red-hot discomfort in their stomach. How to help Kieran focus on the positives, the things that *were* working? He seemed stuck.

What was Nicky doing wrong?

Was Kieran just not a good fit as a client anymore?

It was hard to tell.

"Do you have any idea when we'll be able to do in-person sessions again?" Kieran asked suddenly. "I found those were more effective and useful."

Nicky blinked and refocused. "The stay-at-home order lifts on May 26, and that's when non-essential businesses can have clients show up in-person. Provided, of course, that all parties are wearing masks. Bailey and I are connecting next week to discuss our COVID-19 cleaning policies and our plan for reopening, but I'm thinking mid-June."

Smiling thinly, they reviewed the notes that they had taken so far in the session, looking for inspiration, some way to help them redirect Kieran's focus.

"You mentioned that things have been going well with Wanda, the person you started dating last month. What about your relationship with her has been most joyful?"

As Kieran began sharing more about Wanda and their unfolding kink dynamic, Nicky let out a silent sigh. At last, things were back on track. Even if just temporarily.

* * *

Another relationship that had become more challenging was Nicky's connection with Paco. The two of them had reconnected in late March, and it seemed they were both soothed by talking with each other. For health and safety reasons, they weren't meeting in person. So, every Friday evening at six o'clock, the two of them chatted on the phone. Sometimes, it was fun and friendly banter. Other times—and more often—it turned into Nicky providing Paco with free emotional labor.

"I sent her that email last week, right? I haven't received a response yet. I don't know if she's going to respond. She said she wanted to be friends, but I don't know if she was sincere about that or not. Either way, I wish she would just tell me what she actually wants."

Nicky sighed. Paco was talking about his ex-girlfriend, Catalina.

Again.

It was exhausting.

"Have you thought more about talking to a therapist about this, Paco?" Nicky asked tentatively. "Or looked at the list of people I sent? It's been a full year since the two of you broke up."

Silence.

"I don't know if therapy is for me," he said evasively after a moment. "I don't really feel like sharing my entire life story with a stranger. Besides, I'd need to find somebody in-network."

"That's understandable," Nicky said. "It took a bit before I felt comfortable opening up to my therapist, Emma."

"That's nice," Paco said, cutting them off. "I'm glad you have that. But honestly, I'd rather just talk with you about it for free instead."

Nicky stopped walking and looked at their phone incredulously.

"I can't believe you just said that."

"Oh, come on, Nicole. It was just a joke. Lighten up."

Maybe it was that they had listened to *their* ex lament over another woman dozens of times over the past year. Maybe it was that they had already provided Paco with the equivalent of thousands of dollars of free coaching. Or maybe it was that he just called them Nicole for the umpteenth time.

Whatever it was, something inside Nicky snapped.

"No, it wasn't a joke, and you know it," they said coolly.

"Seriously, it was just a joke, Nicole. I don't understand why you're so upset."

"My name is *Nicky*, Paco, not Nicole."

"Okay, fine, *Nicky*," he spat.

"Look, I've got to go. It's your choice not to see a therapist, but I'm done with this conversation."

With that, Nicky pressed the button to end the call, turned on their Metal Mayhem playlist, gripped their phone tightly, and began to run.

* * *

Later that day, Nicky was in front of their laptop, an open beer next to them. A Belgian. Kieran would approve.

"Thanks for seeing me on such short notice, Emma," Nicky said.

Over video chat, Emma just smiled. "Of course, Nicky. It's always good to connect with you. I'm just glad that I had someone cancel so you could get in right away. What do you want to talk about?"

Nicky sighed. "Paco. COVID. Other things."

Emma raised her eyebrows. "Paco? That's a topic we haven't covered in awhile. Are the two of you still in touch?"

"Yes," Nicky admitted after a moment. "He reached out to me a few weeks after the pandemic started, sharing that he was feeling lonely and disconnected because of COVID-19. We ended up talking on the phone, and it turned into a weekly thing."

"You don't sound that thrilled about it."

"I didn't mind at first, and some of our conversations have been okay," Nicky said. "But mostly, it's turned into me counseling him about his ex. I didn't mind supporting him shortly after the two of them broke up, but he's processing the same loop every goddamn time. They're not going to get back together. She wasn't transparent about why she broke up with him. He deserves better. Him pining over her is not supportive for either of them. More than that, I'm not even getting paid to listen to him gripe about the situation. And I'm sick of it."

"Did you ever tell him that topic was off-limits during your conversations?" Emma asked thoughtfully.

"No," Nicky mumbled. "So that's on me."

Emma smiled with compassion. "Setting boundaries with certain people in our lives can be challenging. Doing so in a way that feels supportive to both parties is even harder."

"Tell me about it," Nicky muttered, taking a swig of their beer. "Every time I'm around Paco, I feel like I revert back to my twenty-two-year-old self."

"Sounds like a trauma response," Emma said.

"How so?" Nicky asked, frowning.

"Well, when there's trauma attached to a certain event or relationship, younger parts of us can show up because they want healing. We haven't done parts work together yet, but we can incorporate it into your therapy if that would be supportive."

"It might," Nicky admitted. "Maybe next session."

"Sure," Emma said. "So, let's go back to what you said about not asserting your boundaries with Paco. It sounds like you were trying to please him, to put his needs and desires above your own. He wanted to talk about his ex, and you wanted to tell him to stop, but you let the pattern continue."

"That's accurate."

"Have you and I talked about codependent relationships, Nicky? Or attachment theory?"

Nicky shook their head.

"We don't have time for both topics today, so I'll just share about codependent relationships. Would you be willing to research attachment theory before our next session?"

"Definitely. Also, if we could meet in two weeks' time, that would be great. COVID fucking sucks."

Emma suddenly looked sadder, older, and more tired. "A lot of people out there are hurting. That's for sure. We're going through a collective trauma."

"Yeah," Nicky echoed.

They were both silent for a moment before Emma launched into describing what codependent relationships were, and how to identify them.

"Let me get this straight," Nicky said, after Emma had finished her explanation. "Codependency, at its simplest, is when one person needs the other and the other person needs to be needed."

"Yes," Emma said.

"And one sign of codependency that you see in my relationship with Paco includes me continuing to be friends with him even though he's said and done hurtful things—like ignoring my chosen name and my gender pronouns. Another sign is my historic tendency to try to please him, no matter the cost that it has to me. Like I did by listening to him go on about his ex."

"Exactly," Emma said. "Keep in mind that relationships are not black-and-white, that elements of codependency can exist in relationships that are mostly healthy. Ideally, though, you're creating relationships that exist independently of that toxic dynamic... where there's mutual value in the relationship, you honor yourselves and express your boundaries without attacking the other person, and you don't need to feel needed. That need to feel needed can become an addiction."

"Thank you, Emma," Nicky said, as they smiled sincerely. "This really helps a lot. I have a lot to think about."

"Excellent. I'll see you virtually in two weeks."

"Can't wait," Nicky said.

* * *

After their therapy session, Nicky walked another loop around the neighborhood. Once they returned to their parents' house, Nicky went straight to their mom's bedroom, sighed, and plopped dramatically onto the bed.

"Mom," Nicky announced, "I need something new to do."

Donna paused her TV show and looked over at Nicky. "Like what?"

"I don't know," they said after a minute. "I'm just tired of working, running, and watching Netflix. I thought maybe you could give me some chores or something."

"Give you chores?" Donna chuckled. "You *really* must be looking for things to do."

"*Yes,*" Nicky said emphatically. "I am."

Donna chewed her lip thoughtfully, then with a small groan, rolled over and sat up on the bed. She began walking toward the door. "Follow me."

The two of them made their way down the hall, through the living room, and down the stairs to the basement. Donna entered her old craft closet where boxes upon boxes stood, and Nicky followed. Some of the boxes were labeled with Nicky's name, others with Nicky's sister's name, and still others with the ever-obscure Miscellaneous.

Donna reached for a faded cardboard box no bigger than a laptop that was several inches high.

"Here," she said, handing the box gingerly to Nicky. "Your grandparents' old love letters. I've been meaning to type them up as a Christmas gift for the family, but every time I reach for the box, it's like I'm not supposed to. Like they're not mine to read. Maybe you'll have better luck. Besides, your *abuelita* sometimes wrote in Spanish to your grandpa, and he sometimes wrote back in Italian. Goodness knows you read and write both languages far better than I do."

This had sometimes been a sore spot for Nicky's mom. Both sets of Nicky's grandparents had decided to speak with their children exclusively in English as they were growing up. As a result, Nicky's parents could only speak basic phrases in what had been their parents' mother tongues: Spanish and Italian for Donna, and Spanish for Mateo, Nicky's dad.

Nicky, on the other hand, had studied Spanish all throughout high school and college, graduating with a Bachelor's degree in the subject. After graduating, they'd taken a few online courses in Italian. Even though they were rusty in their second language, Nicky usually described themself as bilingual in English and Spanish.

Every time Nicky went to the local cantina with their mom, Nicky saw both the pride and pain on Donna's face when Nicky spoke in Spanish with the wait staff. Nicky had decided that, should they ever have children (which was highly unlikely), they would raise them to be bilingual from birth, despite English still being their native language.

Even just holding the box of letters, Nicky felt closer to their cultural heritage. They could almost hear a ghostly whisper of their *nonno*'s hearty chuckle. Nicky's heart ached. "I do like stories," they said. "Especially old-fashioned love stories like Grandma and Grandpa's."

A small grin lit Donna's face. "I know. That's why I think this would be the perfect pandemic project for you. When you need a break from work, of course, or being outside."

Nicky smiled back and cradled the box gently against their chest, almost as if they were rocking a newborn.

"Thanks, Mom," Nicky said. "I promise I'll take good care of them."

Donna touched Nicky's cheek, then their shoulder. "I know. I know."

* * *

Breezy May faded into balmy June, and before Nicky knew it, they were packing their things to move back to Madison, the letters in tow. Nicky had only made it through a fraction of their grandparents' correspondence, so they were taking the box with them to finish transcribing—and, where necessary, translating—the contents of the letters.

There was something inspiring about the relationship that Nicky's grandparents had before they passed—the way they teased each other so easily, had fun together, expressed their affection through silly pet names. Even just through their writing, it was clear the two of them had loved each other deeply.

Their grandpa's devotion came through when he planned to drive nearly five hours to visit Nicky's *abuelita*, writing letters after a long workday. It also shone through when their *nonno* took the entire summer to visit his beloved; work in Baresi, Chicago; and rent a small studio flat because that's all he could afford. Even when Nicky's grandpa was in Chicago, he still wrote to Nicky's grandma. Sure, the letters were fewer since they lived in the same city, but they were all the sweeter. More playful, less informational. Sometimes, they bore no stamps. Sometimes, it was just Grandma's silly poetry or Grandpa's kitschy drawings.

This is the kind of relationship I want, Nicky thought, as they placed yet another letter in the 'done' pile. Connection, intimacy, understanding, trust. Their grandparents had had that overwhelmingly.

Nicky paused.

Did they have all of that with Paco? Any of it even? Maybe they did once upon a time. But now? Emma had shared her professional opinion that the relationship reeked of toxic codependency. Plus, at the end of each of their phone calls with Paco, Nicky felt drained and irritated.

Was it supposed to feel like that? Was it *okay* that it felt like that?

Maybe they could just be friends?

Nicky felt like their guides were trying to give them a message, nudge them in a direction, but Nicky just felt foggy-brained and confused.

So Nicky called up the one person they knew they could trust: Bailey.

"I just don't know what to do," Nicky lamented over video chat. "I'm so tired of him talking about his ex-girlfriend, and she's not going to choose to be with him. He's cycling through the same patterns without resolving anything. I've listened to him as he's processed, and I've held space for him, but he doesn't seem to realize just how much emotional labor it's been. I don't enjoy our chats anymore, and I don't have fun when I'm around him."

Bailey bit her lip. "My guides are really urging me to speak up here."

Nicky shook themself, and they refocused their gaze on their screen, where Bailey looked distinctly uncomfortable. She kept taking her long blonde hair out of its bun, combing through it with her fingers, re-stacking it, and putting it back in the bun.

"And you want my consent?" Nicky asked. "It's about Paco?"

"Yes," Bailey said.

Nicky shrugged. "Okay, shoot."

"He's not the one," Bailey practically blurted out. "He's not your 100% match, your Divine Match. The one you're waiting for. Paco isn't even half of what you want."

"I know," Nicky said, now a bit agitated. "I know he's not. He's not poly, he's not kinky. He's still hung up on his ex, and when I suggested he see a therapist, he didn't do anything about it. Even when I sent him a list of potential people to see in the area."

"He's choosing to stay where he is," Bailey said gently. "You value personal growth, doing the work, and self-awareness. You deserve a partner who meets you where you're at. Someone who's equally passionate about working on themself."

"*Yes*," Nicky said emphatically. "But I haven't known where to set the boundaries with Paco. It's hard. He was my first partner, my first love. So many firsts. I don't want to cut him out of my life entirely."

Bailey smiled sadly. "I know. But you're holding on more than he is."

Nicky felt a rising urge to say something biting, so they took several deep breaths.

"When you clear the relationships that are no longer serving you," Bailey continued, "you make way for this Divine Match to come in."

There was something potent about Bailey's words that Nicky couldn't ignore.

"Where do I find this Divine Match?" they asked.

"It's not about looking for him," Bailey said. "The more you look for your Divine Match, the less he'll see you. Just do the work. That's how he'll find you. The more you do your work, heal from your own stuff, the more visible you'll be to him."

It wasn't what Nicky wanted to hear. To shed the comfortable, worn blanket that was their relationship with Paco and not have anything in its place, to be *completely* single...

Was *exactly* what Nicky had wanted back in February.

Damn pandemic. It had changed everything.

"Makes sense. Anything else?" Nicky asked after a moment.

"My guides want you to know that your next relationship is coming soon. He won't be The One, but he'll find you adorable. You should give it... a year," Bailey said carefully, after a moment. "It'll be in motion before that, but give it a year."

"And do the damn work," Nicky said humorlessly.

Bailey smiled. "Yes. And do the damn work."

Chapter Eleven

“Tell me, what's happened since we last connected?”

It was late June, and Nicky was sitting across from Kieran, both of them wearing masks. Nearly a month had passed since their last session because of scheduling conflicts.

Kieran smiled. “A lot. My therapist got set up with telehealth, my divorce was finalized, and my relationship with Wanda has had some potholes. She started dating one of my roommates, which is fine. But when she comes over to see me, I need transition time between work and doing kinky things. And if I don't give her what she wants, she'll spend time with my roommate instead and ignore me.”

“You need time to shift from a work mindset to a kink headspace,” Nicky reflected. “And when you don't have that transition time, it doesn't work for you.”

“Exactly,” Kieran said. “I've told her this several times. But she wasn't getting it. To the point that it's become a consent issue. She'll expect me to be in Daddy mode right after I get done with work. It's hard to switch headspaces right away, and it's even harder when she's bratting.”

Nicky frowned. “Bratting?”

“Teasing, being cheeky, seeking fun-ishment,” Kieran explained.

“Fun-ishment?”

“Behavior correction that's supposed to be fun, rather than upsetting. With Wanda, it's a spanking that's not overly hard. But right after work, I just don't have the capacity to deal with that behavior from her. I just want to connect with her, talk with her, cuddle for a bit. Sometimes it feels like she wants me in that Daddy Dom headspace no matter what, my desires be damned. ”

Nicky's gaze softened. "That sounds like a lot to handle, just in a single month. Especially with your divorce being finalized, too."

"Yeah," Kieran murmured, his eyes locked onto Nicky's. "It has been."

His hazel eyes were intense, unyielding. After a few seconds that seemed to stretch into minutes, Nicky looked away, their cheeks flushed.

"Is it all right if I ask you a challenging question?" Nicky asked.

"Sure," Kieran said.

"If consent is so important to you—and I know it is, because it was when you and I did that scene together—why are you tolerating this behavior from someone that you're dating? Why are you with someone who's violating your consent?"

Silence. Nicky looked at him after a few moments and saw Kieran's lips were a thin line.

"If this were a kink scene, what color would you be at? Green, yellow, or red?" Nicky asked tentatively.

"I'm okay," Kieran said.

"That's not a color," Nicky replied. "Are you yellow?"

Kieran shrugged.

"Okay, I'm going to say that you're yellow," Nicky said. "Do you feel comfortable with me guiding you through some deep breaths? Until you're green again?"

Kieran nodded.

The two of them inhaled and exhaled together. After just a few rounds of breath, Kieran's body relaxed visibly.

"What color are you at?" Nicky asked again.

"Green," Kieran said. "Thank you for leading me through those breaths."

"Yeah, no problem." Nicky paused. "Do you feel comfortable revisiting the question I asked before we did the deep breathing?"

He nodded again. "I felt activated because I just realized I've been creating a relationship that isn't what I want. And while I want to give Wanda the benefit of the doubt, I haven't been happy the last few weeks. It hasn't been working."

"You haven't been happy, and it hasn't been working," Nicky echoed. "What would a relationship that worked look like for the two of you?"

"She'd respect my boundaries. She wouldn't push for scenes when I've expressed that I'm too tired. There wouldn't be any drama. Or at least, a lot less of it. I understand that people get activated and have unprocessed trauma they're dealing with—hell, I do too—but it's frustrating when they don't take *any* action to fix their circumstances and just sit there. Or they blame or attack me for things *they* created in their lives."

"I'm guessing there's been some drama in your relationship with Wanda," Nicky said.

"Yes," Kieran said. He was leaning forward in his chair, his face less than two feet from Nicky's. "I'm happy to support my partners through their stuff, big stuff even—divorces, moving, finding a new job—but if I'm giving my all and they're not doing anything, it's frustrating. I end up sacrificing my health for their happiness or their comfort when they're just rotting in place."

Nicky was suddenly reminded of their therapy session with Emma back in May.

Codependency, at its simplest, is when one person needs the other and the other person needs to be needed.

Apparently Nicky wasn't the only one in the room who had had a codependent relationship before.

"How much of your frustration right now is leftover from your marriage with Jamie? Or from other relationships besides the one you currently have with Wanda?" they asked.

Kieran's shoulders sagged. "At least half. Probably more than half."

"So this was a pattern in your other relationships."

"Yes," Kieran said, looking at the floor.

For a moment, Nicky was at a loss. They saw so much of themself in Kieran. He was giving so much of himself for his partner's benefit, to the point that it was sapping his physical energy, his mental health, when he already had so many challenges he was navigating.

He deserved so much better.

Nicky bit the inside of their cheek to prevent themself from saying so.

"I'm hearing," Nicky said after a moment, "that you want to be in a relationship where your partner is taking action to improve their life."

"If it's necessary," Kieran countered. "More than anything, I want to be with someone who doesn't take me for granted, but I seem to keep attracting these people regardless. I want to be with someone who wants to be with *me* rather than someone who cares first and foremost about all the things I can do for them."

"You're done with codependent relationships," Nicky reflected.

"Yes," Kieran said simply. "They just don't work."

"No," Nicky murmured. "They really don't."

* * *

That night, Nicky paced their apartment. They'd messaged Paco asking to talk on the phone, and he said he'd call sometime after seven o'clock. It was quarter after, and he hadn't called.

Typing a quick message, Nicky asked if he had a more specific time-frame in mind so that they could plan their night accordingly. Normally, it wouldn't matter a whole lot, but their energy was very focused on what Paco would have to say in response to their conversation, and they couldn't seem to focus on anything else.

At last their phone began ringing. It was Paco. Nicky slid their finger across the glass screen, unlocked it, and put it on speaker.

"Hey, Paco," Nicky said, "Thanks for giving me a call."

"Yeah, no problem," he said. "What's up?"

Nicky began pacing their apartment again, and could practically hear the wood being smoothed beneath their feet as they wore grooves in the same small patch of flooring.

"I just wanted to talk," Nicky said. "I've been doing a lot of thinking and wanted to let you know where I'm at."

"Okay." Despite his best efforts, confusion seeped through Paco's voice.

"Great, thanks." Nicky took a deep breath, said a quick prayer to the Universe, and dove in. "So, when you and I first broke up four and a half years ago, I didn't take a whole lot of time to grieve. You and I met up in person just six weeks later, even though we had dated for eighteen months, and I wasn't really over you.

"Since we were in contact as I was dating Camden, and then we've had this on-again off-again relationship, I've never really allowed myself to get to the root of the healing that should have happened immediately after our breakup. And I really need to do that for myself."

There was a pause. "What are you saying, Nicole?"

If Nicky had any doubt that this was the right decision, Paco calling them Nicole instead of Nicky sealed it. "I'm saying that I need to be out of contact for a while," they said. "I don't want to have these blurry boundaries with you anymore. It's not supportive for me."

"So, I get where you're coming from. I really do," Paco said. "But it seems a *bit* unfair. Like this is a unilateral or one-sided decision. I thought what we had was supportive. It's been nice talking with you every week."

"I just... I just need this for me," Nicky said simply. Their heart started beating more quickly in their chest, and their breathing started to increase.

"Fine, whatever," Paco said acidly. "It just sucks and I feel like I don't get a say."

The tears were welling, and it felt like Nicky couldn't breathe. They weren't sure what would happen if they stayed on the phone call much longer.

"Look, I have to go," Nicky said quickly. "Thank you for your time and the phone call. I wish you the best."

With that, they tapped the 'end call' button on their phone, and tossed it gently onto the other side of the bed before slipping on their shoes, grabbing a mask and their spare set of keys, and going for a walk outside.

The crisp, fresh air helped Nicky clear their head, helped them ground, and helped them remember why they were doing this. Their Divine Match was out there, and by continuing to be in this pattern with Paco, Nicky was preventing this person from coming in, making themself known.

Besides, Nicky already knew where a long-term relationship with Paco led: sexual dissatisfaction, frustration, and anxiety. No use treading the same worn path yet again.

That night, after Nicky returned from their walk, they recreated the night when they had first broken up with Paco. Just as they had four and a half years ago, Nicky ate Ben and Jerry's and binged romantic comedies. One after another after another after another until their eyes watered. The hollowness Nicky felt was muted, numbed by the movies and the ice cream.

In time, they would heal. In time, perhaps they could have a healthy, boundaried relationship with Paco. But for now, he was not part of the vision.

For now, Nicky would focus on themself, on their business, and on doing the damn work.

∗ ∗ ∗

With each passing day, Nicky missed Paco less, and their resolve strengthened and grew. Initially, Nicky found themself wanting to text Paco, saying they were sorry and that they'd changed their mind. Ultimately, Nicky blocked his number and deleted their message history. It was the only way that they could have a sense of peace.

Not having those weekly conversations with Paco freed up so much emotional space for Nicky that they found they had energy they hadn't had in awhile. They braved their fear to work out at the gym (masks were required unless Nicky was on a machine), did more journaling than they had in a long time, and began developing a group program to support their private coaching clients at an even deeper level by building a like-minded community.

During this time, Nicky also realized just how much they missed kink and BDSM. The clubs had closed in mid-March, and it was now July. Almost five months since they had attended a play party, and it had been seven months since their delicious birthday scene.

Groaning, Nicky pulled out their phone and typed an all-too-familiar query into Google.

When will the pandemic end?

They didn't even have to finish typing the question. So many other people had clearly been wondering the same thing. Dozens of articles came up, some of them recent. Others had been published back in March or April, and Nicky skipped them entirely. The situation with COVID-19 was continuing to evolve so quickly that even a two-month-old article was irrelevant.

Nicky clicked on an article that had been published two weeks earlier. The writer had interviewed several different experts who relayed different prognoses for the pandemic.

Having the pandemic end by the fall was incredibly optimistic, most of them agreed. Overall, the U.S. and the rest of the world were looking at a twelve or eighteen-month timeline. Perhaps even two years before things would be normal.

Through the end of 2021, at least.

Which meant that public kinky play parties probably wouldn't be happening for another year and a half. Nicky's heart fell a little at the realization. They shut off their phone and plopped themself on their couch, looking out the window.

Nicky could, of course, always trawl FetLife and meet new people in the area with whom to do kink scenes. But that option didn't really feel appealing during a global pandemic. Especially when not everyone was taking the same precautions with masking.

What was a solo kinkster to do in the time of COVID-19? Nicky mused.

* * *

Their answer came barely a week later during their third-to-last coaching session with Kieran. Although he'd renewed his contract with Nicky once already, he'd been hesitant to commit to another three or four months of coaching. Between his divorce and the pandemic, his budget had changed. On Nicky's end, something felt sticky. Renewing Kieran's contract didn't feel in alignment for them, either. But it wasn't until they asked how things had been going in his relationship with Wanda that Nicky understood why.

"Wanda and I actually had a disagreement a few weeks ago," Kieran commented, his voice muffled slightly beneath his mask.

Nicky paused in the middle of the note they were writing.

"I was tired and not in the mental headspace to do a scene," he continued. "But Wanda kept pushing, asking me why we couldn't do some impact play."

"What happened?" Nicky asked, looking at Kieran's eyes intently.

"I should have listened to my body," he said, not quite meeting Nicky's eyes. "I wasn't as careful as I normally am during a scene, and Wanda called 'red.' We ended the scene, and I gave her the aftercare we'd agreed on, but—"

"The damage had been done," Nicky supplied.

Kieran nodded.

Nicky's heart panged uncomfortably.

"She hasn't wanted to do a scene with me since," he admitted. "And we had a Daddy-little dynamic, too. She hasn't felt safe or comfortable being in littlespace with me either."

"What's been most challenging about the situation?" Nicky asked.

"Not doing kink or BDSM. It's been three weeks since we've been intimate, and I'm not playing with any of my other partners right now."

"Why not?"

Kieran sighed. "The pandemic. Some of my partners have family members who are immunocompromised, and others are trying to keep their bubbles small. Or they live further away and scheduling has been a challenge. Plus, I have my son to think about. Until there's a vaccine and COVID becomes less of a threat, I don't know there's a whole lot that I can do."

"That sounds challenging. Emotionally, I mean."

He smiled ruefully. "It is, but all I can do is be mindful of my own risk. Mask up. Use hand sanitizer. Get tested if I've been exposed. At least they've made that easier."

Silence hung heavily between them. In that moment, Nicky felt Kieran's emotions more fully than they ever had. Felt the stickiness in his third-eye chakra, the weight in his heart chakra.

"I'm sorry," Nicky blurted out.

Kieran lifted his eyebrows. "What for?" he said. "You didn't have anything to do with what's going on between me and Wanda. And you certainly didn't cause the pandemic. In fact, working with you during this time has been a lifeline. Especially before my therapist was set up for telehealth, I was floundering."

"I just wish this pandemic would end soon. And I wish people would realize that their actions affect others. I keep waiting for things to end, for things to go back to normal, and they just haven't yet," said Nicky.

"I agree wholeheartedly," Kieran said.

From there, Kieran continued to vent about COVID-19, the pandemic, and his anxiety around being in public spaces—even though Wisconsin had a statewide mask mandate. How he hadn't been to the gym since February. All the things he missed doing with his son during the summer. Nicky could relate to Kieran's frustrations all too well.

But at the end of his coaching session, it wasn't what Kieran had said about being in public spaces that Nicky was turning over in their mind. It was something else he had said.

What's been most challenging about the situation with Wanda?

Not doing kink or BDSM.

That refrain, which played in Nicky's mind the entire car ride home, planted a seed.

* * *

"Hey, Bailey. Do you have a minute?"

Nicky was leaning in the doorframe after what was looking to be their penultimate session with Kieran.

Bailey looked up from their scheduler. "Sure, yeah. What is it?"

"Is it alright if I share something personal?" Nicky asked tentatively.

Bailey chuckled. "Of course, Nicky."

"Great, thanks." Nicky took a deep breath, clenching their hands together. "I've decided to ask Kieran to be my play partner."

The surprise and confusion in Bailey's eyes was plain. Nicky felt their cheeks flush. They already felt self-conscious about asking Kieran to be their play partner, and Bailey's judgment—her surprise, Nicky corrected themself—didn't make it easier.

But they hadn't come to this decision lightly. In fact, it had taken a few weeks of journaling, meditating, seeking counsel from Emma, and weighing pros and cons before Nicky finally admitted to themself that yes, they did in fact very much want to do kink with Kieran.

The energetic release of impact play, of pain play helped Nicky clear their head and stay connected to their body. And their scene with Kieran back in December had helped them ground more than any other kink scene ever had. His connection to energy, to chakras, and his presence and power and control were magnetic.

More than that, recent changes in Kieran's life had also paved the way for this shift in his relationship with Nicky. Today, he'd still been hesitant to commit to another three months of coaching, and his relationship with Wanda seemed to have dissolved entirely.

"I've thought about this a lot," Nicky said, a bit defensively.

Bailey smiled. "I'm sure. I know you take a lot of care with your decisions. But I don't know what a play partner is."

Nicky blushed. "Oh. Um, it's someone with whom I'd do kink and BDSM on an ongoing basis. Kieran recently ended things with the person he was dating, and with the pandemic, there aren't any in-person kink events happening right now. He misses it, and I miss it, so I was thinking of approaching him at the end of our next session and suggesting that he and I do kinky scenes together after some time passes."

"That's great," Bailey said after a minute. "I hope the conversation goes well."

"Thanks," Nicky said awkwardly. Apparently their inner monologue had become defensive for no reason. "I hope it goes well, too. It would be purely platonic. I don't like him that way—romantically, I mean—it's really just because I miss kink and BDSM."

"Sure," Bailey said. "Was there anything else you wanted to share?"

Nicky shook their head. "How were your client sessions today?"

Sighing, Bailey turned their full body away from the scheduler. "Every time I have a session that's more physical—you know, it's a massage or it incorporates bodywork—it drains my energy. Even if it's with a client I like. Fortunately, there's been an uptick in Reiki clients, but even that isn't quite as fulfilling as it used to be."

"Sounds like you're in the middle of a transition and starting to look for your next thing," Nicky said.

"Yeah, you could say that." Bailey's eyes suddenly sparkled with mischief. "Almost like I'm transitioning from a coach and client relationship to what was it? A play partnership? But in my business?"

Nicky rolled their eyes, but they laughed a little. "Touché."

* * *

The day of Kieran's final client session, Nicky's heart stuck in their chest like a lemon lozenge. Nicky hoped that deep breathing would shake it loose, but their heart still thudded more than usual during the session.

Was it even ethical to ask Kieran if he wanted to be their play partner? After all, he was a client, and maintaining strict boundaries with a client was important.

But he won't be a client anymore, another voice reassured them. *Besides, it's not like you're going to be having sex with him. It's just kink. Just impact scenes. Isn't that how things started between the two of you, anyway? Before he became a client?*

Throughout the session, Nicky found themself redirecting their thoughts multiple times to be present with what Kieran was sharing. He was still feeling frustration around how things had ended with Wanda—how he hadn't honored his own boundaries consistently throughout the relationship—and wanted to attract higher-caliber partners.

"I'm hearing that you're frustrated with the situation and how things ended," Nicky reflected. Their body felt detached from their throat. It was like someone else was speaking. "Sometimes, looking at the lessons gained from a situation can help soften frustration or anger. What do you feel you learned from this situation with Wanda?"

Kieran answered, but the response seemed to be coming through water; blood was whooshing too loudly in Nicky's ears. They checked their watch. Forty-five more minutes. Thirty. Fifteen.

Ten.

Five.

At last, the two of them were wrapping up, and Nicky guided Kieran through a final round of deep breathing. Once they ensured he had regrounded, Nicky paused, pressing all of their fingers together.

"Kieran, do you have a few minutes?" they asked. "There's something I'd like to discuss with you."

"Sure," he said, an easy smile on his face. "What's up?"

Nicky sat straight in their chair and looked him in the eyes. *Courage, Rivera. You've got this,* they told themself.

"You mentioned a couple sessions ago that you really miss kink and BDSM. That it's been hard during the pandemic. That a lot of your play partners live further away or aren't meeting with lots of people right now."

Kieran leaned back in his chair. "Yeah, I did say that."

Nicky took a deep breath. "Well, I miss kink, too. It's been a long time since I've gotten my ass flogged. There haven't been any play parties for months. And the thought of connecting with someone random from FetLife feels really gross to me. So, I was thinking... today's our last session, and we haven't discussed you renewing your contract again. We both really miss kink. I'd like to propose that we terminate our coach and client relationship and instead become play partners."

His face was inscrutable. Nicky's cheeks and neck were hot. They pressed on, speaking more quickly now, determined to finish their piece before their wits failed them.

"Obviously, we would give it some time before playing together," they said. "As a client, you've shared some emotionally intimate things with me over the past several months, and there's an inherent power dynamic in a coaching relationship. I was thinking about checking in at the beginning of October... forty days from now. How does that sound to you?"

Nicky forced themself to keep their head level, looking at Kieran.

He didn't say anything for a minute. When he finally spoke, his voice was friendly, but plain.

"I'd be open to that," he said simply.

Admittedly, it wasn't a *negative* response. But it wasn't a 'yes, that sounds great, I'd love to' or 'wow, Nicky, what a wonderful solution.'

Nicky didn't know what they were expecting, but not that.

Maybe he was just humoring them. Maybe they shouldn't have asked.

"I wouldn't want you to feel like I'm pushing this on you," they added quickly. "If you want time to think about it, we can discuss it forty days from now when we check in."

Kieran shrugged. "Okay."

Nicky's cheeks flushed deeper. "Right, well. So, until then, I'm thinking it would be good if we have minimal contact. Just to create a better transition and stronger boundary between our coaching relationship and whatever comes next."

"Sounds good to me."

It felt too easy. Unsettled, Nicky grabbed their hands and started fidgeting. "Okay, well... I guess I'll talk to you forty days from now."

Kieran stood up to leave. "Sure."

"Have a good September."

From the doorway, Kieran grinned. "You too. Try to stay cool."

"Thanks," Nicky mumbled.

They waited until they heard the door to the office suite close behind him, then shut the door to their office and slumped in their chair.

I'd be open to that. Okay. Sounds good to me. Sure. You too.

Nicky groaned, letting their head fall back. As they did, all the adrenaline and cortisol that had been pumping through their body dissipated, and suddenly, Nicky felt very, very weary.

* * *

After stopping by Mon Ami to pick up a crowler of their favorite beer, Nicky replayed the day's events in their mind. Over and over and over.

It wasn't that big a deal, they reassured themself. *If Kieran thought it was inappropriate or a breach of boundaries, he would have said something. He's an adult. He understands the nuances of consent—he's been part of the kink community for seventeen years. He's not going to do anything he doesn't want to do.*

But every time Nicky settled those anxious thoughts through logic, another fear would crop up, and they began soothing the anxious parts of them once again.

Eventually, out of frustration, they began bingeing one of their favorite shows, *POSE,* in an attempt to calm the chatter of self-critical thoughts. It worked. Even though the plot took place in New York's ballroom scene in the early 90s and not a dungeon in the early 2020s, there was something reassuring about seeing other trans people on screen. Hearing their stories, witnessing their pain, celebrating their triumphs.

It was familiar. Different, of course, since Nicky was a light-skinned Latinx person, and most people assumed they were white. Nicky had privileges most characters on the show never would. But the characters' challenges and their euphoria were familiar nonetheless.

Another ballroom scene appeared on the screen. The music, the celebration. Their half-drunk beer forgotten, Nicky closed their eyes and imagined for a moment they were at the local dungeon wearing one of their favorite outfits—thigh-high fishnet stockings, black lacy underwear, and sparkly heart pasties over their nipples. Kieran was there, the same subtle smile on his face.

I'd be open to it.

The living room began to darken as it got later, and only snippets of the TV show filtered through now.

"And the category is…"

Fishnets.

Chapter Twelve

When Nicky asked Kieran if he wanted to be their play partner, it didn't particularly surprise him.

In hindsight, he supposed he actually should have expected it.

During his final coaching session, Nicky's face colored a few times, and they didn't maintain eye contact like they normally did. At one point, Nicky even asked him to repeat what he was saying, which had never happened before.

Then they asked him to stay.

"Kieran, do you have a few minutes?" they asked. "There's something I'd like to discuss with you."

"Sure," he said. "What's up?"

Nicky sat straight in their chair and looked at him more directly than they had during the entire session. How different they were from when he'd first met them a year and a half ago. Their body, while awkward, had lost much of the rigidity he'd seen in it the night they had volunteered together.

They'd grown so much in that time. Become so much.

"You mentioned during our last session that you really miss kink and BDSM," Nicky replied. "That it's been hard during the pandemic. That a lot of your play partners live further away or aren't meeting with lots of people right now."

Kieran leaned back. He wasn't sure where they were going with this. "Yeah, I did say that," he said slowly.

"Well, I miss kink, too," Nicky said in a rush. "It's a long time since I've gotten my ass flogged. There haven't been any play parties for months. And the thought of connecting with someone random from FetLife feels really gross to me."

A faint warm glow ignited in Kieran's heartspace.

It had been awhile since he'd felt that.

"So, I was thinking… today's our last session, and we haven't discussed you renewing your contract again. We both really miss kink. I'd like to propose that we terminate our coach and client relationship and instead become play partners."

Kieran's chest grew warmer. His heartbeat accelerated, just a touch. And for the first time since Nicky's birthday scene back in December, he let himself wonder if there could be more between them.

More than friendship. More than just pickup play. More than a professional coaching relationship.

Tapping into his years of experience as a Dom, Kieran smoothed his face into a blank mask. Friendly still, of course. But pushing down any desire he felt so that it wouldn't be obvious in his words, his glances.

Self-restraint was crucial.

Consent was crucial.

"Obviously, we would give it some time before playing together," Nicky added. "As a client, you've shared emotionally intimate things with me over the past several months, and there's an inherent power dynamic in a coaching relationship. I was thinking about checking in at the beginning of October… forty days from now. How does that sound to you?" Nicky asked.

"I'd be open to that," Kieran said simply.

For some reason, Nicky immediately began fidgeting.

"I wouldn't want you to feel like I'm pushing this on you," they added quickly. "If you want time to think about it, we can discuss it forty days from now when we check in."

From where Kieran was standing, that wouldn't be necessary. He would be a yes to playing with them tomorrow if they were okay with it. But he suspected the transition time would be important for them. That *they* needed to make sure they were certain about their decision.

"Okay," he said.

Nicky's cheeks flushed deeper. "Right, well. So, until then, I'm thinking it would be good if we have minimal contact. Just to create a better transition and stronger boundary between our coaching relationship and whatever comes next."

Whatever you need.

"Sounds good to me."

Nicky was fidgeting again. "Okay, well… I guess I'll talk to you forty days from now."

This was his cue to leave. Kieran stood up. "Sure."

"Have a good September," Nicky said.

From the doorway, Kieran took a final look at Nicky. They were so beautiful. Their short, dark hair framed their pale golden face and amber eyes, and even though their cheeks and ears were stained deep pink, he felt such power and presence radiating from them.

Tonight, Kieran knew he would imagine all sorts of things he might say to make Nicky blush intentionally. Imagining his lips on theirs, winding his hand through their dark hair.

He blinked.

"You too," he said. "Try to stay cool."

"Thanks."

Kieran left his final coaching session humming. Forty days from now, Nicky might just be his play partner.

But he would let Nicky lead, he decided firmly. He'd wanted to be intimate with them since December, at least. Kieran would scare them off if he was assertive or indicated that he had any deeper feelings right now, and it also wasn't the kind of relationship Nicky was consenting to.

I'm going to be present with what our relationship is, Kieran told himself. *Not what I want it to be. I'm not going to bend, mold, shape, or manipulate it.*

He enjoyed Nicky's company no matter what. If all that happened was the two of them became casual play partners, he would enjoy their scenes together. And if it evolved into more, because *Nicky* wanted it to be more than a play partnership, he would cherish that, too.

* * *

When nearly forty days had passed, Kieran reached out to Nicky, asking if they still wanted to connect and chat about being play partners. They might be self-conscious about initiating, he reasoned. They needed to know that having this conversation was important to him.

Fortunately, Nicky agreed to meet with him, and they set a date to connect virtually. After spending a few minutes catching up, Kieran dove right in. No time like the present, he reasoned.

"In August you suggested that we become play partners," he said. "Are you still interested in that?"

"Of course," Nicky said, their brows knitting together. "Are you?"

Kieran nodded. "I feel like I have a pretty clear idea of what you want, but I'd like to hear you share your intentions, what you'd like to experience during our play."

"Sure," Nicky said, their face smoothing out. "I really miss impact play, and I really enjoyed our scene back in December. I like that you know how to play with energy; it helped me get into subspace. I'd really like some flogging. I have a padded bat that I like."

"It sounds like a mix of thuddy and stingy," Kieran commented.

"Yeah," Nicky said.

"What about bondage?"

"I haven't done a whole lot of bondage," Nicky admitted. "I liked it when you tied my wrists to the Saint Andrew's cross back in December, but other than that, I haven't done a lot of rope play. I'm definitely open to it, though."

Light impact, some rope play, check. "What about massage?"

"I don't know. Maybe," they said.

"And what boundaries do you have? Regarding where and how you'd like me to touch you?"

Nicky's cheeks colored slightly. "Probably the same boundaries we had during our scene back in December. Not touching me under my underwear with toys or your hands. No touching of my breasts. No spanking."

"Fair enough." Kieran paused, surveying Nicky for just a moment. "One thing I want to be careful about, especially with any rope scenes that we do, is trauma bonding. Are you familiar with what that is, Nicky?"

"Nope."

"It's when you experience a trauma with someone, and you form an emotional bond with them as a result. Some people find they want to be romantically or sexually intimate with that person just because they shared that traumatic experience together. The trauma is literally bonding you together."

"Can you give me an example?"

"It often happens in toxic relationships, but it can also happen if there's some external event. Like a war, or a bomb scare."

"Or a pandemic," Nicky said slowly.

"Exactly," Kieran said. "Or certain kink scenes that are emotionally intense. For example, you might come to associate me with rope and want to be more intimate with me because you want to experience more of that activity. It's not because you actually want to be in a relationship with *me*, but because of what I can do for you."

Nicky looked straight at him. "My therapist and I have been doing parts work for the past couple months, so I'm pretty aware of where I have wounds and unhealed trauma. I don't think it will be an issue. Our relationship is platonic. I've done kink with other people platonically without developing the attachment you described, so I'm not concerned."

"Excellent," Kieran said. "So, when do you want to connect for the first scene?"

"Wait a minute," Nicky said. "I shared what I wanted. What do *you* want from us being play partners?"

He shrugged. "I enjoy a lot of things. What you've outlined sounds good to me."

Nicky frowned, but didn't press the issue.

Before leaving the call, Nicky and Kieran had decided to aim for doing two scenes together in October. A warm-up scene in the middle of the month to gauge Nicky's pain threshold and preferences, and a longer, more intense scene on Halloween. The first one would take place at Nicky's apartment, and Kieran said he would try to book a space at the local dungeon for their Halloween scene.

"I'd like to set a powerful intention for our Halloween scene," Nicky explained. "I've been working on increasing my financial abundance, and that scene will be taking place right in the middle of Conscious Kink Bootcamp. In Spanish, Halloween is even called *El Día de Las Brujas*—the Day of the Witches—so it's a powerful day for using magic to set intentions. I'd like to use the energy we create to support me in building greater financial abundance in November and December."

Not that they planned to share this part with Kieran, but Nicky had recently accepted a loan from their parents because they hadn't been making ends meet, even with their group program and a couple other clients they had. Building financial stability was important to them.

And after their group scene in December, where the energy had been so intense, so powerful, they knew just how much energy could be built during a kink scene.

Why not channel that energy toward creating financial abundance? Nicky reasoned.

Kieran shrugged. "Works for me."

"See you Wednesday for that first scene, then."

Nodding, Kieran smiled. "See you Wednesday."

* * *

Wednesday came quickly. Twenty minutes before Kieran was set to arrive, Nicky began throwing some of the papers and clothes on their living room floor haphazardly into the second bedroom. Even so, the common areas still looked a bit of a mess. Clean towels were strewn across the loveseat in the living room (Nicky cursed themself for not folding them earlier in the day), and food wrappers and dirty dishes littered the coffee table. In the kitchen, Nicky had piles of dirty dishes completely covering the available counter space. On their dining table, their laptop was open, along with a few piles of papers.

Nicky grabbed a few of the wrappers and an empty juice box as the doorbell rang. They closed their eyes in frustration. Shit. At least they'd thought to set out the massage table and some sheets in case Kieran wanted to use them for tonight's scene.

They quickly threw away the trash they were holding, scanned the apartment, and grabbed one of their cloth masks (a black one with gold stars) before flying out the door and down the few stairs to the main entrance.

"Hey," Nicky said breathlessly, as they opened the door.

Kieran was wearing a heavy fleece jacket, earmuffs, and a nerdy facemask. Usually, during their in-person sessions, he'd worn a Star Wars mask that tied at the back of his head. But this one was different—navy blue, covered with several different kinds of dice, including the super-multi-sided kind a person might use when playing Dungeons and Dragons.

"Can I come in?" he asked. He gestured to the bag across his shoulder. "It's small, but it's actually kind of heavy."

"Oh, uh, sure." Nicky opened the door to the building wider so Kieran could pass through. "Up these steps and to the left. The door that's open."

After both of them had entered the apartment, Nicky shut the door and locked the deadbolt. Kieran was already taking off his jacket, gloves, and earmuffs.

"I can take that for you," Nicky said awkwardly. They snatched it from him, strode to a closet in the small dining area, and hung it up.

When they returned, Kieran had set up the massage table and put sheets on it. "Were you wanting to do a massage scene tonight?" he asked. "I was under the impression that you just wanted to do some impact play."

"Yeah, just impact. I just don't have a bench or cross, so I thought this would be easiest."

"Fair enough."

It was strange, being so close physically in Nicky's apartment. There was a weird intimacy about it. "This is the first time you've been here," Nicky commented.

"Yes, it is," Kieran said, looking around. "Nice place that you've got. I'm envious of the fireplace."

"Thanks," Nicky murmured.

The silence that followed was too uncomfortable. After just a few seconds, Nicky found themself moving to the kitchen. "Do you want any water?" Nicky called.

"Nope, I'm fine. I'll get out my toys like last time so you can pick out what you want me to use on you."

After Nicky was hydrated, and after Kieran had laid out all his toys (this was just the portable set, he explained), the two of them discussed the scene in more detail. A little bit of light massage as part of the warm-up. Like last time, Nicky approved the finger floggers, the thuddy bat that Kieran had, a crop, a paddle, and some toys used to increase sensation. Once again, Nicky had passed on all the canes.

In addition to Kieran's toys, Nicky had also set out a soft suede flogger as well as their homemade bat.

"If I remember from last time, you like impact more on your back than your butt," Kieran said, as Nicky began pulling off their clothes. "So, I'll just use the flogger on your back."

"Sounds good. Usually, spanking is part of my warm-up when I do impact scenes, which makes flogging more tolerable on my butt. But I only do that with people I'm dating."

Once they'd finished stripping, only wearing a pair of black cotton underwear, Nicky hopped onto the massage table face down, as Kieran had instructed during their scene negotiation.

"Are you going to take off your necklace?" Kieran asked.

Nicky lifted their head and chest, twisting to look at him. The dark green cross, with a hole in the middle, swung out. "Do I need to?"

Kieran looked away. If he looked at the necklace right now, it would seem like he was staring at their breasts. "No, just asking."

Satisfied, Nicky put their head back down, tucking the necklace beneath them, and placed their head on their arms. "Okay, I'm ready."

Like the last time, Kieran began with a warm-up, just to help Nicky acclimate to the sensation of the toys on their skin, the sting and the thuddiness. Just to gauge what their pain tolerance was right now. What they were ready for. What they could handle.

Next, he dragged the finger floggers across Nicky's back so they could feel the leather falls against their skin. They shivered.

"Cold?" Kieran asked.

Nicky shook their head. Then they paused. "Maybe a little. But I'll be okay."

He kept going, beginning to swing the finger floggers across their back.

"Yellow," Nicky said after a minute, wincing.

Kieran stopped, pulling the floggers away from Nicky's skin. "What's wrong?" he asked.

"I-that hurt a lot," Nicky said. "I think even having the floggers on my back is a bit much tonight."

From then on, Kieran focused more on thuddy sensations, using the bat, the paddle, and watched as Nicky's shoulders loosened and softened down. They'd been away from kink and impact play for so long that their nervous system was much more sensitive to it.

Kieran was also willing to bet that some of the positive associations that Nicky's brain had made with physical pain when they were doing impact more often had been disrupted. It might take a few scenes before they reached their pre-pandemic threshold again.

Another good reason for them to be doing this scene before Halloween. Not only did Kieran get a sense of Nicky's physical limits, but tonight's scene would help Nicky's body remember that yes, flogging was pleasurable. Paddling was pleasurable. Getting hit with a crop was pleasurable. There was pleasure in the pain.

After he'd finished the warm-up, Kieran checked in with Nicky. They said they were good for another round, but halfway through the second round, they called yellow. When he paused and checked in, they admitted it was probably more of a red.

"I'm not triggered," they clarified, as Kieran set aside the toys. "I think my body's just had enough for tonight."

"Makes sense," Kieran said. "You haven't done an impact scene since—"

"February," Nicky finished. "That's what? Eight months?"

Nodding, Kieran grabbed Nicky's water bottle. "Do you have a blanket nearby?"

Nicky shook their head. "Blankets are in my bedroom. I'll snag one as I'm getting into my pjs."

A few minutes later, Nicky returned wearing flannel pajama pants, a hoodie, and fuzzy socks. In their arms, they balanced a juice box, a box of graham crackers, Ollie the Otter, and a thick blanket. Their mask still covered the bottom part of their face.

"Do you still want to watch a movie together?" Kieran asked.

Nicky nodded and queued up the streaming platform. As they scrolled through the list of titles, Nicky hovered over one that featured a determined Hawaiian girl holding an oar, with waves in the background. Disney's *Moana*. "I know it came out like five years ago, but I still haven't seen it."

Kieran's eyes widened. "If you haven't seen *Moana*, we absolutely have to watch it. You'll love it. You'll love the music."

Pressing the center button on the remote, Nicky selected the title. As the music and opening sequence started, Nicky slowly began to relax. Kieran sat next to them, watching as their eyes moved imperceptibly, drinking in the movie, just as they drank their juice box and ate their snack.

Once Nicky was done eating and drinking, they slid their mask back over their face.

"For your aftercare, you mentioned you'd want me to give you head scratches," they said. "Do you want that now?"

Kieran nodded, and he slid off the couch and positioned himself in front of Nicky. A few seconds later, he felt their fingers scratching at his head, tentative, even a bit awkward. Kieran closed his eyes nonetheless. It felt really good. He could feel the Reiki energy flowing through Nicky's fingers, and his own nervous system started to settle and rebalance.

It took such focus to be present like that—watching a person's bodily movements, making sure he was hitting in the right places and with the right amount of pressure. Even though it wasn't discussed as much, many Doms and tops needed aftercare just as much as bottoms and submissives.

"Is that good for now?" Nicky asked after a couple minutes.

Kieran nodded. "Thank you." He pushed himself back onto the couch, sitting in the same spot as he had before.

"Thank you for the scene," Nicky replied.

"My pleasure," he said.

Nicky slid into the corner of the couch, and their eyes became heavy-lidded. They yawned, clutching Ollie to their chest and pulling their blanket tighter around themself.

Kieran felt that warm glow in his heart again. Nicky was so adorable right now.

"You know so much about kink," they mumbled.

He smiled. "Nearly two decades of experience should be good for something."

Nicky's grin matched his own. "It is."

As the two of them continued watching the movie (surprisingly, Nicky stayed awake until the end), Kieran had a strong suspicion he might remember this moment, this night, for a while. Even though he'd seen *Moana* before, to share it with Nicky like this felt special, maybe even sacred.

And though Nicky wouldn't have told Kieran if he asked them, they had a strong suspicion that they might come to associate this movie with him, too.

Chapter Thirteen

The rest of October passed in a blur between Nicky working with new coaching clients (a couple this time), running their group program, and creating new sex-positive content.

Specifically, Nicky was working on creating a trauma-sensitive BDSM limit list. Many of their clients had massive sexual trauma, or had even been sexually abused. Still, they'd expressed curiosity in kink and BDSM after reading, watching, or hearing about *Fifty Shades of Gray*. But when Nicky had pointed their clients to existing BDSM limits lists online so they could identify what they wanted to explore, they'd felt overwhelmed. Which was, of course, understandable.

After all, most limit lists had nearly three hundred inventory items. It was a lot.

In response to their clients' feedback, Nicky decided to create something new, something that had mechanisms to more actively support people with trauma. And thus, the Erotically Empowered Limit List™ was born.

As part of the limit list, Nicky had created filters, and had sorted the inventory items as Mild, Hot, Spicy, and Edge Play. They had even created a way that people could sort by the category of the item: Bondage, Physical Touch, Fetish, Pain Play (S&M), Power Play (D/s), and Miscellaneous.

Once it was complete, Nicky decided that this limit list was a work of art indeed.

Very *kinky* art.

More than the pride Nicky felt about developing something so useful, though, it was a great exercise for them to fill out their own limits using the tool they'd created. It took a few hours to complete, but they were able to section it out. *Okay, I'm completing these twenty. Oh, and these twenty. Now these twenty.*

Pretty quickly, those individual sets of twenty inventory items added up, and Nicky had completed the entire thing. They sent their limits over to Kieran in an email.

Hey, it read, *I know you didn't ask for this, but I thought this might be supportive since we're playing together. Also, I designed the template for this document. What do you think?*

Kieran had responded kindly, and had also sent over his own limits. *I include definitions in mine,* he wrote back. *That way people know what the activity is without going on a Google hunt.*

It was good feedback, and Nicky told him so. They also made a mental note to include that in the next version of their document.

From there, the email thread quickly turned into a conversation about their scene on Halloween. As he had the time before, Kieran quickly deflected and asked Nicky what they wanted to do. *I have fun doing a lot of things,* he replied, when asked. *What do you want to do?*

Nicky wanted to do more impact. While being tied to a cross. They'd loved that first scene with Kieran, and wanted to do something similar. And *goddamn,* it had been nearly a year since that scene.

Kieran also shared that he'd reserved a space for them at the one local dungeon that was still open despite the pandemic. The facility had updated its policies to keep people safer, Kieran explained. The two of them would rent a designated area of the event space and could only play in that section of the facility. In addition, Nicky and Kieran still planned to wear their masks, as they had earlier in the month when the two of them had scened at Nicky's apartment.

Nicky wasn't sure *exactly* how much good it did to wear the masks since they were within two to three feet of each other when they were doing their scenes, but wearing masks made Nicky *feel* more comfortable, at least. The last thing Nicky wanted to do was infect their sixty-something-year-old parents with the virus, so wearing masks around everyone else seemed like the best protocol.

Admittedly, the safest thing would be *not* to play with Kieran at all, but that didn't feel like an option. Nicky's body craved the physical touch, the impact. It was purely platonic, of course, not romantic or sexual *at all*, but Nicky's most recent scene with Kieran had just felt so damn good even though it had been intense.

Pandemic or no, Nicky wasn't giving that up.

* * *

On Halloween, Nicky was working late. *Again.* Nicky didn't think anything of it until they glanced at their phone out of pure habit. It was twenty minutes before seven o'clock. To be on time for their scene with Kieran, they needed to leave in less than five minutes.

"Damn it all," Nicky said as they quickly closed their laptop. "I'm going to be late."

Flying through their apartment, they shrugged on some leggings, slid on their boots, and shoved their toys—handheld vibrator, anal plug, padded bat, and flogger—in their backpack along with Ollie and some lube. Scowling, Nicky brushed a hand through their hair before dashing out the door.

The late October air was chilly, even with a coat, and Nicky's heart was beating fast as they began driving toward the play space where they were meeting Kieran. It had been just two weeks since their last scene, and yet it felt like an eternity.

While Nicky was driving, they sent Kieran a quick text and pulled a purple cloth mask out of their purse. They placed it over their nose and mouth, pinching the nose piece tight. As soon as Nicky parked, they grabbed their backpack unceremoniously, slammed the car door shut, and power-walked into the event space to the front desk.

"Nicole Rivera," they said breathlessly, pulling their ID out of their wallet and flashing it to the two volunteers sitting behind the desk. "I'm here with Kieran Jackson."

Looking at the computer, a woman with cat-eye glasses and turquoise hair nodded and clicked the mouse. "You're good to go in. He's already here. Follow the blue tape marks on the floor, and that will guide you to the space you've reserved for tonight."

"Great, thanks," Nicky huffed. They hurried into the main dungeon space, following the blue tape marks on the floor.

Sure enough, Kieran was there, masked, in a short sleeve shirt and kilt, tying rope around a St. Andrew's cross. Nicky noticed that he'd also already placed rope along a suspension rig.

"Sorry I'm late. I lost track of time," Nicky said.

Kieran turned toward them. Though Nicky couldn't see his mouth, they imagined he was smiling beneath the mask. "You're fine," he said. "It gave me time to set up."

"You need any help?"

Shaking his head, Kieran tied one more knot on the cross and stepped back. "Nope. We're all set. Ropes are tied, and I've cleaned the equipment already. The volunteers clean everything after each Saturday's event, and no one's used the cross or massage table since then. Even so, I wiped it all down. Can never be too careful."

"Thank you," Nicky said, a bit surprised. "That was really… proactive of you."

"I try."

Nodding, Nicky slid their backpack onto a nearby table. "I brought some toys for tonight's scene. Can I show what I have?"

"Sure," Kieran said, walking toward them.

Pulling out all the toys, Nicky held up a medium-sized black, silicone anal plug. Kieran noticed it had a rhinestone on one end. Cute.

"If it's okay with you," Nicky said, "I'd like to wear this during our scene. It's new, but since I'm working on creating more abundance in my coaching business right now, I thought it might be helpful. You know, to help open up the root chakra? How do you feel about that?"

Kieran shrugged. "It's your body. Do what you want."

Nicky blushed. "Um, okay. Thanks."

Next, they showed him their handheld vibrator. "And I thought, you know, if you wanted, that you could use this on me."

Kieran surveyed Nicky carefully. He noticed that their feet were pointed in, their cheeks were flushed, and their body was rigid. "Is that a hell yes for you?" he asked quietly.

Nicky hesitated.

Okay, so it was *not* a hell yes. Beneath his mask, Kieran quirked a smile. "How about this?" he said. "If you've got an itch you *really* need to scratch, you can use it on yourself."

If possible, Nicky's cheeks became even redder. "That works."

That being settled, Kieran walked toward the massage table. Just like he had a couple weeks ago, he asked Nicky to select which toys he would use on them. Nicky immediately set the floggers, padded bat, and a plush paddle off to the side. Then, delicately, they picked up one of the many canes that Kieran had set out on the table for Nicky to look at. This one was thick, translucent, clear, made of acrylic. From the little that Nicky knew about canes, the thicker they were, the less they stung.

"What do you think about using this on me?" Nicky asked, holding up the acrylic cane and tapping it on the inside of their forearm.

Kieran looked at the cane thoughtfully. If he remembered correctly, caning had been only a five out of ten on Nicky's limit list. It was neutral. Undecided. Unknown.

Not a hell yes.

"Have you ever done a caning scene before?" he asked.

"No."

Kieran paused. Nicky was hitting themself *very* lightly with the cane as they tested it.

"Cane strikes can be quite intense," he replied. "And that wasn't something we explicitly discussed before you arrived. Since it's something new for you, I'd suggest we hold off."

"So that's a no?"

"If you still want to do a caning scene in a couple weeks," he said carefully, "we can try it then."

"Sounds good."

Next, Kieran walked Nicky through the setup of the scene. "So, here's what I was thinking: we start you off with a massage to help you relax and ground, and then we do some impact on the St. Andrew's cross. Maybe some more impact on the suspension rig. You can lean against the ropes like this."

Folding his arms inward, Kieran placed them on the rope and leaned into it. "It's great if your arms get tired on the cross but you still want more impact. Then we can end with another massage to help you integrate. The massage at the end will be gentler because you'll be sensitive after all the impact.

"How does that sound?" he asked.

"I'm all for it," Nicky said. "Should I go put my anal plug in now?"

"Yeah, if you want to use it. Go ahead."

Nicky gathered their lube, anal plug, and gray cotton robe and headed to the single-occupancy all-gender bathroom, turned on the light, and locked the door.

Looking in the mirror, Nicky exhaled deeply and set both items on the edge of the sink. They noticed that the eyes of their reflection were wide and sparkling. Fear and excitement. This scene was *definitely* going to be an edge.

Something new. Something that stretched them.

"The only thing that separates fear and excitement is the breath," Nicky muttered as they stripped and began slathering lube over the anal plug. "Okay, Nicky, you can do this. Deep breaths. Just keep breathing."

It pinched a bit as the anal plug went in, and Nicky noticed momentary anxiety. They kept breathing, and as the plug went *all* the way in, they exhaled. It felt comforting, expanding, stretching. *Just keep breathing,* Nicky reminded themself. *Just keep breathing.*

"Okay, here we go," Nicky said, and they grabbed their items, put on their black lacy undies once more, tied their gray cotton robe, and walked out of the bathroom.

When they re-entered the dungeon, they saw that Kieran had re-moved his shirt. They breathed. There was something uncomfortable about this all, and Nicky didn't know what it was.

Not something to call yellow about, exactly. Just... different. Surprising.

"Are you ready?" Kieran asked.

Nicky nodded.

They took off their robe, lied face-down on the massage table, and took another deep breath. *Just keep breathing.*

After dripping lotion onto them, Kieran began massaging Nicky's shoulders with his hands, inviting them to relax. Slowly, gently, Nicky began to sink into the table.

It felt nice to be touched. To receive a massage. It had been awhile... in fact, they hadn't received a massage since early March, just before the pandemic. Nearly eight months ago. Two weeks before the governor had announced the stay-at-home advisory.

God, that seemed a *lifetime* ago.

Nicky sighed, exhaling out, releasing even more tension, wiggling down and into the vinyl of the massage table. Kieran pressed his hands even deeper. Nicky's energy had been erratic, rushed when they'd first entered the space. They hadn't been in their body. But between the touch and the energy work, Kieran saw Nicky's energy soften and set-tle, their breathing grow deeper.

He kept touching their neck, their shoulders, their back, their legs until Nicky was floating at the edge of subspace. When Nicky gave a soft sigh, almost a moan, he paused, holding his hands on Nicky's upper back.

"How are you feeling?" he asked.

"Mmm?" Nicky said.

"Are you ready for some impact?"

A soft, almost sleepy nod.

"Great. Take your time sitting up. There's a bottle of water right here for you." Kieran gestured to a nearby side table.

"Thank you, that's perfect," Nicky said, slurring their speech just slightly.

Yep, Kieran thought with a grin, Nicky was in subspace. Slurred speech and a bit of drowsiness were some cues. This was going to be fun. He couldn't wait to see their reactions.

Once Nicky finished their water, Kieran guided them toward the St. Andrew's cross, tied rope around their wrists, and made sure they were comfortable. "If you start to feel any tingling," he said, "let me know immediately. I can get you out of there very quickly."

Prior to tonight, Nicky had expressed most of their boundaries, and those were largely still in play. Underwear would stay on. No touching of their swimsuit areas, as Nicky called it—their breasts, ass, or genitals. No spankings. Overall, it was similar to the first time Kieran had played with Nicky, except that there was more rapport here. It wasn't an isolated scene.

Kieran began touching Nicky's shoulders gently with a piece of faux fur. Nicky shivered, and their shoulders began to open up even more, and they started sinking deeper under the touch. After just a minute or so, Kieran spoke, his voice muffled behind the mask.

"We're going to do two or three rounds of impact, okay?" he said. "Ten minutes each. I'm going to use all the toys on you at least once, and then I'll check in."

Nicky nodded, their head heavy. So open. So relaxed. This was way more fun than watching a horror movie by themself, or even with their parents. More than that, it had been so long since they had physically engaged with someone who had such awareness and mastery over their own energy. It was just wonderful to receive. To be.

To dive deeper.

God, how Nicky had needed this.

Soon, the softness was replaced with a sting. A flogger. On their butt. Then their back. Nicky sighed and rested their head on the cross, allowing the impact to lull them in. A padded bat replaced the flogger, then a paddle, then a crop. Back to a flogger, but a different one.

"Yellow," Nicky said.

Kieran stopped immediately.

"The flogger on my butt is still too much. It's fine on my back, though."

Nodding, Kieran resumed the flogging, focusing strictly on Nicky's back. After another minute, he stopped and began rubbing Nicky's shoulders.

"We're not done, are we?" Nicky asked.

"No, that was just the warm-up," Kieran said with a gentle chuckle.

And he began the cycle again, once more with the faux fur. The finger floggers. The padded bat. The paddle. The crop.

It was interesting, Nicky noted, halfway through the cycle, but they were really wet. They felt their pussy opening up, despite the lack of direct contact, and they felt the energy building.

And it needed some sort of release.

Of course, it was just kink, and this was just Kieran, so it was almost like a tease. Nicky knew nothing sexual was going to happen. Hell, Nicky didn't *want* anything sexual to happen. Even though they brought their massage wand, Nicky knew they would feel self-conscious using it on themself in front of Kieran.

But yet they were turned on and *so* wanted to be touched.

It was a Catch-22, doing a scene like this.

After the second round of impact, Nicky said their wrists were getting tingly. True to his word, Kieran untied them immediately, and they moved to the suspension rig so that Nicky could just lean against the rope.

Nicky felt drunk. They giggled as they leaned into the strands of rope. Almost fell into the rope. Started swinging back and forth. Feeling like a five-year-old. Playful. Curious.

Nicky was in littlespace, and *boy* were they having fun.

"Bet you wish you could spank me," Nicky teased Kieran, in a singsong voice, as they wiggled their ass, while leaning into and out of the ropes.

The next thing Nicky knew, they felt heat. Kieran was pressing his bare chest against their back. His energy radiated shadowy dominance, exuded control, *demanded* to be obeyed. Even without Kieran saying anything, Nicky felt a bit stunned.

This was new.

There was an electric energy, just in that moment. For an instant, it *did* seem almost sexual. Like Nicky was glimpsing behind some curtain.

Kieran leaned in further and placed his lips near their ear. "If you wanted me to spank you," he murmured, "you *really* should have negotiated that beforehand. Because right now, you're in subspace and you can't consent."

Just as suddenly as he had leaned in, he leaned out. And the dominant energy that had been there before shifted just as quickly.

"Are you ready for another round of impact?" he asked.

Nicky nodded silently, then shivered. Soon, the familiar *fwip fwip* of the floggers was cracking through the air, and the sting was sinking into their skin. Nicky settled into the impact once more, allowing themself to float even higher.

Tomorrow, Nicky would wake up with a horrible headache, feel listless and unwilling to get out of bed. They would need massive amounts of dark chocolate to feel human again because of the sub drop. And it would be the worst sub drop they'd ever had.

And once they returned home, after the aftercare, Nicky would still be so wet, so turned on from the scene that they wouldn't be able to focus or sleep. At least, not until they had brought themself to their own crashing crescendo of an orgasm using their black vibrating wand.

But in that moment, with Kieran wielding the floggers in double-time, none of that mattered. Regardless how Nicky felt later, they knew this scene was completely worth it.

Nicky was soaring. Like Icarus, they were flying toward the sun, stretching and playing with their edges.

Chapter Fourteen

Sure enough, Nicky awoke with the worst sub drop they'd ever had. Standing was hard. Walking seemed even harder. Listless, Nicky swaddled themself in a big blanket and continued to lie in bed.

It was around ten o'clock when Nicky finally dragged themself to the kitchen, still wearing their pajamas. Even then, it was only to grab a chocolate bar.

At noon, Nicky was lying in bed again staring at the ceiling.

At two, Nicky was back in the kitchen making hot chocolate and toast and finally texted Kieran back. He'd asked Nicky how they were doing in the late morning, but they hadn't known what to say.

Nicky had never dealt with depression, but they had to imagine that it was a lot like an ongoing sub drop. Twelve hours was bad enough. They couldn't imagine weeks or months of this on end.

I'm surviving, they replied. *Sub drop has been brutal. Hoping I'll be functional in two hours for the masterclass I'm leading for Conscious Kink Bootcamp.*

Two minutes later, Kieran had responded. *Do you want to talk and connect? We can chat on the phone if that would be supportive.*

Nicky stared at their phone, uncertain and uncomprehending. Meanwhile, the milk they were warming for their hot chocolate started overflowing out of the pan. It bubbled over onto the burner and continued to flow until Nicky snapped to attention at the noise.

"Shit," Nicky muttered. In a flash they had turned down the temperature, taken the pot off the burner, stirred the milk, and replaced it. They sighed.

For some reason, taking Kieran up on his offer to connect over the phone seemed… well, uncomfortable. Nicky knew they were perfectly capable of taking care of themself. They messaged him back telling him so, and finished making their hot chocolate.

***

In the two weeks that followed, Nicky stayed primarily at their parents'. Somewhere along the way, between work and transcribing their grandparents' letters, Paco reached out to them via email. He wanted to talk. He was sorry about what had happened earlier that year and wanted to make it up to Nicky. A little wary, Nicky agreed nonetheless.

"I've missed you, Nicky," he said once they were on the phone. "How have you been?"

Nicky glanced around their makeshift office in their parents' basement. "I'm fine," they said. "Back at my parents'. You?"

Paco shared that he'd largely been out of contact with his other ex, Catalina, and that he'd gotten a new job. "It's much more enjoyable. The office space is better, and they gave me a good-enough laptop so that I can work remotely without it being a pain."

"That's great, Paco," Nicky said.

Throughout their conversation, something felt off, but Nicky wasn't sure what it was. Paco hadn't said anything harmful or offensive, and it should have been just like old times.

Eventually, the two of them finished catching up, and then Paco spoke again. "I've missed you. Do you want to meet up and go for a walk sometime this month? If you're making a trip into Madison anyway?"

Nicky didn't know what to say. Back in March or April, they would have leaped at this opportunity. They *had* leaped at this opportunity. Even still, while part of them was excited about seeing Paco in person, other parts were unsure, hesitant.

Those parts were yellow. They wanted to pause.

"Let me get back to you," Nicky said. "I'm not sure when I'll be in the area next."

After a brief, friendly goodbye, Nicky ended the call.

Over the next several days, Nicky continued to process their conversation with Paco. After chatting with him, certain parts of them wanted to date him again, be his partner again. Even though he was monogamous and Nicky was poly. Even though Nicky was kinky and Paco was vanilla. After all, Paco had been their first love.

Ultimately, after a lot of reflection, Nicky emailed Paco requesting that the two of them not be in contact until the new year. Maybe that was the kind of space that Nicky needed. A lot could change in two months, and maybe when they reconnected, it would feel more joyful to be friends with him.

* * *

Given how emotionally draining it had been to reach a decision on what to do about Paco, Nicky was surprised they somehow had the capacity to respond to Kieran's texts about doing a scene in November. It was just the distraction that they needed.

The two of them agreed to meet at Kieran's new apartment midway between Madison and Milwaukee, and confirmed that—in addition to impact, rope bondage, and massage—Kieran would introduce Nicky to caning. Nicky was nervous and excited; their heart was beating rapidly as they knocked on the door to Kieran's apartment, then rang the doorbell.

A shuffle of feet, then a click. The burgundy door swung open to reveal a masked-up Kieran. This time, he was wearing a Lord of the Rings mask with Frodo and Sam and other characters that Nicky didn't recognize.

"Nice mask," Nicky said, stepping through the door.

Kieran closed it behind the two of them. "Thanks," he said. "But it's not as great as the shirt."

He held the material of the t-shirt away from his body so that Nicky could see it more clearly. *Never Too Late for Second Breakfast*, the shirt read in block letters, with an image of Sam at the bottom.

Nicky snorted. "You are such a nerd," they said.

His eyes sparkling, Kieran nodded. "Yup."

Then he climbed up the stairs, and Nicky bounded behind him. When they reached the landing, Nicky felt their chest squeeze and tighten.

It was one thing to do a scene at the public event space. Especially since that's where they'd first done a scene with Kieran. Or even for Nicky to do a scene with him at *their* apartment. After all, they could always ask him to leave.

But it was something else entirely for Nicky to be sceneing with Kieran here, in *his* home, *his* private space. It seemed even more intimate.

The knot in Nicky's chest and gut squeezed tighter.

"So, this is what I was thinking," Kieran said, and he began launching off, describing how they could set things up. Began pulling out impact toys. Asked Nicky what they wanted during the scene, what aftercare they would need.

Nicky was grateful to focus on the logistics. It distracted them from the fact that they were in Kieran's living room about to do their first caning scene. Nicky was excited, of course. Otherwise, they wouldn't be doing the scene. But for the longest time, using canes had been a hard limit, something they thought they would *never* try. Just the thought of them had scared Nicky. Plus, Nicky knew canes hurt, *really* hurt.

Funny how Nicky's desires could change so radically over time.

"Are you ready to get started?" Kieran asked.

Nicky nodded. "I'd like to use a couple toys again tonight, if that's okay with you. The anal plug from last time, and one of my yoni eggs."

"Like I said last time, it's your body. You don't have to ask for consent on that."

"Right," Nicky said slowly. "I'll be back in a minute, then."

Nicky grabbed their backpack, headed into the bathroom, and locked it. After stripping, adding some lube to the anal plug and inserting it, they pulled out their medium-sized rose quartz yoni egg, rinsed it, and sat on the toilet.

And then Nicky started breathing.

With yoni eggs, the rule was not to push the crystal into the pussy. When Nicky had first purchased their yoni eggs two years earlier, that had been clear in all the literature. It was important to make sure that the yoni *wanted* the egg.

Continuing to breathe, Nicky placed the larger end of the egg toward the entrance of their pussy and began doing Kegel exercises, contracting and releasing their pelvic floor muscles. Following each Kegel, the egg slid in a little, and Nicky held the rose quartz crystal in place. After several rounds, the egg slipped out.

"Must not be wet enough," Nicky muttered. They placed a finger to their yoni and felt the wetness and the heat. On a scale of one to ten, Nicky was probably at a six. Maybe a seven.

Holding the yoni egg with one hand, Nicky stroked their clit with the other, tracing circles and rubbing back and forth, every so often bringing more lubrication up from their pussy.

Nicky's tits began feeling more tender, calling for attention. They moaned and gently stroked their breasts. Then took another big deep breath and began the process again.

Again, the yoni egg slipped out almost at the point of being fully inserted.

Nicky let out a frustrated exhale. This was taking too long. Kieran was waiting for them.

Patience, a voice seemed to say. *There's all the time in the world. Be present with your body and focus on your breathing.*

Sure enough, on the third try, Nicky released their expectations and the rose quartz crystal slipped in easily. Once it was in their yoni, it seemed to be sucked up completely.

After doing a couple more Kegels for good measure, Nicky wiped themself up, washed their hands, put their underwear back on, tied their gray robe around themself, and exited the bathroom holding their black backpack, their toy bag, in one hand.

In the living room, Kieran had also changed. Just like last time, he was wearing his green and black plaid kilt and was shirtless. The massage table was set up, the toys spread out along it. Attached to the closet door was the restraint system.

At that moment, Kieran turned around to face Nicky, still masked, the edges of his eyes crinkling with what Nicky knew to be a smile.

Nicky swallowed.

"I'm sorry to have kept you waiting," Nicky said apologetically, setting down their bag next to Ollie. They were half-tempted to pick Ollie up and snuggle with him right now.

Kieran's crinkles increased. Nicky assumed his smile was wider beneath the mask.

"You didn't keep me waiting," he said. "I was setting up for the scene and just finished a couple minutes ago. Are you ready?"

Nicky nodded. "We're starting with the massage, right?"

"Yes," Kieran said, and he pulled back the sheets on the massage table. "I want to make sure that you're grounded and relaxed before starting the impact."

"Right," said Nicky, pulling off their robe. "Face down?" they asked.

At Kieran's nod, they got onto the table, their stomach and breasts pressed into the sheets and took a few deep breaths.

When he began using the oil on their neck and shoulders, Nicky groaned as Kieran touched a tender spot.

"You have a big knot right here," he said, touching it with a tad more pressure.

Nicky winced. "That hurts."

"Good ouch or bad ouch?"

"It's okay," Nicky said, their voice muffled by the sheets. "Just not any harder than that."

"You have a lot of stress and tension in your neck and shoulders," Kieran commented as he continued touching them. "Lots of sitting and working?"

"Yeah, it's been a full week."

They settled into rhythmic silence after that, but then Kieran moved into a pattern of movement that felt especially soothing. Nicky felt an electric tingle every so often.

"You're flowing energy into me, aren't you?" Nicky asked after a moment.

"Yes," Kieran said.

Nicky could practically hear the smile in his voice.

If anyone had asked Nicky how much time had passed while they were lying on the massage table, Nicky would have said it was both ten minutes and two hours. It was soothing being in that energetic space, being touched, receiving Reiki or whatever form of energy healing Kieran was incorporating into the massage.

Such a great way to start a scene.

Nicky had a feeling they were *quickly* going to become spoiled if they kept playing with Kieran.

Once Nicky had gotten off the table and had some water, Kieran began tying them up, as they'd discussed. First, he tied Nicky's wrists together with rope, and placed ankle cuffs on them. The cuffs weren't attached to anything, so Nicky could move their legs and feet freely.

"Does that feel comfortable?" he asked.

Nicky nodded.

Kieran guided Nicky to the closet door. From there, he showed them how to hold the loop hanging off the restraint system, and reminded them to let him know if they started to feel any tingling or numbness in their hands, fingers, or wrists.

"Next, we're going to attach the ankle restraints to a spreader bar," Kieran said. He placed a metal bar about three feet long and one inch wide on the floor. Then, using the clips on the restraints, he connected Nicky to the bar.

"How does that feel?" he asked.

Nicky noticed just a touch of nervous energy in their stomach as they approached the spreader bar, and Kieran clipped them to it. Though Nicky had been wanting to try a spreader bar for a long time, it was still new.

"It's okay, but a little weird."

His eyes crinkled. "Yeah, it can be uncomfortable the first time."

Then, after getting the music set up, Kieran began the impact scene.

It was similar to the scene they'd done just two weeks before—a warm-up with gentle flogging, the padded bat, paddle, and a couple other toys. Nicky was sinking in, and energetically they were open, expanding.

Such beautiful, buoyant white light. It made Kieran smile. He wished he could see Nicky's smile and more of their physical response beneath their mask.

After the first round of impact, Kieran checked in. "How are you doing, Nicky?"

"I'm doing great," they said, and their words were slurred just a bit.

They were entering subspace. He would start the second round of impact, get a good portion through, and then use one of his thin, wooden canes on them.

At a fraction of his full power, of course. Nicky wouldn't be able to handle him striking them with his full strength.

He'd check in after a single cane strike.

After all, this was new for them. He didn't know what they would be able to handle. And padded bats and floggers didn't even come close to the pain that a cane caused.

Seven minutes later, after more flogging, gentle beating and paddling, Kieran picked up the cane. He held it in his hand.

"I'm about to use the cane now," he said.

Nicky nodded.

Then, holding the narrow piece of wood in one hand, Kieran struck Nicky's right hamstring, halfway between their glute and their knee.

Quick and firm.

Nicky immediately cried out with pain; their body leaned forward involuntarily.

Kieran paused. "What color are you?"

Nicky felt nauseated, and the edges of their vision seemed to be going black.

"Red."

Chapter Fifteen

Kieran sprang into action the moment that Nicky called red. First, he set down the cane, then helped Nicky unhook themself from the resistance system. He guided them to the massage table.

"How can I be supportive?" he asked.

Nicky didn't say anything for a minute, just stood there, leaning against the massage table, taking a few deep breaths. Their vision was still off, black at the edges, and the pain of the strike was overwhelming.

"I need a minute," they said.

They stayed there for several minutes, practically lying on top of the massage table as the black spots faded and their vision returned to normal.

Gingerly, Nicky touched the mark the cane strike had left. And hissed.

"Yeah, it can sting a bit," Kieran said.

"More like a lot," Nicky muttered. "Can you unhook me? And untie my wrists?"

Kieran nodded, detaching the spreader bar from the ankle cuffs, and then helped Nicky take off the ankle cuffs. Then he untied the rope from their wrists.

Once they were free, Nicky stood up and carefully walked toward their clothing, gathered up their pajamas, and went into the bathroom to remove their toys and to change. While naked, Nicky glanced at the back of their right thigh and saw a nasty welt. They touched the bruise and hissed again. God, that *really* fucking hurt.

It would be awhile before they did another caning scene, Nicky thought ruefully. That cane strike was a *bitch*.

After washing their toys, getting dressed, and taking a few more deep breaths, Nicky came back out into the living room. Kieran was folding up the massage table and had already taken care of the sheets. When he saw Nicky emerge, he paused with what he was doing.

"How are you feeling?" he asked.

"A bit better," Nicky said. "Thank you for untying me so quickly."

"Of course. I set a water bottle out for you on the counter," he added, pointing.

Self-conscious, Nicky wrapped their arms around themself.

"Thanks."

Kieran carried the massage table back to the closet, closed the door tightly, and looked back at Nicky. They were still holding themself, arms wrapped around their middle, the water bottle forgotten on the counter.

Nicky was definitely having a shock response. Kieran had gone lightly with the cane, but with the anal plug, yoni egg, bondage, *and* cane strike, Nicky had clearly gotten overstimulated.

Grabbing the water bottle from the counter, Kieran handed it to Nicky. "Here. Drink."

Nodding, Nicky accepted it wordlessly and cracked it open, taking a long sip.

"Do you want to watch a movie? You talked about *Frozen* last time."

Nicky looked up, and a small smile graced their face. "Yeah, that sounds great. Let me grab Ollie and my blanket."

"Where are they? I can grab them."

Nicky pointed across the room, and Kieran fetched them.

"Do you want to sit in the chair during the movie?" Kieran asked, handing Nicky both Ollie and the blanket.

Nicky hesitated. It was the one piece of furniture in the living room. They didn't want to be a nuisance or make Kieran uncomfortable. After all, it was his space. "No," they said quickly. "I'm fine on the floor."

Settling on the carpet, Nicky pulled their fuzzy purple blanket around themself and pressed Ollie into their chest. As the movie started, they took some deep breaths and drank some more water.

"Thank you for doing that scene with me," Nicky said after a few minutes. "And thank you for being so responsive when I called red."

Kieran nodded. "You're welcome."

"Is there anything that you want for aftercare?" Nicky asked.

"Just some head scratches. But it doesn't have to be right now. Finish your water first."

"Okay."

The movie played, and Nicky felt their body start to soften. Nicky's right thigh still smarted from the cane strike, but they felt safe. Tipping their head back to drain the water bottle, Nicky turned to look at Kieran.

"Do you still want head scratches?" Nicky asked.

"Yes, please," he said.

So Nicky stood up, walked over to Kieran, and stepped behind the chair, gently running their fingernails over his scalp, scratching his head.

As Nicky did so, a strange thought popped into their head: *I kind of want to kiss him.*

The thought surprised Nicky. Things with Kieran were platonic. Always had been platonic. They had never thought of him romantically or sexually and never would. So, instantly, Nicky quelled that instinct.

He warned you about trauma bonding through kink, they chastised themself. *That's what this is. You said you would be mindful of those trauma parts of you. This is just a response to the impact scene that you just did with him. That's all.*

Nicky paused with the head scratches. "How's that?"

"That's good, thank you," Kieran said.

So Nicky headed back to their spot on the floor to continue watching the movie. It must have been a really intense scene that the two of them did together, they thought, because the small part of them that wanted to kiss Kieran was present during the rest of the film.

Trauma bonding, Nicky reminded themself, pulling their blanket tighter. *That's all it is.*

* * *

It was two full months before Nicky's next scene with Kieran. Because of the holidays and Dane County's pandemic advisories, Nicky didn't see Kieran for the rest of 2020.

Fortunately, the thoughts about kissing Kieran had evaporated overnight, so Nicky was able to keep themself focused on work. They'd had their largest revenue month, and cash flow finally seemed to be stabilizing. Overall, Nicky was doing well. Despite the pandemic, they were happy.

Even so, they still wanted to be in a relationship.

Nearly every day, they thought back to Bailey's most recent prediction: *He's out there, Nicky. Be patient. Give it a year. And do the damn work. That's how he'll see you.*

And every time that Nicky thought about this prediction, they sighed and refocused on their business, their healing work, and being a better human.

Nicky's birthday came and went. Unlike last year's celebration at Mon Ami, this year was a quiet affair. Nicky, their mom, and their dad all had homemade veggie lasagna and a glass of red wine. It was nice to gather as a family (sans Nicky's sister who was working), but Nicky was tired of COVID-19. It had affected so many people, so many aspects of normal life.

Even Mon Ami had recently closed because of the pandemic, and that was a real shame.

At last, though, the number of COVID-19 cases had dropped enough that Nicky was willing to go back to Madison and scene with Kieran again. Nicy had gotten a couple free tickets for an upcoming virtual play party and asked if he'd like to join them. Kieran said yes, and he suggested that the two of them meet up in person and do a scene together during the event.

We can meet at the kink space if you feel more comfortable with that, one of his messages read.

Nicky did feel more comfortable sceneing at the local dungeon than having Kieran in their apartment. But, at the last minute, the kink space had a COVID-19 scare and canceled all reservations for the night.

And so, that was how Nicky found themself ushering Kieran into their newly minted queer playroom in the middle of January. Nicky called the guest bedroom their queer playroom now because a hand-painted rainbow geometric mosaic covered one of the walls and a black massage table stood in the center.

"Good to see you, Kieran," Nicky said, leaning in for a quick hug. "How have you been?"

His eyes sparkled, a clear sign he was smiling behind his mask. This one was covered with rainbow dice, all shades and hues. Some of them were multi-sided, just like they were on the navy blue mask he had.

God, he was *so* nerdy.

"Holidays were good," Kieran said. "It was great to spend time with my son. I also started dating someone, and she spent a few days with me just before New Year's. That was nice, too."

"What's her name?"

"Jade. She's studying at the university," Kieran said.

"How did the two of you meet?"

"FetLife."

"And she's poly?"

Kieran shook his head. "She knows that I'm poly, and I've explained to her what that means, that I might have other partners at some point, but she's not interested in that for herself. She's also really busy with her studies, and I don't think she has time for more than one relationship right now."

"Well, I'm glad it's going well," Nicky said finally.

"Thanks," Kieran said. He surveyed the room. "What do you want to do tonight?"

"I figured we could do some bondage, since you've been wanting to do that for awhile, and we didn't do a ton of it last time. Also, maybe some impact? And maybe massage?"

Kieran nodded. Pretty standard fare. "Do you have any specific intention for this evening?"

Nicky froze. "I don't know. I hadn't thought that far ahead," they admitted.

"That's okay. How about you take a few minutes to decompress, meditate, get dressed in whatever makes you feel most comfortable right now? I'll go into the bathroom and put on my kilt."

"Do you wear underwear under your kilt?" Nicky asked.

Kieran looked at them. Nicky could see the amusement in his eyes. "Sometimes."

"Will you be wearing something under your kilt tonight?"

He raised an eyebrow.

Nicky turned bright red and shook their head furiously. "You know what. Never mind. I'm going to get into some more comfortable clothing myself."

Their face still flushed, Nicky strode out of the playroom to get changed.

* * *

Just ten minutes later, Nicky was lying on the massage table in the playroom, wearing nothing more than a pair of lacy black underwear, looking up at Kieran as he began tying their hands together with purple nylon rope.

He was shirtless, as he had been the last two times they'd played together.

"How does the rope feel?" he asked.

"Good," Nicky said. "I can move my wrists some, so we're fine."

"Excellent," Kieran said. "You said your intention was to ground before the play party, to come into your body. I want you to feel snug, not overly restricted."

Kieran continued weaving the rope around Nicky, over their chest and their breasts so they could only lift their head. Then their legs were tied down as well. Then, their feet.

By the time Kieran was finished, Nicky felt the rope pressing on all sides. They breathed in deeply, and exhaled. The ropes might as well be vines, pulling them into the ground. And the massage table was a planter bed. And Nicky was a ghost.

Or corpse.

Savasana.

They blinked rapidly, and Kieran smiled down at them. "How are you doing?"

"I-I don't know."

"Green, yellow, or red?"

"Green," they said decidedly. "I'm just not sure how I feel."

"Grounded?" Kieran asked.

"Yes, but there's something else," Nicky said slowly.

"Are you up for a head massage?"

Nicky nodded.

Grabbing a chair, Kieran sat down and slowly began massaging Nicky's scalp using his fingers. After a couple moments, Nicky closed their eyes and took a deep breath. For some reason, this part of their head was very sensitive.

"I've been thinking about Paco recently," Nicky said at last. "I told him I wanted to be out of contact until the new year, and I'm not sure whether or not I should message him."

"Mmm," Kieran said. "Has he started calling you Nicky instead of Nicole?"

Nicky winced. "I forgot I told you about that. Sometimes. At least he's not rolling his eyes when I correct him."

"Hmm," he said, continuing to massage Nicky.

Soon though, making conversation was difficult. Nicky was simultaneously more relaxed and also more acutely aware of the pressure in their head, especially in their temples. How it felt like Kieran was being rough with them, that his fingers were digging in.

Then Nicky started crying. A wave of emotion was coming up, and they couldn't handle all the energy coming into their head. Like they were at the edge of a cliff and trying to hold on, but their fingers kept slipping because the rock was wet.

"Yellow."

Kieran paused immediately, stopping the massage, then he lifted his fingers from Nicky's scalp.

"Do you need to stop?" he asked.

Nicky didn't respond for a moment. They just felt the wave of grief, how the trickle of tears flowed more steadily. Felt the ropes along their skin. Finally, they nodded.

"Do you want me to untie you?"

Nicky nodded again, sobbing.

They began to breathe more fully as the ropes came off. Nicky felt raw, exposed, vulnerable. It was uncomfortable. Like Kieran could see the shiny red parts of their emotions and soul that were still healing.

And for once, there wasn't a steel wall blocking those shiny red healing parts from Kieran's view. There wasn't that same level of holding, resistance, firm boundaries.

That awareness, though, was subconscious. All Nicky truly felt in that moment was grief. Waves and waves and waves of it. The need to let go of an old relationship. The desire to be present with what was. To stop changing themself in the hope that someone would love them more, that Paco would finally accept them, treat them differently.

Nicky felt driftless. Ungrounded.

"Is there anything I can do to be supportive right now?" Kieran asked.

Shaking their head, Nick sat up. "No, no. I'm fine. I just need—I just need some space."

"Okay," said Kieran, folding his hands.

"I'm going to get dressed," Nicky said.

"Okay."

Then slowly sliding off the massage table, Nicky left the playroom and shut the door. They continued breathing. Inhale, exhale. Inhale, exhale. Inhale. Exhale.

When Nicky finally reentered the playroom, they saw immediately that Kieran had put on a shirt. He was still wearing his kilt, but he was coiling up the rope and drinking from the glass of water that Nicky had given him earlier in the evening.

Nicky tugged the gray cotton robe tighter around their frame. Even though Kieran had seen them nude before, somehow they suddenly felt shy.

It was weird.

After closing the door, Nicky untied the robe, held it open with one hand, and looked up at Kieran curiously. "What do you think?"

Kieran surveyed the pink babydoll negligee and the thigh-high black and white striped socks. The socks had panda faces embroidered at the top with black puff balls for the ears. He'd seen the socks before, but this was the first time he'd seen Nicky wearing lingerie like this. Usually, they opted for pajama pants.

Their breasts were poking out, and it gave Nicky some really wonderful cleavage. More than that, Nicky looked innocent, young. Hesitant. Adorable. And it showed off their ass and legs. Overall, it was a great outfit.

Behind his mask, Kieran simply smiled. "Very cute. Someone's in littlespace."

Nicky ducked their head, and looked up at Kieran from the side, their neck still bent, blushing.

"How are you feeling?" Kieran asked.

"Better," Nicky admitted. They held up their other hand, which held a glass of water. "I'm hydrating, which helps."

"Good," Kieran said.

Nicky stood there awkwardly.

"Do you want to sit down?" Kieran asked.

Hesitating, Nicky finally nodded, then gingerly sat down next to Kieran on the daybed.

"That was an intense scene," they said at last, sipping some water. "I wasn't expecting those emotions to come up when you massaged my head."

"You set a powerful intention. You wanted to get grounded," Kieran said simply. "And you had a lot to release."

"Yeah, I suppose so."

Their conversation shifted some after that, became lighter, about how they'd celebrated New Year's Eve, what their goals and intentions were for the year ahead.

"My word for the year is visibility," said Nicky. "I've been afraid to share the work that I do, especially my creative writing. I want to publish my poetry chapbook this year. Be on podcasts. Create financial flow in my business."

Kieran smiled. "I just want this year to be better than last year. Get vaccinated. Get back to the gym. Start seeing people again."

Nicky could relate. It was more challenging to run outdoors during the winter. Thankfully, their parents had a treadmill.

Before long, it was time for Nicky and Kieran to log on for the play party. Nicky grabbed their laptop and set it on the massage table, positioning it so that the two of them were visible to the webcam. When Nicky sat down again, they held their hands to their elbows, rocking slightly.

Nicky's energetic walls were back up, Kieran noticed. Not as high as usual, but that scene had upset their emotional equilibrium. That hadn't been his *intention*, of course, but that didn't matter. It was the impact the scene had had that mattered.

"Have you ever attended a virtual play party before?" Nicky asked.

Kieran shook his head. "Never any need to before COVID-19. And recently, I've been playing with you and Jade."

"Mmm," Nicky replied, fiddling with their robe, then their computer.

The play party began, first with the facilitators introducing themselves and stating the agreements for the event. They explained that the first forty-five minutes would be games and get-to-know-you exercises, and then there would be roughly two hours of virtual play.

"The first activity," said one of the facilitators, "is Mildest to Wildest. First, you'll name your mildest desire, the tamest thing that could happen tonight that would make this event a success. Then, you'll name your wildest desire, the greatest thing that could happen tonight that would still be fun, sexy, and bring you satisfaction. After a few minutes, we'll bring you back from the breakout rooms. And go!"

Almost immediately, Nicky and Kieran were matched with two other people. Finally, it was Nicky's turn to share.

"My mildest is to just enjoy the space, talk with people, and connect with my body. My wildest is to touch myself and have someone else witness my orgasm."

One of the other participants cheered in response. Nicky smiled. They weren't sure how they actually felt about their wildest desire, but they liked the fantasy of it, anyway.

Just as they were about to rotate, so that Kieran could go, Nicky and Kieran saw a notification to return to the main event room.

"Looks like we're all being called back," Nicky said. "It was nice meeting all of you!"

After they'd returned to the main room, Nicky placed the two of them on mute.

"You didn't have a chance to share, Kieran," Nicky said, as the facilitator began asking people to share about their experience in the chat. "What's *your* mildest and wildest?"

"My mildest is to spend time connecting with new people, having great conversations."

Nicky nodded. Pretty mild. Pretty standard. That often happened at a play party.

"And your wildest?" they prompted.

Kieran paused, watching Nicky carefully. "To bring you to orgasm."

Chapter Sixteen

Nicky froze. Their face was hot. They didn't know what to do, what to say. Orgasms were something they experienced with their partners. Lovers. Romantic interests.

Not Kieran.

"I'm going to need to sit with that," Nicky said at last.

"Understandable," Kieran replied.

Nicky found themself unable to look Kieran in the eye. While part of them wanted to pretend Kieran hadn't said anything, their face and cheeks were flushed.

Dammit.

It took several minutes for Nicky's nervous system to reset, before they could relax and their shoulders dropped again. The virtual play-rooms finally opened, and everyone at the event went off to play, exploring their sexuality, being voyeurs or exhibitionists, or simply chatting.

Nicky and Kieran landed in a breakout room with several other people. It was a room dedicated to kinky play, and there was a couple demonstrating and talking through a bondage scene on their screen.

The couple, a blonde-haired Black man and a Native woman with long, silky auburn hair were chuckling and laughing and playing to the camera. They'd clearly played together before, were probably lovers, and were both very attractive. But after a few minutes, Nicky found themself a bit bored.

They wanted to play, not just watch other people playing.

Specifically, Nicky wanted Kieran to tie them up and flog them as he had back in November.

That scene had been two months ago already, Nicky realized. It had been far too long.

"There's not a lot happening here," Nicky said finally, turning to Kieran. "It feels a bit awkward to play in this room since they're doing a demo. Even though it's the kinky breakout room."

"Do you want to go to a private room?" Kieran asked.

"Yeah. Or a semi-private room at least."

Clicking on another room with just a few other people in it, Nicky and Kieran were transported away from the bondage demo into a space where people were sitting and chatting.

"Hey, everyone!" Nicky said, waving to their webcam. "I'm Nicky."

"And I'm Kieran."

After everyone had introduced themselves and chatted for a bit, Nicky asked, "Kieran and I were thinking about doing an impact scene. Is everyone here up for witnessing that?"

With enthusiasm and nods all around, Nicky moved their laptop to their desk so that the massage table was in full view. Then, unceremoniously, they began stripping.

After all, Kieran had just seen them practically naked half an hour ago. And Nicky had been to plenty of play parties where strangers had seen their breasts and most other parts of their body.

"I'm going to start by tying Nicky's hands together," Kieran explained. "Then I'm going to bend them over the massage table for the impact scene."

"Do you want me to take off my underwear before you do that?" Nicky asked. "It's going to be easier to see where the toys land if my ass is bare."

Kieran shrugged. "It's your body. Do what you want."

With a shrug to mimic Kieran's, Nicky slid off their black lacy panties and then leaned over the massage table, sticking their butt in the air. They knew it was perfectly visible in the webcam so that everyone in the breakout room could see, but they didn't mind.

Nicky was actually kind of looking forward to doing this demo with Kieran.

"Great, so now that Nicky has taken off their underwear, I'm going to tie their hands together."

Kieran spun Nicky part way toward the camera, and they were standing facing him. He had a bemused look on his face as he tied them up. Then, playfully, he gently pushed them back into the massage table.

It took Nicky's breath away just a little bit.

"Okay, so now, I'm going to start with a warm-up with the impact. I typically start with flogging, and I want to make sure that the falls, that's the individual suede or leather bits of the flogger, land here."

Fwip.

The falls landed on the fleshy part of Nick's butt, a few inches away from their sacrum, which Kieran was covering with one of his hands.

He began flogging Nicky more fully after that, and also used the crop on them, demonstrating the use of that toy. It was light as far as their impact scenes went, Nicky thought. They could take a lot more.

After some time, people began drifting out of the room until the two of them were alone. Nicky was feeling bored, felt less inclined to continue with impact.

"It feels like the scene is kind of done," they admitted.

"I agree. What do you want to do now?" Kieran asked.

"Go to a private room, I think. Are you okay with that?"

Kieran nodded.

After he untied them, Nicky changed the settings on their laptop, adjusted which breakout room they were in, and for good measure, added "DO NOT JOIN" to their screen name, hoping that would deter possible visitors.

"Okay, I think we're set," Nicky said.

They looked beautiful, just standing there. Kieran had only seen them nude once before, during their birthday scene a little more than a year ago.

Nicky was truly stunning.

"We're going to do another bondage scene, right?"

Kieran nodded, and gestured to the massage table. "If that's what you want."

Hopping onto it, Nicky lied on their back, breathing deeply. They couldn't quite place what they were feeling, but magic and intimacy seemed to permeate the air.

Nicky wriggled into the vinyl, feeling the cold material along their back, butt, and thighs.

They shivered.

"Are you warm enough?" Kieran asked.

"Yeah," Nicky said.

"Are you ready?" he asked.

Nicky nodded. "Can we put on some music, though?"

"Sure. Anything in particular?"

"Just something soft. Meditative. Maybe Divine angelic codes or something like that? Or the happiness frequency."

The music flowed from Nicky's laptop, and Kieran began tying them, slowly. With intention. A certain grace that Nicky wasn't sure he'd possessed even the last time he'd tied them, just earlier that evening. Fluidity marked his movements, and there was a softness in them, too.

With a deep inhale and exhale, Nicky sank into the vinyl of the massage table just a bit more.

Kieran looped the rope through and around the table, restricting Nicky's chest and thighs and feet. Like their birthday scene, Nicky was fully restrained and wouldn't be getting up anytime soon.

Placing a hand on Nicky's shoulder, Kieran looked at their face. Even half-covered by their sparkly purple mask, it was beautiful. Two gentle lines on Nicky's forehead spoke to their age and experience, and even though their eyes were closed, Kieran was in awe of them.

He didn't often allow his brain to delve deeply into the feelings he had for Nicky, but here, in this moment, Kieran allowed himself to experience that care and tenderness, just a bit.

Nicky didn't jerk at the movement, as he caressed their shoulder, as he gently brushed his hand along their stomach, then along their thigh.

A question. An invitation.

He hoped Nicky would say yes.

* * *

It was the first time in a little over a year that Nicky had been touched this way. Like a lover. Nicky also knew that Kieran wouldn't touch them any further or more intimately unless they gave consent. Nicky felt that promise in his touch, knew he wouldn't touch their breasts or yoni unless Nicky agreed to let him bring them to orgasm.

The intimate touch awakened something in Nicky, and they wanted to feel more. Could feel their body aching for it.

But more than that, Nicky could feel an energetic presence. Their future self. Their authentic self. Silently, Nicky asked if they should go through with it. Allow Kieran to give them an orgasm. Surrender.

And Nicky's authentic self seemed to nod. *Yes*, they said with a smile.

Nicky took a deep breath.

At that moment, Kieran felt, more than heard, Nicky's breath hitch.

"Do you still want to bring me to orgasm?" Nicky asked.

"Yes," he said.

Their eyes opened for just a moment, and they looked at him shyly. "Okay," they said, nodding.

Kieran knew without any doubt that it was Nicky's consent, and a part of him opened up and expanded, feeling immense joy and peace. It was humbling and beautiful that Nicky was willing to surrender in this way.

Suddenly, the energy from a year ago December seemed to flow into the space, to merge with the music that was playing softly from Nicky's laptop speakers, to weave its way through the two of their bodies.

But it was different, Kieran knew. The trill of the flute and the crescendo, the swell he was starting to feel now, it was more intimate.

Because tonight, it was just him and Nicky. No one else.

He brushed his hand over Nicky's breast, and they gasped, moaned. Then, weaving just a sprinkling of energy through his fingers, he traced their ribs, stomach, hip bone, pelvis, thighs.

Nicky's breathing became ragged, and small gasps and moans peppered their inhales and exhales.

Still touching them lightly, he pinched one of their nipples.

Another gasp. Louder this time.

"God, it's been so long," Nicky moaned, tipping their head back.

"How long?" Kieran asked quietly.

"A year ago December. That was the last time that Arthur and I were intimate. Things were strained between him and me when Sofia and I were fighting a lot, and then the pandemic happened."

Gentle. He would be gentle tonight, soft, and listen to Nicky's body. Help them open up and release. Be vulnerable.

Let go.

"What time is it?" Nicky asked suddenly.

Kieran looked at them. "Why do you want to know?"

"They're going to close the breakout rooms at ten-thirty, and all play is supposed to end at that time so that everyone can rejoin the main lounge area," Nicky explained. "And I don't want to be interrupted in the middle of our scene."

"It's ten after," Kieran said. "Do you want me to leave the meeting?"

Nicky nodded, and with a few more button presses, they saw their webcam shut off.

The soft, meditative music continued playing, seeping into Nicky's muscles. They inhaled, and then with a deep exhale, released some of what they were holding onto. Their fear, their anxiety.

They could trust Kieran. After all, he'd seen them in a lot of different spaces. He knew about Paco. And for fuck's sake, he'd shared unabashedly and openly with them when Nicky was his coach. Nicky knew about his past trauma, at least in part, and had seen him tremor in those moments of his deepest release.

As Nicky's energy began to unspool and unfold like a flower, Kieran began touching them. Down there.

Barely brushing their clit. Their labia.

Nicky felt their back arch ever so slightly. God, they were so sensitive.

Kieran continued to bring in more energy, intention. After a couple moments, he was using one hand on their breasts, grazing them, pressing and pinching their nipples, and with the other hand, he was rubbing their clit and fingering them.

As Nicky's brain began to respond to all the pleasure, they felt their body continue to open and expand. They wondered if somehow the music was getting louder. It felt like the meditative melody was wrapping its way around Nicky's middle, into their core, pooling in their abdomen, spreading warmth and heat through their pelvis.

But even with the warmth and the pleasure, Nicky still felt the rigidity in their body. Minutes passed, and the resistance seemed to grow. Fear at what might happen if they came in front of Kieran. Unwilling to let go. Holding on. Clenching.

Admittedly, Kieran was new to touching them, but Nicky knew on some level that it wasn't him. He was present, fully in the space, opening up their yoni, touching all parts of their vulva. But Nicky knew they wouldn't orgasm. Couldn't orgasm.

"You know," they said after a moment, opening their eyes, "it's a vulnerable thing to orgasm in front of another person. I don't know if I can do this. Maybe we should stop."

Kieran's eyes crinkled, and he placed a hand on Nicky's hip, and the other on their shoulder. Nicky felt a faint stickiness where his hand landed on their skin.

"Nicky, you are so strong. And courageous," Kieran said. "Look at what you've done in the past year and a half—come out as being trans and non-binary, started working in a whole new industry. You are strong enough to be vulnerable in this way, in this moment. I know you are."

Inhale, exhale. When Nicky breathed out, they felt the tension shrink from their shoulders, their back, their spine. Their cells seemed to become one with the music, vibrating at the exact same frequency, moving in tune with the world around them.

It seemed like Nicky's authentic self was in the space at that moment, flowing energy toward them, helping them relax and release just a little more, to continue moving through the scene.

Even after that, Nicky almost called "yellow" just a few minutes later. To ask Kieran for a pause. They were on the verge of something and didn't know what. It would have been "red" shortly thereafter to stop.

Days, weeks, and months later, Nicky wouldn't know what made them decide to keep going with the scene rather than stop it. To lean in. Surrender. Go deeper.

Perhaps Divine forces were at play, or perhaps Nicky was simply too stubborn.

Or perhaps it was Kieran's belief in them, the care and tenderness in his eyes when he said Nicky was strong.

Either way, Nicky realized what was missing, and understood why they hadn't yet orgasmed. It was the deep, profound emotional connection that was lacking.

Love.

Nicky had almost always been in love when someone had brought them to orgasm. There were a few exceptions, of course, but toys had typically been involved, and it was different.

This scene was different.

It was intimate.

And Nicky knew they needed something from within to feel safe and willing to surrender.

To let Kieran witness their orgasm.

All of a sudden, Nicky felt that familiar energetic presence of their authentic self more firmly again. Almost like this future self was hovering above the scene and the massage table, in the room, in the air. Protecting, guiding, witnessing.

Nicky tuned in to see what the message was.

If you go forward with this, Nicky's authentic self said gently, *you can't go back.*

In their mind, Nicky saw the loosening of a red ribbon on a box and gads of energy pouring out. Like the myth of Pandora's box.

The voice was loud and clear, and there was no mistaking the intuitive guidance.

This moment was a precipice, and Nicky could either stay on the ledge, or jump off.

Even though they didn't quite know what that all meant, and what would happen, Nicky knew they wanted to orgasm in front of Kieran. To be vulnerable and release in that space there with him.

I love Kieran, and he loves me, they told themself. *I love Kieran, and he loves me.*

Nicky said this to themself over and over and over again.

On repeat.

Like a mantra.

Until they felt their mind settle and release and open. As though Nicky had tricked their subconscious with some untruth that somehow, in this moment at least, felt very believable.

More than believable. It felt *true*.

Just a moment later, Nicky felt their body start to tense up in a way that was new. They leaned into the rigidity and felt the orgasm begin to build from their yoni to their abdomen, and radiate out. Up through their heart, then their head and their arms until they reached the peak.

The ocean waves in the music seemed to crash into Nicky's heart, to fill them, and they began to wail, cry, sob. The energy filled them and poured out, kept pouring, kept releasing.

Nicky shivered and trembled and just wanted to feel Kieran pressed to them. Feel that closeness. Tears rolled down their cheeks, and almost as if he knew exactly what Nicky needed at that moment, Kieran leaned forward and pressed his bare chest into Nicky's.

The waves of grief continued to wash over Nicky, nurturing and carrying away their tears. All the while, they felt the warmth of Kieran's body against theirs. It was the first time they'd been pressed chest to chest like this. Love and care and intimacy radiated through them.

As they continued to be in the moment and with their tears, Nicky heard the voice of their authentic self ringing through their mind.

If you go forward with this, you can't go back.

You can't go back.

Chapter Seventeen

Several minutes later, as Nicky's sobs subsided, Kieran peeled himself off the top of them. Silently, he untied the ropes. Released one knot, then another. It was clear that Nicky was complete. Their release had been huge, and their nervous system was practically shot.

When Nicky sat up, they saw that Kieran was coiling the ropes. But their energy felt distracted and scattered, and Nicky felt dazed, confused. They brought their attention to their hands, where they gripped the edge of the massage table. Their feet where they dangled.

One thing was clear: things wouldn't be the same.

Nicky felt they had just the barest hint of understanding around what their authentic self had said. These feelings, these big emotions, the rawness and vulnerability—their relationship with Kieran had moved into different territory.

It felt like the orgasm had cleared Nicky out. That Nicky had had so much energetic residue, so much clogging them, so much unhelpful emotion filling them. The release from the orgasm had reconnected Nicky to pleasure, to touch, to intimacy, to surrender, and to themself.

And as much as it confused Nicky, now they had feelings for Kieran.

A switch had flipped.

Clearing their throat, at last Nicky spoke. "I'm curious how this changes our dynamic moving forward."

Until they did speak, Nicky wasn't sure what they would say. Thoughts were swimming through thick molasses in their mind, barely peeking above the surface before they submerged again. But this ache in their chest, this rawness, this need for closeness, that was evident.

Kieran looked up from where he was coiling the rope. "I don't think it needs to. I've done orgasm scenes with play partners before."

Nicky's chest contracted. It was like exposing their raw skin to cold steel. They simply nodded, feeling sadness, and another wave of grief overcame them. What else was there to say?

"And if you *do* want it to change our dynamic," Kieran said, "that's a conversation best had when you're not coming down from a couple of orgasms."

Again, Nicky could only nod. It was a sensible thing to say. They'd done three scenes with Kieran tonight, and the sub drop tomorrow would probably be wretched. Anything they requested right now or wanted right now couldn't be trusted. Nicky continued sitting on the edge of the massage table, just feeling the openness and the emptiness and the sadness. At last, Kieran finished coiling the rope, and he looked at Nicky.

"Do you want your robe?" he asked. "Or Ollie? Or even some water?"

Nicky closed their eyes for just a minute. "I just—I'm just really confused right now. Normally, I only experience orgasms with people I'm dating, people I'm romantically involved with. That's part of me being demisexual—I just don't get there if I don't have a deep emotional connection with someone."

"I hear that, and if you still feel this way in a few days and want to talk about it, I welcome that conversation," Kieran said. He paused. "Can I please get you some water?"

"Sure," Nicky said.

A moment later, he was gone.

Once Kieran had left the playroom, Nicky pulled on their panda socks and robe. They went to their bedroom and grabbed a comfy pair of pajamas—a knit shirt and flannel pants—as well as Ollie. When Kieran returned with the glass of water, Nicky accepted it gratefully.

"Thank you," they said, pulling down their mask so they could take a sip.

"You're welcome," he said.

Nicky hesitated. Normally, aftercare for scenes involved water, chatting, and Nicky scratching Kieran's head. Head scratchies, as he called them. They never cuddled. Even as they both sat there on the daybed, facing the massage table and rainbow mosaic, Nicky recalled the time a year ago December. After their first scene together, Nicky had tried leaning into Kieran to cuddle with him and it felt uncomfortable, weird, and awkward.

For awhile, the two of them just spoke with each other, recapping their holidays more fully, talking about the virtual play party, and just getting to know each other.

Nicky realized it was the first time they were choosing to engage with Kieran in more conversation. Where they actually wanted to learn and know more about him. Instead of simply responding and engaging politely.

It was a revelation.

"What's your favorite color?" Nicky asked suddenly.

"Green," Kieran said.

All the little getting-to-know-you questions that they had somehow skipped because they hadn't met under traditional circumstances. Because they'd never gone on a first date. Or dated. Or, in Nicky's mind, even truly been friends.

As they talked, Nicky felt their body was pulling them toward Kieran, inviting them to lean into him. After a scene as intimate as the last one they'd just done, it felt jarring *not* to be physically connected to Kieran.

"Is it alright if I lean into you?" Nicky asked finally.

Kieran nodded. "Of course."

It was strange leaning into Kieran like that. Nicky felt none of the resistance they had before. Cuddling with him like this felt a little strange, sure, but not bad. Not uncomfortable.

In fact, it was very soothing.

Nicky couldn't remember the last time they'd felt this comforted being next to another human, cuddling. Probably the last time they'd been with Arthur. With Paco, things had felt stagnant—more like a safety blanket. With Kieran, it felt like stardust was settling between and around the two of them, binding them together.

"I don't think things will ever work between me and Paco," Nicky said finally.

Kieran looked over at Nicky, and saw that their brows were knitted together. He knew how challenging it could be to end relationships that had become toxic. How hard it could be to say goodbye and let go.

They were beautiful, stunning. More so because he knew their personality, saw how diligently they prioritized communication, self-love, and creating conscious relationships. He'd seen how Nicky had sought to honor themself over the past year and a half, and how they had also continued to struggle with their attachments to past partners, especially Paco.

Nicky finally letting go of Paco? It was a big deal.

"What do you think?" Nicky asked at last.

Kieran paused before speaking; he didn't want to sway Nicky unnecessarily. "I made a commitment only to spend time with people whose company I enjoy more than my own. I figure if I don't like spending time with them at least as well as spending time by myself, it's not worth it."

The crease in Nicky's brow deepened. "That's really helpful," they said slowly. "I'm not sure if that's how I feel about Paco. We used to have such fun together, and I loved spending time with him. But over the last year, it hasn't felt the same."

The two of them stopped talking about Nicky's relationship with Paco after that, but Kieran could tell that Nicky's mind was still at work, mulling over what he had said.

Their conversation turned to more light-hearted topics. Nicky asked about his favorite childhood memory, his son, how he'd gotten involved in kink. To Kieran, the openness in Nicky's demeanor was a stark change from the rigidity he'd so often seen in them. There was curiosity, compassion, excitement. Their entire body lit up with that light, buoyant white energy, and there was nothing restraining it.

Overall, though, it was a lot of fun. Nicky even teased him a little bit, and made a couple flirtatious comments. They'd never flirted with him before, and he'd been very mindful not to flirt with them. Even tonight, he restrained himself. Nicky was in subspace, and their feelings could change tomorrow. Kieran had almost sworn the last time they did a scene together that Nicky was feeling something toward him, that the energy between the two of them was softer, but Nicky hadn't said anything about it afterward.

In this case, Kieran was following Nicky's cues.

"It's getting pretty late," Kieran commented. "How are you feeling?"

Nicky blinked. "Oh, I'm okay. You know, you're welcome to stay the night, sleep in the second bedroom here. Just so you don't have to drive home right now."

Kieran checked his phone. It was almost one o'clock in the morning. The offer to stay at Nicky's was tempting. He could drive back once it was light out, and he wouldn't be at risk of hitting any deer.

But he also wanted to be in his own space. More than anything, though, Nicky hadn't invited him to spend the night prior to their final scene, and he didn't want to impose on them and their space. In the morning, Nicky might feel differently and be upset that they'd asked him to stay.

He didn't want to risk that.

"It's okay," he said. "I'm okay to drive, and I'll head back tonight."

"Are you sure?" Nicky asked.

"Yes," he said. Kieran began gathering his things, placing them near the door. Nicky followed him, their arms wrapped around themself.

Just before leaving Nicky's apartment, Kieran glanced back at them.

There was a part of him that didn't want to leave.

Instead, he said, "I'll text you tomorrow, see how you're doing."

Nicky nodded silently.

On the drive home, Kieran kept replaying the final scene that Nicky and he had done. The way their body had softened, the way their toes had curled, the way their back had arched during the moment of climax. The way they had broken open and sobbed while he pressed his chest to theirs.

It had felt so good. It had felt so right.

Kieran took an exit off the Interstate, turning onto a country road that he commonly used during the final leg of his journey home. A bit of a shortcut. After a mile or so, once there were no other cars in sight, he flicked on his brights.

Instantly, he braked.

Hard.

Before him were three deer, blinking into the headlights, completely frozen.

He had almost hit them.

At this speed, that would have been a serious injury.

Kieran took a few minutes to let his heart rate slow and his breathing settle.

Once his body settled, and the deer had moved out of the way of the car, Kieran slowly pressed down the accelerator and continued home.

Nevertheless, he couldn't help but think: maybe it was a sign he should have stayed the night with Nicky.

* * *

Nicky couldn't sleep after Kieran left. Their mind was racing, and their yoni was throbbing. They'd just had an amazing orgasm, yet they didn't feel satiated.

It was confusing, maddening, and frustrating.

After tossing from side to side for a good thirty minutes or more, Nicky finally stood up, went to the closet where they kept their sex toys, grabbed their silicone vibrating wand, and stomped back to bed.

Settling beneath the covers once more, Nicky squirted some lube onto their vibrator. Then, turning it on, they began rubbing the vibrating wand over their clit.

Soon, the lube merged with their wetness, and Nicky began moaning. They thought about earlier that night when Kieran had touched them, how good it had felt, how much they had *needed* to be touched, missed being touched. Nicky thought back to the moment of release, how Kieran had pressed his chest into theirs almost by instinct...

And Nicky came, their moans transforming into whines, gasps, and soft screams.

Shortly after, they turned off the toy, placed it on the nightstand, and breathed.

They wished that Kieran would have spent the night. They'd felt disappointment when he said he wouldn't. But maybe it was for the best.

Maybe.

Another thirty minutes later, Nicky still couldn't sleep. They punched their pillow in frustration.

Sighing, Nicky grabbed their vibrating wand from the bedside table, placed a dollop of lube on it, pressed the 'on' button, and began the process all over again. They thought once more about the scenes they had done with Kieran earlier that evening, and this time they imagined him in bed there with them, going down on them, sucking their clit, sticking his thumb in their yoni.

Nicky came even faster and harder this time, and they pressed their free hand over their mouth so as not to wake their upstairs neighbor. Nicky allowed the orgasm to stretch on, to expand, to lengthen.

But after just thirty seconds or so, Nicky had reached their threshold and shut off the toy once more, breathing heavily.

This time, as they settled, they fell asleep at last. A keen observer might suspect that Nicky's sleep was still a bit fiful, but between the late hour and the multiple orgasms, Nicky's body could do nothing else but breathe more deeply, rest, and integrate.

* * *

The next morning, Nicky felt the familiar slowness and listlessness they associated with sub drop. But unlike the scene they'd done with Kieran back in November, they still had feelings for him today.

Right on cue, Kieran messaged Nicky to check in.

How are you doing? the text read.

There were so many ways that Nicky could respond to that simple question, starting with that they didn't sleep well last night, or they needed to use their vibrating wand to come twice more after he'd left, but both felt inappropriate and too vulnerable to share. Especially over text.

Besides, it wasn't as though they'd masturbated because of Kieran. There had just been so much energy during the scenes that the two of them did, and it needed somewhere to go. Nevertheless, Nicky told Kieran they wanted to meet up with him and discuss how they were feeling. Kieran said he was open to it, and the two of them agreed to meet on Wednesday.

When the day arrived, Nicky felt nervous. They weren't sure how this conversation would go or what would happen. Or even entirely what they did feel for Kieran. Over the past few days, their brain had been going back and forth.

It was just the scene. No, it was more than that. Actually, they weren't really sure.

Because their brain was a jumbled mess, Nicky decided to bring over their new chess set so that they could do something non-kinky with Kieran. Kink had been the bulk of their relationship. Aside from watching animated movies together (which was part of Nicky's aftercare), the two of them hadn't done *anything* vanilla together, and it felt about time to correct that.

After all, if there *was* a possibility that Nicky was attracted to Kieran and *might* want to be more than just his platonic play partner, the two of them needed to have more in their relationship than just a mutual love of kink.

Nicky rang the doorbell again. As they waited for Kieran to open it, they bounced on their feet, impatient.

It had been a long three days.

Soon, Kieran answered the door, masked-up, and he ushered Nicky in. At the top of the stairs, Nicky paused.

There was more furniture than the last time they'd been over. A large leather sofa, and a massive tawny bean bag that looked like it could fit two adults comfortably.

"Nice additions," Nicky said. They fiddled with their fingers underneath the chess box. "I've never seen a bean bag so big."

"Yeah, it's pretty great, isn't it? I got it from my buddy for a couple hundred bucks. Can I get you anything to drink?" Kieran asked.

"Water would be great," Nicky said.

After Kieran had handed them a bottle, they both sat down on the sofa. Nicky turned to face Kieran.

This was uncomfortable.

"I don't really know what to say or where to begin," they said, wringing their hands. "I just—something switched for me on Saturday. Before that, things were platonic between us, and now—I mean, it felt different after the scene when you gave me that orgasm. It was a very intimate scene."

"It was," Kieran agreed.

"And I don't do that kind of scene with just anyone. So, my brain's a bit confused. And I don't know if my feelings are real, or if it's because the orgasms hacked my biochemistry or what," Nicky said.

"Sure," Kieran said. "I can understand that."

"More than that, I haven't had *anyone* give me an orgasm in more than a year, so I don't know if it was just the orgasm, or you, or both, or what it was. And you had talked about trauma bonding, and we had done a bondage scene earlier that night, and I was vulnerable with you, so I'm worried that my feelings might be affected because of that."

Then Nicky clammed up. They felt like they were rambling.

"Can I ask some questions? And reflect back what I'm hearing?" Kieran said.

"Sure."

Kieran looked at Nicky, his gaze level. Nicky found they could only glance at him before looking away.

"What I'm hearing is that Saturday's scene was like flipping a switch, but you're not sure what you feel. Part of you is concerned that your feelings might be a result of trauma bonding, or because of the orgasms from Saturday's scene. Especially because you hadn't been intimate with anyone like that for over a year."

Nicky paused. That *was* what they had said, but it wasn't *completely* accurate to how they felt. Something was niggling at their subconscious, asking for attention. But Nicky didn't know what it was or how to communicate it.

"I guess so," Nicky said doubtfully, frowning. "More or less."

They glanced back at the chess set. And back at Kieran. He was still studying them openly, his eyes curious, his expression otherwise unreadable. Nicky wondered what expression was on the lower half of his face.

Damn masks.

Damn pandemic.

"One thing I do know," they said, "is that I would like to do more friendship things with you. We've done a lot of kinky scenes together, but we haven't ever played board games together or cards, or even watched a movie together that wasn't animated."

"That's fair," Kieran said.

"So, where does this leave us?" Nicky asked, setting their empty water bottle on the counter. When they returned, they plopped down in the bean bag so that they could face Kieran. "How does this change things?"

Kieran hesitated for just a moment.

"I tend to have unconventional boundaries for friendships," he admitted. "I'm also a play slut and reaction junkie—I like seeing how people respond to touch, to energy, to kink. It isn't uncommon for me to do scenes like the one you and I did on Saturday with people that I consider to be friends. The lines between sexuality and friendship are a bit more fluid for me. I'm actually more likely to give someone an orgasm than to kiss them. I have a story that you're less accustomed to that kind of dynamic."

"It's more that that's not how I'm wired," Nicky said. "I'm demisexual. For me, sexual play and orgasms require such emotional intimacy and trust, that it takes me a couple of months dating someone to do that with them. Before I want to, before it's appealing, before it feels good. For me, romantic feelings and attraction almost always precede sex and orgasm. You and I haven't had that, which is why I'm so confused."

"Thanks for clarifying. It's hard to be vulnerable. Sex, romance, intimacy… It's important to experience it with someone you trust. I've had too many times where I've opened up to people too early on and they didn't respond well, or I felt betrayed afterward. I identify as demisexual, too, but more as a result of that trauma."

Kieran paused. It was clear that some big emotions were coming up for Nicky, but only three days after their scene together, Nicky wasn't entirely sure what they felt. If Kieran were to share that he'd been attracted to them and interested in them for more than a year, he suspected Nicky would freak out. Shut down.

More importantly, being in a relationship with Nicky would be far different from simply being their play partner. And there were still many things Kieran didn't know about Nicky. Specifically, their attachment style.

"Before I date someone, it's also important to me that I understand their attachment style. If our attachment styles are incompatible, it makes the relationship more challenging to navigate. For example, I have a secure attachment style now, but growing up, I had a dismissive avoidant attachment style. As a result, it's harder for me to understand and anticipate the needs of someone who has an anxious attachment style."

Nicky nodded. That made sense.

"I do have an anxious attachment style," they shared, "but between the work I've been doing as a coach and the work I've been doing with my therapist, Emma, I'm better at communicating my needs than I used to be."

Kieran's eyes crinkled. "Good to know. Thanks for sharing."

A long pause. "Where does this leave us?" Nicky asked again.

"I see you as a friend," Kieran said simply. "I'm also willing to continue having conversations on this topic if and when that feels supportive for you. If your feelings change, we can revisit this conversation."

Nicky felt a sharp blow to the chest.

Kieran saw them as a friend.

Disappointment overwhelmed them for a moment, and then Nicky nodded. "Thank you for letting me know," they said.

Thankfully, Nicky recalibrated quickly, and they smiled at Kieran just a moment later.

"I brought my new chess set," Nicky said. "Ever since watching *The Queen's Gambit* on Netflix about a month ago, I've been *obsessed*. So, I'm starting to learn how to play, and I thought it could be fun to take you on in a game."

"Sure, I'm up for that," Kieran said. "But you should know that when I was younger, I won regional chess trophies for under-14, and my rating was over 1400."

Nicky's eyes widened. Based on the computer bots that they'd been playing online, their rating was about 1000. That 400-point gap was a lot.

"This is probably not going to end well," they sighed.

* * *

Nicky was sorely beginning to regret taking Kieran on in a chess game. They had decided on a bold opening (one of the two that they had already learned), and Kieran had pounced in response. He'd very quickly and decisively begun taking Nicky's pieces, and even though white supposedly had an advantage in the game, Nicky felt that they'd lost any small advantage they'd had, and then some.

Nicky had been staring at the board for nearly ten minutes, lying flat on their stomach on the floor, debating their next move. They'd put themself in a very vulnerable position, and no matter where they moved, they couldn't save their queen.

They were fuming. They were competitive, and Kieran was just smiling cheekily at them.

It was maddening.

Good thing Nicky hadn't suggested they do kinky chess. Kieran would have slapped or beat or struck them several times already. Or, if it had been strip chess, Nicky would be nude.

And given the conversation the two of them had had earlier that evening, Nicky wasn't sure that being naked around Kieran or doing kink with him would be supportive right now.

"I give up. I resign." Nicky tipped forward their king and covered their face with their hands.

They hadn't even made it to the endgame with Kieran. Really, they hadn't even made it much into the middlegame.

Just barely beyond the opening.

"Are you sure?" he said, frowning. "It's not completely lost at this point."

"I'm sure," Nicky said. "You're several points ahead, and I don't have the skill or expertise to see myself out of this one. Besides, it's demoralizing."

He shrugged. "All right. If you're sure."

"I am."

The two of them began to put the chess pieces away into their two mesh bags, and then Kieran folded up the game board. By the time everything was back in the box, Nicky's breathing had regulated itself, and their frustration had abated.

Some, at least. It had abated *some*.

"That was rough," Nicky said, moaning. "I can't believe I agreed to that."

"You just attacked really quickly without thinking through your moves in response to my play," Kieran said. "And you brought your queen into the game really quickly. That was probably your biggest mistake. Chess requires patience and discipline."

"Ugh," Nicky said, and they rolled over on the floor.

Finally, they dragged themself up to look at Kieran. He was looking at them, his eyes crinkled, his body shaking, soft ripples of sound coming from him.

He was *laughing*.

"Ugh," Nicky said again, standing up. "I better head home before my pride is *completely* demolished."

Kieran immediately became sober. "Please be careful," he said. "I almost hit a few deer when I came from your place a few days ago. These country roads attract a lot of them, and they tend to be most populous this time of year. Text me when you get home."

"I will," Nicky promised. They put on their coat, grabbed their chess set, gave Kieran a quick hug, and headed out.

It was a good thing Kieran had said something. About two miles after they had turned onto the country road, Nicky's headlights illuminated big yellow eyes, brown fur, and antlers.

Three deer were standing in the middle of the county highway, frozen in front of Nicky's car.

Nicky braked. Hard.

After a few minutes with the car at rest, the deer moved out of the roadway, and Nicky let out the breath they'd been holding.

They called on their guides and angels, asking that they would have a safe remainder of the journey home, then gently pressed their foot into the accelerator. But the entire way back to Madison, Nicky was a bit more alert, and their heart was still beating just a touch faster than it had been before.

Chapter Eighteen

Over the next few weeks, Nicky gradually thought less and less about the orgasm scene they had done with Kieran. He saw them as a friend. It didn't mean anything beyond that he'd wanted Nicky to feel pleasure in their body.

He was just a platonic play partner.

That was all.

Nicky still felt a twinge of annoyance when Kieran messaged them out of the blue or said hello to them without Nicky initiating the conversation. Of course he meant well, and it was kind and sweet and thoughtful, but it was uncomfortable.

To distract themself, Nicky continued learning to play chess, worked long hours, and picked up a new Netflix show.

Bridgerton.

Everyone was talking about it. Bailey was obsessed with it, and even Nicky's mom had watched it.

Pride and Prejudice meets steamy erotica. That was how Bailey had described it.

Nicky had to agree that description was on-point.

Not only was the cinematography stunning, but the characters were well-rounded and believable. The story was also relatable. Daphne Bridgerton, a wealthy young woman who lived in Regency-era England, was searching for a husband on London's marriage market. At the beginning of the series, she didn't know anything about sex and hadn't even touched herself before. But then, she started having feelings for a powerful, older, sexually experienced man—the Duke of Hastings—who was just supposed to be a friend, a co-conspirator. After immersing herself in scandal by kissing this man, Daphne ended up marrying him, falling in love with him, and then having a child with him.

As a sex and relationship coach, Nicky justified it as research. It was important to know about pop culture that was informing their clients' perceptions of sex and intimacy.

But in reality, it was Nicky's own form of escape.

A way to experience a sexy, smutty happy ending while Nicky was still keeping their head down, doing the damn work, and making themself more visible to their own Duke of Hastings.

Your next relationship is coming soon, Bailey had said. *Give it a year.*

Six more months to go, Nicky thought.

One night while Nicky was bingeing *Bridgerton* and eating mint chocolate chip ice cream, they connected with Kieran and scheduled another scene. Rope bondage, light on the impact. Maybe no impact.

The caning scene Nicky had done with Kieran back in November had made impact play less exciting.

Kieran was game, and the two of them planned to do the scene at his place. After all, Nicky had upstairs neighbors, and if they played in the queer playroom again, they had another neighbor alongside of them, just a thin wall separating them.

It was a sound-sensitive situation all around at Nicky's.

As they were making their plans, though, Kieran shared he'd like Nicky to spend the night. Because each of them had almost run into deer recently, it was safer if Nicky went home in the morning once it was light out. Kieran had a second bedroom, the place his son slept when he was there, and Nicky was welcome to use it.

Fair enough, Nicky said, texting him back. *See you next Wednesday.*

* * *

The day of their scene came quickly. As they had the last time, Nicky rang the doorbell, and Kieran let them in. He was wearing another super nerdy mask (this one looked like Star Trek), and it put Nicky's plain purple one to shame.

Not that Nicky minded, of course. They also had plenty of masks that reflected their interests. Nicky had a few with various constellations, a few rainbow-striped ones, and even a couple that used Harry Potter-themed fabric. All that was missing in Nicky's mask collection was their newest obsession: *Bridgerton*.

"Nice mask," Nicky commented when they finally reached the top of the stairs. They glanced around Kieran's apartment, and lifted up the couple bags in their arms. "Where do you want me to put my overnight stuff?"

"In here."

Kieran guided them to a carpeted room that Nicky hadn't yet been in. Minecraft posters decorated two of the walls, and a twin bed was pushed into one corner. There was also a small, gray desk, and an oversized wooden chest of drawers.

It was simple but functional.

"Thanks," Nicky said. They dropped their bags. "I'll just get changed in the bathroom, and I'll be ready for tonight's scene."

"And we're doing rope bondage and massage, right?"

"Yes, and no orgasms. And no touching in my swimsuit areas," Nicky said firmly. "I don't want to hack my biochemistry like we did during our last scene back in January."

"Fair enough," Kieran said easily. "I'll get the massage table set up and ready for you."

* * *

Nicky emerged, wearing their standard lacy black undies and gray cotton robe.

Hearing the click of the bathroom door, Kieran turned around and looked at them. He held the massage sheets for the table in his hands. "Are you ready?" he asked.

Nicky nodded and took off their robe. Once the sheets were on the massage table, they laid down, just wearing their underwear.

No orgasms. No sexual touching.

To Nicky, those boundaries made sense. Bondage was standard fare for kinky scenes. Orgasms were more intimate, and there was a stronger, more potent energetic experience during climax. More oxytocin was released. More bonding was possible.

And things with Kieran were purely platonic.

At that moment, Kieran began weaving the purple nylon rope over Nicky, restraining their chest, restraining their legs and feet. It was familiar. Grounding.

While Kieran was tying rope over them, Nicky decided to chat with him. During past scenes, they had asked about the ties that he was doing or how he'd learned certain techniques. But today, Nicky felt like sharing.

"I've been thinking a lot about this coming year," Nicky said. "And I really want to have a more formal D/s relationship with someone. I've wanted that for so long. Tried to create that with a couple of my partners. But I've never really had that—you know, the deep psychological journeying and understanding. Someone who supports me by stretching my edges. I want that."

Nicky was so open as they were sharing, but Kieran didn't know how to respond. It wasn't like they'd said they wanted that kind of relationship with him. Just in general.

"It sounds like you're pretty clear on what you want," he said after a moment. He finished tying the last knot. "Are you comfortable?"

"Yes," Nicky said.

After adjusting the rope slightly, Kieran stood at the end of the massage table. He began touching Nicky, kneading their neck and shoulders, digging in with his thumbs and knuckles, helping to release tension.

Nicky hissed. "That hurts," they whined.

Kieran let out a small chuckle. "When's the last time you got a professional massage?"

"Before the pandemic," Nicky mumbled.

"And how much have you been working the last couple weeks?" Kieran asked.

"A lot," Nicky muttered. They saw where this line of questioning was going.

"Well, that's why you're so tense. You sit at a desk for most of your work, when you meet with clients, and do marketing-related tasks, and that's not supportive for your body."

Note to self, Nicky thought darkly, *get a massage from someone other than Kieran and begin booking regular massages.*

"Can you use less pressure though, please? I'm super close to calling yellow."

"Sure," Kieran replied.

Now that his touch was softer and a bit more sensual, Nicky breathed into it. Leaned into the discomfort and pain. Sometimes, they thought Kieran tried to play their edges a bit too much rather than touching them well within their comfort zone. Just because *he* could take intense pressure didn't mean that Nicky could.

Nicky continued breathing in and out, letting the background music of ocean waves lull them into deeper relaxation, allowing their body to unwind and open. The condensation from their breath made their cloth mask feel warm and wet.

Like their pussy.

Even though Kieran wasn't touching Nicky's breasts or genitals like he had during the scene back in January, Nicky still felt themself spooling out, their energy softening into a lake of white light.

They continued breathing, softening, opening.

Nicky moaned, and their back arched slightly.

As Kieran continued massaging them, weaving Reiki in through the tissue manipulation, Nicky opened their eyes and looked up.

Kieran's face was just above them, visible if Nicky craned their neck enough.

Immediately, several things became obvious to Nicky.

The first was that they had feelings for Kieran. That the feelings they thought they'd had during January's scene and a few days later were still present now, somewhere in their subconscious. So it wasn't just a kink thing. It was something else, even if Nicky didn't understand it and was loath to admit it.

Second, they wanted to surrender to Kieran. Completely. They wanted their energy system to open so wide, crack open so much, that it melted all resistance and all he could feel and see was their soul, just feel Nicky's joy and peace and beingness, showers and rays of bright white light.

Third, they wanted to kiss Kieran. They had a desire to kiss Kieran. Not now, not this evening, because there were health considerations, thanks to COVID-19. Kieran was dating Jade and had a son and he wasn't in Nicky's pod. And Nicky's parents were in their sixties and they didn't want to infect their mom and dad.

Fourth, they wanted to play with his hair. Without him asking. Without it being part of aftercare. Nicky wanted to touch him, to be connected with him, to be fully present with him. To express the care and tenderness for him that he was showing for them.

And without overthinking, because they were so open and aligned and connected, Nicky simply acted on that desire.

They reached above their head, and began massaging Kieran's scalp, touching his hair. Tugging on it, allowing all their feelings to flow through their fingers into his head. Allowing him to feel all that they felt for him at this moment.

His gaze softened, and when he looked at Nicky now, they could swear he wanted to kiss them too. Could feel it in the way he looked at them. Knew and felt that he cared about them as more than a friend. That Nicky wasn't *just* a platonic play partner to him even though he'd said otherwise. Somewhere along the way, Nicky had become *more*.

Unless, somehow, they were reading too much into that tender gaze he gave them.

Either way, it was bliss.

Nicky could have stayed like that for hours, gazing into Kieran's kind hazel eyes, playing with his short reddish hair. Except that reaching over their head was uncomfortable, and the energy between them was electric. The longer they were like that, the greater the charge became, and the less Nicky trusted themself to act rationally.

Eventually, Nicky's shoulders began to ache, and they brought their arms back to their sides.

"If I said I was open to you touching me more intimately..." Nicky began.

"I'd say that we didn't negotiate it before this scene, and I'm not going to do it," Kieran said, his eyes crinkling.

He continued massaging Nicky for a few more minutes, and they closed their eyes, leaning into the touch, just feeling the waves of energy moving through their body, feeling their energy continue to radiate out, pulsing into him, expanding, growing.

They breathed in and out, nice long inhales, nice deep exhales.

At last, the touch began to soften, until it was just a light brushing around Nicky's shoulders, then Kieran was just holding Nicky's shoulders, pressing down slightly.

Grounding them.

"Are you feeling complete?" he asked.

Nicky nodded. "For now, yes. Thank you."

The two of them stayed like that for a couple more minutes as Nicky's breathing continued to regulate, and then Kieran began untying them. Once Nicky was completely freed from the table, they sat up, rubbed at their face and eyes, and took a few more breaths.

"I'm going to get changed," they said at last. "I'll be out shortly."

Then, taking care as they hopped off the table, gathered their clothes, and walked to the bathroom, Nicky focused simply on putting one foot in front of the other.

If they didn't, they thought they might collapse on the floor. Nicky's legs felt just like Harry Potter's arm after Professor Lockhart had removed his bones: rubbery and hard to control.

* * *

Dressed in their pajamas and holding Ollie, Nicky joined Kieran in his oversized bean bag. The two of them thumbed through the streaming catalog, and at last they settled on *A Bug's Life.*

"It's been ages since I've seen this," said Nicky. "I used to love it when I was a kid. In second grade, when I went to Disney World for the first time, I actually got my face painted like Princess Dot."

As the movie began, Nicky noticed they were acutely aware of Kieran's body next to theirs. Nicky's entire body felt warm. Their breathing was shallow.

It had been a long time since they'd felt this way.

They took a deep breath. Inhaled, exhaled.

Refocused on the movie. Chuckled as the film introduced the circus troupe of bugs. Nicky had forgotten how entertaining the German-accented caterpillar had been.

But meanwhile, the heat and the warmth began to grow. Just like the electric energy had grown between the two of them as Nicky had gazed at Kieran and touched his hair, so now it expanded as they leaned into him, laying their head on his chest. As they let him curl his arm around them.

It had been so long since someone had held Nicky this way.

The energy was heady and intoxicating, and Nicky felt like they were floating, not fully in their body. They were present with all the sensations, and for once, their mind wasn't elsewhere. Nicky was simply and fully in the moment.

At some point, Nicky and Kieran began holding hands, and the warmth became a fire that was scorching every part of Nicky's skin. The desire they felt seeped into every cell, creating a hundred thousand fires that would only be sated with more touch.

How wonderful it felt to be so alive, so deeply present, to simply enjoy the closeness. Nicky knew there was something different. At least, they knew they felt differently about Kieran than they had before. And their feelings? This attraction?

It was still here. It hadn't been snuffed out. Or, if it had been temporarily doused, like a candle with more wax to burn, it had been re-lit.

And the flame was growing larger. Stronger. Brighter. More visible in the darkness.

Nicky was just enjoying Kieran holding their hand, their body fitted into his, resting against him while watching the movie when he said the strangest thing.

"You know, I have a story that it would be fun to kiss you sometime."

The comment stunned Nicky, and they could barely breathe. For a couple minutes, their mind wasn't even on the movie. Just last week, he'd said they were just friends. And now, maybe he felt it, too. This overwhelming pull. The attraction.

Like magnets. A cation and an anion. Inescapable.

Nicky's body became rigid as they processed the input. As they allowed the comment to seep in.

When did things shift? For Nicky, it had been again during the scene, when they'd chosen to touch Kieran's hair, looking up at him, with this desire to simply open to him. To share all of their soul with him.

Maybe they *didn't* imagine the tenderness they'd seen in his eyes.

Nicky didn't *think* they'd imagined it, but it was harder to read facial expressions when half a person's face was covered with a mask.

"How long have you had this story?" Nicky asked after a long moment, turning to face Kieran.

The smile in his hazel eyes expanded. "Since tonight."

Nicky's breath stopped again. "Thank you for naming that," they said at last, and they turned their attention back toward the movie.

Chapter Nineteen

That night, Nicky had trouble sleeping. Admittedly, it was a new environment, but Nicky knew it was more than that.

When he had wished them goodnight, Kieran had said that Nicky could come into his room at any point if that felt supportive. Nicky was surprised and noticed some resistance to the idea. They simply thanked him for the offer and politely declined, saying they would be fine.

For a few hours, Nicky slept on the strange sheets (also Minecraft, like the posters) in the strange room in the unfamiliar apartment. But then, around three in the morning, they began tossing and turning and couldn't go back to sleep.

Nicky knew that Kieran was in the other room. Could feel his energy seeping through the walls. Now that they had a label for it, Nicky could feel the sexual tension. And it was strong and overwhelming and distracting and making it damn near impossible to go back to sleep.

Honestly, they did even briefly entertain knocking on Kieran's door and asking him to let them in.

But they didn't know how he felt. Just because he thought kissing Nicky sometime would be fun didn't mean that he really had feelings for Nicky.

Who knew why he had invited Nicky to come into his room if they felt so inclined?

Probably just if they needed something medical. Or had an unexpected sub drop in the middle of the night.

After Kieran had said he thought it would be fun to kiss Nicky sometime, they had flirted with him a bit, and he'd flirted back. He'd touched Nicky's inner thigh during the second movie, as they were re-watching *Moana* together. At one point, he'd even picked Nicky up un-expectedly until they squealed and asked to be put down.

The energy tonight had been different.

It hadn't been that of two acquaintances.

Or platonic play partners.

But it was still so new and unfamiliar. And Nicky just didn't know what was going through Kieran's head. He looked at them in such a level, even way. Unreadable. Inscrutable.

Nicky could also tell their yoni, their entire vulva, was pulsing with this explosive energy.

They moaned, flopped back into the bed, and tried to sleep again.

To no avail.

They tried turning on an audiobook to soothe them to sleep.

Even *that* didn't work.

At last, sighing, Nicky grabbed their phone and drafted their thoughts in an email to Bailey. Nicky might delete the message in the morning, but it was nice to imagine that someone else was on the re-ceiving end.

> *Bailey, you'll never believe what happened tonight.*
>
> *I was hanging out with Kieran, and it's been interesting. Just a couple weeks ago, he shared that he only saw me as a friend. But after tonight's massage and bondage scene, he seems to feel differently.*
>
> *While we were cuddling, he said, "I have a story it would be fun to kiss you sometime."*
>
> *For context, he's said previously that he's less likely to kiss someone than give them an orgasm because he's a "play slut" and "reaction junkie" (his phrases, not mine). So, him saying he thought kissing me would be fun made me pause. It was definitely a shift.*
>
> *The last few weeks have been energetically complex for my body and emotions, so I didn't want to suggest we kiss tonight. That's especially true*

since we just did a scene. I also don't know if him wanting to kiss me means he wants to date me, or that he's even romantically interested in me.

Basically, I have a lot of questions.

Also, logistically with COVID-19... especially since he's dating Jade, too... Do we wait to kiss each other until we're both vaccinated? Do we get tested? How often? Is it ethical to get tested for COVID-19 if we're not having symptoms and haven't been exposed to someone who's tested positive?

I know we have fun together. We both voiced that. I'd like to see him next week instead of two weeks from now. He's also good enough at chess that he'll keep me occupied for a while as I'm learning.

Since we've each almost hit deer coming from each other's places, I'm actually spending the night at his apartment, in the second bedroom. He said that if I got lonely or wanted company I could go bother him, and I said I'd be fine. Which, while true... I can't sleep. I slept about two hours and then have been awake for at least an hour now.

There's a part of me that wants to go into his room, wake him up, kiss him, maybe do more than that... just really feel all the things in my body...

And there's another part of me that thinks it's wise to show restraint... especially since I don't know the full extent of Kieran's feelings for me (or mine for him).

I want to date him. I want to see him weekly, and I want to explore this. I want to go slow and be a full yes to everything. There were a few moments tonight where I wanted to open my body fully to him, a sort of sacred offering. I didn't verbalize that desire because endorphins were flooding my body from the scene, but I thought, "Damn, I haven't felt like this in a long time..."

Because Kieran and I have known each other for more than a year now, and we've seen each other in a variety of contexts, it's different. Dating him would be very different from dating Paco or Sofia. Namely, we knew each other first. Kieran is poly. And kinky. I'm not introducing him to either or pushing him into it, unlike many of my past relationships.

While his energy is different from mine, Kieran has big energy, too. He hasn't directed sexual energy toward me before, so I don't even know what that would look like from him. But, when I tune in, it just feels fun and intense and playful. And it feels like moving slowly would be important here.

So, anyway... that's what's up right now. And my body has been letting me know that it wants me to foster this connection more. Thanks for listening.

After an hour of furious typing into their phone, Nicky's words began to slow at last, and their eyes started to droop. They set their phone on the desk and crawled back into the bed, entering a dreamless sleep.

* * *

Even with a delayed alarm, Nicky still woke up shortly after six o'clock. They made the bed, grabbed their mask, and used the bathroom.

There was no sign of Kieran in the main space, so Nicky went back to the second bedroom where they'd been sleeping and lied down for a bit longer.

Until their body woke them up again.

Once more, they put on their mask as they exited the bedroom. This time, they also got dressed in their clothes for the day since they'd likely leave as soon as they said goodbye.

No Kieran.

So, Nicky returned back to the bedroom, packed up their non-kink items into their small lilac backpack, and their kinky toys into their black toy bag.

This time when they exited the bedroom, carrying their items, Kieran was standing there in the kitchen, wearing a large T-shirt and shorts, one of his typical nerdy masks, and glasses.

Nicky smiled. He looked cute. They felt the temptation to go up to him and wrap their arms around his middle, leaning into him, pulling him toward them.

Taking a deep breath, Nicky shook off that impulse. Instead, they set down their bags and said, "Good morning."

"Good morning," he replied. "How'd you sleep?"

"Not so great," Nicky admitted. "New place and all. I woke up at about three o'clock and couldn't go back to sleep for a while. Finally decided to journal."

"Do you want breakfast? Oatmeal and hard-boiled eggs?" he asked.

"Sure," Nicky said. "That sounds great. Thank you for offering."

He nodded. "You can sit right there at the counter. I'll have it up for you in just a minute."

It was really sweet of him to offer to make breakfast. He didn't *have* to do that. It made Nicky smile. Their body was lit up with joy and peace, pure white light.

Once he'd handed Nicky the oatmeal in a mug, and the hard-boiled egg in a bowl, Nicky braced themself. *Here goes nothing*, they thought.

"I've been thinking, and I'd like to see you more often," they blurted out.

Kieran turned around and looked directly at Nicky. "Okay," he said. "Have you thought about how often you'd like that to be?"

"Once a week."

He looked thoughtful for a minute, then nodded.

"I can do that," he said. "Tuesdays and Wednesdays are easiest for me because of my other commitments."

His response was so level that Nicky wondered if he even *wanted* to spend more time with them. Was he just humoring Nicky?

He seemed to be smiling, but with his mask on, it was really hard to tell.

Even so, Nicky felt like their energy body was curling out in white smoke, and they were giddy that it had been so easy to make that request. Simple.

"Great," they said, and they meant it. Nicky took off their mask and began eating.

The two of them talked about their respective days ahead, and settled on a day and time for their next hangout. *My place*, Nicky suggested, and Kieran's eyes crinkled, which made Nicky's gut turn into goo.

"Is it alright if I ask you something?" Nicky asked. "Well, if we discuss something? It's about last night."

Kieran nodded, holding a rag in his hand, wiping down the counter. "Sure."

"Last night, you said you thought it would be fun to kiss me sometime," Nicky said, picking at their half-eaten egg. "Does this mean that you're romantically interested in me now? And logistically with COVID, how would that work? I mean, do we wait until we're vaccinated? Do we get tested?"

Pausing with what he was doing, Kieran looked directly at Nicky. "I'm going to address those in reverse order, if that's okay."

"Sure."

"As far as logistics, I don't know that there is an answer. I'm getting tested every two weeks before I hang out with Jade, and she's getting tested every three days because she's on campus working in the lab."

Nicky smiled, taking another bite of the oatmeal. "Fair enough. And regarding why I asked if you were romantically attracted to me—I'm not sure what kissing you would bring up for me emotionally, and I want to make sure we're on the same page."

Kieran was silent, just looked at Nicky. It was nice to see their entire face. He'd only seen their full face in snippets during sips of water. Yes, they were in the middle of a pandemic, but Kieran honestly wouldn't have minded if the two of them *didn't* wear masks around each other.

To be honest, he'd half-hoped Nicky might have come into his room last night, but he was just grateful to see them this morning. To be able to make them breakfast.

How did he respond to Nicky's question honestly while omitting that he'd had feelings for them for a year? If he told Nicky he'd been attracted to them for a while, they might shut down.

They were still exploring their feelings, and it was still new.

He didn't want to put that kind of pressure on them.

"My primary attraction to you isn't romantic," Kieran said carefully, "it's energetic and intellectual. Like you, I'm demisexual—there has to be an emotional connection before I'm sexually or romantically attracted to someone. I also identify as sapiosexual—if there's not an intellectual connection, it's really hard for me to be sexually attracted to someone."

Nicky tried not to wince. They knew there were so many different types of sexual attraction, as Kieran said. And Nicky was demisexual, too. But in the spaces between Kieran's words, in the silence, Nicky heard this:

He's not sexually attracted to me. He's not romantically attracted to me.

It felt like a pencil was poking their chest in a few prime places, and Nicky reminded themself to breathe. Not make assumptions.

"So, I'm hearing that our connection nourishes your sapiosexual side," Nicky said. "I'm also hearing that you're open to romantic attraction, that we're both open to and curious about where this can go."

Kieran stopped wiping the counter. "That about sums it up."

Nicky looked down at their nearly empty oatmeal. They felt the immensity of their connection with Kieran. It was big. Very big. Bigger than they'd realized.

But Kieran's even-tempered words made them think that he didn't care. That this wasn't some seismic shift. That their connection was just… curiosity.

He doesn't owe me anything, Nicky reminded themself, but their heart seemed to burn and swell and sink all at the same time regardless.

They mulled this over as they finished eating. Once they'd put their mask on and gathered their things, Nicky turned toward Kieran once more.

"I'm really interested in exploring what's here. It feels like there's something here. Like I said, a switch flipped for me a couple weeks ago. I'm curious where you stand."

To say this, while their heart was beating rapidly, felt so incredibly vulnerable and right at the edge of their ability and capacity. It took all of Nicky's coaching skills and abilities to be present with their fear and be transparent.

Ba-thump. Ba-thump.

This morning with Kieran was so different from everything else they'd known, and it was confusing and maddening, and they wanted to *understand.* Some part of them wanted a bold declaration of love, or at least attraction, though Nicky acknowledged the childishness of that.

Ultimately, though Nicky wouldn't have voiced it, and it wasn't a conscious thought, Nicky wanted to know that they weren't the most vulnerable one.

They wanted to have power, control.

Certainty.

"I see you as a friend, a play partner, and a question mark," Kieran said. "I'm open to exploring what's there, and I value our friendship."

And for Nicky, who had not been romantically attracted to anyone new in more than a year, it felt like rejection. Hot and stingy, and sticky. A rock shoved in their throat.

Nicky did their best not to take it personally.

They nodded and smiled. "Thank you for letting me know where you're at."

Even so, when they finally left Kieran's apartment that morning, the white-light bliss they had felt was muted, and there was a strange ache in the middle of their chest.

* * *

The following Wednesday, Kieran came over sans his kinky toy bag. Nicky had requested as such. After all, if they were going to date (though it was debatable that's what they were doing), Nicky wanted there to be more to their relationship with Kieran than just BDSM.

Nicky ended up making dinner, and then the two of them watched another animated movie together. Afterwards, Nicky went to the kitchen to work on dishes.

"Is there anything I can do to be supportive?" Kieran asked.

Nicky felt a pinching in their gut. *He should just offer to help,* a part of them thought with exasperation. *Be assertive.*

Another part of Nicky didn't want Kieran to be inconvenienced. He was a guest.

"Nope, I'm fine," they said quickly. They turned on the tap and began rinsing the plates, then filling the tub with dish soap. Cooking for multiple people usually exhausted them; without a dishwasher, it was more challenging to keep up with dishes.

"All right then." Kieran pulled up a chair and began working on his laptop.

As Nicky cleaned up from dinner, they encouraged themself to breathe. Up through their feet, into their body, and down and out, releasing anything that no longer served them.

After some time, the annoyance they had felt at Kieran not insisting on helping them with dishes had mostly disappeared. It was silly, anyway. They allowed the chore to be a meditation of sorts, nudging them into relaxation, breathing in time as they washed the dishes.

"What are you working on?" Nicky finally asked.

"My monthly budget. I'm working on paying off my credit card debt. I've got about twenty grand left. With my current timeline, I estimate it will take about two years."

Why the hell is he telling me all this? Nicky wondered. The only person who knew how much debt Nicky had was their mom, who had written them a couple of checks over the past year to help them out during months that had been financially challenging. Nicky's mom had also supported them with starting their bookkeeping system, so being anything less than transparent around finances wouldn't have worked.

"Okay," Nicky said simply. They began putting away dishes.

Kieran continued working on his laptop.

"I can show you the breakdown if you like," he offered.

Despite their confusion and mild irritation, they consented. Kieran walked them through his entire setup, showing Nicky how much he made before and after taxes and other deductions, like child support. It seemed so bizarre that he was sharing this with them.

"Why are you sharing this with me?" Nicky asked.

Kieran looked up, shrugging. "I know that financial stability is important to you."

Nicky left it at that. From their perspective, their relationship wasn't serious or committed enough where having these kinds of conversations around money was appropriate or even close to warranted. After all, they were just hanging out once a week, probably not even dating. Nicky felt a familiar urge to request some space, and felt a little claustrophobic.

"Do you mind if I go for a short walk?" they asked him.

He frowned. "It's dark outside. Do you want company?"

"Uh, no," Nicky said quickly. "Just want to be by myself for a few minutes. I just don't want you to think I'm being rude or anything like that."

"No, that's fine. You said I'd be sleeping in the guest room, right?"

"Yep," Nicky replied, pulling on their coat. Their legs were twitching. They really needed to get out of there. "I'll be back soon. I'll have my phone on me in case you need anything."

Once Nicky was in the fresh air, they began jogging. Even without their running shoes or athletic wear, the urge to run was so powerful that Nicky couldn't ignore it. In hindsight, they should have done a warm-up, at least, but they needed to calm their mind and exhaust their muscles so much that they didn't care.

After about a mile, Nicky's left Achilles tendon began screaming at them. They slowed down to a walk, testing the weight on the left foot. Even walking, it was tender.

"Fuck," Nicky hissed. They began limping back towards their apartment. By the time they saw the illuminated windows, it had probably been a full thirty minutes since they'd left. They hobbled up the stairs, unlocked the door to their apartment, and collapsed on the couch, elevating their left leg. They unlaced their shoes and leaned back with a groan, their right foot still on the floor, helping them balance.

"Goddamn it," Nicky swore loudly, punching one of the pillows near them.

"Nicky, are you okay?"

From their awkward position, Nicky rotated their body just enough so they could turn their head over their shoulder. Kieran was just coming out of the bathroom holding his toothbrush and a container of toothpaste. Nicky's cheeks, ears, and neck flushed with blood.

"I-I injured myself," they said finally. "I was out running in my sneakers, not my running shoes, and I didn't stretch or warm-up beforehand. I think I overstretched my Achilles tendon."

Kieran frowned. "I thought you said you were going for a walk."

"Well, I needed to run instead," Nicky said waspishly.

He didn't say anything, just looked at Nicky lying on the couch. "Can I grab you an ice pack? Do you have any in your freezer?"

At his tenderness, the fight seeped out of Nicky. "I'm sorry. I didn't mean to snap at you," they said.

"I get it. You're in pain," Kieran said. "Can I get you an ice pack, though?"

"Sure. They're in the freezer. Thank you."

A moment later, Kieran returned to the living room with an ice pack and a few paper towels. After he handed these to Nicky, he asked, "Is there anything else I can do to be supportive?"

This time, Nicky just smiled in response.

Chapter Twenty

It was another hour before Nicky calmed down enough to get ready for bed. At one point, Kieran grabbed them a juice box, citing that they needed it.

"Sugar will help. I know you're not in subspace, but if your body's in any form of shock, this will be supportive," he insisted.

Nicky took the juice box with a mumbled thanks.

He also offered to rub their shoulders, massage their neck, and asked if there was anything else he could get for them.

Truth be told, Nicky felt a bit embarrassed with all the attention. The last time they'd overstretched their Achilles tendon, they'd just hopped on one leg to get their ice pack then had binged Netflix until they needed to swap their ice pack for a fresh one.

At the same time, it was nice to be cared for.

Finally, though, Nicky stood up. "I should brush my teeth and get ready for bed," they announced.

"Do you want me to carry you?" Kieran asked. "So you don't have to walk?"

Nicky nodded. First, Kieran carried them to bed, then grabbed their toothbrush, toothpaste, a glass of water and an empty bowl and brought it to them. After Nicky brushed their teeth and rinsed, Kieran whisked away everything but the half-full glass of water.

"Sleep well, Nicky," he said as he left, shutting off the lights. "See you in the morning."

Fucking pandemic, Nicky thought as they turned over onto their side. If they weren't in the middle of a global viral outbreak, Nicky was certain they would have kissed him.

* * *

It seemed like Nicky was thinking about Kieran nonstop. To distract themself, Nicky watched the first season of *Bridgerton* two more times, then read the second book in the series. It had finally arrived from being on back-order.

Even with all of *Bridgerton*'s juicy romance and sexual tension, Nicky couldn't help but feel empty and disappointed. It was a sugar-free, taste-free alternative to their weekly hang-outs with Kieran. The way their skin felt so fiery, the mounting desire to kiss him.

On Saturday, the two of them talked on the phone. There was some light flirting, but overall the conversation was decidedly non-sexual. Yet by the time they got off the hour-long call, Nicky's pussy was drenched. That night, when they used their vibrator, Nicky thought about Kieran touching their hips, their breasts, their clit. It was only after two thigh-shaking orgasms that Nicky fell asleep.

Finally, Wednesday arrived once again, and Nicky packed their overnight bag in a rush. Kieran had said he would make Indian curry for dinner, but Nicky was looking forward to just being in his energy. Just cuddling with him made them feel better. When Nicky was with Kieran, they were fully present in the moment, and very little else mattered.

"What do you want to do tonight?" Kieran asked, as he grabbed Nicky's empty plate. It was still stained orange from the curry.

Nicky shrugged as they put their mask back on. "Watch another movie? On the bean bag? I really enjoy cuddling with you."

Kieran chuckled. "I like snuggling with you, too."

A few minutes later, the two of them were nestled into the oversized bean bag, Nicky leaning into Kieran's side, feeling the heat and blood rush through them. They were only half-aware of what movie they were watching because their body was so bright with desire, and it was far more interesting to run their fingers over Kieran's hand than to watch the screen.

Every so often, they glanced at him, and he looked back. About mid-way through the movie, he asked, "May I remove your mask?"

Nicky froze. The two of them hadn't discussed this. They shook their head.

"Thank you for honoring your boundaries," Kieran said simply, squeezing Nicky's hand.

Once the movie had ended, Kieran and Nicky lingered in the bean bag. At some point, their legs had become entwined. The heat and desire had increased and Nicky felt their clit throbbing insistently. More frustrating than that, though, Nicky still didn't know if Kieran was sexually attracted to them.

No time like the present to find out.

"Do you want to have sex with me?" Nicky asked.

"Do you want to have sex with me?" he countered.

Nicky frowned. They'd asked first, so why was he deflecting?

"I asked you first," they said stubbornly.

"And I asked you second."

Taking a deep breath, Nicky decided to be open, to be vulnerable. "Well, I have imagined you going down on me a couple of times. When you spent the night at my place last week, I could feel your energy seeping through the walls, and I had to touch myself before I could sleep."

Nicky decided to omit the part where they'd also touched themself Saturday night after their phone call with him. Kieran didn't need to know *just* how much their body burned in response to his words, his touch.

Turning to the side, Nicky tucked their face into the cloth of the bean bag. They were getting red. Maybe they shouldn't have said anything. After all, just two weeks ago, he'd said his primary attraction to Nicky was energetic and intellectual. He hadn't said anything about being romantically or sexually attracted to them. Maybe he thought Nicky was ugly. Or, at least, not desirable. Not his type.

The very next moment, though, Kieran pressed into them from behind, and Nicky gasped. Even though Kieran was wearing athletic pants and boxers, Nicky could feel how hard his cock was. His cock pressed into their ass, and immediately, Nicky's body became even warmer, a thousand fires all over.

They could hardly breathe, and their mind had dissolved into a cloud of radiant gas.

"Does that answer your question?" Kieran murmured in their ear.

"Yes," Nicky breathed.

"Good," Kieran said.

The two of them laid there for just another minute before Kieran stood up.

"We should get ready for bed," he said. "It's nearly ten o'clock, and we both have work tomorrow."

Nicky could barely move, let alone stand and walk to the guest bedroom. "I think I need a minute."

"Okay," Kiearn said, shrugging. "If you want company tonight, or if you need anything, feel free to knock on my door."

Nodding silently, Nicky simply rolled slightly more to the side so that Kieran couldn't see their face. They heard him walk away, and a few minutes later, they heard a door close firmly.

* * *

Once again, Nicky had trouble sleeping. After their body had cooled down and their breathing had become less ragged, they finally walked to the guest bedroom, changed into their pajamas, and brushed their teeth in the bathroom. Just like last week and the week before, Nicky could feel Kieran's energy seeping through the walls. But this time, the desire and longing was so powerful that Nicky couldn't stand it.

After lying awake for a couple hours, they put on their gray robe over their tank top and underwear and walked toward Kieran's bedroom. Tentatively, they knocked on the door.

"Come in," a muffled voice said.

The energy in the air was electric. Nicky hadn't been here before; they didn't know what would happen. It didn't matter.

All they wanted, no, *needed*, was Kieran's skin against theirs.

"Hi," they said. "You said I could bother you if I needed anything. And well, I can't sleep. Is it alright if I come in?"

Bleary-eyed, Kieran looked up at them, nodding. "Do you want me to put on underwear?"

Nicky paused, frozen in the doorway. "That would be supportive," they said.

"Hold on a minute."

Looking down at their feet, Nicky forced themself to focus on their breathing as Kieran pulled on some underwear while staying under the covers. Inhale, exhale.

"Do you want me to put on a mask?" he asked, reaching toward his bedside table.

Thoughtful of him to ask, Nicky thought, but they shook their head. "I don't think it makes sense for us to be wearing masks if we're going to be sleeping."

"Fair enough."

With that, Nicky tiptoed into the room and shut the door behind them. When they reached Kieran's bed, they removed the mask they were wearing.

The energy between them was sultry, powerful, overwhelming. Nicky needed to touch him. He was bare chested, and for the first time in months, they were able to see his full face for an extended period of time.

Somewhere between the first time they'd met and now, Kieran had grown a full beard, rather than just sporting a goatee. The part of his beard around his chin was still more pronounced, but it suited him.

For a few minutes, Nicky tried to sleep in the bed next to him. But with the energy crackling between them, they quickly gave up and turned to face Kieran once more.

"Is it alright if I touch you?" they asked.

Kieran smiled. "Of course."

Nicky began running their hands over Kieran's shoulders, his arms, his chest, touching his hair. They still held a bit of distance between the two of them, just enjoying the heady rush of unfulfilled desire.

"May I kiss you?" Kieran asked after a moment.

Blushing, Nicky shook their head.

Yet their legs became entwined, and the energy and the heat seared them together.

It was more than Nicky could bear.

"Do you still want to kiss me?" Nicky whispered after a moment.

Kieran nodded.

"Okay," Nicky said.

Immediately, Kieran's lips crashed onto theirs. They wound their hand into his hair, pressed their body into his, gasped when they felt his cock pressing into them.

But more than anything, Nicky noticed the kiss. The kiss itself wasn't blinding with heat, but it felt natural, easy. Not awkward at all. They continued kissing Kieran, touching him, running their hands over him, just as he ran his hands over them.

"This just feels so right," Nicky murmured between kisses.

"I agree," Kieran said.

He began kissing their neck, and Nicky's robe slid off their shoulder. They moaned, clutching his arm, digging their fingernails into him.

After a moment, Nicky tossed the robe off the bed, and it landed with a soft thud on the carpet.

"I think we've shared past lives together," Nicky said. "It just feels so natural kissing you, touching you."

"I agree," Kieran said. "And we don't have any trauma together that we're healing."

Nicky's body froze. Something about Kieran's words didn't ring true. Their body stiffened, and Nicky rolled onto their other side so their back was facing Kieran.

"Are you okay?" he asked.

Nicky shook their head, and flipped back over to face him. "You can't say that none of our past lives created trauma for either of us because you don't know that. When you said that, it didn't feel true to me."

"Okay," Kieran said simply.

It was a few minutes before the rigidity in Nicky's body softened. Once it did, they nuzzled into Kieran, kissing him again. With a sigh, they breathed out any lingering tension they still felt.

Nicky began focusing on each tiny kiss that Kieran placed on them, their mouth, their chin, their shoulder, their collarbone, and all too soon the aching fire roared back to life from the embers. The two of them pressed their bodies even closer, and Nicky felt Kieran's cock throbbing through his boxer briefs.

They wanted more skin-to-skin contact with him, so next, Nicky pulled off their tank top and tossed it over the side of the bed to join the robe somewhere in the darkness. Pressing their bare chest against his felt so warm, reassuring, settling. At the same time, it continued to stir things even more deeply within Nicky.

"Is it alright if I straddle you?" Nicky asked.

"Yes," Kieran said.

With that invitation, Nicky swung one of their legs over Kieran and landed on top of him. If the heat had been intense before, now it positively seared them. Only two layers of clothing separated Nicky's yoni from Kieran's cock, and it was like nuclear fusion bonding them together, radiating out ripples of heat far beyond their root chakras, far beyond their bodies, even.

And to think Nicky had been so adamant that they weren't attracted to Kieran because he wasn't their type.

How silly that seemed now.

The two of them crashed their lips together once more, their chests centimeters apart as Nicky bent down, still on top of Kieran. He began touching their breasts, their nipples, gently rubbing them, pulling at them, teasing them.

Nicky moaned, all their frustration rising to the surface.

Their body wanted them to have sex with Kieran; that much was obvious. But Nicky knew that if they tried to do that right now, it wouldn't feel fun, joyful, connective. The emotional connection wasn't there yet—sure, they'd bonded with Kieran somewhat, but they didn't love him. And he didn't love them.

No matter what Nicky had told themself during the virtual play party last month, it wasn't love. And Nicky knew they wanted to wait to have intercourse with Kieran until they were a complete hell yes to it.

But *God* did their body want it. It was so maddening.

"My underwear is pretty soaked, I think," Nicky said, pulling away slightly.

"It is?" Kieran murmured. "Mind if I see?"

Again, Nicky's body became rigid. If they took off their underwear, would Kieran take off his boxer briefs? They weren't ready for that. Nicky wasn't ready to see his cock.

Not tonight.

"Will you keep your underwear on?" Nicky asked hesitantly.

Kieran nodded.

Slowly, Nicky climbed off Kieran, still on their knees, and slid their underwear over slightly. Then, grabbing one of Kieran's hands, they placed it next to their yoni. Enmeshed in the hair, and beneath it, slick fluid flowed.

"You are really wet," Kieran commented. "Is it alright if I touch you?"

Nicky shook their head and moved Kieran's hand away.

"Not tonight," they said, moving their underwear back to fully cover their pussy. Then, Nicky leaned down, lied on their side, and pressed themself into Kieran. They moaned. He was still so hard, and once again he began touching their breasts.

Turning to face him, Nicky kissed Kieran once more, feverishly, because they couldn't get enough of him, his skin, his touch. And he, almost in reverence, kissed them back before deepening the kiss, the connection.

This was bliss. This couldn't go on long enough, Nicky thought.

The two of them stayed that way for hours, kissing and touching each other in Kieran's bed, moaning and sighing, until finally the room began to lighten with the gray light of pre-dawn. Every time they'd tried to fall asleep, the fiery energy had kept them awake, and they'd start the entire process over again.

Touching. Kissing. Cuddling. Moaning.

"Maybe I should go back to the other bedroom," Nicky said finally. "So we can get at least a couple hours of sleep."

Kieran looked up at the clock. "It's almost 7:30 a.m. I think we've missed that opportunity."

Propping themself on their elbow, Nicky turned to face him. "What do you propose instead?" they asked, yawning.

"That I make you some breakfast," he said.

After another kiss and a couple more minutes of cuddles, Kieran stood up, grabbed his shorts and a shirt and left the bedroom. Nicky leaned back with a great sigh, and another massive yawn.

This, Nicky decided firmly, was a night they would surely remember.

Chapter Twenty-One

After their first kiss with Kieran, Nicky found they wanted to be in communication with him much more often. They had two phone calls with him that week, and Nicky was riding such a high. When they chatted with Kieran, they felt every nerve crackling in their body. They weren't thinking about being anywhere else. Nicky was completely and totally present in the moment.

Even *Bridgerton* finally seemed to have lost its appeal.

Bailey noticed a definite change in Nicky, too. "When you talk about him, you're glowing," she said with a small smile, the next time they connected over video chat. "Your whole face lights up."

Nicky blushed. "Do I really?" they asked.

Nodding, Bailey chuckled. "It's adorable. I'm glad to see you so happy… I know the pandemic has been hard, especially since you've parted ways with Arthur and Sofia."

"With Arthur it hasn't been so bad," Nicky commented. "He and I actually connected over video chat last month, and I told him I was interested in dating him again at some point. It's been a challenging year for him, though. Between George Floyd's death, Jacob Blake's paralysis, Madison's lack of criminal justice reform, and the pandemic, he's been at capacity. He said he wouldn't be able to think about dating someone new until after he was fully vaccinated or some major legislation was passed in Wisconsin to limit police violence and brutality."

"But with Sofia?" Bailey asked.

"I do feel bad about how things ended," Nicky admitted. "We were so close at the beginning. Connected deeply about our shared interests—I was even teaching her about Reiki and energy healing."

"And?" Bailey prompted.

Nicky paused. It felt like a pulsing wound was in their heart. "I blame myself for how it ended," they said. "If I had just kept my thoughts to myself, and hadn't said anything on New Year's, or if I'd just waited until there was a more appropriate time…"

"Have you talked about this with Emma? Your therapist?" Bailey asked quietly, taking a sip from her mug.

"Yes," Nicky replied. "She's repeated herself multiple times on the issue. It takes two people to create a relationship—whether it's good, bad, or otherwise."

"You're doing such an amazing job navigating all your feelings," Bailey said. "And you've had so many changes in your life the past few months, not to mention the past couple of years. I'm constantly in awe of you and what you've accomplished. I wish you'd be gentler with yourself sometimes."

Beads of water pooled in the corners of Nicky's eyes, and they brushed at them hastily. "Thanks for the reminder. I'm still rewiring my patterns of perfectionism. Breaking the habit of setting near-impossible standards for myself and others."

"You're welcome," Bailey said. Her smile became conspiratorial. "When are you seeing Kieran next? Are you excited? What do you have planned?"

With another blush on their face, Nicky began sharing more about Kieran, how they felt about him, and their next date.

* * *

It was so hard to be separated from Kieran that Nicky asked if they could spend two nights at his place that week. Come over sometime on Tuesday, and leave on Thursday.

Per usual, Kieran said he was open to it.

Does he feel this same pull that I do? Nicky wondered as they drove the familiar route to his place in the early evening. Even though the days were getting longer, the sun was still starting to sink in the sky, which was streaked with pink and purple and orange.

They mulled this over during the entire forty-minute car ride, and the frown on their face became deeper. By the time they'd reached his place, their brow was puckered.

When Kieran opened the door to greet them, the consternation in their face was evident. After last week, they'd both agreed not to wear masks around each other, and for Kieran, it was a welcome change to see Nicky's entire face.

"Everything okay?" he asked.

Nicky shook their head, still frowning.

The two of them tromped up the stairs into the apartment. Once Nicky had set down their backpack and other overnight things, they faced him, biting their lip.

"I've noticed that during the week, I'm more expressive with my texts than you are," Nicky said. "I'll send you three or four messages that are quite long, and you'll send a one-line reply. Like when I shared I'd like to come over on Tuesday because Wednesday seemed too far away. Your reply was just that you'd be open to it. It makes me wonder if you feel the same way I do."

"I'm not the best communicator over text," Kieran admitted. "I'm much better in-person. I read visual cues better. It's something I've been working on, but I'm still not great at it."

Nicky nodded absently, but Kieran knew there was still something amiss.

Sure enough, less than a minute later, Nicky asked, "Okay, but do you want me here? For two nights?"

Ah. Kieran recognized this pattern. Nicky needing reassurance was part of them having an anxious attachment style.

"Yes, I want you here," he said, looking straight at Nicky. "I would have said no to the idea when you brought it up if I only wanted you over for one night."

"You're sure?" they asked.

He nodded. "Yes."

"Okay," Nicky said, smiling.

After the two of them had dinner, lamb stew and asparagus, they sat on the couch, cuddling.

"I was thinking about last week," Kieran said. "How we ended up fooling around until the morning, and how we were both exhausted the next day."

"Yeah," Nicky said. "We probably shouldn't repeat that."

"Unless it's a weekend," Kieran added. "I don't mind staying up late as long as I don't have to be productive the next day. But I had to take a nap in the middle of the work day, and that's not sustainable."

"No," Nicky agreed. "Not for me, either."

"So, how about tonight, we're sleeping by the time it's midnight? At the latest."

"Sounds good," Nicky said with a smile.

After that, the two of them spent a good portion of the evening just talking. At some point Kieran wrapped his arms around Nicky.

"I've got you trapped," he whispered into their ear.

Nicky struggled against the hold for just a few seconds before giving up. He was so strong. Later, Nicky wasn't sure what made them do it—a mix of being playful and wanting to be released, most likely—but they sank their teeth into Kieran's hand.

Rather than him releasing them, the next thing Nicky felt was a sharp bite where their neck met their shoulder. Harder than when their other partners had tried to give them hickeys.

"You bite me, I'll bite you back," Kieran said.

Immediately, Nicky felt their body become rigid, and they became silent. This wasn't something they had negotiated. Now they really needed to escape. They tried pulling away again, like they had the first time, but Kieran's arms held fast.

"Yellow," Nicky said.

Sweet release. As soon as Kieran unwrapped his arms from around them, Nicky leaped up and practically ran a couple paces away from him. They wrapped their arms tightly around their midsection.

Kieran frowned. "Are you okay?"

Nicky shook their head. "That was really hard."

It was clear Nicky was having a trauma response. "What can I do to be supportive?" Kieran asked.

"I need space," Nicky said.

He looked at them blankly. "Do you want me to go into my room?" he asked after a minute.

"No, no, that's not necessary," Nicky said hastily. They were hopping from one foot to the other now. "Just… is it alright if I go to the guest bedroom for a bit?"

"Of course."

Immediately, Nicky left the living room and shut the door to the second bedroom. They sat on the bed and curled into themself, bringing their knees to their chest. It wasn't until they were clutching Ollie that Nicky could focus on their breath. Breathing up from the earth, through their feet, into their body. Exhaling deep out their mouth, sending the breath through their body and back into the earth.

After several rounds of breathing, Nicky's body finally started to soften. They took a few more breaths, stood up, then returned to the living room, still holding Ollie.

Kieran was still there on the couch. He was holding his phone, but looked up when Nicky reentered the room.

"I wasn't expecting you to bite me," Nicky said. "We hadn't negotiated that, and it wasn't something I was okay with."

"I think it was a five out of ten on your limit list," he said. "I don't remember any triggers or warnings noted next to it."

Nicky paused. "You've looked at my limit list?"

Kieran nodded. "Multiple times. How else can I play with you safely?"

At that moment, Nicky felt embarrassed. They didn't know if biting was one of Kieran's limits, or if it was something he just tolerated. *As soon as I get a chance,* Nicky told themself, *I'm looking at his list and checking. Reviewing everything more thoroughly.*

"How often do you look at my limits?" Nicky asked.

"Once every couple of weeks. Just to refresh myself. I won't check it that often forever, but since we're still getting to know each other, I want to make sure I'm staying well within your boundaries."

Nicky didn't know what to say, but they felt a rush of affection and appreciation for him.

I love you, a gentle, melodic voice seemed to say. Nicky brushed it away.

There was *no* way they were telling Kieran that right now. They weren't even sure if they loved him. After all, they'd only been dating a couple of weeks. Nicky had had feelings for him for less than a month.

"Do you want to snuggle in the bean bag and watch a movie?" Kieran asked after a minute.

"No," Nicky said, clutching Ollie tighter. "My little self needs to feel safe with you again before I'm okay with that. Can we just sit on the couch together and watch something from there?"

Kieran smiled. "Of course."

So Nicky sat down, joining Kieran on the sofa, and the two of them queued up yet another animated film.

* * *

The next day went more smoothly. During the day, the two of them worked on their respective projects. In the evening, the two of them went for a walk outside before Kieran started making dinner again. They ate at the counter together, before giving each other a sensual massage.

By the time Thursday came, Nicky was feeling irritated. Claustrophobic. It wasn't until after they'd arrived back at their apartment that they realized they'd probably just spent too much time with Kieran. Two nights together was double what they'd done in the past. And they'd only been dating a couple weeks, if that.

To be honest, Nicky wasn't even sure if Kieran was a good fit for them. There was something that felt a bit off. Nicky wasn't sure what it was, but they just felt anxious and nervous and angry.

Maybe the two of them were better off just as friends. Or as play partners.

Fortunately, Nicky had the foresight to request that they take a week off from seeing each other. They rewatched *Bridgerton* a sixth time. They poured themself into work. But Nicky was restless, unsettled.

Then, they got Paco's email.

Sure, Nicky had blocked his phone number and deleted their message history, but they hadn't done anything about email or Facebook.

It was a simple message, really. He had one of their dishes from the last time the two of them had hung out in person, and he wanted to give it back to them. *I know you might not want to see me, but it's really important that I get this back to you,* his message read.

Torn, Nicky waited a day to reply. Finally, they caved.

Why don't you stop by on Wednesday after work? they said in their email back to him. *I can take the dish, and we can go for a walk and catch up.*

Maybe things had changed in the seven months they'd been out of contact.

Maybe *he* had changed.

A part of Nicky was clinging to that.

Besides, Nicky had already told Kieran they needed space this Wednesday. It would work out perfectly.

* * *

Nicky's doorbell rang promptly at six-thirty. Upon opening the front door to the building, Nicky saw a masked-up Paco standing on the stoop, holding their glass dish, a plastic lid on its top. Hastily, Nicky took the dish, bounded into their apartment, slid on some shoes, shrugged on a coat, and made their way back to the building's entrance.

At first, the two of them simply chatted as they walked around Nicky's neighborhood. Nicky told Paco about some of their recent business successes, and he shared about his holidays. Each of them asked about the health of the other's family, shared what shows and movies they had been watching, and swapped stories about the Christmas gifts that they had received.

It was just like old times. It was settled, comfortable, and Nicky was so glad to have their good friend back. After all, when they were dating Paco, he had been their best friend. It was only recently that Bailey had begun occupying that spot.

Yet, Nicky felt something niggling at them. *I should really tell Paco about Kieran,* they thought, but they brushed it aside.

After all, Nicky had only been dating Kieran a couple of weeks, and Paco knew that Nicky identified as poly. At least, they thought so.

"Have you been dating anyone?" Nicky asked finally.

Paco shook his head. "Everyone I meet just isn't what I'm looking for. Usually, I'm not attracted to them physically. Or they have kids. I don't really want to date someone who has kids."

Nicky could relate. For a long time, dating someone with kids had been a hard limit for them. It wasn't until they decided to date Arthur that they realized there were benefits to dating people who were parents. Namely, from Nicky's perspective, they tended to be more responsible and emotionally mature.

Maybe that was part of the reason Kieran communicated so effectively and was so patient and understanding. He was a dad, too. He'd had so much life experience, had chosen to heal and grow time and time again.

"That's fair," Nicky said neutrally, as they kept walking around the neighborhood. By now, they were passing Monona Bay, winding around Brittingham Park, heading towards the capitol. For some reason, it felt like their energy was pinching into themself, contracting, becoming smaller.

Talking with Paco was fine, but it wasn't fun.

When did it stop being fun?

"Besides," Paco added, "I'm still not over Catalina. We had a really good relationship, and she was so beautiful, too. Did you know she started modeling?"

"No, I didn't," Nicky said evenly, trying not to grit their teeth.

Had anything changed in the last seven months? Anything?

"But I still want to be in a relationship," Paco continued. "So, I'm on the dating sites, going on dates, going on walks, having virtual meetups. But nobody is standing out."

"Have you talked with a therapist about this?" Nicky asked quickly.

Now Paco's energy seemed to contract, to wrap into itself. "No," he said. "I feel funny about telling some stranger about my emotions. I'd rather talk to you about it."

Nicky remembered a similar comment Paco had made almost a year ago. They remembered being on the phone with him, walking on their parents' street, pressing the red 'end call' button. Deja vu.

By now, the pinching in their aura and energy field was unbearable. Nicky took a deep breath.

"This topic of conversation isn't fun for me—hearing about Catalina, I mean," they clarified. "I used to date you, too, and it's challenging hearing about your feelings for her. Especially since I still have feelings for you."

"I mean, you asked if I was dating anyone," Paco said. "But fine, I won't bring it up again, Nicole."

An icy splinter seemed to lodge itself in Nicky's chest. How many times would they have to remind him about their name?

"It's Nicky, not Nicole, Paco."

"Oh, right. Sorry."

The splinter of ice in Nicky's heart grew larger. Almost nothing had changed. Being around Paco was painful.

Why were they still doing this to themself? What value was this connection adding to their life?

None, came the gentle, melodic answer from Nicky's authentic self. *This connection doesn't serve you in any way anymore. It hasn't for a long time.*

"Let's head back toward my apartment. I'm starting to get cold and tired," they lied.

After they said goodbye and parted ways with Paco, Nicky closed the door, shrugged off their coat, took off their mask, kicked off their shoes, and collapsed almost immediately on the couch. They kept opening and closing their mouth as though they needed to gag. Spending time with Paco had left an acidic taste in their mouth.

At the same time, Nicky realized just how much they missed Kieran's laugh. His smile. His touch. His voice. Feeling his arms around them. Pulling out their phone, Nicky decided to text him.

Thank you for giving me some space, they said. *I'd like to see you this weekend, if you're free.*

Kieran responded quickly. *I'll have my son with me through Sunday. How about Monday evening?*

Nicky smiled. *Sounds great. See you Monday*, they texted back.

* * *

After they were done with work on Monday evening, Nicky packed their bags and began the drive to Kieran's. The route was so familiar now that Nicky didn't even bother to look up his address in their navigation app; their muscles guided them along the path instinctively.

When Nicky finally reached Kieran's apartment, they opened the unlocked door, shut it behind them, and climbed up the stairs. The wonderful scent of sizzling onion and garlic pummeled their nostrils.

Nicky dropped their bags, and touched Kieran, gently scratching his back. "Hey," they said. "Can I give you a hug?"

Kieran turned slightly and smiled. God, it was so good to see his smile.

"In a minute," he said. "I don't want the stir fry to burn."

Nicky nodded and grabbed their things. After putting their bags in the second bedroom, they returned to see Kieran doling out food, placing the plates on the counter.

"This looks amazing," Nicky said. "Thank you for making dinner."

He smiled again. "You're welcome."

They kissed each other and began eating.

Just being in the same space with Kieran, Nicky felt such joy. The familiar expansive feeling had returned, and white light was flooding their entire energy body. They loved how they felt around Kieran; appreciated how he made them dinner; loved his strong, gentle presence.

How could Nicky have possibly thought that the two of them were better as friends, or simply play partners?

I love you, a familiar voice echoed.

But Nicky bit back the words their authentic self wanted them to say. It was too soon, only early March. The two of them had only been dating a few weeks. Besides, Nicky still wasn't sure how they felt about Kieran. Sure, they enjoyed dating him, but being in love involved so much more than that.

The two of them finished dinner and rinsed their plates. While Kieran loaded the dishwasher, Nicky thumbed through the streaming catalogs. For some reason, nothing was catching their eye.

"What do you want to do for the rest of the evening?" Kieran asked, sitting down next to them on the couch. "Is there anything that looks good?"

Nicky shook their head, turning to face him. "Not really. I'd much rather just spend time with you."

They touched his face gently, ran their fingers through his hair, began scratching his head.

"Oh, that feels good," Kieran moaned, closing his eyes and sinking into the touch.

It was moments like this where Nicky thought they might love Kieran. When they touched him in a way he liked, not because it was something the two of them had negotiated, but simply because Nicky knew that it made him feel good.

At some point, Kieran began touching them back, and the two of them began kissing. It was deep and slow and scorching, passionate and tender and powerful. Once again, Nicky's skin felt alive with a thousand flames, several degrees warmer than it had been just moments earlier.

"Do you want to take this to the bedroom?" Kieran murmured.

Nicky nodded.

Gently holding their hand, Kieran guided them to a standing position and led them to his room. Once they were there, Nicky peeled off their sweater, their shirt, their jeans. Kieran took off his shirt and athletic pants.

"Do you want me to keep on my underwear?" Kieran asked.

"Yes, please," they said. Nicky hesitated. "Do you want me to keep on my bra and underwear?"

"You're welcome to wear as much or as little as you like," he replied.

The two of them fell into bed together, kissing each other. In quick order, Nicky's bra came off.

"May I?" Kieran asked, gently touching one of Nicky's breasts.

"Please," they moaned.

Kieran took Nicky's nipple into his mouth, gently sucking on it. Nicky's moans grew louder, and they clutched Kieran to them, digging their nails into his shoulder, their hips beginning to buck unconsciously.

The heat continued building, and Nicky both felt and knew that their cotton undies were soaked. Every part of them was being stimulated, even if Kieran wasn't touching it directly. If they weren't careful, Nicky was going to climb on top of him, pull down his underwear, and slide their yoni over his cock.

They hadn't negotiated that with him. And emotionally, Nicky wasn't ready to have intercourse with Kieran, either. Not really. Not even close.

But their body wanted it *so* badly.

Nicky climbed on top and straddled Kieran, keeping their underwear on, not touching his. Kieran, meanwhile, began playing with Nicky's breasts from that position, kissing them, sucking on their nipples one at a time.

Even with his underwear still on, Nicky felt how hard Kieran was. Their skin became hotter, and their underwear clung even closer to the skin because their pussy was so wet. It was too much. They rolled off him and laid by his side, panting, holding his hand.

"Is everything all right?" Kieran asked.

Nicky nodded. "Yes. It was just intense being on top of you."

"Agreed. It's a turn on when you're on top of me."

The two of them laid there for a minute, and the fiery energy began to cool, soften, pool in and out and around them. Kieran wrapped an arm around Nicky's shoulder, and their breathing settled. Nicky turned their head toward him, and he gently stroked a hand through their hair.

"Is it alright if I touch your cock through your underwear?" Nicky asked. They wanted to become comfortable with seeing him fully naked somehow.

Kieran nodded. "Is it okay if I touch you beneath your underwear?"

"Yes."

Pressing their hand against Kieran's underwear, Nicky felt the slightly soft, engorged flesh beneath their palm. They slid their hand lower, feeling his balls through the thin layer of fabric.

Nicky moaned.

Kieran gently began touching them beneath their underwear, reaching into the sopping mess of hair and liquid and skin, stroking circles around Nicky's clit. They moaned again as the energy continued swirling, growing, reaching beyond their yoni and moving through and in and around all parts of their pelvis.

In just a moment, the energy shifted—like Nicky had passed through some unseen portal—and while they knew their body was turned on and their pussy was wet, Nicky's needy, desperate desire for intercourse had dissipated. Now, Nicky felt bathed in white light that was more potent than they'd ever felt. They were one with their authentic self, and they simply wanted to share this energy with Kieran, move it from their body through his.

As he touched them, and they touched him, they began cycling the energy through their body. Moving it from their root chakra, down by their groin, up through to their crown chakra, at the top of their head, and imagining it was passing through them into Kieran. From their hand to his balls. Up his body, into his crown.

Later, Nicky realized how inadequate words were to describe this experience. All they knew was they had shifted into an alternate reality of space and time, where both were clearly constructs. A level of consciousness where they saw the unity of all things—felt, knew, and understood their deep connection with Kieran—and where the only emotions present were peace, love, joy, and radiant bliss.

The two of them stayed like that for several moments, touching each other sexually, feeling and expanding with the energy. It was so light, so freeing to be here, to feel fully liberated, to so intimately share their energy, their being with someone else.

This was the kind of sexual experience Nicky had longed to have for years. Someone who could fully receive them and their soul.

After a stretch of time that was both minutes and hours, Kieran placed a hand on Nicky's shoulder.

"That's about as much as I can take right now," he said. His words shook slightly, as his body tremored.

Even though Nicky was flying so high and could continue running the energy for longer, they shifted the setting of the energy they were channeling and turned onto their side to face Kieran. Nicky touched his beard, his hair, his shoulders, and pressed their body into him.

The thought from earlier kept cycling through their mind. Not once, not twice, but over and over like a mantra.

I love you. I love you. I love you.

Nicky's body became slightly rigid. It was too early, too soon. It had only been a few weeks.

I love you. I love you. I love you.

At last, the mantra was so insistent, so deafeningly loud, that Nicky took a deep breath and looked at Kieran with a small, tentative smile. Having made up their mind, the mantra softened back into an expanse of white light.

"I love you," Nicky said.

Chapter Twenty-Two

“**T**hank you.”

Nicky didn't know what they had expected Kieran to say in response to hearing them say, 'I love you,' but not that. There was a pang in their heart, like a hammer to a geode.

I'd rather he be authentic about his emotions than falsely tell me he loves me, Nicky told themself. *It's okay he's not there right now.*

Though it was challenging, Nicky did their best to focus on the white light energy, on the part of them that knew saying 'I love you' had been the right decision. They hadn't ever had such an expansive experience with any of their past partners. Saying 'I love you' wasn't a forever commitment or promise.

They cuddled there with Kieran for several minutes, talking with him some as well, still feeling the leftover bliss, peace, and joy from the experience they'd just shared together mingled with confusion, hurt, and pain that they didn't want to voice.

Eventually, Kieran clasped Nicky's hand within his own and smiled warmly at them. "It's getting late," he said. "We should go to bed so we're not completely exhausted tomorrow."

Nicky nodded. They grabbed their bra and the rest of their clothes and got into their pajamas. Then, heading to the bathroom, they brushed their teeth in tandem with Kieran, who was still wearing just his boxer briefs.

Playfully, Nicky knocked their hip into Kieran's and he did it back. Amidst toothpaste and water and spit, both of them were laughing when they finally put away their toothbrushes. They kissed, and headed back to their respective bedrooms.

Once they'd tucked the Minecraft blankets around them, Nicky clicked their phone to see what time it was. 1:12 in the morning. Nicky and Kieran would both be exhausted tomorrow, even if they fell asleep right away.

Oops.

But Nicky didn't fall asleep right away. The ache in their heart was still there, and their mind kept reeling.

Before Kieran, Sofia had been the last person to whom Nicky had said that first 'I love you.'

That had been a year and a half ago. In October, five months before the pandemic had started. It had been before Sofia had started dating Ivan, before she and Ricky started having more frequent arguments, before Nicky started overgiving and ignoring their boundaries in that relationship.

Parts of them missed those days.

* * *

The next several days were emotionally challenging for Nicky. They still felt some of the uplifted radiant bliss on Tuesday, the day after their potent, powerful sexual experience with Kieran. At the same time, Nicky felt their energy contracting. Nervous, anxious thoughts swirled through their mind.

That familiar steel wall was closing down around their heart, their energy field. It wasn't safe to be vulnerable with Kieran. They were getting too attached; they needed to create some emotional distance.

Because the two of them had spent Monday together, they opted for a phone call on Wednesday instead.

"The local dungeon is closing this month," Kieran shared while they were chatting. "They've decided not to renew their lease."

"Oh," Nicky said. "That's a real shame. That was the last place in Madison where people could play publicly."

"I know."

The disappointment and sadness in Kieran's voice was evident. He had been good friends with many of the dungeon's leaders for several years. Even with the uncertainty of the pandemic, he'd gotten a year-long membership to help them stabilize their revenue.

"They couldn't hold on until people got vaccinated?" Nicky asked. "It's just a couple months away. June or July, probably."

"No. Their expenses have exceeded their revenue for several months now, and they don't see a path forward. They're not eligible for the grants or loans that many other businesses are."

The two of them were quiet for a minute. Sitting on the daybed, Nicky was staring listlessly at the rainbow mural they had painted on the walls of their queer playroom.

"It's been such a special place," Nicky said. "The scenes that we did there together were so special. It's a shame we won't be able to play there anymore."

"I actually wanted to talk to you about that," Kieran said. "Jade has mononucleosis, so I'm not spending time with her this weekend. I was wondering if you'd like to do a final scene together at the dungeon before they close."

Still looking at their rainbow mural, Nicky nodded. A couple tears were coming to their eyes. "I'd like that a lot," they said.

The two of them spent the rest of the time chatting about what they might like to do for the scene. Bondage, maybe impact, and they agreed that Kieran would come over so the two of them could drive to the event space together. Afterward, Kieran would spend the night.

Even after Nicky got off the phone with Kieran, they felt quiet, reflective, like they needed to journal, go for a walk, take a bath. During pre-pandemic times, there had been four kink spaces; a large play party almost every weekend; and regular munches, workshops, and classes. For a city its size, Madison had had a wonderfully thriving kink scene.

And now, there would be nothing for who-knew-how-long.

It was a sobering reminder of just how much the pandemic had changed the world—even those pockets that had seemed certain, definite, stable.

Doing this scene just a week before the dungeon closed was, in many ways, an homage to how their relationship had started and evolved. Nicky's first-ever impact scene with Kieran was what inspired them to ask Kieran to be their play partner last August. The Halloween scene was when things started to shift. In hindsight, Nicky realized that their pussy might have been so wet during the scene not just because of the energy of the kinky play, but because—on some level—they already had feelings for Kieran.

In any case, Nicky was glad they were doing a final scene at the dungeon. Three was a powerful, sacred number, and their budding relationship with Kieran seemed to be powerful and sacred as well.

It was only fitting that they did a third scene together at the dungeon before it closed.

* * *

Saturday night, Kieran parked his truck on Nicky's street and dropped his overnight bag in the second bedroom before the two of them set off for the local dungeon. Both of them were wearing inconspicuous clothing and planned to change once they reached the dungeon. For their part, Nicky's current ensemble was black skinny jeans, their black Oxford knock-offs, and a black t-shirt. Kieran was wearing athletic pants, but the rest was covered by his thick winter coat.

"How's Jade?" Nicky asked while they were in transit. "Is she feeling any better?"

Kieran sighed. "She's still feeling pretty awful. I brought her a care package, and I hope that helps. She's hoping we can spend time together at the end of the month."

"What about next weekend? Or during the week?"

"Jade doesn't drive," Kieran said, "so I usually pick her up from campus and we spend the weekend at my place. As far as next weekend, I'll have my son then. He comes first. That's part of being a parent."

Soon, they were at the dungeon. Kieran grabbed his toy bag and shut the driver's side door behind him, pulling on his cloth mask. Nicky followed, slinging their black backpack over one shoulder and entering the dungeon just behind Kieran.

The two of them checked in, showed their IDs, and made their way to the area of the building they'd reserved. The last two times they'd played together, Nicky and Kieran had been in the main dungeon, which was full of crosses, spanking benches, suspension rigs, and massage tables. This room was smaller, more intimate. Along one wall, there was a small spanking bench, and in another corner, there stood a metal suspension rig. In the middle of the room, there was a small bench. It was wide enough for a person to lay on, but only just, and it was much lower to the ground than most massage tables typically were.

Overall, it was quite a simple layout.

"I'm going to change," Nicky said. "If that's okay."

Kieran nodded. Exiting the room they'd been assigned, Nicky walked to the all-gender bathroom and closed the door behind them.

Their heart hurt so much. Even though they'd spent time coaching the part of them that was upset that Kieran hadn't said he loved them back, it still sucked. Sure, Nicky was used to being the first person to say, 'I love you,' but the person had almost always said it back. The one exception was Arthur, and he'd quickly explained he didn't like to put a lot of pressure on that phrase, that for him saying 'I love you' might mean something different than it meant to Nicky.

Plus, if Nicky was honest with themself, Arthur was never someone who might, someday, become a primary partner. He was not someone with whom they would build their life, share their home, mingle finances. Nicky's spiritual views were radically different from Arthur's. Besides, he already had a nesting partner with whom he co-parented his daughter.

With Kieran, not hearing him say 'I love you' had been a hundred times harder.

Taking a deep, shaky breath, Nicky opened their backpack and pulled out the clothes they'd chosen for tonight's scene. They stripped. Through the pain and the grief, Nicky fastened their white corset; combed a hand through their short, dark hair; changed their cotton underwear for gray, lacy panties; pulled on their fuzzy striped panda socks; and slipped into their filmy, barely-there white robe.

* * *

When Nicky returned, Kieran paused. So did his breath. There was something about the white satin corset that made Nicky seem particularly ethereal and innocent.

And gorgeous.

"You look amazing," he said.

Nicky ducked their head down, their cheeks turning pink. "Thanks," they said.

"You're welcome."

Sitting on the bench, Nicky looked up at Kieran. Once again, he was wearing his signature black and green kilt and was shirtless. On his feet, he had thick woolen socks. After all, the room was a bit chilly (at least by Nicky's standards), and it was technically still winter.

"We spoke previously about doing massage and intimate bondage, maybe some impact if that felt joyful," Kieran said. "You also wanted to use toys, but not have me touch your clit or pussy. Is that still the case?"

Nicky nodded.

"Right. I was thinking we would start out on the bench with some massage, energy play, and bondage before moving into impact."

Tucking their knees into their chest, Nicky felt the deep ache pressing inward. They felt closed-off from Kieran.

Not a great place emotionally to start a scene.

"Before we start, can we do a more formal check-in?" Nicky asked. "While doing some Tantric poses? With music in the background? Maybe sitting on the bench?"

"Of course," Kieran replied. He made his way to the bench.

Nicky leapt up and grabbed their phone, bringing up some meditation music. As the gentle, healing music began to play, they resettled themself on the bench, facing Kieran.

Both of them were sitting cross-legged, and Nicky guided Kieran's hands into the appropriate position for the pose. Right hand facing down, touching the other person's left hand. Left hand facing up, touching the other person's right hand.

"Next," said Nicky, "we gaze into the other person's left or non-dominant eye. That's the receiving eye, the window to the soul. For some reason, though, when I do this exercise, I'm always drawn to the person's right eye."

"My nondominant eye is my right eye," Kieran said.

There was an odd pang and flutter that rustled through Nicky's chest. What a strange synchronicity.

Nicky took a moment to settle in, breathing deeply. In this position, sitting across from Kieran, gazing into his right eye, their hands clasped with his, Nicky felt so close to him. Yet Nicky's heart still hurt. Monday was the first time they had opened up to someone new in nearly two years.

Before beginning the scene, it felt absolutely critical to share everything that was on their heart and mind with him. Even if it was uncomfortable. Vulnerable. Hard.

"There's a couple things that I'd like to share with you, if that's okay," they said after a moment. "Before we start the scene."

"That's fine," said Kieran.

"Is that a hell yes?" asked Nicky.

Kieran smiled. "That's a hell yes."

Nicky took a deep breath.

"The experience that we had on Monday was a big one," they said. "I felt *so* connected to you as you were touching me, as I was touching you. I felt so connected to my own Divine light, and was just radiating pure white energy out of my body into yours. It was the most spiritual experience I'd ever had, and it was truly fifth-dimensional.

"The phrase 'I love you,' kept playing in my mind over and over and over, and I couldn't not say it," Nicky added. "I didn't say it expecting to hear anything back. I said it because I felt it, because not saying it felt out of alignment. But not hearing you say it back was hard."

They felt completely open, exposed, like Kieran might be able to see the rubbed-raw energy in their heart chakra.

But not to speak these emotions into the space tonight felt inauthentic. This scene was different from the others they'd done at this event space. Tonight, the two of them were unmasked. They were dating. They were here as a couple.

And Nicky loved him. It was still new and scary, and Nicky was afraid they were moving too fast and didn't know what to expect because the control games they'd used in other relationships just didn't work here, but Nicky loved Kieran.

It was overwhelming, to be totally honest. And a total mindfuck.

Because Nicky had *so* not seen this coming.

Until January, Kieran just hadn't been on their radar.

At all.

But now that they were here, surrounded by these flickering LED lights, about to do another scene, Nicky wanted to know they weren't alone in this. Because after not hearing 'I love you' the other night, Nicky felt deflated.

Kieran continued looking at them, his energy sincere and open.

"I cherish that you said those words to me," he said softly, squeezing their hands. "And I care for you, and I adore you, and I have so much affection for you. I just want to be sure that when I say those words to you, I mean them. About you. That's challenging since I'm also dating Jade. It doesn't mean it can't happen, though."

There was something just under the surface niggling at Nicky, hearing those words. Nicky hadn't *necessarily* been expecting some grand declaration of love, and they appreciated Kieran's honesty, but there was still some sadness and sorrow.

After a moment, they realized what it was.

"Part of what's been coming up for me, too," they added, "was that you told Sofia that you loved her. You and I have explored more together physically, we've been involved for a longer period of time, and I have a story that our relationship is deeper and more connective.

"How do I reconcile those two things?" they asked. "That you only want to say, 'I love you,' when you mean it and that you said it to Sofia and not me?"

Then, they inhaled sharply, hoping the breath would be medicine for this gaping wound in their chest.

It hurt so much.

"First of all, I agree," Kieran said, still gazing at Nicky. "Our relationship is deeper. And I've been sitting with that, reflecting on that. I felt so much love that night, coming from so many directions. And I think I associated it with Sofia, especially since she and I were kissing during your group scene and we did a massage scene later that night.

"Does that help?" he asked.

Nicky nodded. "Yes, it does. Thank you."

There was still something sticky about the situation, but the gaping wound seemed smaller. It didn't feel like Nicky was hiding anything from Kieran now. That their thoughts and emotions were out, front and center.

And there had been no blame or judgment or accusation.

This truly was a relationship like no other that they'd had, Nicky realized.

"Are you feeling complete?" Kieran asked. "Or is there anything else that you're wanting or needing right now?"

"I'm complete for now," Nicky said. "I'm ready to get started with the scene if you are."

Smiling, Kieran leaned forward and gave Nicky a kiss.

The kiss started out gentle, just a peck on the lips, but then deepened. Kieran pressed his lips to Nicky's, kissed their top lip, and their mouths parted, hungrily, desperately seeking each other.

"Someday," he murmured, "I'd like to kiss every single inch of your body while you're tied down. Just kiss you everywhere, remind you how beautiful I think you are."

Nicky gasped, leaning and arching back as Kieran held them.

With each kiss that he pressed to Nicky's skin, Kieran wove deep energy and intention through it. A benediction, a message, a prayer. No, he might not be able to say the words to Nicky right now, but action and energy spoke louder anyway.

He pulled Nicky's filmy white robe off them, then stood for a moment and admired them, wearing nothing but their white corset; lacy, gray underwear; and thigh-high, black and white, striped socks with little panda faces at the top.

Nicky blushed when they saw he was looking at their socks. "Warm feet increase the likelihood of orgasm," they said.

Leaning forward, he whispered, "I think they're cute."

Flushing even more, Nicky looked away, but they were smiling.

Pretty quickly, the corset and then the underwear came off. Nicky pulled off the corset, unhooking the closures, and Kieran pulled off their underwear, kissing their hips and thighs as he did so.

In the glow of the dim light, and to the sound of some meditative music, Kieran then began tying a face-up Nicky down to the bench using purple nylon rope.

Before he tied each part of them, he kissed them. He kissed their thighs, caressing them softly. Their knees, their shins. He even tried to tickle their feet through their socks.

"I'm not very ticklish," Nicky said.

"Very well," Kieran murmured in reply.

Then he began securing their torso and arms. Their arms were pinned down near their sides, and he began kissing their stomach, their chest, their shoulders.

Soon, Nicky was fully tied down to the bench, their legs spread apart, and they could move very little. It was a strange sensation this time, different from the other bondage scenes that they had done. They didn't feel grounded in quite the same way, though the ropes around their body did feel nice.

Kieran continued touching them, massaging them now, and Nicky shivered. Whether it was from cold or delight, they couldn't tell. His hands and fingers moved lithely across their form, as though Nicky were a clarinet, and Kieran was the musician. They began moaning, and their back arched slightly, their ribs and torso straining against the ropes.

The next thing they knew, they felt a soft, sudden vibration on their clit and pussy. It moved slightly, in little circles, and Nicky's moans became louder. They didn't know how long Kieran was touching them, but the vibration became greater, the need to orgasm more insistent.

Then, finally, the vibrations were so intense that Nicky was screaming louder than they ever had. It felt like their clit was alive with electric wires, and their body was moving uncontrollably.

Energetically, it felt like a push. Nicky could tell they weren't fully present, and there was something lodged in their heart, their gut. In many ways, this felt like the scene in January, and in many ways it wasn't.

Yes, they screamed and cried and came and had a powerful release, but the energetics that had been present on Monday weren't present now. The orgasm felt empty, devoid of real meaning or the real pleasure and presence that they'd experienced before.

Nicky wanted to keep reaching—recreate what had happened just earlier that week. Maybe if the vibrations were more intense, or if Kieran touched them directly... but something was off. They weren't sure if they wanted to continue.

"Can you stop the vibrator, please?" Nicky asked.

Without the stimulation, Nicky's head cleared just enough. Their breathing began to lengthen.

"You've been tied up for about forty-five minutes. How are you doing?" Kieran asked.

Nicky flexed their wrists, their fingers. They felt funny.

"My fingers are slightly tingly."

Immediately, Kieran began loosening the rope around Nicky, starting with their wrists and arms. He continued untying the rest of them until they could move freely, then began coiling up the rope. Next he brought over an unopened bottle of water.

"Drink this," he said.

Nicky obliged, sitting up and taking a few sips of water. "Thank you."

"Of course."

After a few minutes, Nicky stood up, shivering yet again. "I don't think I'm in the space to do any impact tonight."

"That's okay. I suspected as much."

Kieran began packing up his things while Nicky changed into comfy clothes—flannel pajama pants, the same t-shirt as earlier, and a sweater. They grabbed Ollie and held him to their chest, sitting on the floor as they watched Kieran cleaning the equipment. He sprayed the bench and the rig with cleaner, slid on his athletic pants before taking off his kilt, and then with a paper towel, wiped away the cleaner.

* * *

Once the two of them reached Nicky's apartment, they sat on the couch and put on some animated movie. *Moana*, perhaps. Both of them were so exhausted that what was playing on the screen in front of them barely mattered. Nicky curled into Kieran, laying their head on his lap. He played with their hair, continuing to run Reiki through them as they wound down from the scene.

Finally, Nicky could barely keep their eyes open.

"Let's get ready for bed," Kieran suggested. "Brush our teeth."

Sleepily, Nicky nodded. Tonight, the two of them brushed their teeth in silence and then kissed goodnight.

After they'd each retired to their separate bedrooms for the evening, Nicky realized why tonight's orgasm scene had felt so different.

They hadn't been open. They hadn't surrendered like they had so many other times. They had closed their heart, just a little bit, because they were so afraid of being hurt.

Whatever this was with Kieran, Nicky wanted it. They wanted all of him, all of it, everything. It felt so immense.

How could Nicky possibly have sex with Kieran if he didn't love them? Intercourse wasn't just something to do for fun. For the longest time, Nicky had wanted it to be this deeply bonding, soul-merging, pressurizing, catalyzing experience that cracked them open beyond what they could even imagine or fathom. To laugh, to cry, to be in complete Divine oneness.

Here, with Kieran, Nicky could finally create that reality. Given enough time, Nicky knew they *would* experience deeper healing, transformation, and growth than ever before.

And, Nicky suspected, deeper love.

Nicky was grateful that the fan was on to block some of the noise, and that Kieran was a heavy sleeper. Because as they laid there in bed, rather than close their eyes and sleep, Nicky cried and cried and cried.

Chapter Twenty-Three

In the two weeks that followed, Nicky felt their chest and back seize up. They felt more tightness throughout their body. They were resistant, less willing to engage with Kieran. He'd explained it carefully, and honestly, but it still hurt that he'd said 'I love you' to Sofia and not to them.

The two of them still spent time together, but Nicky didn't know how to process their emotions around the entire situation. Did Kieran love Jade? Would he ever be able to love Nicky? Did him dating Jade mean that he'd only say those words *if* he was no longer with Jade? Should Nicky have sex with Kieran since they loved him, even though he hadn't said it back?

These questions cycled through Nicky's brain almost on repeat, and it took conscious effort for them to pull their mind away from the anxiety-inducing thoughts.

"You sound upset and disappointed," said Bailey, when Nicky was sharing about their scene with Kieran just a few days after it happened.

"Yeah, I am. I mean, I'm glad we had the conversation, and it helped give me clarity, but I definitely still feel less connected to him. My entire body tenses just thinking about our last scene together."

"Have you tried yoga? Epsom salt baths?" Bailey asked, frowning.

"Both," Nicky said ruefully. "I'm not sure what it's going to take to melt the resistance here. Maybe it's just better if Kieran and I have something casual."

But even as they said it, Nicky knew that something casual with Kieran was impossible. Ever since the night they kissed, their gut had told them that this was something big, something massive. Something of the magnitude that Nicky could barely even fathom.

If you go through with this, you can't go back, a ghostly whisper echoed.

If only they had listened and taken their authentic self's guidance seriously, Nicky thought glumly, then maybe they would have been spared some of the ache and frustration they were experiencing now.

"I'm confident you'll move through this," Bailey said. "Give it time. Let it marinate in the background. Talk to your guides."

But Nicky was skeptical. Even with meditating, yoga, and their near-daily run, the anxious thoughts continued cycling through their mind. Was it worthwhile continuing to invest in their relationship with Kieran? Maybe it was better to end it. Maybe it was better to take a break. Nicky had recently emailed Paco and let him know they'd be blocking his email address and unfriending him on Facebook, so if Nicky wasn't dating Kieran, they'd be truly unattached.

But when Nicky laid in bed at night, and was really honest with themself, they *knew* that avoiding a relationship with Kieran wasn't going to make them happy. Nicky also realized, though, that having intercourse with Kieran before he told Nicky he loved them would threaten their emotional safety.

Nicky needed certainty. If that meant that they never had sex with Kieran, then as physically frustrating as that might be, that's what they would choose.

* * *

"Are you okay, *bella?*" Nicky's mom, Donna, asked over the phone. It was nearly two weeks after Nicky's last scene with Kieran. "You sound sad."

Nicky bristled a bit at '*bella*,' but took a deep breath. It was exhausting correcting their mom every single time she misgendered them.

"Mom, can you please use gender-neutral pet names in English?" Nicky asked, for what seemed like the hundredth time. "I'm your child, not your daughter."

"Oh, right. Sorry. But how are you doing, really?"

They debated for a moment, wondering whether or not to share. "It's Kieran. The new guy I'm dating. I told you about him last time. He's poly, like me, and we met about two years ago when we were volunteering for an event together."

"But the last time we talked, it seemed like it was going really well between you two," Donna said.

Nicky couldn't help it. The tears started rolling down their cheeks. "It was," Nicky said. "And I still like him, and I still enjoy spending time with him… it's just…"

Their breathing was shaky. Nicky didn't want to hold the phone up to their ear, but their earbuds were in the other room. They compromised, putting the phone on speaker and laying it on their lap. A couple tears splashed onto the screen. Thank God for waterproof phone cases.

"Do you want me to come up?" Donna asked. "Do you want to talk about this in person?"

Nicky hated being an inconvenience. They hated feeling like they were a burden to their mom, Bailey, or even Emma. Honestly, Nicky didn't understand why they couldn't just navigate this Kieran thing by themself. *I'm making too big of a deal about it. I'm being too sensitive about it*, Nicky told themself.

They didn't say anything for a minute or so.

"I don't want to be an inconvenience," Nicky said between their tears. "It's an hour either way, and it's already afternoon. You hate driving once it's dark."

"You're not an inconvenience, Nicky. If you ever become a parent someday, you'll understand. I would do practically anything to make sure you and your sister feel happy, healthy, and safe. That's all I want for you.

"Do you want me to come up to Madison?" she repeated.

"Yes, please," Nicky sobbed. They wiped at their nose with the back of their wrist.

"Okay, I'll leave in just a few minutes. I'll be there in a little more than an hour."

The two of them said goodbye and hung up. Then, tossing their phone onto the coffee table, Nicky sat on the couch with their knees tucked into their chest and continued to breathe and cry.

Their mom arrived just when she said she would, rapping on the window outside. Nicky bounded down to the main door and let her in. Unsurprisingly, she carried a small cooler and a few Styrofoam containers.

"I brought lunch. I figured you might not have eaten yet, so I stopped at the nearby brewpub and got a salmon burger and sweet potato fries. I also packed some lasagna that I made the other night and some water bottles."

Nicky smiled. "Thanks, Mom."

Once Donna had finished putting away the extra items in the fridge, she joined Nicky in the living room, sitting on the loveseat as Nicky ate from the couch. Until Nicky began digging into the salmon burger, they hadn't realized how hungry they were. The burger and fries were gone in a few minutes.

"Tell me what's going on," Donna said at last. "You sounded really upset on the phone. You said it was about Kieran—this new guy that you've been dating. What's wrong?"

Immediately, tears started rolling down Nicky's cheeks again. "I told him I loved him," they said, "and he didn't say it back."

"Oh, sweetie," Nicky's mom said. "I'm so sorry."

"It's okay," they replied, brushing away their tears. "I just—I haven't felt that way about anyone new since I was dating Arthur and Sofia right before the pandemic, and it was hard being that vulnerable with him. He and I talked about it a week afterward, and he was very transparent, very honest."

"What did he say?"

Nicky hesitated. Their mom had grown a lot over the past few years and had done her best to be accepting of Nicky and their lifestyle, but polyamory was something that was challenging for her to grasp.

"He said he didn't want to say he loved me unless he meant it. Since he's dating someone else, I don't know if he can even feel that way about me while he's dating her. And I realized the other day that I need him to say he loves me before we have intercourse."

Donna looked at Nicky carefully. "Are you planning to talk to him about this?"

"Yeah, I was planning to message him later this afternoon to see if he could come over tomorrow afternoon. He'll be in Madison anyway, so he probably can."

"Do you want to practice what you'll say to him?" Donna asked. "I can pretend to be him, just listen so you can get it all out."

It was a long moment before Nicky nodded, brushing another tear from their eye. "Yes, I think that would be helpful."

"Where do you want me to sit?"

"Where you are is fine," said Nicky.

Then, taking a deep breath, Nicky looked at their mom and imagined that Kieran was sitting in front of them, dug into the raw achiness of their heart and pulled out all the words, all the thoughts they'd had over the past two weeks.

How they needed him to say that he loved them before they could have intercourse. That doing it any other way didn't feel emotionally safe to them. How, for them, mutual love was a prerequisite to greater intimacy. How they'd rushed sex in the past and it had ruined a couple of their relationships. How they wished they could spend their weekends with him.

There were a couple times where Nicky almost censored themself, knowing this was their mom. Maybe they shouldn't allude to the kink scene they'd done, or talk about the sexual experience. But Nicky knew the more they poured out, the more they emptied themself now, the easier it would be tomorrow.

With the stopper released, Nicky kept sharing and crying, all the while being present with the ache in their heart that just hadn't gone away.

How they weren't sure if they wanted to have sex with him unless the two of them were sexually monogamous. How part of them thought they might need him to pick between them and Jade. How they wanted to leap off the edge with him, but they needed him to be there on the ledge with them, too.

At last, Nicky's tears began to slow, the heaviness in their chest was lighter, and their words trickled off. They wrapped their arms around their knees.

Nicky's mom smiled. "That was really great, Nicky," she said. "Just be careful that whatever you say to him doesn't come across as an ultimatum."

"Thanks for listening, Mom," Nicky said. "I really needed that."

Their heart felt so much more open, cleared out, emptied. At least if they were going to sob this much tomorrow, they knew what to expect.

Smiling, Donna leaned over and gave Nicky a hug. "You're such a smart girl, Nicky. I know you'll do great tomorrow."

Nicky grimaced. "Thanks, Mom."

"Is there anything else I can do? Do you want to go out for ice cream? My treat."

Silent for a moment, Nicky looked at their mom. She seemed hopeful, eager. It had been awhile since she'd seen Nicky, and they hadn't spent this kind of time together since Nicky was last living with her in Illinois—probably four months ago now.

"Sure, we can do that."

Shrugging into their coat, snagging their keys, and grabbing their mask, Nicky followed their mom out the door into the bright March sunshine.

* * *

When Nicky finally messaged Kieran, he responded quickly. Yes, he could come over tomorrow afternoon and the two of them could talk. It would probably be somewhere around three or four o'clock, but he'd let Nicky know for sure when he was in Madison.

The next morning inched by. Even after going for a run, stretching, and taking an Epsom salt bath (Nicky's left Achilles tendon was tender), it was still barely noon. The dishes that were stacked on the counter seemed overwhelming, but Nicky had no way to make themself lunch unless they washed some of them. So, Nicky put on a podcast and washed most of the dishes before making a hearty tofu scramble. After that, Nicky played some of their favorite music and kept cleaning. First the living room. Then their bedroom. Then the guest bedroom. Then the bathroom.

Finally, it was close to three. Nicky showered and changed their clothes and sat themself on the couch, just like they had yesterday. They pinched the skin on their wrist. Caught themself and pressed their hands tightly into each other and started breathing.

This was going to *suck*. Even with the roleplay yesterday, they were dreading this conversation. This might be the end.

After all, how could Nicky jump off the ledge, be willing to dive deep, submit, and surrender if they didn't feel safe? And what if what they needed to feel safe was different than what *he* needed to feel safe?

Even just thinking about this conversation, Nicky wanted to run to the bedroom, pull the covers over their head, and hide. Was this *really* the best time to have this conversation? Should they postpone it? They paused and breathed, even though their body was screaming at them to run, to disappear. To pretend this day had ended and just move to the next one.

"I'm yellow, and I'm having a trauma response," Nicky said aloud. "I'm scared that Kieran is going to laugh at me. I'm afraid he's going to say he doesn't value me and this relationship more than the other one he has."

Taking a deep breath, Nicky inhaled and exhaled. Let go and release. After a few rounds of breath, they had calmed down enough that they were able to grab their phone, put on a guided meditation, and began listening to it through their earbuds. Continuing to breathe, inhale and exhale.

Bring, bring! Bring, bring! Both a few seconds and a few hours later, Nicky was jolted from the meditation; they'd been drifting. When they looked at the screen, they saw it was Kieran. Nicky accepted the call.

"Hey, I'm here," he said. "You must not have heard me knocking. Or gotten my text."

"Nope," Nicky said. "I was meditating. I'll come let you in. See you in a sec."

They ended the call, took off their headset, stood up, and unlocked the door. Nicky bounded down the few steps to the front door of the apartment building and pushed it open. And there was Kieran, a mask covering his face, sunglasses covering his eyes. He took off his sunglasses.

"May I give you a hug?" Nicky asked.

Kieran nodded, and his eyes crinkled, sparkling. Nicky leaned in and wrapped their arms tightly around him, pulling him into them. Comforting, strong, grounding. Nicky imagined their nervous energy was sinking through their body, through their feet, into the floor. After a moment, they pulled back to look at Kieran.

"Shall we go inside?" he asked. Nicky nodded, and holding Kieran's hand led him up the steps into their apartment.

The two of them sat down, Kieran on the loveseat and Nicky on the couch, just like Nicky had roleplayed with their mom the day before. Kieran removed his mask. Even though today's conversation would be different, Nicky felt relieved knowing that the energetic setup was the same. He was over there, and Nicky was here. It eliminated one variable, at least.

"I'm nervous to have this conversation with you," Nicky shared, folding their hands together. Without his mask, Kieran's smile was easier to identify. His energy was full of peace and calm, white light. Even so, and even though they'd thoughtfully curated their outfit of corduroy jeggings, fuzzy socks, and a hoodie to add to their comfort, Nicky felt vulnerable, raw, exposed.

Must be residual from yesterday, Nicky thought wryly.

"May I hold your hand?" Kieran asked. Nicky shook their head and tucked their arms into themself.

A pause, then, "Is it alright if I just get into it?"

Kieran nodded. "Sure."

Nicky took a deep breath, forced themself to place their feet on the floor and their hands on their knees. Curling into a ball would just make Nicky feel more uncomfortable, more likely to give into their trauma response.

"First of all, thanks for being willing to come over for a little bit," Nicky said. "I appreciate being able to have this conversation with you in person."

"Of course." A kind smile.

Looking into Kieran's eyes, Nicky allowed themself to lean in. Somehow, in being present with his smile, Nicky just knew what to say, and their nerves abated.

At least somewhat.

"I've been sitting with what you said the other night, when we were at the kink event space and did our final scene there. I've also been sitting with what I want and need from this relationship to feel safe, especially when it comes to certain aspects of physical intimacy.

"We haven't had intercourse yet. And it seems like you're onboard with us having sex, and I know you're attracted to me, and I'm attracted to you. But for me, it's important to be mutually in love with someone before I have intercourse with them for the first time. If I haven't been, I've regretted it. Maybe I thought I was in love, or I thought it was okay to do it anyway, but I always ended up wishing I'd waited. It's part of me being demisexual," Nicky added. "That emotional connection is such an important prerequisite."

Kieran just continued smiling, listening.

It was amazing how Nicky felt so seen and understood, just by looking him in the eye. Honestly, it was unnerving.

"For me, sex is this really intimate thing. Or, at least, I want it to be. This merging of souls that just blinds me with ecstasy and joy and connection. That expression of love is such a vulnerable one... it requires so much trust to let someone see me that way, to open so fully to someone, and if I—if I do that with you, I need to know that you're there with me. That we're at the same spot. That we're willing to jump off the ledge together. I might have a really big emotional release, and I might cry, so I need to trust that you'll hold me and be there with me, in the trenches.

"That's what I need to feel safe having sex with you," Nicky said simply.

The smile on Kieran's face hadn't dimmed at all; if anything, it had only grown brighter, more luminous. That somehow, Nicky's sharing had awoken something in him, connected to some deeper part of him that Nicky didn't yet know and understand.

But still, he said nothing, waiting for Nicky to continue.

"When we were at the kink space last week, what I heard and understood is that you don't want to say you love me unless you're absolutely certain that's how you feel about me. That those feelings aren't coming from someone else. And, since you're in another relationship, that makes things complex."

Kieran nodded. "Yep, that's right."

"What I inferred is that as long as you're dating Jade, you won't tell me that you love me. Or, I shouldn't expect you to say that to me."

As Nicky expressed the last part, it felt like someone was twisting the stiletto icicle that had wedged itself into Nicky's heart during their last scene with Kieran. Nicky shivered, and gripped their arms around themself.

This was torture. Pure torture. And not in a fun, kinky way. Nicky was standing on the edge, wondering if Kieran would join them, or if he might push them off.

"No," Kieran said. "That's not what I meant."

Nicky looked up. A big part of them still just wanted to curl into the couch, put their head down, and disappear entirely.

Instead, they held Kieran's gaze.

"It's not?" they said.

"No, it's not," he replied, shaking his head. "When I tell you I love you, I want it to be because of my relationship with *you*. I don't want my feelings from any other relationship to influence me saying those words to you. It doesn't mean I can't or won't get there with you, even if I'm dating other people at the same time—just that right now, I'm not."

The demands and ultimatums that had been running through Nicky's head quieted. They dissolved like sugar in water. They were irrelevant.

"Oh," Nicky said. "Okay."

To be honest, they felt just a *bit* foolish. Like they'd made a big deal out of something that they could have just cleared up by asking Kieran, *Hey, what did you mean by that?*

Leaning in with curiosity really *did* solve a lot of issues.

"May I reflect back what I'm hearing?" Kieran asked.

"Yeah, that's fine," Nicky said, but it came out more like a mumble.

Regardless, Kieran must have heard what Nicky said. "I'm hearing that you haven't always honored your boundaries when it comes to sex, and you want to do it differently in our relationship," he said. "Specifically, you want to wait to have intercourse until after I've told you I love you."

A part of Nicky felt bad for saying so, felt bad that they needed that. After all, so many people—Sofia, for example—could just go out and have sex on the third date and it was okay. Or on the first date.

But Nicky needed more than that.

"Yes, that's right," Nicky said quietly, staring at their knees.

"You are worth waiting for," Kieran said simply. "I want your hell yes."

When Nicky looked up, they saw Kieran was looking at them with such affection, it stunned them. Knocked their breath out of them. *Trust your gut*, Nicky's authentic self was saying. *Trust Kieran.*

"Thank you," Nicky said, wiping at their eyes. They'd begun to sting a little bit. Allergies probably.

"I mean it," Kieran said, still smiling. "Your consent is sexy. When you honor yourself and your boundaries, that's sexy."

None of Nicky's past partners had ever expressed something quite like that. Had never told them that they were worth waiting for. Except for Arthur, Nicky's past partners had usually expressed impatience and frustration at their need to move slowly in relationships.

"You know, Kieran, when you say those things to me, I only half believe you," Nicky murmured.

His smile, if possible, grew wider and gentler. "That's okay."

The two of them continued gazing at each other for several long moments before Nicky finally scooted over on the couch and patted the spot next to them. Kieran stood up from the loveseat and sat next to Nicky on the sofa.

"May I wrap my arm around you?" he asked.

Nicky nodded, and Kieran wound his one hand around their waist, pulling them into him. He smelled like soap and musk, and Nicky leaned in and buried themself in his chest.

"Well, that was a lot easier than I thought it would be," Nicky said dramatically, throwing their hands in the air. "I did a dress rehearsal with my mom yesterday, and I was *sobbing*. The center of my chest felt so raw. Today, it was so easy. So simple. Not complicated at all."

Chuckling softly, Kieran held Nicky even closer. "That's understandable," he said. "From what you've shared about your past relationships, you were used to feeling attacked."

"Feeling attacked," Nicky echoed. "I suppose so. I think it's my anxious attachment style, too. My tendency is to assume the worst, to catastrophize. You didn't say you loved me, so it's the end of the world as I know it."

"You know, there's no destination in our relationship. There's no place that we have to get to or go," Kieran said. "There's nothing we have to do. We get to choose and create our relationship as it feels most joyful to us. And if that doesn't include intercourse, that's okay."

What Kieran was saying was sweet, yet Nicky felt exasperated.

"It's just—my automatic response is to try and control because I need certain things to feel emotionally safe, and I want to have sex with you and feel like we're both in it. We're not there, and that's okay, but it makes things emotionally challenging right now."

Kieran paused, but when he spoke, Nicky could hear the amusement and care in his voice. "From my perspective, we're moving toward a committed relationship. But you like to rush things—build the whole castle in a week—and that's not how things work."

That was an astute observation.

Maybe Kieran knew them better than Nicky realized.

"I feel both *so* called out and *so* seen by that statement," Nicky said.

No, Kieran hadn't said 'I love you,' but what he had just shared was more profound. He knew and understood Nicky's patterns, and he still wanted to be with them.

More than that, Kieran felt the two of them were creating a committed relationship. That they were building something deep, meaningful, lasting. He *was* in this with Nicky. Maybe not in the way that they wanted right now, but in some way.

"You really feel like we're moving toward a committed relationship?" Nicky said, turning toward him.

Kieran nodded.

Nicky gazed at him for a few minutes, just taking him in. Kieran's reddish hair glinted gold with the sunlight behind him, and his smile kept widening. Nicky felt some of the white light energy from a few weeks ago creep in, slowly at first, then faster. It soothed their energy field and made their body feel larger, lighter, more expanded.

They wanted to be closer to him, more connected to him. The physical distance separating them was too much, too great.

"Is it alright if I straddle you?" Nicky asked.

Kieran grinned. "Of course."

Climbing over him, Nicky placed one knee on either side of his lap, sitting on their butt. They stroked his hair, his face, his beard. Then, in one gentle motion, they leaned forward and kissed him. Sweetly, gently, purely.

That kiss illuminated more joy, more bliss, more peace than Nicky had ever felt before. Even more than that one Monday a few weeks ago. Nicky's entire body was buzzing, and they felt like they were one with Kieran's energy body, like no physical space separated the two of them. Like their souls were dancing, flowing into and around each other, merging in cosmic prayer.

Nicky was completely present, completely open, completely here. The two of them were moving toward a committed relationship. It was okay to savor this moment, this space where they both were right now.

As Kieran said, they didn't have to get anywhere. There was no predetermined destination, just a winding road ahead of them, with an infinite number of branches. The two of them got to choose where they went and when.

After several long minutes, Nicky broke the embrace, gazing at Kieran once more.

"I love you," they said.

"I adore you," Kieran replied.

And in that moment, that was enough.

Notes

Chapter Two

sex and relationship coaching, page 31: I currently offer private sessions to a limited number of individuals, couples, and moresomes who want to create fulfilling, spiritually-driven kink and BDSM dynamics and relationships by stretching their edges, communicating more thoughtfully, and healing related trauma (e.g., sexual trauma, attachment trauma). Learn more and apply at empowerederotic.com/private-coaching.

Chapter Four

a cross-legged position, page 54: The Pose of Recognition in *Urban Tantra: Conscious Sexuality for the Twenty-First Century* by Barbara Carellas. Over the past several decades, Carellas has worked as a gender-inclusive, kink-affirming neotantra practitioner, and this book has been a powerful foundation for my own journey into sacred sexuality. I often recommend this book to my private clients. Learn more about Barbara's offerings and her approach at barbaracarellas.com.

into another pose, page 54: The Heart Connection as outlined in Barbara Carellas' *Urban Tantra*. I highly recommend this book for anyone who wants to become more connected to their own energy body and sexuality, whether or not they're partnered.

Chapter Eight

what the design was, page 96: the Flower of Life, a design associated with metaphysics and sacred geometry. The flower of life is said to be the origin of all life and is similar to the shape of a blastocyst, which is the shape an embryo takes immediately before cells begin to differentiate. In energy healing, the Flower of Life is a powerful shape, and it's often used as the outline for crystal grids.

Traffic Light Trauma Framework™, page 98: a framework and series of protocols developed in late 2019 by the author, Kelly Noel Zeva. Although this framework has its roots in the traffic-light safeword system commonly used in kink, the Traffic Light Trauma Framework™ is used during coaching and healing sessions to support clients with going deeper. This framework includes a series of protocols and how to support a client with rebalancing their nervous system once they've had a trauma response. I teach this system in my practitioner training programs, including Zeva System™ Levels 1 and 2. To learn more and join the program's waitlist, visit empowerederotic.com/zeva-system.

Chapter Nine

Sexual Healing Challenge, page 115 Originally a series of livestreams over Facebook, our team recorded a version of the challenge in December 2020 that's currently available for purchase. The program includes my signature 5-Day Sexual Trauma Healing framework and several bonuses, including a past life regression. Learn more at empowerederotic.com/sexual-healing-challenge.

Chapter Eleven

group program, page 137: This group program, Zeva System™ Level 1, was originally led from September 2020 through February 2021, and helped students identify, unravel, and heal their body's trauma patterns around sexuality, money, and relationships. Since then, some of the content has been modified to make this a practitioner training program. Learn more and join the waitlist at empowederotic.com/zeva-system.

Chapter Twelve

Conscious Kink Bootcamp, page 152: a nine-day workshop series that features my signature five-day "BDSM for Beginners" framework. This framework covers consent, scene negotiation, healing through kink, crafting an authentic scene, and aftercare. The workshop series ends with topical masterclasses on specific kink topics, including bondage, D/s, pain play, and ageplay. Our team occasionally leads this workshop series live; however, lifetime access to a recorded version of the masterclass series is currently available for purchase. Learn more at empowederotic.com/ckb.

Chapter Thirteen

Erotically Empowered Limit List™, page 158: a first-of-its-kind trauma-sensitive BDSM limits checklist that I developed in October 2020. I was tired of limit lists that weren't beginner-friendly and weren't designed for people who had experienced (and were still healing from) physical, sexual, or psychological abuse or violence. Whether you're new to BDSM or a veteran kinkster, this tool will help you to be more mindful as you negotiate your play and build your dynamics. Learn more at empowederotic.com/limit-list.

Chapter Fifteen

Mildest to Wildest, page 186: a negotiation icebreaker game made popular by sex educator Reid Mihalko. Reid credits the icebreaker games of the Pu'uhonua community in Escondido, California, and Monique Darling, which gave birth to Mildest to Wildest. During 2020 and early 2021, Reid co-facilitated several virtual play parties with Crista Reid of Permission Productions, and I was privileged to attend two of those events in 2020. Learn more about Reid's work at reid-aboutsex.com.

Chapter Twenty-Two

the pose, page 258: the Pose of Recognition, as outlined in Barbara Carellas' book *Urban Tantra*. Learn more about Carellas' gender-inclusive and kink-affirming approach to neotantra at barbaracarellas.com.

Glossary

abuse: a non-consensual form of physical, emotional, psychological, or sexual violence toward oneself or another living being.

aftercare: the care a person gives or receives after a scene to help a person integrate. Aftercare helps the body and nervous system rebalance and lessens the impact of top drop or sub drop. Aftercare may include water, food, cuddling, sexual play, or other items and activities that make the person feel cared for.

ageplay: a form of consensual kinky play where adults (people 18+) will take on mental, emotional, and physical characteristics of someone who is younger or older than their current biological age. Most commonly, ageplayers "regress," and do things mainstream society associates with childhood such as wearing onesies or comfy pajamas, watching animated movies, or drinking juice boxes. Ageplayers who regress are often divided into Littles (2-11) and Middles (12-17).

anxious attachment: one of the three types of insecure attachment. Roughly 25% percent of adults have this attachment style. For people with anxious attachment, they tend to assume the worst in relationships and often catastrophize. They tend to view relationships as being unstable and fragile. People with anxious attachment also seek closeness with their partners, are sensitive to criticism, and respond negatively to emotional unavailability. When their attachment system has been activated, a person with anxious attachment may respond with blame and criticism, withdrawing, seeking reassurance, or emotional manipulation. However, when they feel secure in their relationship, these people tend to make devoted partners, and may be better at anticipating their partner's needs.

anxious avoidant attachment: also known as 'fearful avoidant' or 'disorganized,' roughly 5% of adults have this attachment style. For people with anxious avoidant attachment, they oscillate between pushing away their partner because they are afraid of being too close (avoidant) and seeking reassurance about the stability and committedness of their relationship with their partner (anxious). Ultimately, this attachment style is a blend of *anxious attachment* and *dismissive avoidant.*

attachment style: how a person connects with others in relationships. A person's attachment style is largely formed during infancy and childhood, but it can change over time in response to therapy, personal growth and development, supportive relationships, or toxic relationships. Typically, there are four kinds of attachment styles that exist: secure, anxious, dismissive avoidant, and anxious avoidant. However, it's often more helpful to think of a person's attachment style as having a certain level of anxiety and avoidance, which could be plotted on a two-dimensional coordinate plane.

authentic self: the part of a person's consciousness that exists beyond pain and trauma. Depending on your psychological, spiritual, and religious beliefs, you may also refer to this part as your superego, soul, Divine self, or ideal self. Even while having a trauma response, it is often possible to remain partially connected to your authentic self. Doing so can reduce the length and severity of dissociation, avoidance, and other trauma responses.

BDSM: acronym that actually includes three shorter acronyms: B&D (bondage and discipline), D/s (dominance and submission), and S&M (sadism and masochism). Multiple facets of BDSM may be present within a single scene.

blue (safe word): In the context of a kink scene, this means, "We can keep playing, and I'm done with that particular toy or that kind of touch." Definition courtesy of the real-life Kieran.

bottom: a person who is on the receiving end of the scene. Just because a person is a bottom for a scene does not mean that they are a submissive. Being a bottom is scene-dependent.

chakra: the Sanskrit word for "wheel," this word refers to key energy centers within the body that spin and rotate like discs. Most sources refer only to the seven primary chakras that show up along the spinal column: root, sacral, solar plexus, heart, throat, third eye, and crown. However, other chakras do exist both in a person's body and in their auric field.

conscious kink: a form of kink/BDSM where full-bodied consent, presence, and showing up as a spiritually empowered being are valued. Often, conscious kink considers this question: "What can we do with kink beyond having fun and feeling good? What deeper healing or growth can this facilitate?"

consensual non-monogamy: a relationship style where all parties involved have consented to a non-monogamous dynamic and adhere to mutual agreements set forth by relationship members. Consensual non-monogamy (CNM) is in direct contrast to cheating, which is done without the awareness, agreement, or consent of at least one party who is part of the relationship. CNM is an umbrella term that includes polyamory, swinging, open relationships, and other similar relationship styles.

consent: a full-bodied *yes* to any activities taking place or language being used. A person cannot give consent if they are under the influence of substances, are already sexually aroused, are already in subspace, are being persuaded or coerced, or are having a trauma response. There are two kinds of consent: enthusiastic consent ("hell yes") and amicable consent ("sure, sounds good"). In general, I advocate seeking enthusiastic consent as often as possible, especially if one or more people are untangling and healing past trauma.

D/s: Dominance and submission. The "D" is capitalized to show authority in the relationship, and the "s" is lower-case to show the surrender of power. In healthy kink relationships, the D/s dynamic is always consensually negotiated and can be reevaluated, as necessary.

DDlg: Daddy Dom, little girl. The most common and fetishized form of a Caregiver and little dynamic; the Caregiver and little dynamic can have people of any gender in either role. DDlg is often a power dynamic, incorporating elements of D/s. Rather than instructing through harsh punishment, Daddies/Mommies/Caregivers guide and discipline their littles in ways that support their growth and development as people. It is often a softer, more nurturing dynamic; however, it doesn't mean that the little experiences no consequences for misbehavior.

demisexual: a person who needs a strong emotional connection with a person before they can experience sexual attraction for them. (Note: sexual attraction is different than arousal.) Demisexual people often only experience sexual attraction to people they know very well, such as intimate friends. They may also take longer to be sexually intimate with prospective partners. Some demisexual people rarely experience sexual attraction; others experience it more frequently. Like any group of humans, not everyone is the same, and many people experience their demisexuality in different ways.

dismissive avoidant: one of the three insecure attachment styles. Roughly 20% of adults have a dismissive avoidant attachment style. A person who has dismissive avoidant attachment will push away their partner when their attachment system has been activated. If they feel too much closeness in the relationship, they may start to disengage with the person they care about by stonewalling, passive aggressive behavior, condescension, or frustration. People with a dismissive avoidant attachment style need plenty of space to be independent; if they feel like they're being controlled, or their autonomy is being threatened, it will activate their attachment system.

dungeon monitor (DM): a person who is trained to ensure that kinky play at an event remains safe, sane, and consensual. Many kink spaces require that any especially risky play must receive the sign-off of a DM before it can occur.

dynamic: refers to the relationship between two or more kinksters. Common dynamics in kink/BDSM include D/s, DDlg, M/s, and Owner/pet. Each of these dynamics is also defined in this glossary.

electric play: also known as electro play. A form of consensual kinky play where the top runs an electric current through themself or through metal items into the bottom's body. In many spaces, electric play is considered a form of edge play and should only be done with proper training or supervision of an experienced top.

emotional labor: any form of labor, work, or effort that requires presence and emotional capacity. For example, if a friend shares about challenging things that are going on in their life, the person listening and offering support is providing a form of emotional labor. Emotional labor can also involve educating non-oppressed people. For example, queer folx provide emotional labor any time they educate non-queer people about sexual orientation, queerphobia, what it's like to be a queer person, or how to be a better LGBTQ+ ally. While there is going to be some emotional labor that people provide in relationships, it should ideally never feel too unbalanced.

energy play: a form of play where energy healing (e.g., *Reiki*), mindful breathing, and/or *neotantra* are incorporated into *conscious kink* scenes (e.g., impact, bondage) to heighten the emotional and erotic experience, and to deepen healing.

ethical non-monogamy: see *consensual non-monogamy.*

FetLife: a social networking site for kinksters. FetLife lists a number of events, including workshops, play parties, and conferences. It also has numerous groups and forums. As such, FetLife is a great place to learn about your kinks and to connect with other kinky people. It's common to add people on FetLife after meeting them in person at a *munch, slosh,* workshop, conference, or *play party.*

green (safe word): "Keep going." Within kink, green means, "I'm good to keep playing at this intensity. I'm feeling good, I'm feeling safe." If you're playing with someone new, it can be helpful to check in with them even when you know they're green so that you both get comfortable using safe words.

impact (play): a form of kinky play where the top hits the bottom with part of their body or an implement. Spanking, flogging, paddling, and caning are all common forms of impact play.

kink: an umbrella term for play that includes BDSM, fetishes, voyeurism, and exhibitionism. In mainstream culture, people often associate kink and BDSM with sex; however, it is not necessary to include any form of sexual play in a kinky scene, and many people don't. *Asexual kinksters are valid.*

limit list: a document or spreadsheet that details the kinksters' limits, or what they will and won't do and how much they enjoy certain activities. Exchanging limit lists, or filling them out together, is common when players transition to an ongoing dynamic.

M/s: A *consensual* Mistress/Mixtress/Master and slave dynamic; people of any gender can be in either role. This kind of relationship is negotiated justly, without pressure, manipulation, or coercion, and both parties enter into the relationship with full knowledge and awareness of what they're agreeing to. Both parties also have ways to communicate what's not working and ways to modify/end the relationship, if necessary. Often, the Mistress/Mixtress/Master and slave will have had a trial or training period, or a preexisting D/s dynamic before becoming entering an M/s dynamic. M/s relationships often involve formal agreements or contracts (not legally binding), or a collaring ceremony, where the slave (submissive) will earn and wear a piece of jewelry or brand that marks them as property of the Mistress/Mixtress/Master (Dominant). In some cases, a slave will choose to give up aspects of their vanilla life in order to serve their Mistress/Mixtress/Master more fully and consistently.

meta: short for metamour. My metas are any other partners that my partner(s) have with whom I'm not involved. For example, at the beginning of the novel, Ricky is Nicky's meta because they're both dating Sofia, but Nicky isn't involved with Ricky. Likewise, Arthur is Sofia's meta because she's dating Nicky, but not Arthur. Once Nicky and Kieran are play partners/dating, Jade becomes Nicky's meta. In more open poly circles, it's common for metas to be friendly with each other. This more open approach to poly, where metas know each other, get along, and are involved socially with each other is sometimes referred to as 'kitchen-table poly.'

munch: a kink meetup where people share a meal together at a restaurant or tavern. Typically, most newbies to kink attend a munch before a *play party.* Attending a munch is a less intense way to connect with people from the kink community, and it also gives community members an opportunity to vouch that newbies are safe to welcome into a play party.

neotantra: a Westernized version of *Tantra* that focuses almost exclusively on sacred sexuality, using breathing, movement, touch, sound, and energy to deepen and heighten the erotic experience. For example, neotantra may involve consciously working with a person's energy body and their *chakras* to expand their conscious awareness or using sex and eroticism to increase bliss. One key component of neotantra is 'mindful presence.' Referring to neotantra as 'Tantra' is a form of cultural appropriation and should be avoided. Likewise, most (if not all) practitioners who are not from Southeast Asia should refer to themselves as 'neotantra practitioners' instead of 'Tantrikas' to avoid cultural appropriation and perpetuating the harmful impact of colonialism. See '*Tantra*' to learn more about neotantra's origins.

nesting partner: a partner with whom a person lives. Often, there are shared financial, emotional, and day-to-day responsibilities and commitment. However, some people maintain relative independence even within nesting relationships and partnerships. "Traditional" markers of commitment that exist in a monogamous relationship (e.g., sexual or romantic exclusivity, amount of time spent together) are still often negotiated, rather than assumed.

Owner/pet: A D/s dynamic that often involves *petplay*. The Owner will take care of their pet by cuddling with them, playing with them, training them, disciplining them for misbehavior, and other assorted activities.

past life regression: a form of energy healing where a person is guided into their subconscious mind so they can access other timelines that their soul has lived. A past life regression (PLR) is often done with the intention of uncovering and releasing trauma that originated in other lifetimes.

petplay: a form of play where someone acts the part of some animal, often through their behavior and attire. Common forms of petplay include kitten play, puppy play, and pony play; however, there are many kinksters who identify with other animals instead. Any form of consensual petplay is valid. See *Owner/pet*.

pickup play: a more casual form of kinky play. Pickup play often occurs spontaneously at an event or play party and is negotiated just before the scene takes place, often between people who do not have an ongoing kink dynamic or other kind of relationship.

play partners: people who have an ongoing relationship and engage in kink/BDSM with each other. Play partners may be platonic or romantic, or the lines may be a bit fuzzy. A play partner may be someone you play with a few times a year or a few times a month; however, it's usually a less committed dynamic than most D/s relationships.

play party: an event where consensual kinky and erotic play takes place. Some people host private play parties out of their homes, and there are also public events where kink/BDSM takes place. Rules and etiquette vary from space to space, so be sure to inquire about the rules, protocol, and dress code before attending.

polyamory: also referred to as 'poly' or 'polyam,' polyamory is a relationship style and practice where people may have multiple partners with whom they are emotionally, physically, romantically, and/or sexually intimate. Polyamory is one form of consensual non-monogamy (CNM). *People who identify as asexual and/or aromantic can still be poly, and they are valid.*

primary partner: a partner with whom a person shares finances, property, a residence, significant emotional investment, co-parenting, and/or other aspects of their lives that often require a greater level of priority and commitment. Some poly people prefer to use "nesting partner" instead since the term "primary partner" can emphasize and reinforce hierarchy that may exist between different relationships.

red (safe word): "Stop." During a kink scene, calling "red" means the scene immediately stops and aftercare begins. In many kink spaces, "red" is considered a universal safe word, which means it will be honored even if other safe words are being used in that particular scene.

reflective listening: a form of active listening, where a listener repeats back what they heard the speaker say. This strategy helps minimize either party making assumptions since they can check those assumptions in the moment.

reflection: a key component of reflective listening, where the listener makes a statement that mirrors back what they heard. For example, "I'm hearing that you're feeling frustrated with yourself because you didn't call your safe word during that bondage scene. As a result, you're not feeling safe."

Reiki: a common, flexible form of energy healing that was rediscovered in the early 1920s by Usui Sensei of Japan. A Reiki student receives attunements or placements where they are connected with the Reiki energy and can share the healing energy with others. Once a person becomes a Reiki Master, they are able to teach Reiki classes and help others connect with the Reiki energy. Because it is so flexible, Reiki is often incorporated into other healing modalities, including *past life regressions* and *conscious kink.*

safe word: a word that kink players use to express their limits, and to make sure that all kinky play remains consensual. Many kinksters use the traffic light system, which has three safe words: green, yellow, and red.

scene: a kinky encounter. Scenes begin with a negotiation, where all parties involved express what they'd like to experience during the scene, as well as share their limits, triggers, aftercare needs, and other physical and emotional constraints/requirements. Scenes end with *af-*

tercare to help the players integrate the experience and rebalance their body and nervous system.

scene name: a pseudonym that a person uses within the kink community. Often, this may be a portion of their FetLife username. Not everyone uses scene names, or they may not use them universally (e.g., not at a local/private play party, just at larger conferences).

secure attachment: the attachment style that roughly 50% of the population has. A person with secure attachment is less likely to take things personally; gives feedback without attacking, criticizing, or blaming; and actively communicates their needs, desires, and boundaries rather than resorting to protest behavior (e.g., manipulation, withdrawing, stonewalling). People with a secure attachment style tend to view relationships as being resilient. It is possible to become more secure in your attachment style by recognizing your existing trauma patterns, learning to communicate more effectively, investing in relationships that help you become more (not less) secure, and improving your relationship with yourself.

solo poly: a type of polyamory where a person does not have a primary partner. Typically, a solo poly person does not have (or wish to have) a partner with whom they live, share finances, own property, or co-parent. However, some people who have a live-in partner with whom they share finances and co-parent may still identify as solo poly if their relationships are non-traditional in some other way. A solo poly person may be single or be in relationship(s) with other people.

slosh: a meetup for kinksters that occurs at a bar. Typically, people chat about kink and BDSM and connect socially between play parties.

sub drop: the experience a person has when the neurotransmitters that flooded their brain during a scene have worn off. Depending on the person and the intensity of the scene, this could be later in the night, the next day, or even a couple days after the scene occurs. For some, sub drop results in sadness, lethargy, headaches, or tiredness. Water, food, chocolate, and other self-care activities help mitigate sub drop.

subspace: an altered state of consciousness that can result from being on the receiving end of dominance, impact play, bondage, or any other form of kinky play. How people experience subspace varies on the length and intensity of the scene as well as their personal biochemistry. For some people, it results in relaxation, giggles, or extreme euphoria since the brain is usually being flooded with serotonin and dopamine.

Switch: a person who isn't either a Dominant or a submissive; they prefer both sides of the slash. A Switch may be more dominant with some partners, and more submissive with others. A Switch does not have to be 50% dominant and 50% submissive; they may lean one direction or another. For example, Nicky identifies as a "sub-leaning Switch" because they are naturally more submissive than dominant.

Tantra: Sanskrit for 'principle, doctrine.' Tantra is a series of esoteric practices that originated in Hinduism and Buddhism in the first century CE, and was developed in Southeast Asia, specifically India. Tantric practices include yoga, worship, meditation, mandalas, and sacred eroticism. In contemporary times, Tantra is often confused with *neotantra,* a Westernized version of Tantra that focuses almost exclusively on 'sacred eroticism.' Referring to neotantra as 'Tantra' is a form of cultural appropriation; likewise, most (if not all) practitioners who are *not* from Southeast Asia should refer to themselves as 'neotantra practitioners' instead of 'Tantrikas' to avoid perpetuating the harmful impact of colonialism.

top: the person who gives and facilitates the kinky scene/experience. When a person is topping, it's crucial that they know and understand how to keep the bottom safer within the scene. For bondage, this includes knowing how to make ties that mitigate the risk of nerve damage. For impact play, this means knowing how and where to hit the person safely. If you want to be a top, please take workshops and/or engage an experienced mentor within the community first.

top drop: less often discussed than sub drop, top drop occurs when a person who was topping experiences a drop in the level of neurotransmitters that were in their brain. Top drop is just as valid as sub drop, and it's important that tops practice self-care and request any aftercare that they might need from their bottom or from other willing partners.

top space: the mental, emotional, and energetic space a person inhabits when they are topping a scene. For some, this may include a deep sense of focus, power, and control. For others, it may mean unleashing their inner sadist, brat, or Dominant. Much like subspace, top space can involve a change in biochemistry as neurotransmitters may flood the brain.

toy: within the kink community, a toy is anything used during a scene to increase, heighten, or expand sensation. Kink toys may include common sex toys like dildos and vibrators, but also include floggers, canes, handcuffs, and other similar implements.

Traffic Light Trauma Framework™: developed by Kelly Noel Zeva in late 2019, this framework gives healers, coaches, and therapists a way to check in with their clients and ensure ongoing consent within a session. This framework prevents healers, coaches, and therapists from taking a client deeper in a session than their body and autonomic nervous system can handle that particular day.

trauma: "too much, too fast, too soon" or "too much or too little for too long," trauma typically results from some sort of distressing event. Trauma can result from major events (e.g., abusive relationships, major physical harm, pandemic, homelessness) or from minor events (e.g., isolated microaggression, minor physical harm). There is also 'short trauma,' which results from an isolated incident (e.g., car crash) and 'long trauma,' which is an ongoing, traumatic experience (e.g., living through the COVID-19 pandemic). Trauma can be physical, emotional, psychological, spiritual, or cultural.

trauma bonding: when a person develops an attachment to another person because they have shared a traumatic experience with them. Trauma bonding is often part of the reason that people have trouble leaving toxic or abusive relationships; once they have established this bond to another person, it is challenging to release this attachment. Trauma bonding can also create or deepen codependent patterns within an existing relationship.

trauma response: also known as fight, flight, freeze, or fawn. When the body experiences a trauma response, the prefrontal cortex (the thinking brain) shuts down. The body goes into survival mode, and only basic, routine, highly repeated patterns are accessible or available to the person.

vanilla: can refer to a person or an encounter. If it's a person, they're someone who is not interested in kink/BDSM. If it's an encounter, the experience does not involve kink/BDSM. People who are vanilla may be willing to engage in the occasional kinky scene if it's initiated by their partner, but it generally doesn't turn them on. Likewise, kinksters can and do have vanilla experiences with some (or all) of their partners.

yellow (safe word): "Pause." Using this safe word during a kink scene can mean a number of things, so it's important to establish what yellow means to you and to anyone else involved in the scene. Yellow can mean that "the intensity is too much," or "I need a breather," or "I know that something is off, but I don't know what." This safe word often pauses play so that I can do a more thorough check-in with my body.

yoni: the Sanskrit word for a person's vagina and vulva, which translates to 'sacred temple.' Yoni is a word often associated with *Tantra* and *neotantra* as well as some other branches of conscious and sacred sexuality.

yoni egg: an egg-shaped gemstone or crystal that can be inserted into a person's vagina to support and deepen their healing as well as strengthen pelvic floor muscles. Traditionally made from Nephrite Jade. Do not use yoni eggs for extended periods of time, while pregnant, or while menstruating, and ensure that any crystal yoni eggs you purchase are 100% certified authentic.

Bind: Coming in 2023

Crystalline Kink Series, Book #2

Less than four years after their sacred journey to Peru, non-binary Nicky Rivera has not only met but has started dating their Divine match—the kinky, sadistic, polyamorous Kieran Jackson.

Despite their shared values, energetic compatibility, and potent sexual connection, Nicky's relationship with Kieran is far from simple. Jealousy, trauma, and insecure attachment styles quickly rear their ugly heads as Nicky searches for certainty within non-monogamy. After all, Nicky isn't the only partner in Kieran's life, and they fear their time with Kieran may forever be relegated to weekday tete-a-tetes.

Energetic forces beyond Nicky or Kieran's control are also driving their relationship into hyperspeed, even before they've had intercourse. Ultimately, the two of them must decide: do they want to bind themselves immortally to the other? And if so, how far are they willing to go—and how much are they willing to heal and surrender—to create what they most desire?